THE THIRTEENTH MAN

Also by J.L. Doty

THE TREASONS CYCLE (hard science fiction)

Of Treasons Born (prequel to *A Choice of Treasons*)
A Choice of Treasons

THE GODS WITHIN (YA epic fantasy)

Child of the Sword, Book 1
The Steel Master of Indwallin, Book 2
The Heart of the Sands, Book 3
The Name of the Sword, Book 4

THE DEAD AMONG US
(contemporary urban fantasy)

When Dead Ain't Dead Enough, Book 1
Still Not Dead Enough, Book 2
Never Dead Enough, Book 3

Note: sample chapters for all of these books are
available on the author's web site at www.jldoty.com.

THE THIRTEENTH MAN

J.L. DOTY

HARPER

VOYAGER
IMPULSE

An Imprint of HarperCollinsPublishers

This is a work of fiction. Names, characters, places, and incidents are products of the author's imagination or are used fictitiously and are not to be construed as real. Any resemblance to actual events, locales, organizations, or persons, living or dead, is entirely coincidental.

EPub Edition AUGUST 2016 ISBN: 9780062562081
Print Edition ISBN: 9780062562104

10 9 8 7 6 5 4 3 2 1

Beware the curse of the thirteenth man,
for should he not fall,
all may fall before him.

PROLOGUE
HOMECOMING

Charlie awoke with a start, peered into the utter darkness of the ship's hold, and realized someone sleeping nearby had inserted the point of an elbow into his ribs. After five years sleeping chained to his comrades he'd gotten used to that.

Five years in a Syndonese prison camp and you got used to a lot of things.

Charlie shivered—feeling hot and cold all at once—and allowed himself a moment of self-pity. He'd managed to survive five years of the most abominable living conditions, only to succumb to a minor scratch. It had started out as nothing, but had refused to heal. Then it began to fester, and each day grew steadily worse. And now, with his fever returning . . .

He shook himself free of that train of thought and prayed that this time he could remain lucid for more than a few hours.

He closed his eyes and listened to the darkness. Someone jerked nearby, grunted, and started scratching furiously; the never-ending battle against fleas and lice. In the distance someone else snored happily, and close at hand someone wheezed in a restless attempt to breathe through lungs racked with tuberculosis. Two thousand men—chained together in the stinking hold of a ship—made a lot of noise in the darkness.

Five years ago there had been almost five thousand of them, most wearing the livery of Cesare, Duke de Maris, many wearing that of old Rierma, Duke de Neptair, with the remainder evenly distributed among the other seven dukes, and even some from among the king's men—all of them the legacy of a nasty little war that had cost both sides dearly. During those first days in the prison camp they'd lost many to battle injuries, but after that their losses had stabilized at one or two per day, men lost to any of a hundred minor diseases or afflictions which, lacking any medical facilities or supplies, were too often fatal. Before they'd been dumped in the hold of this ship they could remove the dead in some way: bury them, burn them—something. But here, in the dark, the Syndonese didn't bother themselves with the dead, and Charlie and his comrades now shared the chain with close to a hundred corpses, some of them many days old and quite ripe.

Charlie decided to sit up, though he moved slowly to avoid disturbing his comrades. He got his good leg beneath him and rested his back against a bulkhead, then carefully adjusted his hand and leg manacles so he didn't accidently jerk someone else's chain. He fingered the chain for a moment: metal, heavy, rusted, noisy, like the hand and leg irons. The Syndonese could have used plast, which would have been cheaper, stronger, more humane, more efficient, but the Syndonese weren't interested in efficiency—and certainly not in humanity. Plast didn't weigh you down, didn't rattle and chink as you dragged it behind you, didn't abrade your wrists and ankles until they were raw and bloody, didn't drag the spirit down with each painful, shuffling step, didn't . . .

"Commander?" Charlie recognized Roger's whisper. "Is that you? You awake?"

"Morning, Roger," Charlie whispered.

"Is it morning, Commander?"

Charlie shrugged, a useless gesture in the dark. "I don't know. Could be."

"How many days you make it?"

Charlie paused for a moment and considered the question carefully. The Syndonese had long ago deactivated their implants, so their only sense of time came from the distribution of the daily meal of unflavored protein cake and water. Back in the hellhole they'd lived in for the past year and a half—an iron-ore mine on some barren rock somewhere—at mealtime each day he'd gouged a mark in the rock of the mine tunnel where they'd lived. Before that he'd scored their calendar for two years in the stone wall of their cell in some dungeon on some moon circling some planet orbiting some star. And before that there'd been a year and a half in a prison camp on some planet while the Syndonese decided what to do with them. After five years less than half of them remained alive, after five . . .

"Commander," Roger whispered. "You still with me?"

Charlie started. "Ya, I'm still here." In the darkness of the ship's hold, with nothing but plast and steel around them, Charlie had scratched a notch in a fingernail each day at mealtime. "I make it twenty-seven days."

"What do you think this bucket'll do, Commander, two, maybe three light-years a day?"

"If that."

Charlie's former gunnery officer wheezed and went into a fit of coughing—deep, hacking spasms that left him gasping for breath. Back home, a few days in an infirmary and he'd be as good as new. But here, Charlie gave him no more than another month or two before tuberculosis finished him. Roger rested for a moment before continuing. "That's fifty to a hundred light-years. That's the farthest they've ever moved us."

"Well, wherever they're taking us, we're there. We down-transited—I make it six, seven hours ago."

Roger accepted that without question. They'd all learned long ago to accept Charlie's uncanny ability to sense transition, an ability none of them shared. "Maybe just a nav fix, Commander."

Charlie shook his head. In twenty-seven days he hadn't been able to stop making useless gestures in the dark. "No, we haven't up-transited, and a nav fix wouldn't take more than an hour."

"Guess we've come to our new home, huh, Commander?"

Charlie's leg started throbbing again. The pain was relatively manageable at this stage, but after forty odd days of slow, steady deterioration Charlie knew the pattern well. The pain and fever would both steadily grow in intensity, and in another hour or two it would drive him into a semi-comatose delirium. Roger wouldn't admit it, but Charlie knew from the dreams that haunted him at those times that he ranted and raved at unseen ghosts. "Once they park this boat," Charlie said, "I want you to call a meeting of the executive staff."

"Sure, Commander. What for?"

"It's past time we chose a new CO."

"No way, Commander. You're doing just fine. As soon as your leg's—"

Charlie cut him off. "How often am I lucid now? One, maybe two hours a day. And it gets worse every day."

"But the immune augs are helping—"

"The immune augmentation treatments are six years old. Too old to cure gangrene, and not old enough to let it have me quick and clean. They're just prolonging the agony now."

Roger answered with another fit of coughing.

"Shit, Roger. I'm not even going to outlast you.

What have I got? Another five or ten days, maybe twenty on the outside?"

Roger got his coughing under control and sighed heavily. "It could be worse—you could be de Lunis."

Charlie chuckled. That old, childish saying had become their motto.

"Who's it going to be, Commander?"

Charlie looked at Roger, could see nothing in the dark, but Roger seemed to know his thoughts. "Not me, Commander. Hell, you said it yourself. I'm barely gonna outlast you."

"What about Darmczek?"

"He's an old warhorse, Commander."

"He's got the rank, and the respect of the men."

In his mind's eye Charlie could almost picture Roger shaking his head, matted, lice-infested hair hanging well past his shoulders, beard halfway down his chest. "Hell, Charlie, he's got rank over you, but that doesn't make him our CO. Everyone knows that. Even he knows it, and he's not ashamed of it either. Darmczek's a good CO on a fighting ship, but this is a prisoner-of-war camp. Darmczek won't understand how to fight this enemy. I grant you, the CO's got to be someone who knows how to fight a ship. Otherwise, he won't command the respect of these men. But what we need now is someone who knows how to keep us alive with this shit." Roger gave his chains a bitter jerk. Charlie felt it, and no doubt other men along the chain felt it also. "What about Andrews, Commander?"

Charlie had been considering that option for days

now. Seth Andrews had been XO on one of Cesare's ships and had proven he could command. "Seth is right for the job, but he doesn't have the rank, and after I'm dead that'll just put him and Darmczek at odds."

"There's a way to handle that too, Commander."

"And that is?"

Charlie could sense Roger's hesitation. "You could give him a promotion, give him the rank he needs. Decree it . . . as Charles, son of old Cesare."

"Absolutely not. I can't do that."

"Look, Commander, I know we're not supposed to say it out loud—or even admit we know it, or even think it—but we all know he's your father, whether he's acknowledged you or not. We also know you're his favorite, and we know when he needs a military solution he looks to you first, and—"

"But to use his name that way . . . that would be illegal."

Roger laughed into the darkness. "Ya, it would. So are you worried after you're dead they're going to dig you up to hang you?"

Charlie laughed at that. "You've got a point. And Andrews is the right choice."

"Then it's settled."

"Ya, I guess so. But I gotta talk to Darmczek first; try to square it with him. He deserves that. I'll find a way to get him alone, so don't say anything until I do."

Roger coughed for a while, one of those bad fits that lasted several minutes. The pain in Charlie's leg began to intensify and he drifted off into a troubled sleep, but the clang of a docking boom jerked him awake as it echoed through the hull of the ship. From the grunts and groans and intensified frequency of scratching going on about him, Charlie knew his comrades were waking.

Charlie happened to be looking in the direction of the cargo hatch when it cycled open, flooding the hold with a white, incandescent glare. After twenty odd days of pitch darkness it blinded him painfully, and he closed his eyes, covering them with one hand. But in that one instant the glare had etched an image in his memory of several figures standing silhouetted in the open cargo bay. He recalled the image, studied it for a moment against the back of his eyelids: half a dozen people. Oddly enough, one of them was apparently wearing the flowing robes of a churchman.

In that first instant after the cargo hatch had opened, the steaming, sweltering air of the hold had flowed around their visitors and he could hear them as they gasped and choked on the stench of urine, feces, unwashed bodies, and death. For Charlie and the other prisoners, though, *stench* had become a rather academic concept.

They switched on the lights in the hold, filling the entire space with that bright, incandescent glare, forcing all of the prisoners to shield their eyes and cower. Charlie heard their visitors talking among themselves in muffled and distant voices. He squinted through his fingers and tried to catch a glimpse of what they were doing.

To Charlie's surprise one of them appeared to be

a woman. She wore spacer's coveralls, but there was no mistaking the small waist and curves, and she wore her hair much longer than most men—probably some Syndonese bitch-princess come to gloat over the enemy prisoners.

The whole scene took on a surreal air, the half-dozen figures wandering among the seated and chained prisoners, tendrils of steam rising from the bodies on the chain as they picked their way carefully through the men, their hands cupped over their noses. Charlie looked at Roger, who was also squinting through his fingers. Charlie's image of tangled, matted, lice-infested hair and beard had been quite correct. "Do I look as bad as you?" Charlie asked.

Roger looked his way and grinned. "Worse. At least I'm usually kind of cute. In any case, the fleas like me."

He would have smiled, but the pain in Charlie's leg blossomed into a throbbing, fiery burn. He gritted his teeth and forced his hands away from the open, weeping wound. Seeing it for the first time in days, the sight was almost enough to sap any hope from him. The cycle was beginning again, and soon he'd lose all touch with reality.

Charlie looked back at the silhouettes of their guests. One was definitely a woman—he hadn't seen a woman in five years—and another definitely a churchman. That was odd, because the Syndonese didn't embrace the church. And there was something about the churchman too, something familiar, as if he was part of a distant and long ago dream.

"My god, Roacka," the churchman said, shaking his head sadly. "This is the worst we've seen."

Roacka! Charlie knew that name, and the voice that called it, and he knew then that he was hallucinating, that the delirium had begun again.

"Ya, it's the worst, churchman, but then every batch is worse than the last." That voice had the timbre of a crusher turning rock into gravel. Charlie wanted to weep with fear and anger. Roacka, and Paul, such a cruel hallucination.

"Duke Rierma," the Paul hallucination said—Charlie knew that name too. "Look at this. I can't believe they'd be so inhumane."

Charlie removed his hand from his eyes and struggled to see the three men whose voices he knew so well, voices he had thought never to hear again. But his eyes still hadn't adjusted to the light and all they did was tear and weep. He squinted, blinked frantically, and watched their silhouettes approach as they wove among the prisoners. The Roacka hallucination squatted down to examine one of the bloated corpses on the chain. The churchman squatted down next to him. "This one's gone," Roacka said.

The churchman scanned the hold of the ship. "It's unbelievable," he said, his head slowly turning to take them all in. His eyes met Charlie's and his head stopped turning. They stared at one another for a long moment; the churchman frowned and stared more intently.

Charlie spoke to Roacka, his voice barely above a

whisper. "Even a hallucination should guard his back better than that."

Roacka's head snapped around as if he'd been struck. His eyes narrowed, then slowly the large, bushy mustache under his nose rose upward as his lips broadened into a wide grin. He stood, his eyes still locked to Charlie's, crossed the space between them and squatted down in front of him. The churchman followed, glancing back and forth uncertainly between the two of them.

The pain ratcheted up another notch; Charlie couldn't suppress a tremor as a wave of nausea washed through him. Roacka looked down at Charlie's pus-saturated pant leg and shook his head. "Look at you, boy. Let you out on your own and you can't take care of yerself."

The churchman looked at Roacka as if he were mad. Charlie had trouble focusing, but he decided to break the churchman's suspense. "Sorry, Your Eminence. I haven't been very good at keeping up my lessons."

The churchman's eyes widened, then he grinned a grin to match Roacka's. "Oh, Charlie."

Old Rierma leaned over them and spoke without a moment's hesitation. "Charles, my boy. Don't be such a stranger. You should visit more often."

The woman squatted down next to Paul, looking at all of them uncertainly, and with the steadily rising background of pain, any doubt that she was a hallu-cination disappeared. She was far too beautiful to be real. Charlie could feel his words beginning to slur as he spoke. "You brought me an angel, a bona fide, for-real angel."

She reached out and touched his cheek. "You're burning up."

Roger reached out and grabbed her arm. "He's dying."

"Ya," the Roacka hallucination said. "Gangrene."

In that instant, far behind them, still near the open cargo hatch, Charlie spotted another silhouette and his heart leapt, for this was truly the cruelest of hallucinations. He could never mistake the way the old duke moved, the way he bent and carefully looked into the face of each man he passed.

Paul stood, turned, and called out to the old man. "Your Grace, we've found him."

The old duke turned their way, looked at Paul and frowned. "Please, Your Grace. I think you should come here quickly."

Old Cesare frowned and crossed the intervening distance carefully. He stopped in front of Charlie, looked down at him; their eyes met and he nodded. Charlie's eyes started to weep again—because of the glare, he was certain. The Cesare hallucination looked at Roacka and asked, "How bad?"

"Bad," Roacka said. "Might lose the leg at the hip, if he lives."

"Rest easy," the churchman said. "You're home now, part of a prisoner exchange. You're the last group. It's taken us five years to set it up, but you're home now."

Charlie could no longer focus. "Go away," he growled. "Leave me in peace."

The angel frowned and her beautiful face began to twist and distort.

"I knew it," Charlie said at her transformation. "You can't fool me anymore."

Roger's chains clinked as he put a hand on Charlie's arm. "Did you hear that, Charlie? We're home. We're free." Roger lowered his head, buried his face in his hands and wept openly.

Charlie shook his head. "You can't fool me, Roger. You're not real either."

A wave of nausea washed up Charlie's stomach and he vomited bile into his lap, the fever coming on quickly. He tried to focus on that thought, had trouble concentrating. Then he saw the familiar image of his dead brother, Arthur, walking across the deck, the color of life gone from his cheeks, death hanging about his shoulders like a shroud, his body twisted and broken. "Please, Arthur," he cried. "I'm sorry. Please . . . forgive me. Please."

"Charlie," the churchman said, reaching toward him, but as he did so his face slowly dissolved and became Arthur's face. "You failed me," Arthur said. "You failed our father. You failed us all."

Charlie screamed—

During the eight-hundred-year reign of the Plenroix, the Harlburg, and the Stephanov Kings, only twelve men had ever occupied the de Lunis ducal seat, the tenth Duke of the Realm, and without exception each had come to a very tragic, most unpleasant, and certainly untimely end. Some had even brought down their entire family and clan with them. But for the past three hundred years the de Lunis ducal seat had remained unoccupied, the title unclaimed and unwanted, for it had become the stuff of legend that the downfall of the first twelve Dukes de Lunis would pale in comparison to that of the thirteenth, and so no man would accept the title de Lunis. In fact, the legend of the twelve Dukes de Lunis had spawned a common saying, spoken only in the darkest hours of despair when all seemed hopeless:

It could be worse—you could be de Lunis.

The de Lunis legend also spawned a long, rambling poem, often chanted by children when not in the presence of their elders. In stanza after stanza it describes in great and gory detail the demise of each of the twelve, just the kind of thing young schoolboys might take pains to memorize, then chant at young girls to make them blush and giggle. Of particular interest to historians are the final few stanzas of this rhyme:

> *And the twelfth Duke de Lunis, his head*
> *rolling wide,*
> *cried, "Oh my king, oh my king, wherever*
> *shall I hide?"*
> *The thirteenth Duke de Lunis will fare*
> *no better now,*

> *for beneath the headsman's ax he'll lie,*
> *a frown upon his brow.*

There is one more stanza beyond the last of the official verses. But there is some question as to its authenticity, and as to whether it was penned with the original poem, or perhaps added later by some scoundrel bent on demeaning the crown, so it's not commonly published as part of the whole. Though most have heard it at one time or another, and almost all are aware it exists, few remember the lines themselves:

> *But should the headsman miss his prey,*
> *the thirteenth man will rise,*
> *and rule the headsman's ax one day,*
> *no limit to his prize.*

The meaning of this last—unofficial, and often suppressed—stanza is the subject of considerable speculation among historians and academics.

CHAPTER 1
RECOVERY

Arthur's ghost visited Charlie quite regularly, and would often plead with Charlie, "Why did you abandon me, Charlie? I thought you loved me." Sometimes the angel visited him and brought him a certain kind of peace, and sometimes the churchman came and spoke kindly to him, though at other times the churchman berated him for abandoning Arthur. But when the old duke came and stood by him, Charlie could only cry and plead for forgiveness. And then there came a day when Charlie opened his eyes and the oddly distorted sense that he was hallucinating had gone, though the angel sat in a nearby chair reading an old-fashioned book.

Charlie lay in a bed in what was clearly the sick bay of a ship. The angel remained unaware of his gaze and he watched her for quite some time—dark auburn hair, cut shoulder length, blue eyes set in an oval face.

In the hold of the prison ship she'd worn baggy spacer's coveralls. Now she wore a simple knee-length dress, a pair of slippers on the floor in front of her, her legs curled beneath her on the chair, her attention wholly focused on the book in her lap. Maybe he wasn't delirious; maybe she was real. But then again he hadn't seen a woman in five years, let alone been in the same room with one, so perhaps she was an ugly cow and his perspective had changed. In any case it didn't matter.

He asked, "Are you a hallucination?"

She looked up from her book with a start, and her blue eyes sparkled as she stared at him for a moment. "No, are you?" She put her book aside, stood, nudged her feet into the slippers, and crossed the room. "I'll get the others."

"No," he said. "Not yet. Where am I?"

"Cesare's flagship."

"Who are you?"

"You can call me Del."

"My men?"

"I should get a doctor to answer that."

She turned away, but he reached out and caught her wrist. "No. Please. I'll just get a lot of double-talk from a doctor. I need straight answers."

She thought about that for a moment, then nodded. "One hundred and twenty-three were already dead. Two more died before we could get them off the chains, six more during the next two days. The rest—one thousand nine hundred and twenty-seven—are in varying states of health, but they're now stable and so they should do well." The fact that she had such statistics instantly at hand said much for her in Charlie's view.

Charlie shook his head, ran fingers through his hair, and fought back tears. "We started with almost five thousand . . ." For a moment he was back on the chain, going through the ritual of saying a few meaningless words over the daily toll of dead. "I should have done better . . . should have done something different . . ."

She shrugged. "Perhaps. But I doubt it would've turned out any better. From what I saw it's a miracle any of you survived. And you don't strike me as the self-pity type, so please don't start now." She frowned and looked at him oddly. "Those men practically worship you. You're a simple commoner, and yet you've managed to inspire greater loyalty in those men than the king himself."

Charlie couldn't hide his anger. "The king got two million men killed in his pointless little war. The king's a—" Charlie bit back his words; to continue would be treason. He looked at Del carefully. "Do I know you?"

She smiled. He liked it when she smiled. "Not really. We met once, a long time ago, at a dress ball. You were a young cadet, about to graduate from the academy—quite dashing. And I was a gawky sixteen-year-old girl. I made you dance with me, though like the other cadets you were more interested in chasing the more approachable young ladies your own age. But you were nice to me, didn't treat me like some clumsy little girl. So I made you dance with me again . . ." A mischievous glint appeared in her eyes. " . . . though my father did tell me not to waste my time with a penniless bastard." She grinned at him, and that playful look reappeared. He tried to remember dancing with her, but drew a blank.

She said, "Can I ask you something personal?" She didn't wait for his permission. "Why has he never acknowledged you?"

Charlie shrugged. "I'm the son of a servant. It wouldn't be appropriate." He didn't add that he'd always suspected the second duchess—the *witch-bitch*, as he and Arthur had dubbed her—of having his mother killed, and that if Cesare ever acknowledged him, she'd eliminate Charlie as well.

"I'll make a deal with you," he said. "No more wallowing in self-pity for me, and you give me another dance sometime, even though your father thinks you'll be wasting your time."

"Done," she said, nodding and smiling. "But I should get the others." She turned and walked to the door, but paused halfway through it and looked back at him with that mischievous glint in her eyes one more time. "So I look like an angel, do I?"

And with that she was gone.

Alone, Charlie threw back the covers and felt at the bandages on his thigh. Back on the chain the infection had eaten a crater the size of his fist into the muscle, but now, other than some tenderness beneath the bandages, he could find no trace of such massive tissue damage. He flexed the leg experimentally; it was sore, but not as bad as he would have expected. He swung his legs off the edge of the bed, stood cautiously, and limped unsteadily across the room to test it.

"They done good work, eh lad?"

Charlie spun about as the door swung wide and Roacka, Paul, Seth, and Roger were ushered into the room by Del. Roacka, Charlie's lifelong tutor in weapons, tactics, strategy, fighting your enemies, drinking, fighting your friends, fighting with and loving women, and anything else the man took it in his head to fight. Paul, the churchman charged with teaching Charlie the arts, languages, mathematics, history, engineering, politics, diplomacy. Seth, standing almost two meters tall, towered over everyone. He was the brutally handsome one with broad shoulders, but the weight he'd lost only made him look spectral. And Roger, thin and gaunt, but with color back in his cheeks, and no more cough.

Roacka gripped Charlie in a bear hug and lifted him off his feet. "It's good to see you, lad."

Paul said, "You're looking wonderful, Charlie."

Roacka put him down and stood him at arm's length. "No he ain't, churchman. He's looking about twenty kilos short of wonderful."

Paul hugged him as well, though with less vigor than Roacka. "You still look good, Charlie, regardless of what this ignorant lout claims. But he is right. You do need to put on some weight."

Roger just shook his hand, while Seth patted him on the back. "We made it, Charlie," Roger said. "You got us through it." Charlie met both men's eyes briefly, and for an instant their beards and hair were long, matted and lice-infested once more, and they were on the chain. Then the moment passed, but he saw in their eyes that they and the other men who had shared the chain were somehow different. That many things would never be the same.

Charlie thought about their many comrades who hadn't made it, but behind Roger and Seth, Del's eyes narrowed as if she could read his thoughts. With a look she seemed to say, *No wallowing, or you won't get that dance, spacer.* Then she smiled, and Charlie said, "Thanks, Del."

Paul frowned, looked at Del, then at Charlie, then back at Del. Paul's demeanor stiffened. "I get the impression you two have not been properly introduced." He looked at Charlie, and with the understanding of many years of friendship, Charlie read in Paul's eyes a warning of caution. "Charlie, may I introduce Her Royal Highness, Princess Delilah?"

The daughter of King Lucius, a royal princess who might carry tales back to her father. Charlie tried to recall everything he'd said as, Roacka supporting one arm, he bowed formally. "Your Highness, had I realized, I would not have been so familiar."

She almost flinched, as if the wall of formality he'd erected between them hurt her. "Commander Cass," she said, suddenly very much the royal princess. Her curtsy was quite shallow, which was appropriate for the vast difference in their stations.

For some reason, the change in the room took the breath from him.

The door behind her swung open, and a tall, distinguished man in a dark, conservatively cut business suit entered the room. He was thin, almost skeletal, as if he'd spent years on the chain with the rest of them, his eyes dark brown, his hair black with a touch of gray at the temples. He carried a uniform draped over one arm, and he looked disapprovingly at the tableau spread before him. Winston, Duke Cesare's chamberlain, chief of protocol, business manager, frequent legal counsel, and constant source of information on the appropriate this or that. Under his disapproving stare Charlie felt like a bad little boy, and Del dropped her eyes as if Winston were the king and she a mere peasant.

Winston bowed deeply to Del. "Your Highness." He looked at Charlie, standing in the middle of the room in a hospital gown. Charlie suddenly felt naked. "It might be more appropriate for Your Highness to wait outside."

Del curtsied to him almost fearfully, probably more deeply than she would to the duke, and edged out of the room.

Winston turned to Paul. "His Grace will be arriving shortly and I know Commander Cass would prefer to be properly attired. Would Your Eminence be so kind as to assist me?"

Paul nodded. "Of course."

Winston turned on Roacka, Seth, and Roger. "Your presence is no longer required."

Only Roacka, and of course the duke himself, seemed immune to Winston. Roacka winked at Charlie. "I'll be about, lad." He ushered Roger and Seth out of the room.

As the door closed Winston turned to Charlie. "It's good to see you well, Commander. I know you'd not want to appear before His Grace in bed clothing, so I brought your uniform."

Many things would never again be the same, Charlie realized, but Winston was not one of them. "Thank you, Winston. It's good to see you too."

Charlie did all right as long as he didn't have to move around a lot, but he learned quickly that his knees grew weak with any effort, even with something as simple as putting on a new uniform. Paul and Winston managed to get him properly clothed. Then they stood back and examined him carefully. "He does look grand, doesn't he?" Paul said.

Winston nodded. "He looks . . ." Winston hesitated for a long moment. "He looks appropriate." With that Winston reached out, and like a demanding mother put a finger beneath Charlie's chin, lifted his face toward the light, turned his head to the left, then right. "But . . . you are changed. And I think, perhaps, that too is appropriate."

Winston busied himself picking at Charlie's uniform, adjusting the ribbons on his chest, pulling his collar into place. Then he stood Charlie in front of a mirror and even Charlie was shocked at how poorly he filled out the uniform. He was more skeletal than Winston.

Without warning the door swung open and a woman tall enough to tower over any man stepped into the room. She wore the uniform of the duke's personal guard—no visible weapons, but Charlie knew she was a walking arms factory. She probably outweighed most men, but on that tall frame she was a thin beauty. Her skin was a deep olive hue, and her pale blue eyes stood out like beacons in a starless universe. But her most striking feature was her snow-white hair, not yellow-blond, but bone-white, woven into a single braid that hung down her back. And when she stepped forward she walked with the gait of a predatory animal.

A Kinathin *breed warrior*, her prototype had been genetically engineered several hundred years ago with the intent of producing the perfect bodyguard, and through the centuries the strain had bred true. Her name was Add'mar'die, but she was only half of the equation. Knowing she was waiting, and almost as a reflex, Charlie unobtrusively signaled to her in breed handspeak.

No danger here.

She nodded and scanned the room quickly, then called through the open door in breed-tongue, "He is no taller, sister."

Another woman, identical to the first, stepped through the door. Add'mar'die's twin, Ell'mar'kit, looked down on Charlie and shook her head. "And I had hoped he'd grow a bit."

Perhaps because the three of them had grown up together, Charlie was the only person alive who could tell them apart, though not even he knew how he did it. The twins had been the closest thing he'd had to big sisters.

Charlie shrugged, leered at both of them and said in breed-tongue, "I prefer my women a bit shorter."

Cesare stepped through the door on Ell'mar'kit's heels, with Delilah, Seth, Roger, and Roacka behind him. Charlie's leg was stiff, and though it protested painfully he lowered himself to one knee. Cesare tried to spare him. "Stand," he said impatiently.

This was a meeting Charlie had both desired and dreaded for five years. He bowed his head and closed his eyes, and Arthur's ghost hovered in his thoughts. "I said stand, Charlie."

Charlie shook his head. "But it's from one knee that I must beg your forgiveness, My Lord."

"For what?" Cesare demanded, a touch of anger in his voice. "Because you disobeyed my orders at Solista?" Cesare shrugged coldly. "You spotted a lucky opportunity and the trap you sprang on the Syndonese high command turned the tide of that battle, and that battle turned the tide of the war. We were losing before Solista."

Charlie would never forget Solista. He had relived it a thousand times, the ship's hull thrumming like a kettledrum as enemy shells slammed into it, all-

ship blaring the abandon ship order, Arthur unconscious in his arms, his tunic soaked with blood, the
air fouled by ozone and burning insulation. "I tried
to get him to a lifeboat," Charlie said. "I don't even
remember losing consciousness myself. All I remember was that I was carrying him down a corridor, and
then the next thing I knew I woke up in a lifeboat.
Can you ever forgive me?"

Cesare reached down and lifted Charlie's chin to
look in his face. The old man frowned. "What are you
talking about, Charlie?"

"I promised you I'd take care of Arthur, and I didn't.
I must have left him somewhere on the flagship. He
was still on her when they blew her. It was my fault.
I'm sorry. I'm so—"

Cesare nodded. "And how did you learn of Arthur's
death?"

Cesare's question puzzled Charlie. "As new prisoners were brought in they gave us news of the war. 'Cesare's son had bought us victory at Solista,' they said,
'at the cost of his own life.' "

Cesare continued to nod thoughtfully, but it was
Paul who asked, "And you've lived with this grief for
five years? Do you remember any of the final moments
at Solista?"

Charlie shook his head.

Cesare took a deep breath and let it out slowly. But
there was none of the grief Charlie had expected to see
in his eyes, or anger. Only a deep sadness, somehow
tinged with warmth. Cesare leaned down, took hold

of Charlie's shoulders in a strong grip, and pulled him carefully to his feet. "But it was *you* who bought us victory at Solista, by remaining on board a dying flagship and coordinating the final minutes of your trap. And it was you whom we believed still aboard that flagship when she blossomed into a fireball. As for Arthur, apparently you got him into that lifeboat, and into a medpod. We picked him up six days later. He lost an arm, but we've long since cloned him a new one." The Duke was staring into Charlie's eyes. "Those stories were about you, Charlie.

"You were the son who bought us victory at Solista—and we believed at the cost of your own life."

The deck tilted crazily beneath Charlie's feet, but Del appeared at his side, caught an arm and let him lean on her. Add'mar'die appeared at the other arm and kept him on his feet, all of them pretending he didn't need their help.

"He's alive?" Charlie said, his knees close to giving way.

"Yes, little brother," Add'mar'die said. "He's alive." She squeezed the muscle on his arm. "And I doubt you weigh half what you should." She looked around the room and announced, "Ell and I'll fix him up. Regular workouts in the gym, and about five thousand calories a day should do it."

They all fussed over him, then brought in the ship's doctor who fussed some more. Yet none of it mattered. Arthur was alive—that's all Charlie cared about. They could fuss all they wanted, as long as that fact remained

THE THIRTEENTH MAN 29

true. He didn't want to sleep, fearing he'd wake up and learn that Arthur wasn't alive, that this was another hallucination or a dream, but eventually they gave him something and he started to grow drowsy, so they said their goodbyes and left. Del was the last to go and she paused in the doorway. He wondered if she made a habit of exiting that way.

"Why are you here?" he asked, not sure if he should trust her. "The daughter of the king. Why go to all the trouble? Do you really care about us?"

She lowered her eyes. "My father doesn't. He and my mother don't approve of me being here, but I made a public announcement that I'd personally be at every prisoner exchange, and they'd have looked very bad if they'd refused me."

She lifted her eyes, looked at him and asked hesitantly, "Does it make a difference to you, knowing I'm Princess Delilah?"

He was having trouble focusing. "I don't know Delilah very well, but I hope I still have a date for a dance with a girl named Del."

"You do." She grinned, and that mischievous glint appeared in her eyes again. She tossed a hip shamelessly to one side.

"But you have to earn it first, spacer."

Roger preceded Charlie down the deserted corridor on Cesare's flagship, *Defender*, and looking at him reminded Charlie of how emaciated all of them had been, still were for that matter. Even after a tenday Roger walked carefully, the walk of a person weak with illness and starvation. His uniform hung on him like an old rag tossed on a hook, his cheeks sunken and hollow. Charlie knew that if he could step outside himself and look from a distance, he'd see almost a twin to Roger.

Seth Andrews, Noah Darmczek and Chief Petty Officer Tomulka, *Defender*'s security chief, met them in the security commander's office. With the exception of some exercise sessions in his sickroom, this was the first time Charlie had walked anywhere under his own power, and there was much shaking of hands and slapping of backs.

"I won't say you look good," Darmczek said in a voice that sounded more like a growl, "but you look a hell of a lot better." Darmczek's voice had regained the strength that had disappeared sometime on the chain.

"I think we all look better," Charlie said. "How are the men? With a few exceptions, I haven't seen any of them yet."

Andrews said, "Like the rest of us, getting better each day."

"And asking about you," Darmczek added. "Let's make sure you get a chance to tell them how you're doing personally."

"Ya," Charlie said, nodding. "Ya, let's do that. But first we have to take care of this nasty business."

Tomulka led the way into the cell block, two rows of four cells each on either side. On a properly organized and disciplined ship, such cells usually saw use only for minor infractions, such as when a spacer returned from shore leave too drunk to report for duty. If the same fellow repeated the offense one time too many he might be thrown into a cell to sleep it off, and for a few days more to sweat about his punishment.

The only occupants of the cells today were four men—Turnman, Crowley, Smithers, and Johansen—housed in separate cells. They were all seated on their bunks, and stood nervously as Tomulka led the four officers into the block. They too showed some signs of malnutrition, but nothing close to the real starvation the rest of them had suffered. Crowley gripped the plast bars of his cell and said, "Commander, what'd I do to get locked up? I didn't do nothing wrong."

In the cell next to him Turnman shook his head, lowered his eyes and said, "Cut the crap, Crowley. You ain't fooling nobody."

"But I ain't done nothing," Crowley pleaded.

Darmczek leaned close to him, their noses only inches apart. "You were a fucking snitch, Crowley. And if I could, I'd wring your neck myself."

Crowley backed away from Darmczek. "You can't prove that."

Darmczek shook with rage. "You don't think everyone knew, Crowley? You don't think we all knew exactly what was going on? The only reason we didn't kill you in the camps was because the Syndonese would retaliate."

"Captain Darmczek," Charlie said. "Please."

With visible effort Darmczek swallowed his anger and adopted a calm he clearly didn't feel. He stepped back from the cell.

Charlie said, "You four men collaborated with the Syndonese. You know it, we know it, all the men knew it then, and know it still. The rest of us on the chain grew absolutely skeletal, while the four of you thinned out a bit, but miraculously stayed rather healthy. I'll bet they even treated you against infection and some of the other things we suffered. I could probably prove it in a proper military court, though I admit the evidence would be circumstantial. But I don't have to prove it to get you punished. I can just release you, let you go back to your bunks among your comrades . . ." All four of them cringed noticeably.

Turnman said, "Please, Commander. Don't."

Andrews spoke up. "He won't. But the rest of us would. We'd like you tried and executed. And you've got Commander Cass to thank for your lives."

That wasn't exactly true. Charlie had wanted them dead as well, had wanted to come down here and personally put a bullet in each of them. But Cesare had talked him out of it. "Those men don't matter anymore, Charlie," he'd said. "But if you kill them, even though they deserve it, you won't be able to put them behind you. I know you, and coldblooded murder, that's not you. Their blood on your hands will haunt you for the rest of your life. It's your decision, but think it through carefully."

Darmczek growled at Charlie, "And I still don't understand why."

Charlie didn't look at Darmczek as he answered him. "They were on the chain with the rest of us. I guess I can understand the need to survive, and the temptation to sacrifice your honor.

"But I can't understand betraying your comrades," he said firmly. Charlie looked at the four men carefully. "As such, you're being held here in protective custody. You will not be mistreated, and you'll continue to be held until we reach Traxis. At that time we'll issue you your back-pay, and transport you to a place of your choice, as long as it's outside any de Maris holding. And be warned: should you ever return, you'll be arrested, tried, and executed."

As Charlie turned to leave, Turnman called out to him, "Commander."

Charlie stopped, half turned and looked over his shoulder at the man. Turnman said, "For what it's worth, Commander, I'm sorry . . . and thanks."

The man seemed sincere, but Charlie couldn't find any kind words for him, so he turned and left.

CHAPTER 2
MEMORIES

Charlie back-stepped as the knife hissed past his nose. He spun, caught Ell with a vicious kick to the side of her thigh, but in that instant her knife cut a furrow across his ribs and an agony of fire lanced up his side. They separated, circling warily, she limping on the damaged leg, he clutching at the deep cut in his side, simblood soaking his sparring suit. He too limped badly.

"Come on, Ell," Add shouted. "Finish him. You're getting sloppy. He shouldn't have lasted this long."

He tried to ignore the pain, tried to remember that he wasn't actually hurt. The fabric of the sparring suit was soft and flexible, but with power reinforcing its fibers it could sense the moment of impact, turn into a rigid shield in the immediate neighborhood of the blow and protect its wearer. However, as Add and Ell were wont to remind him, he'd learn nothing about fighting if he didn't feel the pain of his mistakes. So the suit fed false sensory signals to the pain centers of his brain, telling him he'd badly sprained his left ankle, he'd been cut painfully across his ribs, he was bleeding and he was weakening. The simblood was an illusion fed directly into the cerebral cortex, adding to the psychological impact of the simulation.

Charlie and Ell continued to circle, looking for an opening. At least her sparring suit treated her no better, though he knew his kick had been a lucky one.

Add coached from the sideline. "He's gotten sloppy about his left side. Remember how long we worked to create balance? And now he's forgotten it all. Give him a good lesson."

On Ell's worst day, and Charlie's best, he was just barely a match for her, but not today. She came in low with a cut to the knees. He spun with a heel kick to her ribs, only to realize at the last instant her cut had been a fake. She sidestepped the kick and buried her knife to the hilt in his chest. He dropped to his knees, blood welling down the front of his sparring suit, a lance of pain in his chest so intense he almost lost consciousness. He fell forward to his hands and knees, lay down and curled up as darkness began to envelop him, thankful that with unconsciousness the pain would end.

In his last moments of consciousness Add stood over him shaking her head sadly. "You've forgotten everything." She lifted a small instrument in her left hand, touched a switch on its face and the pain suddenly vanished from his body, though not from his memory. Charlie sighed and decided to lie there for a moment.

Ell took up Charlie's defense. "He's improving, Add. Don't be so hard on him." Ell sat on the mat rubbing her knee, slowly overcoming the psychological effects of her own sparring suit. "He's only recently come back to his proper fighting weight. And he's doing far better than he did even a tenday ago."

The twins had begun torturing him only two days after he'd regained consciousness, and they'd been at him for a solid month while Cesare's flagship drove toward Traxis, home planet of the de Maris ducal seat. The two breeds were bound and determined to see him properly fed, healed, and exercised, and spent about two hours every day beating up on him, or standing over him forcing him to eat what they considered a proper meal, which to Charlie seemed enough to feed ten men. Then Roacka would usually join them, and all three of them would beat up on him again for a few hours more.

Add grabbed him by the collar of his sparring suit and lifted him to his feet. Facing him, looking down at him from her commanding height, she grinned and said, "I suppose you're right. And in any case, we can never expect too much of him—he's so short."

"Short, tall," Ell said as she pulled herself to her feet. She leered knowingly at Charlie's crotch. "That's not the measure I'm interested in."

Charlie blushed, but Add ignored it and spun on her heel, heading for the corridor. "Roacka's got you next.

Fighting staffs, I think, both powered and antique. Then after that you're to meet with the duke."

Cesare sat alone in his office and thought of the bargain he'd made more than twenty years ago when Charlie was only seven. It had been shortly after Gaida had murdered Charlie's mother. Cesare had been furious, and the argument that ensued . . .

"Do not try my patience, woman. I know you were responsible for her death." Cesare struggled to remain calm, but the loss of Katherine—the knowledge that he'd never hear her voice again, never hold her in his arms—ate at his soul and tormented him constantly.

The Lady Gaida, his wife, a cold witch of a woman, turned her head slowly toward him. As always, her face held no expression, and he wondered how he could ever have shared her bed. "You can prove nothing," she said. "But even if you could, she was no more than a servant, and at most I'd have to pay some reparation to her family. And the only family she has is that whoreson—"

"Don't call him that," Cesare shouted. Gaida grinned, and he knew he'd let her get the better of him. They were alone in her sitting room after he'd dismissed her servants and ladies with a shout, and he realized he'd chosen his battleground poorly.

She spoke with an unnerving calm. "I speak only the truth, and he stands between my son and his rightful inheritance."

Cesare suddenly understood, and he felt foolish for not having realized from the moment the marriage contracts were signed that Gaida was a viper. Granted, a beautiful viper spawned of a powerful and influential family—hence the marriage—but still a viper. If the balance of power on the ducal council weren't so precarious he'd be rid of her, but to do so now would alienate her kinsmen, and that could destroy the delicate equilibrium of the Realm's power structure.

He knew now that the ducal seat was in danger, that the life of his eldest son, his heir Arthur, hung in the balance. Rather than being overcome with fear, though, knowing his enemy had a calming effect. "And what is your son's rightful inheritance?"

She answered quickly, "Why, he's in direct line to the de Maris—" She caught herself and realized her mistake.

"Woman, your son is not my heir."

"He's your son too. Your second son."

Cesare knew the proper goad. "My *third* son," he corrected her.

"The whoreson is illegitimate and unacknowledged," she shouted, "and I'll not have him standing between my son and the ducal seat."

Cesare lowered his voice and spoke calmly. "But my first son, my Arthur, my legitimate heir, does stand between your son and the ducal seat."

Gaida's eyes widened as she realized her mistake. She wisely chose to remain silent.

Cesare turned squarely toward her and used a

deadly tone of voice that had brought down kingdoms. "Perhaps we should have a bargain, woman."

She took the bait. "A bargain?"

"Yes," he said, turning away from her and pacing thoughtfully back and forth. He needed to give her a reason to allow Charlie to live. He wanted to have her and her small child killed, to be rid of her quickly and easily, but even if she was clearly responsible for the murder of Charlie, he couldn't go that far. After all, Charlie was the son of a servant, and unacknowledged he was still just a commoner. So Cesare improvised. "Should Charlie, my second son, die—and should I have even the faintest suspicion of complicity on your part, or that of your son—then you and your son will spend the rest of your lives in near poverty." Her family was powerful and influential, but not wealthy.

"I will not have a whoreson standing above my son in the line of succession."

"Very well," Cesare said. "I'll not acknowledge Charlie, I'll not legitimize him, I'll never call him son and he'll never call me father. I'll not bestow upon him property or wealth, and in return, you'll see to it that he remains alive and healthy. I will, however, make sure the boy is financially comfortable, though nothing close to what's appropriate for a son of House de Maris. I think I'll also buy him a career, perhaps a commission, and I'll see to it that he's educated and given appropriate training."

"And my son and I?"

"As long as Charlie remains healthy, you'll remain

the supreme lady of House de Maris. For your son, I'll buy him some title, something significant, and unlike Charlie, I *will* bestow upon him property and wealth." He turned toward her again and faced her squarely. "Do we have a bargain, woman?"

She thought carefully for an instant. "Do I have a choice?"

"No. You don't."

With that he turned and strode for the door, pulled it open, but paused in the doorway. "There is one more thing."

She didn't look his way.

"Your son will *never* inherit the ducal seat. For should Arthur, my legitimate heir, die before his time, regardless of the circumstances, and whether you're implicated or not, your death, and that of your son, will be long, slow, and agonizing. Do we understand one another?"

She hesitated, then nodded . . .

The knock on the door brought Cesare out of his reverie. That had been so long ago, the bargain they'd struck. Charlie and Arthur had been but children, and he, Cesare, had still been young and vital. Three sons, Arthur, then Charlie, then Theode. Arthur, son of the first duchess, whom Cesare had even loved, in a way. Arthur was bookish, intelligent, noble, kind, a diplomat by nature, a politician by instinct; he'd inherit the ducal seat and would carry the responsibility well. Theode, son of the second duchess, had turned out to be no less a viper than his mother, self-indulgent, spoiled, calculating. And Charlie, born between Arthur and Theode of the only woman Cesare had ever truly loved. Charlie, condemned by a bargain struck more than twenty years ago to a life between lives, more than a commoner, but less than a nobleman's son. Charlie was what Cesare had made of him: the warrior, trained to stand at Arthur's right hand, the man who would enforce Arthur's policies when the diplomacy of politics would not suffice. Cesare wondered if Charlie was truly a warrior by nature, or if the boy had merely followed the path laid out before him.

Again, a knock on the door brought Cesare back to the moment. He hadn't meant to keep Charlie waiting.

The computer acknowledged Charlie's knock. "You may enter."

He took an instant to adjust his tunic, to make sure all was right and proper before entering the duke's presence, then pushed the door open and stepped into the duke's study. The computer closed the door behind him. Charlie immediately bowed. "Your Grace, you wished to see me?"

"Stand up, Charlie. Let me look at you. And relax."

Charlie straightened and saw the duke clearly for the first time, seated behind a large desk. He looked tired and old, but he smiled and said, "You're starting to look like the old Charlie, though I noticed a slight limp."

Charlie grinned back at him. "Add, Ell, and Roacka beat up on me almost daily, when they're not trying to force-feed me."

Cesare stood and came around the desk. "It seems to be doing you some good." He patted Charlie on the shoulder, led him toward two large, comfortable chairs in the corner.

"Ya, but I'm not about to admit that to them."

"Of course not. Sit down." Cesare pointed him to one of the chairs, and without asking his preference, turned to a small bar and splashed whiskey on ice in two glasses. It was a ritual Charlie had forgotten, and seeing it for the first time in years reminded him that he was truly home. "They tell me you still have nightmares."

Charlie shrugged as Cesare handed him one of the glasses. "And they tell me the nightmares are natural, and they'll pass with time."

Cesare sat in the other chair. "And they tell me you won't accept any of the standard therapies for such difficulties. You know they could end the nightmares with a few hours of treatment, end them once and for all."

Charlie shook his head. "Yes I know. But neural probe therapy will also destroy some of the associated memories. And I don't want that."

"Are those memories so good?"

"Of course not." Charlie sipped at his drink; it burned his throat wonderfully. "But they're part of what I am, and I don't want to lose that. I know that sounds trite, or maybe just stupid . . ."

Cesare nodded thoughtfully and considered his drink for a moment. "Do you know that all the men who came back with you, once they heard you refused the neuronics, have also refused them? And they've asked to serve under you. Even those sworn to other noblemen have requested release from their oaths."

"I don't have a command."

"That can be changed in an instant."

"I don't want a command."

Cesare finished his drink and stood to fix another. Like the first drink, this one was small, just a splash over ice, more a ritual than a drink. While he stood at the bar with his back to Charlie he said, "I need a strong military presence behind the ducal seat. Once again Lucius is playing at emperor, demanding levies from the Nine, and if he gets them he'll start something . . . possibly another war."

Charlie asked, "Another war with the Syndonese?"

Cesare turned back to Charlie, holding a fresh drink. "No, I don't think President Goutain wants open war. The last one cost him dearly, and he and his Syndonese sycophants have carefully avoided any saber-rattling. Our dear king has something up his sleeve regarding Aagerbanne and the independent states. I don't yet know what, but Arthur should have more information when we get back to Farlight."

Charlie said, "And once again you're the primary opposition to Lucius's posturing."

Cesare smiled and shrugged. "Guilty."

"If you resist him, he might accuse you of treason."

Cesare paced back and forth across the small room. "Treason is a relative term. If House de Maris is weak, then I'm guilty of treason, and will probably lose my head. If we're moderately strong, then I'm merely an obstinate advisor to the king, and I must eventually capitulate to his desires. If we're truly strong, then I'm the king's most trusted counselor, whose advice he will certainly heed. In any case, Lucius has exhausted his own treasury, so at the moment he's quite weak."

"And what are we?"

Cesare stopped pacing and faced Charlie squarely. "Before your return, we were strong. Now, we're very strong."

"I can't see how two thousand men changes things. It's ships that make a difference."

Cesare nodded his agreement. "And the men that fight them. I have ships aplenty, and I have experienced crews for them, and with your two thousand—all experienced fighting men—we *are* stronger. But they're not the key, Charlie. You are."

"Me? Why me?"

Cesare sipped at his drink. "Lucius glorified your deeds rather unashamedly, after we thought you dead. I'm sure that had you lived, he wouldn't have gone to such excess. But he did, and here you are, returned from the dead with a reputation that I can put to use against him. I should add, this puts you at some risk. Know then that I intend to use you."

Charlie bowed his head and said, "You have but to command."

"But to be *very strong*, Charlie, I need more than your obedience. I need your active support, I need your counsel, and I need your understanding of the men who may need to fight for us."

Charlie had only one question. "Do you intend to make war?"

Cesare looked him in the eyes and spoke plainly. "No. I seek to stop Lucius from wasting another two million men on his petty ambitions at empire. And to stop him I need you. But I warn you, war may be a means to that end."

Charlie stood, put his drink down, dropped to one knee, took the duke's hand, and kissed the ring on his finger. "As I said before, you have but to command, my liege."

CHAPTER 3
FARLIGHT

"Now, that's much better," Add shouted.

Charlie bent down, picked up Ell's saber and handed it back to her, hilt first. She was having a bad day, and he was having a good one, so they were almost evenly matched. She had killed him twice, but he'd managed to kill her in the third match, and disarm her now in the fourth.

Charlie backed out of the ring. "That's enough for today. I have orders to be at the main airlock when we dock." He started peeling off the sparring suit.

Ell flipped the saber to her twin sister, who caught it casually. "You still have a ways to go. But at least now we can let you out on your own, knowing you have half a chance of keeping yourself alive against an assassin."

Add, always the more critical of the two, mumbled,

"*Half a chance* is pushing it a bit, sister. I wouldn't give him more than one in three."

Charlie tossed the sparring suit to Ell, left the two of them in the gym, and hurried to his cabin. He showered, shaved, put on a freshly pressed uniform, shoved a small palm gun into the holster hidden beneath his left armpit, and stuffed a plast knife into the sheath in his right boot. "Remember," Roacka and the twins had reminded him, "a body scanner will catch a power knife or the palm gun, but a plain old plast blade has a good chance of passing unnoticed."

At the airlock Cesare acknowledged him with only a nod and a gruff "Commander." There would be no first names or familiarity in front of others, though when Charlie took a position behind and to the left of the old duke, Cesare said, "Stand at my right hand, Commander."

Winston appeared magically at Charlie's right. "Are you ready for this, Charles?" Winston, Paul, Cesare, and Charlie had discussed "this" carefully. Upon return to Traxis, Cesare could bypass normal entry procedures. They could take up a restricted orbit close to Traxis, and an armed gunboat would shuttle the duke and his entourage down to the ducal estates at Farlight, all under the watchful and protective guns of *Defender*, Cesare's flagship. But with the announcement of Charlie's resurrection, Winston felt that the duke should make a public appearance with Charlie at his side. So, like so many other ships, they'd docked at Traxis Prime, the main station orbiting Traxis. And while they'd certainly get VIP treatment, Winston had made sure that certain members of the media knew where to wait if they wanted to be the first to shove a microphone into someone's face.

"Ya," Charlie answered. "I'm about as ready as I can be."

While docking booms clanged through the hull, Charlie tried to imagine what awaited him. So many times he'd thought to never see home again. He'd believed he'd die nameless on some unknown planet, though after a time the dying part hadn't bothered him so much as the nameless part had. But now a piece of him was afraid to be there when the airlock opened, afraid to step through and find that everything had changed. Paul, standing behind Charlie, seemed to sense his unease, though he misinterpreted it. "Don't worry, Charlie. It'll be easy. Remember to nod politely, and keep any answers you give benign and meaningless."

Meaningless answers, he thought. *Sounds like a contradiction in terms.*

The hatch cycled open without warning. Add stepped through it before it completed cycling, followed by four of Cesare's personal guard. Ell remained just on this side listening to her implants. After a few seconds Charlie saw her subvocalize a response to Add, then she nodded to the duke, while to Charlie she signed in handspeak, *This will be no fun, little brother.*

The hatch opened onto a private dock maintained

for VIPs, and containing Winston's carefully selected group of media hypes. As Cesare's retinue marched through them they rifled questions at him. Cesare responded with practiced ease to questions about Lucius, himself, and the returned prisoners. Charlie was happy to be ignored and beginning to hope he might be overlooked completely, then one of the hypes stepped in front of him, blocking his path and forcing him to come to a halt—clearly something not in Winston's prearranged script. "Lieutenant Commander Cass," the hype demanded. "Do you intend to support the king in his negotiations with Aagerbanne?"

Never answer a dangerous question, Winston had warned him. *But try to avoid, "No comment." If you don't like the question, then think of a question you do want to answer, and answer it.*

"I've always been a loyal subject of the crown," Charlie said.

One of the guards politely edged the hype out of Charlie's way, and Winston got the retinue going again. But the hype persisted, "Even if it means war, Commander?"

Another hype shouted, "Even if it means alliance with the Republic of Syndon?"

Charlie halted, turned on them, tried to look displeased, and suddenly everything came to a stop as the hypes waited for him to say something newsworthy. *Alliance with Syndon,* he thought. *Where did that come from?* With the dukes withholding levies, Lucius just might be that desperate. Charlie mentally clamped down on what he really wanted to say. "I've always supported my king. Do you question my loyalty?"

"Of course not," the hype said, unruffled by Charlie's counter. "But our viewers are wondering . . ."

Winston quickly turned Charlie around, started the retinue up again, and with the hypes firing questions at their backs they passed into a VIP lounge where a door slammed shut behind them. Cesare kept moving, though he looked over his shoulder at Charlie and commented, "Well done, Commander."

The hypes' questions had brought on a cold, sinking feeling in Charlie's gut. "What did they mean, Your Grace, by *alliance* with the Syndonese?"

Cesare frowned, turned away from Charlie, and commented over his shoulder, "Don't worry about it, Charlie. We'll discuss it later."

As they boarded a shuttle for the trip down to the planet's surface, the sinking feeling deepened.

We sure as hell will *discuss it later*, Charlie thought.

Once their shuttle settled onto the ducal estates at Farlight, Charlie headed straight for Arthur's study. Charlie found him with three of his assistants, all leaning over some sort of designs on Arthur's desk; they were in the midst of a rather heated discussion. They didn't notice Charlie as he slipped into the study, and it wasn't until he cleared his throat that Arthur turned around, looked at him, and froze in midsentence. A big grin spread across his face. "Come back from the dead, eh?"

Charlie shrugged. "I could say the same about you."

"Yes," Arthur said. "I heard about that, you idiot."

Arthur sprinted across the room, gripped Charlie in a bear hug, and lifted him off his feet. "Damn, Charlie! I couldn't have wished for more." Arthur was taller and bigger than Charlie, though not as athletic, and he swung Charlie around once before putting him down. He held Charlie at arm's length and looked him up and down. Charlie saw the big brother he had thought dead. He was a little older than Charlie remembered, with a few added pounds around his waistline . . . and had never looked better. "It's good to have you back," Arthur said. "We need you now more than ever."

Charlie frowned. "I've been getting dire little hints like that, but no one has bothered to enlighten me as to why. Would you care to?"

Arthur looked over his shoulder at his assistants, nodded at the designs on his desk. "If you don't mind, we can continue this later."

They all replied with an "Of course, Your Lordship." They gathered up the designs and disappeared quickly. Arthur closed the door behind them. "Computer," he called over his shoulder as he strode back to his desk. "Full privacy and surveillance scan, no recording, no monitoring."

"All entrances are sealed," the computer replied. "Surveillance scan verifies a monitor free environment within the confines of your study. Vocal monitoring will be disabled upon your verification. You'll have to reactivate manually when you're finished, Your Lordship. Please verify."

"Verified," Arthur said.

"Confirmed," the computer replied.

He turned to Charlie. "Okay, Charlie. We can talk. There'll be no record kept."

"That bad?"

Arthur shrugged. "We're going to discuss the Realm's dirty laundry. And some of what we say might be construed as treason."

That bad, Charlie thought.

Arthur began with a question. "What do you know of the situation with Aagerbanne?"

This time it was Charlie who shrugged. He had heard bits and pieces on the trip back from the prisoner exchange, but not much. "Lucius is negotiating for unlimited access to the Aagerbanni port facilities on Aagerbanne Prime, which would give us access to all the trade routes into the independent states. But there's been some sort of snag."

Arthur sat down behind his desk. "On the surface, you've got the gist of it. But the Aagerbanni Cabinet Minister for Trade thinks the crown might take the position that, since Aagerbanne was originally colonized with funds from the royal treasury, it's a candidate for annexation as a Crown State Holding."

"That's ridiculous," Charlie said. "Aagerbanne has been an independent state for more than five centuries."

"Yes," Arthur said. "But once it's done, and crown

troops are occupying Aagerbanni nearspace . . ." Arthur finished with a shrug.

"Lucius is insane," Charlie said.

"No," Arthur said. "Foolish, yes. Idiotic, maybe. But this is calculated. The Syndonese war badly depleted the royal treasury. If he pulls it off, it would be a financial windfall. So Lucius's real game is to push the negotiations into stalemate, feed appropriate amounts of misinformation to the media, and when the time is right, forcibly annex Aagerbanne."

Charlie shook his head, couldn't believe what he was hearing. "He might get away with it. Even with advance warning Aagerbanne can field only a few hundred thousand troops and maybe a dozen warships. What about the independent states?"

"They're moving carefully," Arthur said. "Finalsa and Allison's Cluster have signed a mutual defense alliance with Aagerbanne. Toellan and Istanna are arming themselves now, and the other states are simply watching the situation nervously. If Lucius—"

The computer interrupted him. "Your Lordship. Forgive me for interrupting, but Lord Theode is demanding admittance."

Arthur sighed. Charlie grinned and asked, "How is Twerp?"

"Unchanged. And please don't call him that to his face. It'll only start a fight, and he'll go whining to his mother."

"And the Lady Gaida?"

"The witch-bitch is also unchanged. Oh, Charlie!"

Arthur laughed. "I haven't called her that since you got killed."

"Again, Your Lordship, I apologize for interrupting, but since my monitoring systems are deactivated at the moment, if you have replied to my earlier request, I am unaware of it and cannot respond to vocal instructions."

Charlie sighed. "You might as well let Twerp in and get this over with."

Arthur reached over and touched a switch on the console buried in the surface of his desk. "Computer, reactivate standard monitoring and security procedures. Then admit Lord Theode."

"Well, if it isn't the whoreson," Theode announced as he strode into Arthur's study with two friends following him. "And newly risen from the dead. Quite a miracle, especially considering the lineage." He glanced at his two friends and raised an eyebrow, which appeared to be a signal that he was being witty, and they were now supposed to laugh. They did.

As Arthur had said, Theode hadn't changed. Small, slight of build, dark hair combed and oiled, an impeccably trimmed goatee. He sported an expensive green tunic, with the coat-of-arms of House de Maris tastefully embroidered on the lapels, and cream colored pants stuffed into soft, leather, knee-high boots. Theode had always been conscious of fashion, and spared no expense to ensure that he was properly attired.

"I'm told the conditions you survived were rather atrocious." In the Syndonese prison camp Charlie had remembered Theode's voice as a nasally, high-pitched whine. But he'd convinced himself that his dislike for Theode had colored his memories, that no one's voice could be that irritating. He realized now that his memories had been all too accurate. "Now, that, I think, is genetic. One must have the appropriate genes to survive happily in filth and muck. And we never doubted your genes, Charlie."

Theode was smaller than Charlie, and to Charlie's knowledge had never bothered with any kind of exercise. As boys, Charlie had once responded to Theode's insults by beating him soundly. Gaida's retaliation had been harsh and cruel, teaching Charlie to respond not at all to such taunts, and Theode had learned that he had free rein to deliver them.

Charlie looked at Arthur, bowed slightly from the waist as was appropriate for a vassal—long ago they'd learned to conceal any affection in the presence of Theode or Gaida. "With your permission, Your Lordship, I must go."

Theode sneered, "You don't have my permission."

Arthur came to his rescue. "But he has mine."

Charlie bowed again to Arthur. "Your Lordship." And though it galled him greatly, he offered the same courtesy to Theode. "Your Lordship."

He turned, and as he walked out of Arthur's study he heard Theode demand, "What were you talking about?"

Charlie threw one comment over his shoulder, "You, Twerp."

"You're not supposed to call me that," Theode shouted after him. Then to Arthur he asked, "You were talking about me? What did you say?"

As Theode's whining dwindled in the distance, Charlie felt bad about putting Arthur in such a predicament. Still, he couldn't help but leave with a huge grin on his face.

CHAPTER 4
SUMMONS

Charlie paused outside Arthur's study and asked a passing housemaid what room they'd assigned him. She frowned and said, "Why, your old room, sir."

At the look on his face she lowered her voice and said, "His Grace wouldn't allow us to change it. Made us leave it exactly as it was the day you left, said we could clean it regularly along with the other rooms, but that was all. He always insisted you'd be back."

Charlie couldn't exactly recall the condition in which he'd left his room, but it did appear unchanged. He had a closet full of old uniforms, though they were probably all outdated. He spotted a bunch of mementoes on a shelf, reached up and grabbed one at random: the sleeve insignia for the uniform of a spacer first class. He'd been so proud to receive that promotion at a very young age, and he had to think for a moment to recall his first time aboard a fighting ship, and the old chief who'd looked after him. That had been so long ago . . .

"Teach him well, chief," Rierma said, then turned and left young Charlie in the care of the grizzled old spacer. At the age of ten, Charlie barely stood chest-high to Chief Dekker.

"Come on, boy," Dekker said, "follow me."

Charlie had to hustle to keep up with the larger man as they headed deeper into the bowels of the ship, a task made more difficult by the fact that crew members going the other way paid deference to the old chief while they ignored Charlie, and he had to dance around them or get stepped on. Charlie was completely lost when Dekker finally came to a stop in a small barracks. There were about twenty other crewmen in small groups, all busy at one task or another. One group had some sort of weapon disassembled, with pieces spread out across the deck. Dekker halted in the middle of the barracks, and Charlie caught up to him.

"Listen up, you assholes," Dekker growled, and one by one they all looked away from their work. Dekker stepped aside, leaving Charlie the center of attention. "This here's Spacer Apprentice Charlie Cass. He's gonna learn how to be a pod gunner. And you assholes are gonna teach him."

Dekker turned to a spacer leaning casually against a bulkhead. "Stipko, get Spacer Cass his first weapon."

Stipko retreated into some sort of supply closet, returned with a bucket and a sponge, and handed them to Charlie. Dekker looked at Charlie. "The first enemy a pod gunner has to learn to kill is dirt, 'cause if there's any dirt during the next inspection the CO comes down hard on our department head, then our department head comes down hard on me, then I—" Dekker hooked a thumb over his shoulder at the other spacers in the barracks, "—come down hard on them, then they come down hard on you. Got it, Cass?"

"Yes, sir," Charlie said nervously.

"You don't call me *sir*, kid. You call me *chief*."

"Yes, sir," Charlie said, "I mean chief, sir. I mean chief, chief."

Several of the other spacers chuckled. Dekker turned on them slowly. "If the kid does his job, and one of you makes problems for him, I'm gonna be real unhappy. Then again, if he don't do his job, he's fair game."

Charlie didn't wait for orders, got down on his hands and knees, wetted the sponge in the bucket and started scrubbing the deck.

"There," Dekker said. "The kid ain't too smart, but he seems to have a good attitude. Maybe we'll make a spacer of him yet."

Charlie scrubbed decks and polished brightwork. There was a bit of hazing, but not much, and he had the feeling that Dekker was always in the background to make sure it didn't get out of hand. But after six months they put him in a pod and turned him into a lower deck pod gunner, and later that year he got his first confirmed kill in the border skirmishes with Istanna. And with the kind of pride only an eleven-year-old boy could feel, he'd gladly participated in "gunner's blood," the ancient rite in which a half-chevron is cut into a gunner's arm for each confirmed kill in combat, and his blood is spilled onto the deck of the ship in memory of comrades who had died before him. Charlie still had the scars of two chevrons, which was the only rank acknowledged among pod gunners, and rare for an officer to possess.

He'd served as steward's mate, machinist's apprentice, engineering mate—every kind of job on every kind of ship they could think of. But after the first few years there'd been a vast difference between his duties and those of the other spacers. He spent half his time tutored by the officers on ship, or Paul and Roacka when he wasn't on a ship. And if his ship saw action, afterward, regardless of his rank, he was always called to an officer's cabin, usually the executive officer, to review the results of the action, and the strategies and tactics employed by both sides, whether successful or not.

It was common practice to swap officers between duchies with longstanding good relations, and Charlie served for three years with Rierma, Duke de Neptair. He spent two years in service with pinch faced little Sig, Duchess de Plutarr, an amazing, hard-edged little woman who was the most demanding taskmaster he could remember. There were two years with Band, Duke de Merca, a towering giant of a man who had demonstrated the most amazing patience with a little boy just growing into a young man. And a short stint with Faggan, Duke de Jupttar, who was undeniably eccentric, and considered by everyone a bit crazy, though Charlie had liked him in an odd sort of way. Then he'd gone to the academy on Turnlee, and for the first time rubbed elbows with people whose rank among the nobility was all that counted. It was there that he first became aware that Cesare, Duke de Maris, was one of the most powerful people in the Realm, though none of that rank rubbed off on Charlie.

After Charlie graduated from the academy, he'd been serving with Cesare's guard for more than three years when the Syndonese war broke out. All of the senior officers on Cesare, Rierma, Sig, and Band's ships understood that Charlie was to be included in any command decision, though more often than not he merely observed and kept his mouth shut. And when he did speak, like any junior officer he never did more than politely suggest and recommend. *Begging your pardon, sir, but might I recommend* . . . And if ignored, or told to shut up, he was careful that it never got back to Cesare.

By the time of the battle at Solista he'd made lieutenant commander and was serving on the flagship of a flotilla of five capital ships with associated tenders and secondary vessels. Cesare had put Arthur in command of the flotilla, and Arthur had brought Charlie along, making it clear that Charlie's politely spoken recommendations were no less than direct commands from the duke. Their mission was to support a badly maimed fleet of His Majesty's ships during an orderly withdrawal from a battle that the Syndonese were winning decidedly. But as they approached Solista nearspace, their arrival had been unanticipated, and with the element of surprise Charlie saw an opportunity and took it. They flanked the Syndonese fleet, hit them hard without warning, and were able to inflict considerable damage before taking any themselves. Charlie's memories of the latter stages of the battle were still vague—a byproduct of his injuries, they told him—and he didn't remember much until he awoke in the hold of a Syndonese prison ship . . .

Charlie stood in his room in Farlight, looked one last time at the sleeve insignia from so long ago, and had no problem recalling old Dekker's face.

"Lieutenant Commander Cass," the computer said. "His Grace would like to see you in his study right away."

"Has he moved his study since I was last here?"

"No, Commander. You should have no trouble finding it."

When Charlie stepped into Cesare's study he found him in a heated argument with Arthur, who turned to Charlie and said, "He wants to make you an admiral."

"Please, Your Grace," Charlie said. "No admiral's stripes."

At Charlie's objection the duke's face hardened. "Why not?" Cesare asked. "You earned them, and none of your fellow officers would object."

Cesare was probably right about that, at least when it came to the men he'd shared the chain with. But other officers might regard such high rank on a young officer as undeserved. And he had to consider Gaida and Theode. "While I'm not too worried about my fellow officers, I'm concerned about Tw—" He'd almost said, *Twerp and the witch-bitch.*

"Father," Arthur said, coming to his rescue. "Nadama has plans, and giving Charlie too much rank could make Gaida his ally, and Charlie a target. And don't forget Gaida's family is still quite influential. It would be an unnecessary complication."

Cesare emitted a low growl. "Ahhhh."

Charlie asked, "What's the Duke de Satarna up to?"

Arthur raised an eyebrow. "He wants to marry Dieter off to Delilah. Lucius is getting old and can't last forever, or Nadama could help him along a bit—then Martino could die of an overdose after he takes the throne, or something of that nature."

At hearing Nadama wanted to marry his son and heir to the princess, Charlie felt a pang of jealously. And Charlie had heard that at any official function Lucius's heir, Martino, was never without a full drink and usually ended up stumbling about. His predilection for drink, drugs, gambling, and women was apparently no secret.

"With no heir," Arthur continued, "Delilah would

become queen, Dieter her consort, and in a few years he could be properly crowned."

Charlie asked, "Could he really get away with that?"

"Oh yes," Arthur said. "He'd have to move carefully, and patiently, but if he did it right, yes he could."

Arthur turned back to Cesare. "Please, no admiral's stripes."

"All right," Cesare said, "but I'm promoting him to full commander, and I won't hear any argument on the matter."

Cesare needed appeasing, and Charlie could see that Arthur understood that as well.

Cesare continued. "And I've got a flotilla I'm putting under his command: two heavy cruisers, two medium frigates, and three destroyers."

Arthur started to object, but Cesare cut him off. "Charlie's my wild card. I want everyone to see him in charge of a significant force that won't question any order he gives. That's why I'm assigning his fellow POWs to him. That's two thousand men who'll do almost anything he says. That'll keep Lucius and the rest of the Nine on their toes. But it won't elevate his rank so much they'll fear I might elevate him further."

Cesare turned to Charlie. "I want that flotilla in fighting shape, and ready for deployment anywhere in the Realm."

It felt good to have Cesare barking orders at him again, almost as if the intervening years on the chain had never happened. Strangely enough, that simple return to normalcy made him feel more at home than all the welcoming embraces. The one thing keeping him from feeling truly happy, though, was the thought of Dieter and Del. He did want to have that dance with her, but the likelihood that would ever happen grew less with each passing day.

Charlie took command of the flotilla, and after a little over two months on deep space patrol, he and his officers had it ready for whatever Cesare might throw their way. Cesare had sent Add, Ell, and Roacka with him to continue beating up on him, and Charlie was back in full health, though all three reminded him constantly he was one of their worst students.

Charlie was at his desk in a small office in the flagship reviewing performance reports when the computer said, "Commander, Captain Darmczek wishes to speak with you. He says it's urgent."

An hour ago they'd down-transited for a nav fix. It was standard procedure to contact the nearest de Maris outpost or relay buoy, from which Darmczek had probably received orders of some kind. "Patch him through."

Darmczek's face appeared on a screen embedded in the surface of Charlie's desk. "Good afternoon, Captain," Charlie said politely.

"We've got new orders," Darmczek said. "We're to make for Traxis and proceed with all due haste. We're setting up the new heading now and realigning the flotilla. We should up-transit within the hour. There's also an urgent message for you, coded private and sealed with a de Maris encryption key. I've forwarded it to your console."

"Thank you, sir. Is there anything else?"

"Nothing," Darmczek said, and killed the circuit.

As the screen went blank, Charlie isolated his console from *shipnet*, sealed his office, and activated the security monitor. He brought up the encrypted message and entered the proper decryption sequence, then leaned back to watch the message. Cesare, Arthur, and Winston appeared as half-sized three-dimensional projections, Arthur seated casually on a large, plush couch, Winston standing calmly beside him, and Cesare pacing back and forth, an intense furrow on his brow. He stopped suddenly and looked at Charlie— Charlie had to remind himself that Cesare was actually looking at a recording camera.

"Charlie," Cesare said. "I'm sure you're wondering why I've contacted you with such urgency. Lucius has summoned me to attend high court at the Almsburg Palace on Turnlee."

High court, Charlie thought. That meant all nine dukes would be attending, with family and heirs.

Cesare continued. "Lucius's advisors have dropped some rather unsubtle hints that you're to attend with me. The royal summons conspicuously doesn't state when my attendance at court will no longer be required, so we'll have to be prepared for an extended stay." Cesare looked over his shoulder. "Winston?"

Cesare's chamberlain stepped forward. "It's highly

unusual, Charles, for the king to directly summon a commoner who's sworn to one of the Nine. This is an appropriate, though indirect, means of summoning you into the presence of the king, perhaps even for an official audience. His Lordship might have something to offer there."

Winston stepped aside and Arthur took up the narration. "My agents inform me that, for your gallant deeds during the Syndonese war . . ." Arthur grinned and raised a mocking eyebrow at that, " . . . Lucius is going to bestow upon you some minor title, but no properties, which is an extremely unusual thing to do. Now, we know he'd never have made such a hero out of you if you'd been alive." Arthur turned his mocking eyebrow on Cesare. "And he's quite annoyed that you've managed to return from the dead, which has resurrected the myth associated with the Charlie Cass name. So why does he choose now to bestow further honors upon you?" Arthur let the question hang.

"What game is he up to?" Cesare demanded. He looked at the camera. "Winston thinks Lucius purposely leaked the information about bestowing a title, and that it's a cover for some other trick he's planned."

Charlie's paranoia ramped up a notch.

Arthur added, "I think he just wants to irritate our dear stepmother, sow a bit of dissention in the de Maris household. He knows that any kind of title granted to you will really piss her off, and it's interesting that no other information is leaking out concerning this. The whole thing smacks of Adsin—Lucius really can't keep a secret. I'm not sure you know Enrik Adsin. He's chancellor to the crown, one of Lucius's closest advisers, and a real snake in the grass. In any case, we have no choice but to answer the summons. We'll have to let them play their hand, then counter appropriately when we know more. Winston is having formal attire and dress uniforms tailored for you now. We'll all attend as part of Cesare's retinue."

Cesare stepped in close to the camera. "Charlie, you're just a pawn in this." Both Arthur and Winston suddenly found something of great interest on the toes of their shoes. "I wouldn't use you so if there were any other course, but we suspect Goutain and his Syndonese followers are involved somehow. And I may have to use you badly indeed. Forgive me." The projection ended.

Charlie marveled that Cesare's final words didn't bother him more. He resented being a pawn, but he'd been raised to serve House de Maris, and he felt every bit a part of the de Maris legacy. Cesare, without a thought to the contrary, had dropped him right back into his allotted slot in the de Maris household. And until that moment Charlie hadn't questioned that, had responded without thought to a lifetime of conditioning. He'd lay down his life for House de Maris, but he began to wonder now where this was going. With the Syndonese involved did that mean another war? Another prison camp? If not for him, then maybe for others.

Charlie didn't have to work hard to suddenly feel

very paranoid, and it occurred to him that a healthy dose of distrust might be the best thing he could do for House de Maris. He decided to make sure he had a backup plan for everything. He'd feel a lot better if he could figure out a way to have some firepower on hand when they went to Turnlee. But it would require Lucius's permission to bring anything more than Cesare's flagship.

It occurred to him there might be something he could do, and if he was sneaky enough, Lucius need never know. However, it might be wise to first have a chat with Darmczek and some of the others with whom he'd shared the chain.

We from the chain certainly understand survival, Charlie thought, and he smiled. *We can always apologize later . . . or they can assume we were sorry when we're dead.*

CHAPTER 5
NICE DIGS

The weather report for the vicinity about the Almsburg Palace described a cold, late-autumn day with a nasty windchill, and as the shuttle dropped through the outer reaches of Turnlee's atmosphere Charlie couldn't put aside his sense of unease. Perhaps he'd gotten a bit too paranoid of late; certainly the precautions he'd taken were extreme, provoking a raised eyebrow even from the normally reticent Roacka. And Darmczek had warned him that he was breaking the king's law by violating Turnlee nearspace. The twins had been his only supporters in this.

He'd had Darmczek split up the individual units of his small flotilla. They were under orders to keep their power plants operating well below that of a warship, to approach the Turnlee system independently from different directions and times, to fake up their electronic identifications and claim to be noncombatant vessels—merchantmen, freighters, and the like—to shut down all nonessential systems so their emission signatures matched their supposed identities, and then drift slowly into Turnlee nearspace. They could get away with that because they could generate their own fake clearance codes. His hope was that nothing would happen, in which case his ships would quietly turn around and leave the system the way they'd come. On the other hand, if something did happen, he'd have some serious firepower at his disposal.

He'd also enlisted the aid of Taggart, captain of *Defender*, which had brought them all here and was in orbit around Turnlee, though he'd had to lie to Taggart and claim that Cesare was privy to, and supported, his paranoid fears; just one more complication among many. Taggart knew Charlie was lying, but if Charlie's head rolled, Taggart could claim Charlie had misled him.

Charlie's plan was simple: as soon as the shuttle dropped them off it would return to *Defender*, pick up a squad of fifty marines in full combat armor, then return to Almsburg where it would park in an unobtrusive corner of the palace's landing field. The marines would be kept in the cargo hold of the shuttle in stimsleep, from which they could be awakened in moments, fresh and ready to fight. That meant Charlie had some firepower on the ground, close at hand, with a response time of minutes. Looking out the window of the shuttle he breathed a long sigh. He had to agree with Darmczek: he was probably just paranoid.

Better paranoid than dead.

The shuttle landed, they disembarked into a diamond-clear, bitterly cold day. A band struck up a rousing chorus as Cesare's foot touched the soil of Turnlee, though Charlie was thankful there were no speeches, if for no other reason than that the stiff collar of his dress uniform was decidedly uncomfortable, and without an overcoat the uniform did a poor job of keeping out the cold. They marched across the tarmac of the landing field to several waiting grav cars. Cesare, Theode, and Arthur were escorted each to his own limousine, each accompanied by two members of Cesare's household guard, while a fourth limousine carried important members of the retinue. Out of habit Charlie rode with the rest of Cesare's guard in a big grav truck equipped for troop transport. They'd be barracked somewhere in the bowels of the palace, ready to relieve the guards that shadowed Cesare, Arthur, and Theode.

The troop transport pulled up to a side entrance near the back of the palace, and Charlie spilled out of the truck with the rest of the guard. They were met by a servant who gave them room assignments—most of the guard were assigned to a common barracks, while NCOs and officers were given private or semi-private rooms, depending upon rank. However, when Charlie gave the servant his name, the man frowned, hit the search key on his pad several times, and asked Charlie, "Are you sure about the spelling, sir?"

Charlie frowned back at him and the man said, "Oh, of course you are, sir. If you'll give me a moment, sir." The man stepped aside, put a finger to one ear, and subvocalized into a com implant. A moment later he turned to Charlie with a smarmy smile. "I'm terribly sorry, sir. There's been some sort of mistake. You're not being housed with the staff. We'll have someone down here in a moment to escort you to your suite."

The servant who escorted Charlie to his *suite* bowed and postured incessantly. And as they climbed higher and higher into the palace, and as the décor grew steadily more ornate and expensive, so grew Charlie's discomfort.

In the middle of a long hallway the servant opened wide double doors three meters high, and ushered Charlie into his suite. He had a study, bedroom, private toilet, and shower. Both the study and bedroom sported the luxury of an old-fashioned hearth with a blazing wood fire that took the chill off the cold winter day. Charlie had never been quartered in the upper palace before, and the sudden change fueled his paranoia.

He shrugged it off and decided, *I might as well enjoy it while it lasts.*

"Dinner will be at eight this evening, Commander Cass," the servant said. "Dress is formal. Duke Cesare sends his regards, and asks that you join him in his apartments at the third hour." The servant backed out of the room, leaving Charlie standing before the blazing hearth.

Charlie looked at his watch. He had an hour before seeing Cesare. Might as well take a shower and put on a fresh uniform. He tossed his spacer's bag on the bed and stripped down.

The shower was lavish, plenty of hot water, no shipboard rationing. He toweled off, found a luxurious, warm robe hanging on the back of the fresher door, threw it on, wandered into the bedroom, and stopped in front of the fire to enjoy the warmth. He was thinking he might enjoy this after all, just go with it and let Winston do the worrying. He stood in front of the fire and let the warmth relax him a bit.

Something made a sound behind him, a click and a whir, and he froze. *Click, whir, tap, tap,* there it was again. He tried to imagine what it might be, but his mind drew a blank. It was probably something of no consequence, something to do with grand suites in palaces, of which Charlie had little experience.

But his training wouldn't let him accept that. *Assume the worst,* Roacka seemed to whisper in his ear, *and play it like yer life depended on it, boy.*

Standing there like a statue and not moving seemed to be acceptable. So with infinite patience he turned slowly about, taking several seconds to complete the motion. He didn't have to look carefully to find the source of the noise. He spotted a small bot on top of his spacer's bag where he'd thrown it on the bed. It was shaped like a six-legged spider, sharp little mechanical legs poking and prodding at the bag and the uniform he'd tossed there. His heart climbed up into his throat—this was not benign.

It was probably looking for a thermal signature combined with motion detection, perhaps with a hormone or DNA sniffer, which was why it had focused on the dirty clothing. It was pure luck that he'd immediately stepped in front of the fire. The heat radiating from it swamped Charlie's own low-level thermal image.

There was a small, spinning globe on top of the mechanical spider. It rotated full-circle every two or three seconds. Again, with infinite slowness he lowered into a crouch in front of the fire, hoping to further obscure his thermal signature. He had no weapons, nothing near at hand to throw or use as a club. He had the robe he was wearing, and the warmth of the fire was becoming uncomfortable. He carefully peeled off the robe, held it close to the fire until it was starting to give off little tendrils of smoke. It should give off its own thermal signature now.

Maintaining his crouch, he tensed, then tossed the robe into the air to one side of his position. The bot responded instantly, scurried across the room with blinding speed and leapt at the descending robe before it hit the floor. The force of the bot's leap was such that bot and robe together slammed into the wall then dropped to the floor. The bot, tangled in the robe, thrashed about furiously as Charlie scrambled across the floor on hands and knees. He gathered up the edges of the robe, lifted it like a sack with the bot trapped inside, swung the robe around his head once and slammed the bot into the wall. Taking no chances he swung again, and again, and again, until finally sparks and smoke erupted from the dead weight trapped in the robe.

He dropped the bundle on the floor, and as the rush of adrenaline subsided and his knees turned to rubber he sat down in the middle of the room, caring nothing for the fact that he was as naked as the day he was born.

If they don't get you with the first strike, Roacka seemed to whisper, *don't forget the backup plan.*

To Charlie's right he heard a pneumatic *whoosh*. He scrambled on hands and knees toward the fresher door, a new spurt of adrenaline goading him on. Behind him he heard a buzzing sound, and he suffered an irrational moment of fear that something would attack his bare ass. The last few steps before the fresher door he got to his feet in a low, running crouch, slammed through the door, and sprawled to the floor in a tumble of arms and legs. He lunged to his feet, caught a glimpse of small reptilian wings rocketing toward him, stumbled toward the door, threw his shoulder into it and slammed it shut.

A tiny reptilian head punched through the door just above Charlie, scattering splinters from the door and transmitting a bone-jarring shock to his shoulder. The little beast's momentum stopped halfway through the door, pinned half in, half out. Its head jerked up and down spasmodically, began spewing a stream of emerald green liquid that shot across the floor of the fresher. Charlie kept his shoulder pressed to the door until the little beast's head slowly jerked to a stop. And only then did he relax, sliding down the door until his bare butt hit the cold floor of the fresher.

"Shit," he said.

Charlie got up and knelt beside the green liquid on the floor, wondering if it was caustic, or something else equally harmful. Staring at it carefully he noticed something moving in the green ooze, and on closer inspection he could see dozens of tiny larva, all squirming and thrashing about in the slime.

Charlie was bruised, sore in a dozen places, but the pain associated with one particular ache on his arm rose to a level above the rest. He lifted his arm, and on it found one small drop of the green ooze.

He stumbled to his feet, and careful not to step in any of the green slime he leaned over the sink, ran water on his arm, washing away the ooze to reveal a small bite mark in the skin. The pain didn't stop, a searing burn that grew steadily. On closer examination he saw that the bite was more of a puncture wound and something beneath the skin moved, writhing and thrashing about.

Charlie stumbled out of the fresher, ran to the bed where he'd tossed the uniform he'd stripped off earlier, started rifling through the clothes. His hand found the hard edge of plast, and desperately he tore the plast knife loose from its sheath. He ran back into the fresher, and leaning over the sink, he slashed the knife across the puncture mark in one smooth motion. His blood flowed freely into the sink as he dropped the knife, and with his free hand squeezed the wound with all the pressure he could apply.

The little creature that had invaded his body popped out of it like a pimple, and the searing burn suddenly disappeared, replaced by the good, clean throb of a nasty cut. The small reptile that landed in the sink was now almost the size of the tip of Charlie's thumb. The tiny creatures he had glimpsed in the green ooze had been a fraction of that, and he realized that in just a single minute the creature had grown within him more than tenfold. He started to shake as he understood the death meant for him, for if the little reptile had spewed the slime all over him, he'd have had hundreds of the tiny things invading his body.

"Clever of them," Cesare said, "separating us like that. We sweep my suite and Theode's and Arthur's, assume our guard will sweep the barracks and any rooms assigned to our staff, and no one realizes you've been sidetracked to a suite in the main palace."

As Cesare's personal physician stitched up the cut in Charlie's arm, Roacka examined the small bot, then the little reptile still pinned in the fresher door. "The hunter probe was just a feint." Roacka nodded toward the little reptile. "The Finalsan flying snake, now that's a nasty one, lad."

Charlie learned that the snake's intent had been to

punch its sharp beak into his torso, then spew its entire brood of young into his body, its last dying act the culmination of its breeding cycle. It might have taken an hour, but the little monsters would have completely consumed Charlie, then consumed each other until there were only a few of them left, a nice means of culling the weak from the gene pool. Charlie didn't say anything to Cesare, but this felt more like something Gaida would cook up.

Roacka voiced Charlie's thoughts. "Gaida?"

"No," Cesare said. "I don't think so. She'd have too much to lose, and almost nothing to gain."

Charlie glanced at Arthur and their eyes met; another little hint of that bargain both of them had always suspected existed. Neither of them said anything, knowing full well Cesare would deflect any inquiry on the subject.

"I agree," Arthur said. "This was cooked up by someone very high up in the palace structure."

Charlie asked, "Lucius?"

Arthur shook his head. "No, my money would be on Adsin; this looks like something he'd try, and he is originally from Finalsa. Of course, we'll never prove anything."

Cesare turned to Major Pelletier, head of his household guard. "Major, I want two bodyguards on Charlie at all times."

Charlie had never had to tolerate bodyguards before, and found them to be intrusive even now. That evening the two men followed him down to a reception he had to attend. At least they peeled off from him as he stepped into a room filled with the Realm's nobility.

He spotted Gaida, looking at him as if he'd brought a bad smell into the room, and across the floor he caught a glimpse of Del. No, he reminded himself, Delilah, the royal princess, daughter of a man who, if he really was conspiring with the Syndonese, seemed more enemy than king. And he couldn't ignore the possibility that Lucius might have been complicit in the assassination attempt with the hunter bot and the flying snake. Charlie didn't want to think about more lives lost in a useless little war.

A few minutes later he found himself drink in hand, chatting with a young woman who insisted on quizzing him about the conditions in a Syndonese prison camp. She'd introduced herself, but he didn't remember her name, probably because he couldn't take his mind off Del, and his gaze kept drifting her way.

"Commander Cass." Charlie turned toward the voice as a short, fat man dressed in flowing church robes descended upon him.

Charlie bowed his head as the briefing Winston had loaded into his implants kicked in. "Archcanon Taffallo."

"Charles—you don't mind if I call you Charles—of course not." Taffallo hooked one of Charlie's arms and looked at the young woman. "You don't mind if I steal this young man, do you, my dear?"

The young woman curtsied deeply, bowing forward, and as she did so the top of her dress opened slightly, exposing some attractive cleavage. Charlie caught Taffallo eyeing it greedily as the young woman said, "Of course not, Your Eminence."

Taffallo dragged Charlie away by his arm. "Now, young Charles, I wanted to ask your thoughts on the Syndonese negotiations. They say you know the Syndonese better than anyone."

At finally hearing solid confirmation that someone was negotiating something with the Syndonese, Charlie tried to keep a neutral look on his face. He shrugged. "I'm afraid that *they* are exaggerating."

"Oh come now, Charles. Don't be modest. You defeated them rather handily at Solista."

Charlie wasn't going to admit he knew nothing of the negotiations. Maybe Taffallo would spill something. "That was luck, Your Eminence. These negotiations require a political savvy that I don't have. Perhaps you should ask Duke Cesare, or Lord Arthur."

Taffallo raised an eyebrow. "I see you're an expert at the fine art of polite evasion. Now, that's the mark of a politician, Charles."

As they talked, Taffallo led Charlie to a rather select group, most of whom he'd never before met, but all of whom were included in Winston's briefing. Protocol demanded that Charlie acknowledge them in order of rank.

Charlie bowed first to Martino, the handsome heir to the throne who seemed to want to make every hour of the day a party. "Your Royal Highness. I'm honored."

Martino swayed on his feet, already a bit drunk, and barely acknowledged Charlie with a nod. He was clearly more intent on the pretty young woman hanging on his arm.

Charlie bowed next to Nadama, one of the three most powerful people in the Realm. "Your Grace."

Nadama merely nodded. The Duke de Satarna rivaled Cesare for power, and the two were almost always at odds.

Charlie turned to Karlok, Duke de Tarris. "Your Grace."

"Commander Cass." Karlok was nowhere near as powerful as Cesare or Nadama, but he was the king's man. Lucius had bought him off by agreeing to marry one of his nieces to Karlok's third son, and to deliver her along with a nice title and a rather sizable dowry of property and estates.

Charlie finished by bowing to Dieter, Nadama's heir and the future head of House de Satarna. "Your Lordship."

Last, he bowed to Theode. "Your Lordship."

Dieter was tall, handsome, and Charlie had heard that, like his father, more machine than human. "Cass," Dieter said. "So, you're the hero."

Charlie shrugged. "I think my heroism is based little on my exploits, of which there are few, and more on the vid coverage contracted for by His Majesty following my demise, though I suspect the vid coverage would've been considerably less had His Majesty had foreknowledge of my resurrection."

Dieter chuckled, Karlok laughed openly, while Nadama just stared. Dieter said, "At least you're not stupid."

"Ah, but he claims to be," Taffallo said, "when it comes to politics. Don't you, Charles? Just the simple soldier, and nothing more, is what you'd have us believe, eh?"

"Perhaps not simple," Charlie said. "But still just a soldier."

Theode chimed in with "Perhaps simpleton is best. Or even whore—"

Nadama silenced him with a look.

"My sister likes you," Martino said, his words slurring a bit. "Thinks you're quite the heroic figure, though from the holos I've seen, that prison ship doesn't appear to have been a very heroic experience."

At Martino's comment Dieter seemed to reassess Charlie carefully and now found him undesirable. Theode threw out another nasty little barb that Charlie ignored. Then Arthur joined them and—clearly more at home amidst the somewhat thorny interplay of court life—rescued Charlie.

"Forgive me," Arthur said. "I have to drag Charlie away."

As they walked away from the group, Arthur leaned close to Charlie and whispered, "I'm guessing Taffallo wanted to see their reaction to you. He's always angling for some advantage, though he'd be better at it if he weren't so transparent."

Charlie couldn't imagine what advantage the man

was angling for, and he could only hope his brother's interference had diverted Taffallo's attention from him.

Arthur led him to two women near the edge of the room. Charlie recognized Telka, Duchess de Vena, a plump little woman with pretty, almost childlike features; and Harrimo, Duchess de Uranna—tall, thin, inscrutable, she reminded him of a female Winston. Arthur made the introductions.

Telka said, "Your family must have been overjoyed that you made it back alive."

When it came to power and wealth, Telka rivaled Nadama and Cesare. And any man who thought her naïve or unsophisticated because of her appearance or stature was a damn fool. Her statement about Charlie's family was a baited trap. He said, "The only family I ever had, Your Grace, was my mother. And she died long ago."

She smiled, and he saw a twinkle of approval in her eye. "I'm sorry, Commander."

"Think nothing of it, Your Grace." Charlie decided he liked the little woman.

Arthur tried to draw the two women out on the Aagerbanni situation. Telka was the wild card among the Nine. She, Cesare, and Nadama constituted the majority of the strength in the Realm. If any two of them agreed on an issue, barring intervention by a serious outside force, the Realm would have to go along. Cesare and Nadama were both lobbying for her support, but so far she remained uncommitted. And in any case, in this venue every word, movement, and expression would be carefully recorded by hidden pickups and analyzed later. Nothing serious could be discussed here.

Across the room Charlie spotted a man wearing the uniform of a Syndonese general, speaking with a fellow whom Charlie's briefing identified as Enrik Adsin, the king's chancellor. Adsin, wearing an expensive business suit, was a short, stringy little man, with an impeccably trimmed goatee, and sharp, sour features. He had a big cheesy smile on his face showing a lot of white teeth, but it didn't extend to his eyes, which made it seem more like a leer. When he saw Charlie looking his way, he leaned forward and whispered something in the general's ear, then the two turned and crossed the room to join Charlie, Arthur, and the two duchesses.

Adsin greeted the women and Arthur formally. Telka said nothing, while Harrimo nodded politely and said, "Chancellor." The word came out wrapped in a cold chill.

"Commander Cass," Adsin said. "We finally get a chance to meet." He reached out and tugged at Charlie's hand to shake it.

Charlie let him do so and lied. "A pleasure to meet you, Chancellor."

Adsin turned to the Syndonese standing next to him and said, "Let me introduce General Tantin, chief of staff to President Goutain."

With the exception of a hook nose, Tantin appeared

rather average looking. He smiled at Charlie and looked him over carefully. "Commander," he said in a thick Syndonese accent. "Your reputation precedes you."

They chatted for a while, none of them saying anything of substance, Adsin always displaying the big smarmy grin. Somehow he managed to talk around a mouth full of flashing white teeth. Eventually, he excused himself and escorted Tantin away, again whispering something in the general's ear.

Watching Adsin's back, Telka said, "Why is it that after I've been in the company of that man, I always feel the need to bathe?" She nodded toward Charlie's hand. "And you, Commander, should probably wash that hand."

Harrimo's impenetrable calm broke and she chuckled. A moment later they were called to dinner, where Charlie was relieved to be seated "below the salt" amidst a group in which the verbal barbs were kept to a minimum. Later that evening, with his suite freshly swept clear of any unwanted devices or dangerous predators—and with two of Cesare's personal guard stationed in the hall outside—Charlie fell into an exhausted sleep.

CHAPTER 6
FRIENDS INDEED

Charlie started each day with Add, Ell, and Roacka pounding on him for a few hours in a gym in the basement of the palace. His first morning on Turnlee, Roacka wanted to work knives: plast knives, power knives, even old-fashioned steel knives; knife fighting, knife throwing—Charlie was surprised they didn't do knife swallowing. Del showed up to watch, applauding whenever Charlie got the best of his opponent—which wasn't too often. Still, Charlie knew he'd have to put up with a bit of ribbing from Add and Ell about her. Dieter showed up near the end of the workout, clearly didn't approve of Del's presence, and managed to drag her away in short order.

"Enough," Winston said, bringing everything to a stop. Somehow he managed to cow even Add and Ell.

"Eh, Chamberlain," Roacka said. "We're having a good workout with the lad."

Winston shook his head. "That'll have to wait. I bring orders from His Grace. Charles, please come with me."

It felt as if Winston was dragging him away for a spanking. He stripped off his sparring suit and quickly joined Winston, who took him by the arm and led him back toward their apartments. Winston leaned close to Charlie's ear. "In a little over an hour and a half you're to meet with the king."

Charlie's eyebrows rose involuntarily. "An audience with Lucius?"

Winston made a point of saying, "No. There'll be no *audience* with the king. This is informal and unofficial, an encounter that will happen purely by accident. At half past ten you'll be strolling in the Winter Garden. At half past ten His Majesty will be strolling in the Winter Garden. The two of you will meet, purely by coincidence. You'll chat briefly, and then you'll part. We have barely more than an hour in which to clean you up, brief you, and get you to the Winter Garden, so let's not waste any time."

"Ah! Commander Cass! Fancy meeting you here."

"Your Majesty," Charlie said, pretending surprise. He bowed deeply from the waist.

Lucius dismissed Charlie's bow with the wave of a hand. "Tut, tut, Commander. No need for such formalities here."

Lucius was accompanied by Adsin. The chancellor

acknowledged Charlie with a nod, and again he wore a cheesy grin. Charlie recalled that Arthur thought Adsin was responsible for the hunter bot and the flying snake in his room.

"Come," Lucius said. "Walk with Us a bit." The *Us* clearly did not include Adsin, and was instead the majestic plural.

Adsin dropped to the rear, leaving Charlie on Lucius's left. Charlie wasn't sure if he liked having Adsin at his back.

"You're a lucky man, Commander," Lucius said. "Luck seems to accompany you, and my generals tell me that luck is important for a military man."

"Perhaps if I'd had more luck, Your Majesty, I wouldn't have spent so much time in a Syndonese prison camp."

"Ah, that." Lucius stopped to admire a large, yellow flower. "Do you blame me for that, Commander?"

"No, Your Majesty," Charlie lied. "Of course not."

"Then it's the war itself. You blame me for that?"

Charlie chose his words carefully. "It's not my place to judge, Your Majesty, therefore I do not blame. But if I may presume to ask, what did the war accomplish?"

Lucius looked up from the flower. "We defeated the Syndonese, did we not?"

"Yes, and what did that buy us?"

Lucius was at a loss. "Why—we won."

"But what did we win? What did we gain?"

Adsin intervened. "Your Majesty, I think I begin to understand this young man. In fact, the war accomplished nothing. At great expense we held a war, defeated the enemy, then returned to the status quo, our situation unchanged. And I believe Commander Cass's concern is less with the expense and more with the fact that we paid for the goods without receiving them." Adsin smiled at Charlie, a truly friendly smile, as if he and Charlie were kindred souls and understood one another completely, which left Charlie feeling a bit unclean. He recalled Telka's comments at the reception.

Lucius smiled also. "So, Commander, in our next war you would have us conquer territories, annex states, or something of that nature?"

"Is there going to be a next war, Your Majesty?"

"We would hope not, Commander. But let's be realistic. War, or sometimes merely the threat of war, is one of the most powerful tools in the diplomat's kit, is it not?"

"I'm no diplomat, Your Majesty, so such concepts are beyond me. I'm a soldier, plain and simple. And yet—perhaps *because* of that—I'd have there be no next war."

Lucius sighed heavily. "We all would have there be no next war, but we often have no choice, do we? Thank you for the insight, Commander. It's been most enjoyable chatting with you."

Lucius turned away from Charlie and continued walking. Adsin rushed to catch up.

And Charlie simply stood there, replaying the scene.

As Charlie left the garden, he still wondered what that little meeting had been all about. Perhaps Lucius was just curious about him since they'd never met. Or maybe he was reconsidering the minor title he was supposedly going to bestow on Charlie.

As soon as he stepped into the palace he was accosted by Rierma. "Charles, my boy. You know, since you've returned from the dead we've not had a chance to truly chat. Come with me."

One didn't just happen to run into one of the Nine, any more than one might happen to run into the king in the Winter Garden. Rierma, with his personal guard at his heels, chatted amiably as he led Charlie through the palace. Charlie knew Rierma almost as well as he knew Cesare; his first years in the navy had been on one of Rierma's ships, and Rierma had been a frequent visitor to Farlight. The benign nonsense the old duke spewed as they walked was the face he put on for all who didn't know him well. But when they entered the wing of the palace that housed Rierma and his retinue, the captain of his guard, a man named Silas, stepped into place behind the bodyguards accompanying them. Rierma nodded at the man.

Rierma's chatter ended abruptly as they walked into a sitting room in his personal suites, where Sig and the captain of her guard awaited them. Charlie had also spent time on one of the Duchess de Plutarr's ships, and her presence confirmed Charlie's belief that there was nothing coincidental about this meeting. With the doors to the palace proper closed behind them, Silas stepped up to Charlie and asked politely, "Commander, may I search you?"

Charlie glanced at Sig and the little woman showed nothing on her face. He cocked an eyebrow at Silas, and Rierma said, "No insult meant, Charles. But who knows what sort of listening devices might have been planted on you without your knowledge?"

Charlie nodded his permission, and the guard captain patted him down with some sort of scanning device. Silas announced, "He's clean." Then he searched himself, the two guards, and lastly Rierma. Apparently, they'd adopted a standard procedure of searching anyone who'd been outside Rierma's suites, no matter how briefly. Silas finished by telling Rierma, "We've recently re-swept the entire suite, and for insurance, we're jamming."

Silas dismissed the two guards, leaving Charlie, Rierma, Sig, and their guard captains. "Now we can talk," Rierma announced. "Something to drink, Charles?"

Charlie declined. Rierma poured an amber liquid into a glass while Sig introduced her guard captain: Talcott. Charlie didn't know Sig as well as Rierma, but when she inquired about his health, then made a few comments on the weather, he politely interrupted her. "Forgive me, Your Grace. Ordinarily we might begin with some small talk, then slowly work our way around to the really serious stuff. But after such a dramatic entrance to these suites, don't you think small talk is somewhat anticlimactic?"

She threw her head back and laughed. She was a pinch-faced little woman, and he'd never before seen her laugh so heartily. "You are your father's son."

Charlie had had years of experience ignoring such baited comments. "May I ask why I'm here?"

Rierma swirled the drink in his glass. "I've known you a long time, watched you grow up, even helped raise you a bit here and there."

Sig said, "I don't know you as well as Rierma, but I recall that you were a good spacer—smarter than most—and he says you're a man of honor. We wish to consult you on a matter of some delicacy."

"And that matter is?"

"I warned you he'd not vacillate," Rierma said. Rierma looked at Charlie, and all pretense at cheerfulness disappeared. "Sig and I . . . are somewhat uncomfortable with the situation here at Almsburg. We're concerned for our safety."

Silas said, "Pelletier and Roacka, per Cesare's orders, briefed us all on the attempt on your life. And I'm told Arthur suspects Adsin."

Charlie now understood. "But that was a mixture of carelessness and gullibility on my part. Now that we're forewarned there should be no issue."

Sig shook her head. "You're not that stupid, Commander, so I must assume you're cautious."

Charlie smiled at her. "When one treads a path among kings and dukes and duchesses, caution is a survival trait."

"Charles, my boy," Rierma said. "I'll bet you could hold your own among the best courtiers. But there is more than merely security at issue here. Lucius is up to something sneaky, and he's about to do something. He's not a subtle man, and rather transparent to those of us who've known him long. We fear for the Realm, our duchies, and our personal safeties."

Sig said, "And I didn't like seeing Tantin there the other night. Adsin and that Syndonese officer have been thick as thieves, and I don't trust either of them."

Rierma turned to pour himself another drink, saying, "I find it surprising that even Lucius trusts that snake, but then our king has never been terribly perceptive. Flatter him the right way and he'll believe anything."

Charlie glanced at Silas and Talcott, was surprised to see that the two guard captains showed no discomfort at a discussion bordering on treason. "Do you think Tantin is working on his own, without Goutain's knowledge?"

Sig shook her head. "No. Tantin's a bootlicker, and his presence here is too visible. If he was sneaking around behind Goutain's back, he'd be far more discreet."

"And let's not forget Nadama," Rierma said. "He's playing some game as well, something far more serious than getting Dieter married off to Delilah."

Charlie waited for Rierma to say more but nothing came. The silence stretched out uncomfortably as they waited for him. Rierma was a friend, both to him and House de Maris. Sig he knew not well, but Arthur attested to the fact that she was a friend. So he felt he had no choice but to trust them.

"We can do little to protect the Realm from Lucius's machinations," Charlie said. "And the best protection for your duchies is if you yourselves are free to see to their welfare. Now, if I were a cautious man, and the captain of the guard responsible for the welfare of my liege," he looked pointedly at Talcott and Silas, "I might wish to have a stronger, more personally loyal response close at hand, a response that could react quickly and be at my side in seconds."

Talcott was a short, slightly plump little man. "My guard contingent is not inconsiderable."

"Nor mine," Silas said.

"But your guard contingents are not marines in powered combat armor and heavy combat kit. And having such, close at hand, rather than a thirty-minute high-G drop away, might make all the difference in the world."

Silas shook his head. "His Majesty will never allow us to maintain armed troops on the premises."

Charlie looked pointedly at Talcott, then Silas. "You both know Roacka?"

Both men nodded.

"I suggest you talk to him."

Talcott's eyes narrowed and Silas nodded again.

Charlie realized then that he'd have to bring Major Pelletier in on this. He'd been reluctant to do so because he didn't know the head of Cesare's household guard well, but had no choice now. He resolved to brief the man immediately.

"Furthermore," he said, "should some difficulty arise, I suggest we act in unison. And the only way to accomplish that is to have only one commanding officer." He smiled. "And that should be me."

Add cut high with her saber. Charlie ducked beneath her blade, saw an opening, charged in and buried his shoulder in her solar plexus. A *woof* escaped her lips as he lifted her off her feet and dropped her on her back on the floor, his shoulder still buried in her abdomen. But he'd forgotten her knee, which managed to find its way into his groin, and as he landed on top of her he took as much injury as he dealt. They rolled away from each other, both of them groaning and gasping for breath.

"Well done, little brother," Ell cried. "A tie. That's the best you've ever done against her."

Charlie had progressed to the point where he was besting Ell one out of every three or four matches, which was just not acceptable as far as Add was concerned. So Add, the best of the three, had personally taken over his instruction with a certain amount of derision directed at poor Ell. Add was not a pleasant taskmaster, as his groin would attest.

Ell flicked a switch on her control and Charlie relaxed as his sparring suit killed the pain feed. Ell stood over Add. "Sister," she said as Add continued to gasp for air. "Are you in pain? Charlie's such a poor student, he couldn't have hurt you."

Add's reply was "Harruuggghhh."

"What did you say, darling sister? I didn't quite understand you."

"Hurrpain gurrfeed."

"What's that? Oh, *pain feed*. I didn't realize it was still on. I thought you didn't need such things against poor opponents such as Charlie or me. Let me see." Ell looked carefully at the control. "Which button is yours?" She considered the box carefully as Add continued to groan, then finally pressed a switch. Add let out a sigh, then relaxed and lay still on the floor. As Charlie climbed to his feet Ell looked his way and winked, then grinned evilly.

"I'm still waiting for that dance, spacer."

Charlie turned about and found Del behind him, that playful look in her eye. They both knew it wouldn't be politic for him to dance with her at any of the events they'd recently attended. So they limited themselves to this simple little game. "The last time I attended a dance," Charlie said, "I didn't see you there. There was this rather haughty princess, and she did look quite like you. But her name was Delilah, not Del. Let me tell you, though, if this spacer is ever at a real dance, and there's a girl named Del there, then he'll most certainly collect the dance she owes him."

"And tell me, spacer, what's a real dance?"

"Loud," Charlie said with a wink, "noisy, and no waltzes."

"Delilah." Dieter appeared at Del's shoulder. He looked at Charlie and the two breeds with obvious distaste. "What are you doing here?" he asked Del.

"Just watching."

Dieter looked at the saber in Charlie's hand, then held out his own hand. "May I?"

Charlie handed it to him hilt first. Dieter took it and looked at it carefully. "Are you an expert in antique weapons, Cass?"

"Hardly an expert, Your Lordship."

Dieter stepped back, tested the balance of the blade, swung once at an imaginary opponent, and demonstrated a textbook lunge. He clearly knew what he was doing.

"Obviously," Charlie said, "you also practice with antiques."

"Yes," Dieter said, reversing the blade and returning it to Charlie. "It sharpens the reflexes, the timing." He looked at Charlie carefully, his eyes narrowing. "Perhaps you and I, sometime, might test our skills."

Charlie had a strong suspicion he wouldn't want such a match to happen. If Dieter killed him he'd merely have to apologize to Cesare. But if Charlie so much as pricked the skin of the heir to the de Satarna ducal seat, they could hang him. "Perhaps, Your Lordship."

"Come, Delilah," Dieter said, taking her arm and

turning to leave, allowing her no choice in the matter. "I've been meaning to have a chat with you."

Del went along complacently. But as they stepped out of the room she looked over her shoulder and winked at Charlie.

When they were gone Add said, "I think that someday you may have to kill him, little brother."

CHAPTER 7
MYSTERIOUS VISITORS

Charlie had not had the opportunity to bring Pelletier in on his schemes, so he'd asked Roacka to brief the major. The two men were waiting for him as he climbed the ladder to the gunboat's personnel hatch. In the small cabin near the cockpit there was no sign of the fifty odd marines slumbering in their combat armor in the cargo bay. Roacka wasted no time getting down to business. "Darmczek's ships are almost in position," Roacka said. "They're not having any trouble remaining hidden behind false identities. The traffic density in this system is so high, traffic control doesn't have a chance to look closely at anyone. And besides, no one could broadcast proper identity codes without access to classified ciphers."

"So," Charlie asked, "why am I here?"

Roacka grinned. "Darmczek's almost as paranoid as you. Drifting into position slowly like they are, his people got a lot of time on their hands. So he's got them checking out all the ships in Turnlee nearspace, starting with those in the immediate vicinity of Turnlee, and expanding outward. They're taking a close look at each ship, correlating identity and make with emissions—a quarter-million-ton destroyer emits a lot more noise than a quarter-million-ton freighter. And guess what . . ."

"I think you're going to tell me."

Roacka put on that evil grin of his. "Someone else is playing the same game we are."

"One of the other Nine?"

"It would have to be. Or Lucius himself. No one else could provide proper identity codes."

"So we know about them, but do they know about us?" Charlie asked.

"Could be, but not likely. Darmczek's ships are running with a lot of nonessential systems shut down, basically matching their emission signatures to their fake identities. Our friends out there aren't doing the same, so we can assume they haven't caught on yet."

Pelletier asked, "If it comes to a fight, how do we stand?"

Roacka looked smug. "By their emission signatures, looks to be four heavy cruisers and possibly one troop transport. With the element of surprise they could take the system. And forewarned as we are, with our flagship and those of Sig, Band, Rierma, and Faggan all working together, we'd still be outgunned, but could hold our own for a while. Those flagships just don't carry the firepower to stand up to a heavy cruiser. But add in Charlie's flotilla, and a little surprise of our own. As long as there're no reinforcements, we've got 'em reasonably outgunned."

"Band and Faggan are in this, too?" Charlie asked.

Roacka answered him. "After you dropped those rather unsubtle hints to Talcott and Silas, they approached me. And less than a day later it was Esterhower and Corbin, Faggan and Band's guard captains. All four of them now have shuttles on the ground filled with marines, and everyone's ready to take orders from you if the shit goes down."

Pelletier said, "Commander, I gotta say I'm a lot happier taking orders from a paranoid son-of-a-bitch like you, being a paranoid son-of-a-bitch myself."

The man looked pleased, and that made Charlie nervous. This thing was getting out of hand. "Let's not overreact. My paranoia seems to have become rather contagious. If I'm wrong, and they find out what we've done here . . . I've broken the king's law, violating Turnlee nearspace, stationing armed troops on the grounds of the palace without his permission. So let's not let anyone jump the gun."

"Don't worry about my people, Commander," Pelletier said. "And I've had a long talk with Esterhower, Talcott, Corbin, and Silas. They won't screw up either."

Roacka had a 3-D situation summary on one of the shuttle's screens—some serious firepower coming in surreptitiously. Could be benign, and then again not. "Contact Darmczek and tell him to have his ships tweak their positioning. Make sure there's one lined up on each of the intruders, at reasonably close range. I want the ability to put a large warhead into each of them, without warning, should the need arise."

Roacka grinned. "Sucker punch, eh lad?"

"Ya, sucker punch it is. Tell Darmczek that if they start shooting first, he's to use his own discretion and proceed as he sees fit, but only if they start shooting first. And I want him to go as long as he can without playing his hand. If something really bad happens, we have the element of surprise. Let's take maximum advantage of that. But move cautiously. It could be just one of the other Nine bringing a little insurance along, doing no less than us. So let's not get trigger-happy."

Charlie ran his fingers through his hair. If this turned into a screw-up and somebody jumped the gun, they'd hang him for sure.

"Here, lad," Roacka said. "The major here's come up with something for you."

Pelletier handed Charlie an odd looking little gun. "Roacka says you know how to handle antiques. That's no antique, but it's modeled on the principal of antique firearms. It's a chemical-powered slug thrower. Pull the trigger and an explosive charge ejects a slug at high velocity. On impact, the slug expands and fragments, causing quite a bit of damage. Be ready for it to kick like hell and make a lot of noise. It's small and easily concealed, but don't let that fool you; it'll drop a grown man. It probably won't punch through powered armor, but it may have enough impact to make an armored opponent hesitate. No energy sources, no circuitry, all elements but the chemical explosive made of hardened organic materials, so they won't show up on any scanner. Barring a hand search, you can even pass the security around the king. You've got eight shots then throw it away. We don't have a lot of these, so we're issuing them only to key personnel, and the guards immediately responsible for the safety of Rierma, Sig, Band, Faggan, and Cesare."

Next he handed Charlie a small flat card. "It looks like a small personal recorder for keeping notes and reminders, and it'll function to a limited extent as one. You can also use it to communicate with the combat command computer on this shuttle. But if someone were to do something sneaky, like jamming communications in your vicinity, its battery is too limited to punch a signal through any serious electronic countermeasures, and a power source large enough to do so would trigger every alarm in the palace. But this puppy has a special chemical charge in it that won't show up on any scanning or search equipment. It's keyed to your voiceprint. Press the record switch and speak the word 'scramble' into it three times, then drop it, because it's going to get too hot to hold. The chemical charge burns hard and fast, producing enough power for a few seconds to punch a signal through almost any ECM or scrambling, at least enough to get through to this shuttle. The shuttle will relay the signal to Taggart and the other ships. When you activate it that's a signal to us that whatever is going to happen has started, and it'll also tell us where you are if we need to send a hard-target extraction team after you. We're giving these to all key personnel too."

Charlie looked at the device and turned it over in his hand. "Can you modify this?"

"To some limited extent, yes."

"Good. Then I want it to activate on two types of signals. If I say 'scramble' three times, then the shit's hitting the fan and I want those armed marines protecting the dukes and their heirs, and Darmczek goes on full alert. But if I say 'sucker punch' three times, proceed just like the 'scramble' signal and send in the marines, but also, Darmczek is to take out those bogies without warning or delay. He is to immediately put a big warhead into each of them. Can you modify it like that?"

Pelletier nodded. "Not a problem, Commander."

Roacka said to Pelletier, "I told you he ain't as dumb as he looks."

Delilah looked like a goddess that night, dressed in a floor length gown and petticoat styled from another era. She stopped in front of Charlie in a swirl of skirts and lace. "I see you're on my dance card for the next dance, Commander."

A lie, though not one that anyone could call her on. A dangerous folly, to dance with her in front of the eyes of the entire court—not dangerous for her, but for him—though clearly she didn't fully understand that.

And, at the moment, not dangerous enough for him to resist this opportunity.

He bowed properly. "Your Highness."

As the band started a waltz he took her hand, put his other hand oh-so-chastely on her waist just above the curve of her hips, and swirled her out onto the dance floor.

"You're tense, Commander."

"Am I dancing with Delilah or Del?"

"For you, I think I'm always Del. Does that make me brazen?"

"I have a suspicion that you're far more brazen than anyone here realizes. Perhaps even more than I realize."

It was a lively waltz and she threw her head back and laughed as he twirled her about. She looked over his shoulder, and he saw her smother a chuckle. "Oh, Dieter is going to be so disappointed in me—the brazen princess dancing with the penniless bastard. He presumes so much. But then I'll probably end up marrying him . . . for the good of the Realm."

They both understood the realities of noble birth, and it was at times like these Charlie was thankful he had never been acknowledged by Cesare. She'd marry Dieter, *for the good of the Realm,* and if he found someone he could love, and she was common born, or at least not high in the ranks of the nobility, then Cesare would arrange everything for Charlie. But beneath the pretense, he and Del both knew they'd never have *that* dance.

The waltz came to an end. She stepped away from

him, smiled, then stepped back in close and her eyebrows narrowed seriously. "Beware of my father," she whispered. "He is a fool. A kindly fool, a fool I love dearly, but still a fool, and he's planning something sneaky."

She stepped away from him and smiled once more. The entire hall seemed to have come to an uneasy pause. It took Charlie a moment to realize that as long as Del stood in the middle of the dance floor without an appropriate partner—and Charlie was not an appropriate partner—the music would not again start.

Martino suddenly appeared at her elbow, drink in hand. "Flaunting propriety, are we, my dear sister? Well, good, flaunt away. At least you have the balls to do so. I applaud you."

Queen Adan appeared out of the crowd, a strikingly beautiful woman, frowning her disapproval at Charlie. She stepped between him and Delilah with her back to Charlie as if he weren't there. "Come, my dear. I have someone I want you to meet." She hustled Delilah away.

The music started up again. Martino swayed a bit from side to side. "I suggest, Commander," he slurred, "that we leave the dance floor. Otherwise, we shall be forced to dance with one another. And while I might find the scandal a bit enjoyable, it will only put your life in more danger."

Perhaps Martino, though ever the drunk, was a bit more shrewd than Charlie had thought.

CHAPTER 8
THE BETRAYER BETRAYED

The palace was rife with rumors that Lucius's negotiations with Aagerbanne had stalemated. Arthur was of the opinion that Lucius had not negotiated in good faith, and had purposefully brought the discussions to an impasse. There would be an announcement the following day in high court, and Charlie went to bed that night not sure what to expect.

He rose early to prepare for high court. Winston had advised him of the appropriate time to appear: after most of the other commoners were in place, but prior to the arrival of any serious nobility. Charlie put on his best dress uniform—not formal, formal wasn't appropriate for the business of court—but still his best. Then, with his personal guard in tow, he headed for the throne room.

Walking with his guard, Charlie was lost in thought considering the dangerous ramifications of the Aagerbanne situation, when Del accosted him, grabbed his arm, and without ceremony pulled him through a door hidden behind some drapes. His guards followed.

They were in a corridor used by servants, though at that moment it was empty. "Wait here," she said to his guards, then pulled him just far enough down the corridor so they could speak privately. His guards reacted to the princess pulling him into a private conversation with chuckles and grins.

"I have to warn you," Del said breathlessly. "I don't know exactly what my father is planning, but it has something to do with the Syndonese. I think he's actually negotiating with Goutain, not just Tantin."

Her revelation stunned Charlie, though it confirmed some of the more fantastic rumors he'd heard. He asked her a number of questions, but she knew nothing more. She'd heard, purely by chance, a word or two between her father and Adsin, and had drawn a rather broad conclusion from very little data. "Thank you," he said, "but I have to go, and we shouldn't be seen together. Wait a few moments after I'm gone before you leave."

She nodded, and he turned away from her. But he'd taken only a single step when she gripped his arm and pulled him back. Then she kissed him—not a chaste little peck on the cheek or lips, but a full and unreserved kiss, her body pressed against his hot with passion and emotion. She then pushed him away and laughed. "No. *You* wait a moment, then leave." She grinned as conspiratorially as Roacka might have, and walked away.

Charlie's guards had clearly enjoyed the exchange. So he shut them up with a few harshly snapped orders and their smiles disappeared. It was with the utmost respect, then, that the older, more senior one pointed out that he should remove the lady's lip paint from his own lips.

They made their way to the throne room and Charlie took a place among the masses of high-ranking commoners and lesser nobility that lined the periphery of the massive hall, all waiting for the Nine to arrive. The whole time, though, he couldn't stop thinking, *The Syndonese! What are they in this?*

"Eh, lad," Roacka said, appearing at his elbow. "I'd ask you why you're so lost in thought, but I'd be lost too after a kiss like that."

"I take it that's going to make the rounds of the barracks."

"Not *going to*, lad. It's already made the rounds and come back again a time or two."

Charlie leaned close to Roacka and whispered in his ear, "Can you get out of here?"

Roacka knew him well enough to realize that kissing princesses wasn't the subject at hand. "Sure, lad, I'm just a spectator."

"Get hold of Darmczek on a secure channel. Have him cross-check the emission signatures of those bogies against the signatures of known Syndonese warships."

Roacka shook his head. "Nah, lad, can't be Syndonese. They don't have the clearance codes."

Charlie looked at Roacka pointedly. "They do if Lucius gave them to Goutain."

"Shit!" Roacka swore. "That fucking idiot."

"Check it out. Now, not later."

"Aye, lad." Roacka disappeared into the crowd.

A few minutes later, signaling the beginning of events, Archcanon Taffallo appeared at the entrance to the hall. Preceded by two boys in novitiate's robes carrying burning incense, and flanked by churchmen of high rank, all dressed in heavily brocaded robes, they moved slowly up the center of the great hall, with Taffallo calmly throwing blessings to right and left. As they approached the throne they turned right, to what would soon be the king's left when seated on the throne. Taffallo's seat was, in itself, a throne, though lower and less elegant than the seats the Nine would occupy, which themselves were lower and less elegant than the king's throne. Taffallo's attendants would stand, flanking him and behind him.

The Nine appeared, entering to the sound of trumpet fanfare, all dressed in robes of state and marching slowly up the center of the hall in order of precedence, Nadama and Cesare in the lead walking side by side. Drums rolled, cymbals crashed, and as they passed, everyone bowed or curtsied, some more deeply than others. At the throne they turned left, for by tradition they'd all sit at the king's right hand, and there they assumed their appointed places.

A few moments later Charlie noticed Adsin appear from a private entrance hidden behind the throne. As the last notes of the trumpets died, the lord chamberlain of the court struck his staff three times on the floor, and a deep silence descended. "His Majesty, Lucius the First, third to carry the blood of the Stephanovs, thirty-second in succession of the Plenroix, Harlburg, and Stephanov empire . . ." *Empire* was a word Lucius had added. " . . . king of the nine beasts, guardian and protector of the people's faith."

The Nine and Taffallo all stood, and along with everyone else bowed or curtsied deeply as Lucius appeared, Adan at his side, Martino and Delilah and a train of attendants behind them. Like the Nine before them they marched slowly up the center. The fanfare, the drumrolls, the cymbal crashes, the trumpets' blare—they were quite the same as what they'd all suffered earlier at the entrance of the Nine, just louder and longer. The noise continued as Lucius, Adan, Martino, and Delilah ascended to the throne, and it didn't die until some seconds after Lucius sat down. Adan then sat on her smaller throne, with Martino standing on Lucius's right and Delilah standing on Adan's left.

Charlie, as was appropriate for all common men in the throng, had dropped to one knee and bowed his head, while all men of noble station had merely bowed deeply. A profound silence descended as Lucius let them remain so for several seconds, and Charlie realized that one knee wasn't a difficult position for a man to hold, but for the women, an arrested curtsy could be an excruciating affair if forced to hold it for any length of time.

"Rise," Lucius called out. "Please, all rise."

The petticoats of the ladies hissed noisily as everyone stood, and the Nine and Taffallo returned to their seats.

"It's rare," Lucius continued, "for us to have all of our most trusted vassals assembled at once." He nodded regally toward the Nine. "And when we do, there is much that must be done. We have before us . . ."

Charlie tuned him out and carefully scanned the crowd looking for Roacka. Each of the Nine had a bodyguard standing behind them, hidden in the shadows of long, velvet drapes. Charlie could just make out Add's silhouette behind Cesare. Each also had their heir and an advisor standing more visibly behind them, and of course for Cesare that was Arthur and Winston. Charlie couldn't locate Ell in the crowd, but if he had he would've sent her after Roacka. Syndonese! What schemes had Lucius come up with that involved the Syndonese? And was there an immediate threat, or just some conniving power play?

Lucius droned on. There was something about a territorial dispute with one of the independent states. He authorized a minor earl to organize a committee to study the matter so that a peaceful negotiation might ensue. Titles and properties were granted, to which the king gave his blessing. It was all business hammered out previously in private counsel with the king and the Nine, now made public. Charlie continued to scan the crowd for any sign of Roacka, but when the lord chamberlain loudly announced something about

Aagerbanne, Charlie's attention snapped back to the business of the court.

Adsin had stepped forward and stood on the dais to one side of the king and one step down from the throne. "His Majesty has asked me to address the situation with Aagerbanne."

Charlie glanced up and saw Cesare frowning, his eyes narrowed with suspicion.

"As you all know," Adsin continued, "the crown has, for some time, been negotiating for unlimited access to the Aagerbanni port facilities on Aagerbanne Prime, which would give us access to all the trade routes into the independent states. It would be a financial windfall for all nine duchies as well as independent merchants throughout the Realm."

Someone near Charlie grumbled quietly, "But mostly for the crown."

As Adsin spoke, his eyes seemed to focus on Charlie. "The discussions were going quite well until about a tenday ago, and then for some reason progress slowed. After several more days of attempted negotiations on our part, it was determined that the Aagerbanni delegates were not negotiating in good faith, so they were placed under arrest yesterday morning."

A background of whispers erupted from the crowd as Adsin pointedly looked to the lord chamberlain at the far end of the hall. "Lord Chamberlain," he said.

The lord chamberlain rapped his staff three times on the floor and called out, "Charles Cass is called to stand before His Majesty."

There was a moment of near silence, punctuated by shuffling of feet, then the hiss of whispers from the crowd turned into a rising murmur. The fellow in front of Charlie realized he was standing in Charlie's way, and he stepped politely aside. That seemed to be a signal for the rest as the crowd parted slowly and a narrow aisle opened before him. Charlie glanced up to Cesare; the look of suspicion on his face had deepened. Winston and Arthur both shrugged, telling Charlie that connecting him to Aagerbanne was a surprise to them all.

With no choice in the matter Charlie walked forward carefully. He was more than half the length of the hall from the throne as he stepped into the open aisle that ran up its center. He turned to Lucius, bowed deeply, and strode forward. He knew the required formulas, and at the base of the dais he dropped to one knee and bowed his head. "Your Majesty."

"Rise, Commander Cass. Stand and let Us see your face."

Charlie rose and looked up toward the throne. Adan couldn't hide her dislike, while Martino was clearly bored and Delilah appeared nervous and tense. Perhaps it was Lucius's smug, self-satisfied, and self-important expression that gave her cause for concern. Certainly it gave Charlie cause, for it was clear Lucius was about to reveal something.

Lucius scanned the court dramatically and returned his gaze to Charlie. "We know, Commander, that you are greatly concerned about Our negotiations with

Aagerbanne, and the possibility of armed conflict. We know too that you hope for a peaceful resolution to this dilemma. And that's truly admirable in a warrior such as you. Such a combination, the skills of war in a man of peace, is rare indeed, and We see so many ways one such as you might serve the crown. And too, We recognize the debt owed to one who has served Us in the past with such valiant endeavor."

Charlie began to fear the worst. He glanced quickly toward the seated Nine, and all but Nadama were hanging on Lucius's every word. Whatever *it* was, it looked like Nadama was in on it.

"We have sought, therefore, to find the peaceful resolution you so dearly desire. In fact, We've made it imperative, a prerequisite to any solution. We've thought long and hard on this matter, and with counsel from Our most valued advisors . . ." Lucius nodded briefly toward Adsin. " . . . we have, We believe, a solution that satisfies the needs of all."

Out of the corner of his eye Charlie caught some movement in the gallery where the Nine sat. Again he glanced toward them and saw that Add had stepped out of the shadows with Roacka at her side. Roacka leaned forward and whispered in Cesare's ear, while Add stared intently at Charlie, her right hand raised casually up to her left shoulder where Charlie could see it. In breed handspeak she signed *Yes* . . . but before she could go on Lucius continued, "There were many questions that We must answer in these deliberations, but there were two key elements to a peaceful resolution. One, how do We proceed from a position of strength? For if one is strong, the opposition loses its vigor, loses its resolution. The second question: how do We administer a new, and possibly unruly, province in a peaceful fashion?"

The words "new and unruly province" produced a rising buzz from the crowd. Lucius paused, waited for silence to return, and Charlie glanced again up to Add. *Yes*, she signed. *Syndonese. . .*

"The answer to the second question was quite simple," Lucius continued, "and he stands before Us now, a man of peace who is quite capable of war. To that end, We have this day signed and placed Our seal upon documents annexing Aagerbanne as a Crown State Holding. And we appoint you, Commander Cass, as governor general of the province, responsible for all military and police matters, and reporting only to the new viceroy, whom we shall appoint shortly."

The entire hall erupted. Telka, Cesare, and Band jumped to their feet. Faggan, Sig, Rierma, Harrimo, and Karlok leaned forward in their chairs, all but Nadama calling out to the king, some shouting.

Yes, Syndonese, Add signed. *Troops landing now.*

The lord chamberlain rapped his staff on the floor. "Silence. Silence in the presence of the king."

The noise dwindled to a low rumble, then a light buzz, and Lucius continued, "The first question, how to proceed from a position of strength, was far more difficult to answer. But the answer, while not obvious, turned out to be a brilliant stroke that in one move turns a potential source of opposition into a source of strength. Commander Cass, let me introduce His Excellency, President Goutain."

A large, imposing man stepped out from behind the throne, having entered the hall via a private doorway behind the dais. Again the hall erupted into chaos, and as the chamberlain slowly restored order, Charlie and Goutain studied one another. Goutain was tall, close to two meters, athletically trim, though showing the signs of middle age. When Charlie looked in his eyes he saw only hatred and contempt. The Syndonese dictator probably blamed him for the failure of his last war, and Charlie realized that Goutain would let nothing stand in the way of revenge. In that moment they both understood that one must eventually kill the other.

"We have, this day, signed and placed Our seal upon documents declaring a mutual defense pact with the Republic of Syndon, and to that end We appoint His Excellency as king's representative and viceroy of the new province of Aagerbanne."

The eruption this time was thunderous. The lord chamberlain rapped his staff repeatedly on the floor to no effect. In the midst of the noise Charlie looked into Lucius's eyes and calmly said, "Your Majesty, may I ask a question?"

Lucius couldn't hear him, so he leaned forward, cocked his head, and put a hand to one ear. He said, "What?"

That simple action, that visible indication that something more was happening, slowly brought about silence in the great hall. Charlie kept his voice low, though it seemed to echo throughout the room. "Your Majesty, you would appoint a viceroy who has violated king's law by bringing an armed presence into Turnlee nearspace?"

Lucius shrugged. "You're impudent to suggest he's broken king's law, Commander. Like others present here today, his personal ship is armed, and he has my permission to ensure his own safety with its presence."

Charlie knew he had to take a chance now, take a guess and pretend his knowledge was far more definitive than it was, hoping to get Goutain to reveal his hand. "I'm not speaking of his personal ship, Your Majesty. I'm speaking of four Syndonese warships in close orbit around this planet, and a troop carrier that is, at this moment, landing armed Syndonese regulars in the vicinity of this palace."

Even Nadama jumped to his feet this time, shouting with all the rest, and it was clear that Goutain had played them both for fools. If Goutain could take the palace, take Lucius and the Nine and their heirs as prisoners, he'd have the entire Realm in his hands.

Goutain threw his head back and laughed, then he shouted, "Silence, you fools."

His voice carried above the noise and he got his silence, though a background buzz of fear permeated the tomblike stillness of the hall. "Commander Cass, I owe you a great deal."

"What is this?" Lucius demanded.

Goutain said to him, "Shut up, you idiot." Then he

looked over his shoulder, called out, "Tagama," and a Syndonese officer appeared at his side, a pistol held in his right hand pointed at the floor. Pointing at Charlie, Goutain said, "Kill him, now."

The Syndonese raised his pistol, and Charlie knew he had no chance of pulling the small gun that Pelletier had given him quickly enough to save himself. There came a thunderous report and Charlie flinched . . . only to see the Syndonese officer, as if swatted by a giant hammer, topple backward into the drapes behind the throne. Charlie looked up, saw Add had her pistol out and had beaten the Syndonese to the shot. She fired a second shot at Goutain, but he was already moving and disappeared behind the throne. Charlie spotted another Syndonese with an automatic weapon to the left of the throne; the fellow started spraying rounds at the Nine. At some point Charlie had drawn his pistol, though he didn't consciously remember doing it. He aimed, pulled the trigger, and as Pelletier had warned him it kicked like hell and made a lot of noise. But the Syndonese went down. *Eight shots then throw it away.*

Seven to go.

At the entrance to the hall an explosion blew the massive doors off their hinges, throwing shrapnel through the crowd. Charlie stayed low, and using the panicked crowd for cover he pulled out the small recording device, pressed the record switch, and shouted into it, "Sucker punch, sucker punch, sucker punch." He felt the heat of it even before he tossed it aside and scrambled up to the gallery where Cesare had been seated.

The hall filled with smoke and energy bolts tore up the decorations as Charlie dove behind the now empty seats of the Nine, where he found Roacka waiting. "Lad, I scrambled 'em as soon as I saw Goutain."

Charlie grinned. "And I just sucker punched 'em."

Roacka didn't grin back. "Cesare's hurt, piece of shrapnel. Don't know how bad."

It was as if all the adrenaline suddenly drained out of him.

"Take me to him."

CHAPTER 9
ESCAPE FOR SOME

As soon as Roacka had gotten confirmation from Darmczek that the bogies were Syndonese, he'd had Pelletier put Cesare's entire guard contingent on alert. There was a private entrance hidden behind the drapes in the ducal gallery, and the guard had just reached an anteroom there when the shooting started. Roacka led Charlie into the anteroom as Pelletier was issuing orders to set up a defensive perimeter. Charlie spotted Arthur kneeling beside an unconscious Cesare as a medic worked on him. Charlie put his hand on Arthur's shoulder. "How bad?"

Arthur looked up. "Thank god you're here. He'll live, but it was close."

The building shook from an explosion somewhere as Charlie took a head count. Faggan was dead; Telka's heir was dead; Harrimo's heir was unlikely to live out the hour, and barring a few nasty but non-life-threatening wounds the rest of the Nine and their heirs were all present and would live. "Where's the royal family?"

No one answered him. "We have to find the royal family. We can't let them fall into Goutain's hands. Roacka?"

"I'm with ya, lad."

Dieter elbowed his way through the crowd of nobles. "I'm taking command, Cass." He turned his back on Charlie, told Roacka, "Have your marines secure transport. We need to get off planet as soon as possible."

Roacka spoke carefully. "Your Lordship, I have orders from His Grace, Cesare, to take orders only from Commander Cass."

Nadama stepped up beside Dieter. "See here, Roacka—"

"Enough," Telka shouted. The plump little woman's eyes were puffy and red, her cheeks glistening with tears shed for her dead son. "Nadama, why were you not surprised by any of this? I think it's clear you had something to do with it, so I, for one, will not be comfortable taking orders from any de Satarna."

She and Nadama faced off in what Charlie knew was an old argument. Charlie ignored them, turned to Pelletier. "I need two of your best people, armed."

"Right away, sir. But we'll have an extraction team here in five minutes."

Charlie shook his head. "Too long."

Pelletier nodded, handed Charlie one of the little

fake recording devices. "It hasn't been used yet. When you find them, hole up someplace, scramble it, and we'll send a team after you."

"You can't go without us, little brother." Charlie turned around as he shoved Pelletier's device into his pocket, found Add and Ell standing behind him. Add said, "Someone has to come along to take care of you, since you'll probably stumble and shoot yourself in the foot."

"You know, sister," Ell said, "I could just shoot him in the foot now. Then he wouldn't go running off and getting into trouble. He'd be so much easier to take care of that way."

Charlie growled, "Shoot me after we've got the royal family."

Add looked at Ell, one eyebrow raised skeptically. "I think he just wants another kiss from that princess."

Charlie, Roacka, the twins, and the two troopers headed back to the ducal gallery, moving cautiously. The great hall itself was filled with smoke, debris, and a number of bodies, but otherwise empty. The building shook again to a large explosion as they crossed the floor to the throne, leapfrogging in strictest military discipline. Charlie stepped over the body of the Syndonese officer behind the throne and through the private entrance there. He found a short, dark little passage that led to an anteroom not unlike that behind the ducal gallery. It was empty. Roacka was about to proceed on into the corridor beyond when Charlie had a sudden idea. "Wait."

As boys he and Arthur had taken great joy in exploring the servant's passages throughout Cesare's estates. And thinking back to the corridor where Del had kissed him, perhaps she'd done the same. Charlie turned to a wall covered in velvet drapes, pulled the drapes aside, and yes, he found a servant's entrance. He opened the door carefully, stepped into the corridor beyond looking both ways; it was empty. Perhaps he was wrong.

"Little brother."

Ell squatted down and examined the floor. She rubbed her fingers along a dark smear there, lifted them to her face, sniffed, and announced, "Blood."

They continued down the corridor, Ell leading them by tracking the occasional smear of blood. The trail led to a door about twenty meters down the corridor, labeled *Maintenance Supplies*. Charlie opened the door slowly . . . nothing. He stepped through, only to be assaulted by a raging storm of fists and claws and petticoats, and he went down with Del on top of him. Add saved him by plucking her off him as if she weighed nothing. Del struggled like a puppet for a moment, then realized who they were. "Oh, thank god it's you."

Add let her down and turned to Ell. "Is that how they kiss? A rather violent form of affection, don't you think?"

They'd found Delilah with Martino and Adan, but no sign of Lucius. Blood streamed from Martino's nose, the source of the smears they'd tracked.

Del said, "The bloody drunken idiot fell down and bloodied his bloody drunken nose."

"There's a large Syndonese strike force incoming, Commander. Someone gave them Turnlee's encryption keys, so they've got access to the local command grid. They'll be inside long distance bombardment range within the hour."

Goutain's plan had been to take Lucius and the Nine and their heirs as prisoners, use his hidden firepower to hold the planet long enough for a much larger force to arrive and secure his position. But Charlie's *sucker punch* had worked. Darmczek had nailed the four warships without a fight, and got the troop carrier before it landed all its troops. The two hundred regulars that Charlie had at his command had outnumbered the Syndonese decisively. But when Goutain's strike force arrived that situation would change.

"I will not leave without my husband," Adan screamed. They had yet to account for Lucius.

"Mother, please," Del pleaded. "Don't you understand? If he has father he has the king. And if he kills father, then he has nothing. As long as he doesn't have Martino, then he must keep father alive. But if he has Martino also, then father is a dead man. We have to do as Commander Cass says and evacuate before the Syndonese strike force arrives."

Adan screamed at Del, Del screamed at Adan, and

Martino took a sip from a small flask. They were all standing in the royal apartments, trying to get Adan to see reason. Charlie turned to a marine medic and whispered, "I need a palm patch. A sedative. Three of them. Something that won't react with alcohol," he glanced knowingly at Martino, "but something that'll put them down fast."

The marine grinned. He handed Charlie three small patches, started to explain, but Charlie growled, "I know how to use the damn things."

He selected one and slapped it hard between his palms to activate it. He was careful to keep the active surface away from his own skin as he marched up behind Adan, who was busy arguing with Del. He pressed the patch carefully against the side of Adan's neck. It pulsed underneath his hand as she turned on him indignantly. "How dare you? You have no right . . ." She hesitated, then her eyes glazed over and Charlie caught her as she fell.

He lowered her carefully to the floor. "Bag her up and get her out of here."

He turned toward Martino, who offered him a drink. Charlie smiled as he pressed the palm patch against Martino's neck. Martino went down like his mother and Charlie turned to Del.

She held her hands up and backed away from him. "Charlie, you don't need to sedate me like that." Their eyes met and she seemed to read his thoughts. She shrugged and laughed. "Then again, it'll be easier for you if I am sedated. No chance I might turn hysterical at an inopportune moment, eh?" She curtsied. "Commander, I capitulate."

She rose and approached him confidently. He raised the palm patch toward her neck, but she caught his wrist. "No. I'm told it leaves a mark. And I'm so vain."

She turned to one side, swung a hip toward him, angled in a way that no one else could see. She started raising her skirts and petticoats, exposing first her leg, then her knee, then her thigh, and lastly some rather enticing undergarments. "I think I'd rather have it here," she said. All he could say was something to the effect of "Uhh," and while he stood there speechless she grabbed his wrist, pressed his hand with the palm patch against her bared thigh, and closed her fingers, forcing him to squeeze her skin in a most inappropriate way. "I like that much better, don't you? Sometime I'll have to show you . . . if it sca . . ." Her eyes glazed over and Charlie didn't have the presence of mind to catch her as she fell. Thankfully, Ell stepped in and scooped up the princess effortlessly.

With Delilah in her arms, she turned to Add, shaking her head sadly. "Little brother is involved in the strangest courtship ritual I've ever seen, sister."

Charlie strapped himself down in the acceleration seat in the shuttle. "It's gonna be close," the pilot shouted as he firewalled the grav drive and lifted them straight up off the lawn. "*Defender* reports a big transition flare at the edge of the system."

They'd evacuated everyone of importance to their respective flagships, and though he'd tried repeatedly, Charlie couldn't get an update on Cesare's condition. After that Charlie had remained on planet with the marines to sweep the palace and its grounds. Still no Lucius, and no Theode either. It would be ironic if Charlie were killed trying to save the two people for whom he had no liking.

As commanding officer of the ground operations, through long habit he'd hustled everyone else off before jumping on the last boat out. But in the confusion there'd been a mistake: the last boat had already gone out with no room to spare. He and twenty marines had wasted precious minutes finding something to get them off planet. All they'd found was a mere shuttle, not a gunboat: no firepower, no powered shielding, no serious internal gravity compensation, able to drive at no more than about six gravities. It was a bad mistake, perhaps a fatal mistake.

"They're leapfrogging," the pilot announced as he lifted the shuttle's nose.

Like everyone, the Syndonese were blind in transition. It would be suicide to enter Turnlee nearspace on transition drive. The gravitational distortions within the system would warp their heading into the nearest planet or asteroid, and blind, they'd have no way of knowing how to compensate, or even if they needed to compensate. Standard operating procedure was to down-transit at the edge of the system, then spend hours, even days, driving inward on sublight drive. But the Syndonese were leapfrogging: down-transit one ship at the edge of the system. That ship, no longer transition-blind, immediately launched its navigational drones to extend its baseline, then uplinked accurate navigational data to the remaining ships in the strike force, who themselves continued with confidence into the heart of the system at transition velocities. At hundreds, even thousands of *lights*, such ships could cross the breadth of the system in minutes.

"It's a big strike force. I've got thirty, maybe forty transition wakes entering the system. Darmczek's engaging them."

Charlie had a situation summary on the screen in front of him. *Defender* was already long gone with Cesare and the other VIPs aboard. Darmczek had left a small destroyer in orbit around Turnlee to pick them up, then had taken the rest of the flotilla outbound to take potshots at the incoming Syndonese: still in transition and temporarily blind, they were defenseless.

"Big transition flare in near orbit, Commander. A Syndonese, close in, and he came out of transition shooting."

"We're not going to make it out of here," Charlie shouted. "Take us to ground now. Advise Darmczek and tell him to disengage and take care of himself."

The shuttle suddenly lurched badly and listed to port. Charlie didn't need the pilot's "They're firing on us, sir," to know what was happening.

Charlie gripped the arms of his seat. The shuttle lurched again into a wild spin. The pilot managed to pull them out of it, but they were canted at an odd angle, and Charlie didn't need readouts in front of him to know they were losing altitude in a sharply slanted dive with only a few hundred meters to a very hard landing. He braced for a crash, tried to think of something nice, like Del's kiss maybe. It had been a nice kiss. And he did rather enjoy applying the palm patch to her thigh, and . . .

He had no sense of time. He'd been in the dark so long that time no longer mattered. At least someone had shaved off his beard and cut off the matted, lice-infested, shoulder-length hair, though he still had about a two-day growth of beard. Oh, but his face hurt. And his leg hurt, and his arm hurt, and his ribs hurt.

First the arm, his left arm. He explored it carefully with his right hand. It was crudely splinted, so it must be broken. The realization struck him that he wore no manacles, and he was no longer on the chain with his comrades.

He was lying on his side so he struggled to a sitting position. His right leg throbbed painfully. He found that the leg of his trousers had been torn away, and in the dark he could feel a line of crude stitches running up the calf about six inches long. Next he carefully explored his face. The right side was oddly misshapen, and he guessed that his cheek and the orbit of his eye had been shattered. Also surrounding the damage were a number of deep gashes that had been crudely stitched up.

He needed to urinate badly and stood carefully, trying to put as little weight as possible on his right leg. He explored the limits of his cell by touch, and in the dark he had to forcibly remind himself that he wasn't in a Syndonese prison camp. That was his past. Then again, perhaps it was also his future.

His cell measured about three paces by two, with a locked door on one end, a cot on one side, and a bucket in the corner for sanitary facilities. He urinated in the bucket, returned to the cot and lay down.

"Up with you."

They'd turned on the lights in his cell, and after the dark it was blinding. Four Syndonese uniforms entered his cell.

"Up with you, I said."

Charlie tried to sit up, but apparently he didn't move fast enough. They lifted him to his feet, slammed him face-on into a wall, cuffed his hands behind his back—an excruciating process with a splinted arm—then tossed him out of the cell. He landed on his side in the corridor. The sergeant in charge jammed the butt of a rifle with choking force into his throat. "You walk. We ain't carrying you. We have to carry you, you pay for it." Charlie struggled to his feet, and with him limping badly they marched away.

It quickly became evident they were in the palace. Servants scurried out of their way as they marched to some unknown destination. They passed one wall blown away by explosives, but other than that he saw few signs of the recent fight. Then they entered halls he recognized; they were headed for the great throne room.

The massive doors at the entrance to the hall still showed considerable damage, but with that one exception, the great hall appeared fully restored, and filled again with the nobility of the Realm. His guards halted him at the threshold while the sergeant marched forward. Charlie saw Lucius seated on his throne, Goutain standing at his right hand, Adsin at his left, and from that distance he could just hear the sergeant announce, "We brought the prisoner, Your Excellency."

Lucius looked to Goutain, who nodded his approval, so Lucius said, "Bring the man forward."

The sergeant hesitated and waited for Goutain to nod his approval, then he turned about and marched the length of the hall. He rejoined Charlie and the other three and hooked a thumb over his shoulder. "Let's go," he growled, and spun about.

There had been a noisy undercurrent to the crowd, the kind of buzz impossible to quiet when that many people assembled in one place. But a breathless, fearful silence descended upon them as Charlie and his guards crossed the threshold of the great doors and marched up the center of the hall. The only sounds were the thud of his guard's boots on the floor, and the scrape of his own uneven, limping shuffle. They halted at the base of the dais, and his guards separated, flanking him.

He noticed that Nadama, Band, and Telka sat in the ducal gallery, and it was clear they were not happy about the situation. Obviously, their ships had been unable to outrun the Syndonese strike force. He wondered how many others had been unable to do so, or were now just radioactive vapor somewhere between the stars.

"Yes, Commander," Goutain said, looking at the three seated in the ducal gallery. "You did not thwart me."

Charlie looked at Goutain, saw in his eyes that he was going to die, though not this moment. "Three of the Nine, and none of their heirs, and I don't see Delilah or Martino. I'd say I thwarted you rather nicely." Goutain flinched; he'd struck a nerve.

The sergeant clubbed Charlie in the back with his rifle butt and he went down. He lay on the floor for a moment, gasping for breath and letting the pain recede. His guards pulled him back to his feet.

"Your Majesty," Goutain said.

Lucius looked drawn and confused. "Yes, of course. Adsin, read the charges."

Adsin stepped forward, and he didn't seem in the least perturbed that Goutain had taken charge. Charlie realized then that the little shit had probably double-crossed Lucius as well. Adsin flourished some sort of document and read from it. "Commander Charles Cass, you have been charged with high treason, in that you did break the king's law by conspiring to locate armed troops on the grounds of the Almsburg Palace, and that you did conspire to violate Turnlee nearspace with armed vessels without His Majesty's permission. His Majesty, in council, has reviewed the matter in detail, and has found you guilty. You are hereby sentenced to death, and remanded to the custody of the Viceroy of Aagerbanne, the sentence to be carried out at his leisure and by any means he so chooses."

Goutain called, "Dr. Carallo, come forward."

A young Syndonese officer stepped out of the crowd, climbed a few steps toward the throne, halted, and saluted smartly.

"I'm putting Dr. Carallo in charge of you, Cass. It'll be his job to keep you alive, no matter how much pain and damage you suffer. And he'll do a good job of that. You see, his recently deceased father was the commandant of one of the prison camps that you managed to survive. So Dr. Carallo knows firsthand the price of failing me. Do you have anything to say for yourself?"

"And what would I say?" Charlie asked, the words coming out distorted by the damage to his face. He had nothing to lose. Goutain was going to kill him no matter what, and not pleasantly. His one hope was to goad him into losing control and killing him quickly now. "That this is a farce? Everyone already knows it's a farce: the people around me, your own men, this pathetic fool of a king—"

"How dare you?" Lucius cried, rising.

"Shut up," Goutain growled.

"And you," Charlie continued. "You know it's a farce, especially since I got the best of you." And though it hurt terribly, Charlie grinned at him.

The sergeant clubbed him again and he went down. Then the four of them clubbed and kicked him into unconsciousness.

He thought of Del the whole time.

CHAPTER 10
ESCAPE

"Wake up, Commander."

Charlie opened his eyes and looked at Carallo. It took him a moment to remember he was on a Syndonese ship somewhere in space. Carallo was a soft-spoken young man, and Charlie actually pitied the poor fellow his task. The guards, always with Goutain present, would beat Charlie for a while, then they'd call Carallo in to fix him up, just enough to keep him alive. And all poor Carallo could do was apologize.

"I'm sorry, Commander. I have to take you to sick bay again. This is much too serious to handle with just my kit."

"Just let me die, damn it."

"I can't do that, Commander. My wife and children, he'll kill them."

Given Carallo's choices, Charlie would do the same.

Carallo pulled Charlie to his feet, and at some point

Charlie made the mistake of putting weight on his broken, crudely splinted left leg. The pain almost sent him into blessed unconsciousness.

"Put your arm around me, Commander. I'll help you keep weight off that leg."

They adjusted themselves into an odd sort of tripodal state, Charlie with his left arm about Carallo's shoulders, Carallo supporting most of Charlie's weight. Carallo had to shout at the guards to get them to open the door to his cell. "No. I have to take him to sick bay. The shape they've left him in, there's little I can do without the facilities there. His Excellency wants him kept alive. Shall I tell His Excellency he died because you wouldn't let me take him to sick bay?"

Charlie drifted off into a semi-comatose state of awareness as Carallo led him down one corridor then another. The hardest part was squeezing his damaged limbs through a small personnel hatch. "Commander, listen to me. Listen carefully. We're about to down-transit into Tachaann nearspace."

Charlie struggled to grasp reality, managed to hang on to just a thread, but that was enough to tell him that they weren't in any sick bay, and that fact produced a moment of lucidity. "You're in one of the lifeboats."

With that simple statement his surroundings came into focus. Carallo had strapped him into an acceleration couch, one of about a dozen such in the confined space of the lifeboat. "We're about to down-transit into the Tachaann system. I've programmed the lifeboat to launch an instant after down-transition. That may buy you enough time to get away. That's all I can do for you."

Charlie managed to gurgle out, "Why Tachaann?"

"It's the first chance I've had, and it may be the only chance you'll get, so I'm taking it."

"Your family. What about your family?"

"He doesn't know that I know, but he's already had my wife and children tortured to death."

For the first time Charlie truly looked at Carallo, saw a young man about his own age. Carallo had the look of a man going through the motions of life without actually living. Carallo said, "He's afraid of you, you know, in an almost superstitious way, though not so much now that you're in his hands. But if you weren't, if you were free, then he'd fear you more than any other being in this universe. Even if you die, as long as he doesn't have proof you're dead, you'll haunt him for the rest of his life. And if that's the only revenge I can have, then so be it."

That wasn't good enough for Charlie. He didn't want to be a ghost haunting Goutain's dreams. And even through the haze of pain he knew that Carallo's plan would only get them both killed. "I have to leave you now. After down-transition I'm going to try to kill Goutain, though I don't hold much hope that I'll succeed."

Carallo climbed through the small hatch and dogged it shut. Charlie waited only long enough to hear the hatch's lock ratchet into place. Then he popped the restraints holding him to the couch. He staggered to the medical cabinet, rifled through it desperately, and found a *combat kikker*, a cocktail of painkillers and strong stimulants. He slapped the patch against the side of his neck and shivered as drug-induced lucidity washed through his mind. He stuffed a couple more kikkers into his pockets, some antibiotics and painkillers as well. Then he staggered to the pilot's console.

It was minimal at best, but while docked he had access to the larger ship's navigation data. Twenty minutes to down-transition, with the lifeboat programmed to launch one minute later, its autopilot set up to drive at maximum thrust for Tachaann. But the launch of the lifeboat would raise alarms on the bridge, and a warship could easily overtake the lifeboat.

Carallo had opened the pilot's console to command access, and for that Charlie breathed a sigh of relief. He plunged into the boat's autopilot, overrode all its safety protocols, all its fail-safe restraints, especially those concerned with operation of the lifeboat's drive. That done, and praying he hadn't missed anything, he headed for the engine compartment at the rear of the small craft.

Lifeboats were designed to be simple, under the assumption they might be operated by badly injured personnel. Charlie grabbed a wrench and a knife from a nearby toolkit, disengaged a couple of latches, and slid the engine's heat shield out of the way. Cooling lines, that's what he was after. He badly crimped those that were metal or plast tubing in several places, while he cut those that were flexible. He closed the heat shield and limped back to the pilot's console. Two minutes to transition.

He pulled off his tunic to use as a sack, stuffed it full of ration packs and medical supplies, then turned to the hatch. The only way of determining if chance had put someone in the corridor on the other side of the hatch was to open the damn thing. He did so, and luck was with him, or more likely, this close to transition everyone had a required duty station. He sealed the lifeboat's hatch. One minute to go.

There were five more lifeboat hatches in the same corridor, all open for ready access in an emergency. The one he'd just exited was conspicuous in that it was sealed. He chose one of the others at random, climbed through it, and didn't dare be so obvious as to seal the hatch. His one chance was the lifeboat's emergency medical unit, though it felt more like a coffin as he climbed into it and lay down.

He felt the ship down-transit, then its hull thrummed several times as it launched its navigational drones. A short delay, then nearby the hull echoed with the launch of the lifeboat. He manually pulled the med unit's lid down, leaving it open just a crack for air.

The engines on lifeboats were simple rocket motors, fueled by a couple of highly explosive liquid chemicals. If all went well, Charlie's sabotage of the cooling lines would cause the engine to rapidly overheat, and if he hadn't missed any critical fail-safes it would continue to pump fuel at maximum capacity. The resultant explosion would be dramatic enough that no one would expect to find anything left of its one unfortunate passenger.

If all went well.

Charlie didn't dare use the med unit, or activate any of the lifeboat's systems; the pilot's console was always active, but any activity beyond that would trigger alarms in the ship's maintenance systems. And with the lifeboat's hatch open he could leave the med unit only when certain the corridor outside was empty.

After the lifeboat launch, there was an initial flurry of activity. Charlie heard crewmen in the corridor beyond the lifeboat hatch, some discussion, a little shouting, and a few harshly barked commands. At one point a crewman stuck his head through the open lifeboat hatch and glanced about quickly, but didn't stay. Charlie waited until the corridor had been silent for several hours before venturing forth, and then only long enough to check the ship's navigational reports on the pilot's console. No up-transition scheduled yet.

He kept himself conscious with the kikkers he'd pocketed from the other boat, but didn't dare allow himself any painkillers or sleep, nibbling instead on some emergency rations and waiting for the time to pass. At one point he did lose consciousness and slept for a few hours. But once each hour, as long as the corridor outside was quiet, he'd leave the med unit briefly and check the navigational reports. It took a day before they scheduled an up-transition, and that was still another day away.

The wait for up-transition was agonizing. He thought an hour had gone by, but when he checked the pilot's console only a few minutes had elapsed. On the one hand he needed to calm down, but on the other it was even more critical that he not sleep and miss up-transition, so he kept himself loaded to the hilt on kikkers. His heart was racing at this point, had been pumping overtime for a while now, and he knew he was close to his limit, but what choice did he have?

One hour before transition it was time to take the biggest gamble of all: he had to hack into the lifeboat's primary systems, and to do that he had to work at the pilot's console. Hopefully, as transition approached, there would be fewer crew wandering the corridors, but to be safe he appropriated a heavy wrench from the lifeboat's toolkit.

Lifeboats were designed to operate reasonably well even with some damage, and their operating systems were not designed with a great deal of security in mind. Once launched, the pilot console defaulted to command access. But before that the boat's systems would prevent launch in certain extreme circumstances, like while in transition, and somehow he had to override that. He couldn't have hacked a major ship's system in any amount of time, and a minor system would have taken several hours, but he created a back door by fooling the lifeboat into thinking it had already launched, and he got command access.

"Five minutes to up-transition and counting," all-ship announced.

"What are you doing?"

Charlie managed to avoid jumping at the voice, turned away from the console slowly while furtively placing his hand on the wrench in his lap. A crewman stood over him, a common spacer. As Charlie faced him the man cringed at the condition of Charlie's face. "The engine room," Charlie said. "An explosion! Help me—I'm trying to contact the bridge."

If the spacer had taken a moment to think it through, there were a dozen clues to tell him an engine room mechanic wouldn't be sitting at a lifeboat console, trying to use it to contact the bridge about an engine room explosion. "Shit," the spacer growled, and spun on his heel toward the nearest allship link. Charlie rose out of his seat and swung the wrench, catching the man on the back of the head. The spacer went down hard and didn't get up. Charlie checked his pulse; he was alive.

"Four minutes to up-transition and counting," all-ship announced.

Charlie dragged the spacer out into the corridor, though it was an effort getting him through the small lifeboat hatch, and an agony with his own injuries, and he had to listen to allship counting down to transition. Charlie dumped him there.

"Two minutes to up-transition and counting," all-ship announced.

Back through the lifeboat hatch he sealed it: he had

to count on luck that no one discovered the injured spacer or the closed lifeboat hatch.

"One minute to up-transition and counting," all-ship announced.

Charlie sat down at the console. Up-transition was far more critical than down. A wrong vector, incorrect mass, nearby mass distorting the ship's nearspace: too many things could go wrong. And he had only seconds to find that override.

The ship's hull echoed as the navigational drones clamped themselves into their docks.

"Ten seconds to up-transition and counting," all-ship announced.

There it was.

"Nine . . ."

He had it, now he had to override it.

"Eight . . ."

It refused.

"Seven . . ."

"Fuck you," he shouted at the console.

"Six . . ."

"Command override," he shouted.

"Five . . ."

He could only pray the necessary three commands would do the trick. "Override."

"Four . . ."

"Override."

"Three . . ."

"Override."

"Two . . ."

The pilot's console replied with, *Command override access completed. You may now—*

"One . . ."

"Fuck you," he screamed again as he lifted the safety cover on the launch key.

"Up-transition sequence initiated . . ."

He could feel the ship transiting, that weird distortion of his senses. The timing for this was one big guess, one big gamble. The ship would, of course, detect the launch of the lifeboat, and if he launched too soon they'd have time to abort the transition sequence, leaving them both in Tachaann nearspace where Goutain would have no difficulty scooping him up. If he launched too late, the lifeboat would be swept into transition with the ship, a long, slow way to die.

He slammed his fist onto the launch key and explosive bolts fired, violently ejecting the small lifeboat from the larger mass of the ship and hurling Charlie across its cabin. How stupid of him to have forgotten to strap down, he thought as he slammed into a bulkhead and lost consciousness.

Charlie awoke floating in the middle of the lifeboat cabin, bits of debris floating about him. He tried to determine where he hurt most, and settled on "everywhere." He struggled to the pilot's console, strapped down, and brought up the boat's navigational system. He was happy to learn that he hadn't been sucked into transition and there was no sign of Goutain's ship.

The launch of the lifeboat would've raised an alarm on the bridge, but it might not be reported to Goutain, and with or without Goutain they might or might not put two and two together and come up with Charlie. Even if they immediately decided to return and find him, it would take a good hour to set up and make an orderly down-transition, then hours, perhaps even days, of deceleration and then acceleration to reverse course and up-transit again. Charlie had at least a couple of days, maybe longer if his luck held.

His first concern was to kill the automated emergency distress beacon. Since he'd already hacked into the boat's systems, that only took a few seconds. Then he identified several other changes he needed to make to remain undetected once Goutain's ship did return. And he had to assume it would. Then somehow he had to get down onto the surface of Tachaann, preferably alive.

The lifeboat was equipped to keep a dozen people alive for twenty days, so Charlie alone could survive for a long time—that wasn't the issue. *Fuel* was the issue. He was at the edge of Tachaann nearspace, and his uncontrolled ejection from the up-transition had left him with a strong vector at a sharp angle to the plane of the ecliptic. He'd have to do a slow burn now to put the boat into a highly eccentric orbit. Then, taking advantage of the system gravity well, in fifty-seven days another burn would slow him enough for a controlled entry into Tachaann's atmosphere, hopefully with a little fuel left over for a decent landing.

He set up the first burn, fired the boat's engines, confirmed his trajectory, then slept for several hours. When he awoke he stuffed himself into the med unit with instructions for its AI to fix him as well as it could. He had fifty-seven days to wait.

CHAPTER 11
NEW FRIENDS

The planet Tachaann could not boast of any serious strategic or commercial resources. It had a livable atmosphere and reasonable gravity with large land-masses, but the soil was not of sufficient quality to warrant the investment required for large commercial agricultural production, nor were there sufficient quantities of heavy metals present to justify serious mining operations. Its only claim to fame was that it was a convenient supply and refitting point on a major shipping lane, though it wasn't actually a necessary stop. Many ships merely used it as a convenient point to down-transit for a navigational fix and realignment, without even stopping. It had a small orbital station that provided supplies for ships that did stop, and one reasonably large city on the planet's surface. The city, named Ellitah, was an open port, with a reputation as a haven for pirates, smugglers, thieves, and cutthroats. *It could be worse,* Charlie thought. *I could be de Lunis.*

Assuming Goutain's ship did return for him, Charlie was banking on the fact that his highly eccentric, out-of-the-ecliptic orbit would put him outside of their most likely search pattern. With the lifeboat's systems running at bare minimum, he hoped they'd miss him in the vast volume of the solar system. They'd probably search the space between the lifeboat's launch point and Tachaann, then sit in orbit for a while watching for a lifeboat reentry. Charlie hoped that long before the fifty-seven days had elapsed, Goutain would grow bored, assume Charlie had made it to the planet's surface, drop some troops down there to search for him, then go elsewhere with his warship.

What he didn't account for was how bored *he* grew, and by the end of the fifty-seven days Charlie was going stir-crazy. With almost maniacal fervor he set up the reentry burn, excited for something to do. His luck held and the entry into atmosphere and landing went well. The countryside surrounding Ellitah was quite arid with little vegetation. Charlie set the lifeboat down in a small canyon about twenty kilometers from the city. It would never lift again so he stripped it of everything useful. It provided clothing for almost any kind of climate, simple military fatigues without insignia, meaning he'd be reasonably anonymous. He made up a small pack, stuffed it with some ration packs and a careful selection of drugs from the medical cabinet.

He no longer needed them, but he might pick up a little money by selling them on the street. They wouldn't bring in much more than the price of a couple meals, but he was looking forward to something other than rations. The med unit had fixed him up reasonably well, but it had no cosmetic capability, and only limited facility for reconstructing the orbit of his eye. So while everything was once again functional, a field of nasty scars and distorted skin covered the right side of his face. As for weapons, all he came up with was a wrench and a knife.

The twenty klicks to Ellitah was an easy two-day hike, and he timed it so that he entered the city during the anonymous hours of late evening. It wasn't hard to find the district where spacers hung out; he just asked a cabby where a spacer went for a good time. The district itself was a maze of saloons and gambling halls and whorehouses, the streets filled with spacers and prostitutes. He wandered the streets for a good part of the night, trying to get a feel for the place. He could eat ration packs for several days, and sleep in an alley somewhere—the weather was warm and dry—and with the kind of men he saw wandering the streets it would be best to move cautiously.

His second day in the city he traded a couple of kikkers for a heavy overcoat, which improved anonymity, and on the third day he sold some narcotics to pick up a little money. He bought a newspaper printed on old-fashion vellum that would disintegrate in a few days and eagerly scanned it hoping for news of Cesare. Unfortunately there was nothing about the duke, though quite a bit about Aagerbanne.

The occupation had begun with a brutal assault intended to prevent any resistance from arising. And at first it had worked, but during the fifty-seven days he'd been in orbit approaching Tachaann, the Free Aagerbanni Resistance—FAR—had formed and started fighting back with guerilla tactics. At one point they'd brought down a Syndonese troop transport, killing two hundred thirty-one soldiers. The Syndonese responded by executing a like number of civilians. Charlie didn't think FAR could last long without someone on the outside supplying arms and equipment. It was a shame none of the Nine were interested in supporting them.

That evening he returned to his makeshift bed rather content. He slept in the corner of an alley on a soft pile that he'd made by crumpling up carefully selected, nonsmelly bits of refuse. Burrowing into the pile hid him reasonably well from anyone who might wander down the alley.

He lay awake for a while wondering what he would do next. His first instinct was to get back to the Realm as soon as possible, but it would take him quite a while to scrape up the money for an off-planet ticket. And as he thought about it further, he didn't have the protections afforded the nobility. If *Charlie Cass* showed up anywhere in the Realm, Nadama or Goutain would have him quietly executed. No, he'd have to bide his time and scrounge up a false identity before leaving Tachaann, which wouldn't be cheap.

Without a stroke of luck, his options were quite limited, so he'd have to just wait and see. Though, even with those disturbing thoughts, he had no trouble falling asleep.

"You big, strong man. You like suck, or you like fuck?"

Charlie snapped awake at the sound of the voice, but remained still and silent. A whore and a spacer were walking down the alley toward him, and he guessed he was about to get a rather lurid show. But then near him he heard a voice whisper in Syndonese, "Here they come. Be quiet," and he realized three men stood in the shadows just an arm's length from him.

"I like 'em both, bitch," the spacer with the whore growled. He pressed her against a wall and lifted her skirt.

She pressed her pelvis against his hand. "You pay first. Fifty dikkas for fuck, again fifty dikkas for suck."

The three men near Charlie stepped out of the shadows. One of them said, "We don't like your prices, cunt," and all four of them grabbed her. She started to scream, but one of them slapped her hard, stuffed some sort of gag in her mouth, and tied it in place. "We're taking the special discount rate. Four of us, for free."

Shit, Charlie thought. *They're going to assault her.* And as much as he wanted to just lie low—anything he did could bring attention to the fact that Charlie Cass was not, in fact, dead—he couldn't just lie there and let this happen.

He'd kept the wrench and knife from the lifeboat and he waited until three of them had her pinned down, with the fourth between her legs, pulling down his pants, before he erupted from the pile of rubbish. He hit one on the side of the head with the wrench and the man went down. He caught another on the top of the head, kicked the third in the gut, and spun to face the fourth, who'd climbed to his feet and held a knife of his own. With her hands free the prostitute pulled out her gag and started screaming.

The fellow with the knife faced Charlie squarely, but one of the others tackled him from behind and he went down. Charlie slashed the arm of the one who had tackled him and he let go, so Charlie rolled away as his other opponent bore down on him with his knife. "When you're down in a knife or hand fight," Roacka had told him, "don't waste time getting up. That's when they'll take you."

Charlie kicked out in a leg sweep and the man went down between Charlie and the two that were still up. Charlie scrambled to his feet, put his back to a wall, and crouched into a knife-fighting stance. And then the alley filled with a mob of angry, shouting men. Some of them hit Charlie's assailants from behind; others scooped up the whore carefully and carried her away crying. Still others faced Charlie, but with the knife in his hands and his back to a wall they kept their distance. The whore's family and friends had come to the rescue. They had the four assailants disarmed and pinned to the ground, and Charlie surrounded.

They babbled back and forth in a language Charlie seemed to recognize, but they spoke too fast, something about the spacers hurting Janice. He eventually recognized the language, a variant form of one of the more common standards. They were trampsies, and that meant they were all family, and clearly they thought Charlie was in it with the other four. A young one swaggered forward and smirked at Charlie's knife. He pulled his own and bent into a proper fighting stance, showing off by passing the knife back and forth from hand to hand. Roacka would've kicked him in the ass for showing off. The young fellow's friends shouted encouragement—probably their best knife fighter, and they were now going to have a little show as he cut up Charlie.

He feinted at Charlie once, then again. If he was their best he wasn't that good, but good enough considering he'd probably learned in the streets rather than drilling for years with Roacka and two Kinathin fighting machines. He feinted a third time and Charlie pretended to react clumsily, exposed his left side a bit, and the young fellow thought he saw a weakness. His fourth lunge was a legitimate attack. Charlie feinted to the right as if protecting his weak left side and he fell for it. Charlie caught his knife hand just above the wrist, and with a quick tug pulled him forward, adding to his momentum. Then he swung his wrist back over the fellow's head, dropping him neatly on his back in the alley with a nice thud. As his friends surged forward, Charlie bent the fellow's wrist at an odd angle, took the knife out of his hand, leaned down and pressed the edge to the fellow's throat. Everyone froze.

Charlie made an effort at their language. "Me not with them Syndonese."

An older version of the young fellow stepped forward, spit at Charlie's feet and spoke in standard. "You hurt him, you die slow."

Charlie removed the knife from the boy's throat. "I hurt no one," he said as he laid both knives on the ground and stepped back. The boy surged upward, grabbed both knives as he did so, and charged at Charlie. He caught one of the boy's wrists again, but the boy drew a line of fire down Charlie's forearm with the other knife. Someone tackled them both, then they lifted Charlie off his feet and pinned him to the alley wall. The boy stood facing him, holding both knives with no one restraining him.

"Stopping, stopping, stopping," the whore screamed as she came running down the alley, accompanied by two other hookers and a small girl that looked to be in her early teens. "Him not with them. Him them stopping." The four girls pushed the men aside, shoved and elbowed their way between Charlie and the boy with the knives, forming a small cordon around Charlie.

"You ain't hurting him, Willie," the first hooker shouted at the boy, smeared makeup streaming down her face, "or I cut your balls off. Momma Toofat says bring him."

They dragged Charlie off with his arms pinned behind his back, pulled him into a nearby saloon, past occupied tables and into a back room. They sat him in a chair and tied him there, then two of them sat down to watch him and wait.

Charlie never did find out what happened to the four Syndonese spacers, though he assumed it was not pleasant and they did not survive it. But after about five minutes a big, fat woman waddled into the room and sat down facing him. The three whores, the young girl, the young knife fighter, and the older version of the younger man all accompanied her. She barked something in trampsie too fast for him to follow, and one of the men stood and approached Charlie with a knife. Charlie figured this was it, but instead the man cut his bonds, freeing his arms. The old woman reached out and took his injured arm, raised it to look at the slash there and the blood dripping on the floor. "We owe you, stranger," she said in standard. She barked more orders; one of the whores produced a wet towel and a bottle of booze, knelt down in front of him and started cleaning the wound.

The old woman let go of his arm, took his chin in one hand, and turned his head from side to side. She said something in trampsie that Charlie didn't understand, and at the look on his face she switched to standard. "You once pretty boy."

Charlie shrugged. "Not anymore."

"I'm Momma Toofat. You saved Janice Likesiteasy." She nodded toward the whore, who was actually quite pretty, dark curly hair down to her shoulders, big brown eyes.

She smiled at Charlie through dark red lips, the left side of her face puffing up from the slap the spacer had given her. She said, "Thanks. Them fuckers going to hurt me."

Momma Toofat turned on her and shouted, "And you're stupid girl who's going to learn big lesson starting tomorrow." Janice lowered her eyes.

Momma turned back to Charlie, and nodding toward the young boy and the older man she said, "Willie Cutsgood cut your arm, and Willie's father Nano Neverlose."

The whore cleaning his wounded arm smiled up at him. The opposite of Janice, she was all blond hair and blue eyes, wearing a skirt so tight it appeared almost painted on, and a bustier bursting with cleavage. "I'm Sally Wantsalot." She pointed to the third whore, a redhead, frizzy wild hair, black lipstick, green eyes. "Trina Godowna." Then she pointed at the little girl in blond pigtails and what looked like a school uniform. "Becky Neverenough."

Momma interrupted. "I think maybe we change you name to Sally Talkstoomuch."

Sally focused on the chore of cleaning the slash on Charlie's arm.

Momma said to Charlie, "What's your name?"

Charlie hesitated. "Frank," he lied. "Just Frank."

She caught his hesitation and he suspected she knew he was lying, though that didn't seem to bother

her. "No, you Frankie Oncepretty. And we owe you debt. How we pay?"

Charlie considered that for a second. A ticket off planet would cost far more than they were offering, and he had to lie low for a while, at least until he could sneak back to the Realm with a new identity. And all that would take money that he didn't have. So after a few moments, he said, "How about something decent to eat . . . and a place to sleep . . . and maybe a job?"

CHAPTER 12
WAITING TABLES

The saloon belonged to Momma Toofat and her clan. It was a family run combination of bar, restaurant, pawnshop, gambling casino, and whorehouse. The drinks weren't watered down, the food was decent, the pawnshop was more of a side business, the gambling was honest, for the most part, and the whores were all carefully watched over by the family, including Jonjon Hungwell, a handsome bartender who made better money as a male hooker.

To his surprise, Charlie learned that the profession of prostitute was the most highly prized and sought-after vocation among the young trampsie girls. If the clan leaders chose a girl to be a whore, it meant she was among the most beautiful. And since the oldest profession brought in more money than any other job, they were highly valued, highly respected and well taken care of, and none of the girls ever had to bed a john she didn't want to. After all, the whores were all members of the family.

The night Charlie had met Janice Likesiteasy, she got in trouble because she'd picked up the spacer on the street and hadn't bothered to parade him through the saloon so that someone could be assigned to keep an eye on the situation from a distance. And she paid for her foolishness. For a tenday Momma Toofat had her doing all of the dirtiest chores in the building.

Charlie washed dishes, and for that he got three meals and a couple of dikkas every day, and a blanket and a mat to sleep on in the corner of the bar. It was heaven compared to a Syndonese prison camp. There were other trampsie clans in the city, and each owned one or more establishments of one kind or another. Charlie learned that Momma Toofat's clan was one of the oldest, that there was some sort of hierarchy among the clan leaders, and Momma Toofat held a high position within that structure.

When he'd asked for a job Charlie hadn't realized he'd be, in effect, adopted into Momma Toofat's clan. It was kind of nice, being *family*. Cesare and Arthur had always loved him as a son and brother, but he'd never truly been family, and he quickly learned that the trampsies made no such distinction.

Gaida rode Cesare's physician like she'd ridden horses as a young girl on her father's estates. A good rider paced an animal, didn't ride so hard it collapsed prematurely, prepared for and carefully timed the sprint for the finish. As he thrust into her and nibbled playfully on her nipples, she sensed when he was close to exploding within her. Where previously she had backed off the pace to prevent him from climaxing, now she too was ready so she rode him hard toward the finish line, grinding her hips against his erection as he thrust into her frantically. Suddenly he cried out and arched his back; his spasms of ecstasy drove her over the edge and she growled like an animal as waves of pleasure crashed through her. They both rode the tide of physical pleasure for long, glorious moments, then collapsed into the weak lethargy that followed.

After long seconds of silence, punctuated only by heavy breathing as they both tried to catch their breaths, he said, "Oh, my love. That was glorious."

It was good to be back on Traxis, with Cesare still weakened from his wounds, and her own authority greatly expanded because of that. "Yes, my darling Stallas, it truly was."

She rolled off him, lay beside him panting for a moment, then stood unashamedly naked and crossed the room to look in the mirror above her dresser. Her waist was still thin, hips trim, belly flat, breasts firm and glistening with sweat. She had whored herself for many things, had been raised to whore herself for her family; whored herself to Cesare for her father's benefit, but now she whored herself to the fool physician for her own gain. She was much too good for that wrinkled old duke. After he was gone she'd take as many lovers as she chose, men and women, perhaps more than one at a time in her bed, perhaps several. She'd be one of the most powerful women in the Realm.

Without looking over her shoulder, she asked, "How is Cesare, my darling?"

Stallas stood, and she saw in the mirror that his erection had begun to contract. He crossed the room to stand behind her, reached around her and cupped her breasts in his hands. Still breathing hard he had to speak between breaths. "I'm making sure he . . . grows weaker . . . every day. It shouldn't be long now."

"Oh, my love," she said, turning to face him, pressing her breasts against his chest. She grasped his shrinking penis in one hand, stroked it carefully and it started to respond. "When my son inherits the ducal seat, nothing will stand between us."

"Yes, my darling," he said. "Nothing."

She was always amazed at how easy it was to manipulate fools such as Stallas. At least he managed to provide some physical pleasure, though once he'd served his purpose, she'd find a younger man to satisfy those needs.

She knelt down, took him in her mouth, and his erection returned quickly.

Nano pulled Charlie away from dishwashing and asked him in standard, "You know how to pour drinks?"

Charlie shrugged. "You put a glass on the bar in

front of a spacer and you fill it with whiskey, or gin, or whatever he wants."

"No. You don't fill it. You put in a measure. You don't under fill it, you don't overfill it."

Nano handed him a white shirt and a black vest and dragged him to the bar. "Today, you're bartender. Jonjon Hungwell got the clap."

Charlie hoped that would mean a little increase in pay, which would get him the off-planet ticket that much faster.

His first night behind the bar during the evening shift, Becky Neverenough, the little schoolgirl, sa-shayed up to the bar with a big spacer on her arm. Becky and the spacer downed a couple of drinks, then she took him into one of the back rooms with a bottle. It was an appalling thought to think they'd whore out a little girl just barely into her teens.

The next morning while seated next to Sally at the bar, both of them eating breakfast, Charlie tried to broach the subject. "Sally," he said cautiously. "Are things so bad that you need to pimp out a little girl?"

She stopped eating, frowned at him and asked, "Little girl?"

"Ya, Becky."

Her eyes narrowed and she spoke standard with a thick street accent. "How little you think she is?"

He shrugged. "She can't be more than thirteen or fourteen."

Sally threw her head back and roared, tears stream-ing down her face. "Hey Becky," she shouted, and the little girl stepped out of the kitchen, wiping her hands on a towel.

"What you want, Sally?"

"Frankie here thinks you thirteen years old."

Becky's eyebrows shot up. She marched down the length of the bar to stand in front of Charlie. She batted little schoolgirl eyes at him. "Thirteen?" she asked, clearly pleased.

Janice and Trina joined the other two girls. "Thirteen," they said in unison, shrieking with laughter.

"Frankie," Sally said. "Becky's almost thirty." The girls all shrieked as they slapped Becky on the back.

Becky put her hands on her hips, again batted those little schoolgirl eyes at him. "I got some regulars pay good money for this look." The shrieking intensified.

"But they mainly pay good money for what you do on your back," Sally added.

"And sometimes on my hands and knees too," Becky said.

"And sometimes up against a wall," Janice quipped.

The shrieking began anew. The girls walked back into the kitchen, loudly enunciating all the different positions in which they made their living.

Charlie focused on his breakfast.

The Aagerbanne situation was headline news almost every day, though the details were sporadic. The independent states were being drawn into the conflict. Having been through a war himself, Charlie could read between the lines, guessed that some of the information was carefully released propaganda, and some just plain inaccurate. But one thing was clear: both the guerilla tactics and Goutain's brutal suppression were getting nastier, and the Free Aagerbanni Resistance was struggling. Still nothing about Cesare.

On his third tenday working in Momma's, Charlie was tending bar during the slow hours between lunch and dinner. The place was empty, and he was killing time polishing glasses and thinking he might ask Momma for a loan to get a fake identity and an off-planet ticket. Outside it was a hot, dry, summer day, and the light that splashed through the open doorway cast long shadows the length of the bar which, by contrast, made the entire room feel dark and dim.

Two Syndonese soldiers walked in. They marched up to Charlie; one tossed a flat, printed picture on the bar and demanded in Syndonese, "You ever seen this man?"

Charlie spoke in standard, imitating a thick trampsie accent. "Sorry. I'm Syndonese not speaking."

"Ignorant wog," one said to the other in Syndonese. He pushed the picture closer to Charlie and switched to standard. "You ever seen this man here?"

The Syndonese didn't run Tachaann; it was a wild, free port that was just too wide-open. But for the past couple of tendays everyone had been aware of the increased Syndonese presence, with armed soldiers swaggering up and down the streets, throwing their weight around . . . and making sure those who got in their way paid for it. So while they technically had no official status here, Charlie knew that sometimes the only authority you needed was a gun in your hand. As such, he picked up the photo and pretended to examine it carefully. It was a picture of him, face-on, but without the scars and all the damage. He turned his head slightly, giving them a view of more bad side than good. He'd learned quickly that people didn't like looking at his messed-up face, and when confronted with it they tended to look at something else. The soldiers were no exception.

Momma Toofat suddenly appeared at his side, and he noticed that the room was slowly filling with every able-bodied man in Momma's clan, sitting at tables, standing at the bar or in a shadow, none of them paying any attention to Charlie and Momma and the Syndonese. Charlie shook his head and said, "No, not seen him."

Momma said, "Here, let me see." She reached out and took the photo from his hands. She made a show of looking at it carefully, and as she did so Charlie caught her glancing over the top of the picture at him. Standing beside him she could only compare it to his profile, but she was on his good side, and Momma was not stupid. "No, not seen him. Him do what?" She looked inquisitively at the two Syndonese.

"Enemy of the state," one said. "A criminal, wanted for treason. Once we find him he's a dead man." The Syndonese snatched the photo out of Momma's hands, and both abruptly left.

Momma looked carefully into Charlie's eyes, then her gaze turned slowly downward to the antique sawed-off shotgun behind the bar. Charlie's eyes followed hers. He hadn't realized he'd picked it up, was gripping it in a white-knuckled death grip.

The next morning Janice and Sally woke him from an uneasy sleep. "We gonna do you sometime," Janice announced.

Sally added, "So we gonna improve you appearance. Make you even prettier. Make it even more fun for us. Hey Janice, you think maybe we do him together? A threesome?"

Janice shook her head. "No. That'd kill him. He gonna have enough trouble doin' you and me one at a time."

They dyed his hair and eyebrows black, told him to let his hair grow and told him to grow a mustache, which they would also dye black. "I like a man wit a mustache," Sally announced. " 'Specially when he's doin' me the right way." She winked at Janice, and Janice winked back.

CHAPTER 13
CAN'T TRUST ANYONE

Stallas burst into Gaida's chambers, eager to give her the wonderful news. He shooed her maids and servants out of the room and took her in his arms. "It's done," he said. "He died in his sleep last night." He cupped one of her breasts in his hand and planted kisses on her neck.

"Can it be traced back to us?"

"No, my love, not at all. I gave him small doses over a long period of time. If someone knows what to look for, maybe, but since I'm his personal physician, it is I who will be doing the looking."

"Excellent!" she said, stepping away from him. A rather unpleasant smile appeared on her face.

"Computer," she said. "Send in my guard."

He frowned and felt suddenly confused. "What are you doing, my love?"

"Just cleaning up loose ends, darling."

Four men opened the door to her chamber without knocking and marched into the room. They were men with a hard look about them; all were armed, and he'd never seen them in Farlight in all the years he served under Cesare. "My Lady," their leader said.

Gaida pointed at Stallas. "Seize him. He murdered my husband."

One of the men spun Stallas about, slapped him against the wall and pinned his arms behind his back. He didn't understand what she was doing.

"Question him thoroughly," she said. "He conspired with Cesare's son Arthur to murder the duke so Arthur could inherit the ducal seat. And make sure there's something about Arthur growing impatient and tiring of waiting for his inheritance. Use whatever means necessary, but I want a confession to that effect, and don't listen to any of the other lies he spews."

"But my love!" Stallas cried as they dragged him away.

The last thing he heard her say was, "I don't care what shape he's in, so long as I've got a confession and he's alive to stand trial."

The political situation in the Realm had stabilized. It appeared that most of the Nine had come to terms with Goutain's manipulation of the throne. Martino, Delilah, and Adan were still on the loose. Lucius's press secretary pitched the heavy Syndonese military presence on Turnlee as part of the treaty between the

Republic and the Realm. The situation had become just another balance of power, though if Goutain got his hands on Martino that balance could shift dramatically. It was an uneasy peace at best.

Desperate for information, Charlie went to a public kiosk where he could read the latest news without spending his precious dikkas, and his eyes caught and held on a piece of one headline: *His Grace, Theode, Duke de Maris. . .*

Charlie gasped so noticeably that several passersby looked at him oddly. He wasted some of his dikkas, bought the old-fashioned newspaper and took it back to Momma Toofat's. There he sat down at the bar since he didn't have a room of his own, poured a stiff drink, and read it cover to cover several times.

Cesare had never fully recovered from his injury, had lingered on for a time under the care of his personal physician, then died under mysterious circumstances. There were several quotes from Theode and Gaida, all filled with innuendo implicating Arthur in the *mysterious circumstances*. Further quotes from Lucius hinted at a conspiracy between Arthur and the physician, Stallas. But Theode, in a grand show of compassion for his dear, beloved brother, and to protect him from the headsman, had arranged to have Arthur declared mentally incompetent and committed to an institution for the criminally insane. Of course, under the circumstances, Arthur couldn't inherit the ducal seat, and it had passed to Theode. Then the new de Maris duke had thrown his support behind Lucius's annexation of

Aagerbanne. Twerp was getting away with murder because Cesare had been a thorn in Nadama's side, and
all knew Arthur would have followed in his footsteps.

Charlie decided that someday he'd make them
pay for this. They'd taken Arthur and Cesare away
from him, and he regretted that he hadn't gotten off
Tachaann and back to Cesare sooner, hadn't gotten
there in time to save him. And he'd let Arthur down
too, left him in the clutches of Theode and Gaida. Yes,
Theode, Gaida, Lucius, and Goutain; all four of them
would pay, if it was the last thing he did.

"Frankie," Janice said softly. He looked up from the
paper and found her standing next to him, though he
had trouble focusing on her. "You doan look so good,
Frankie. You drunk, and dinner shift about to start."
She reached out and touched a tear on his cheek,
tested it sadly between thumb and forefinger. "An you
crying. You doan need to cry, Frankie. You got friends
here."

For the first time in a couple hours Charlie looked
around. Momma Toofat stood in the doorway to the
kitchen, Nano and Willie in the front doorway, Jonjon
behind the bar. They all had concerned looks on their
faces. Jonjon said, "Frankie, she's right. You got problems, we can fix 'em."

Charlie stood, and as the floor tilted beneath him
he realized he'd been slamming drinks all afternoon.
"You can't fixsh thish, Jonjon," he said, only then realizing how much he'd drunk. "Not unlesh you can
bring someone back from the dead."

"Oh, Frankie," Janice said. "Um so sorry. You take du night off. Le me get you to a bed where you can sleep it off."

"Thank you, Janice," he said, leaning on her and letting her lead him away. "An you goh my name wrong. Iss Charlie."

"Doan worry about it, Frankie. Dats okay. We know."

Charlie woke up in Janice's bed badly hungover. Momma showed him no mercy, made him work through the entire day and into the evening. That night he crashed into an exhausted sleep.

The next day the hangover was gone, but the hole Cesare's death left in his heart remained. He worked through the day, trying to think of some way he could help Arthur, came up with absolutely nothing, and only managed to increase his frustration at his own helplessness. He had trouble falling asleep that night, had been lying on his mat in the corner of the restaurant for quite some time when a soft, curvaceous, fully naked body slipped under the blanket next to him. "Frankie," Janice said softly. "I think it's time I done you."

"Pity fuck?" Charlie asked.

"No, Frankie. Before, I didn't wanna do you. I didn't wanna *not* do you. But still, that woulda been a pity fuck. Now, I just wanna. You and me. And not like a john. I wanna enjoy myself too."

She was beautiful, and sexy, and Charlie realized that he had long ago stopped thinking of Janice, Sally, Becky or Trina as anything but young women who worked hard to make a living and hoped to have families of their own someday.

The next night, at dinner after closing the bar, she announced, "I don't think I can work no more. Someone here . . ." She looked sidelong at Charlie, " . . . been sampling the merchandise, and he's so energetic I don't got none left for no customers no more." They all had a good laugh.

Momma Toofat shook her head sadly. "This bad for business."

Everyone roared.

Charlie was waiting tables and it was a rough night. The Syndonese were especially restless, both the soldiers patrolling the streets and the spacers drunk in the bars. "Frankie," Momma said. "You got a new group at table five."

"I'll get right to it, Momma."

Table five was a booth at the edge of the room. The booths were shadowy, dim places where patrons frequently conducted a lot of illegal business. He delivered a tray full of drinks to another table, then moved quickly to the new group—tips were usually better when they got some attention right away. He was two steps away from the table when he heard her voice, and he froze. He was about to turn around and get someone else to take the table, but one of the men there had noticed him approaching. "Waiter, we'd like a round of drinks."

Charlie didn't recognize the man's voice, though the accent spoke of money and power. He took a step forward, kept his bad side angled toward them and spoke standard with a heavy street accent in imitation of the girls. "Yes, sir. Wadooyouwan?" He couldn't see any of their faces clearly.

"What do you have?"

"We got everything, sir. Only du best."

The woman lifted her head slowly and peered at him through narrowed eyes. She had gone to some trouble to disguise her appearance, wearing faded spacer's fatigues with a floppy hat that shaded the upper part of her face, but Charlie knew Delilah all too well. "Do I know you?" she asked.

"Maybe," Charlie said. "Maybe you done me one night. I ain't real expensive, not with this face."

One of the men started to rise, but another put a hand on his arm and spoke with a heavy Syndonese accent. "Let it go. Remember where you are."

"But he implied—"

Delilah leaned into the light. "Charlie? It's you, isn't it?"

"I don't know what you talkin' 'bout."

The man with the moneyed accent asked, "Who's this Charlie?"

"Bastard son of Cesare," Delilah said.

The Syndonese fellow leaned forward into the light, though his face was still partially obscured by shadows. He asked, "He's the de Maris bastard?"

Delilah said, "Yes."

Charlie had to get out of this quickly. "Look. I got tables to wait. When you wanna order something, you give me a shout."

He turned and marched away, but Delilah called after him, "Charlie, wait. We need to talk."

Charlie kept on walking, headed for the kitchen and passed Sally on the way. "Don't let any customers follow me," he whispered quickly. He went through the swinging doors into the kitchen and behind him he heard Sally say loudly, "Hey. You can't go in there."

"But I want to talk with him. Tell Charlie I want to talk with him."

"Ain't no Charlie here."

Charlie went through the kitchen and into the alley behind the saloon. If Delilah and the Syndonese managed to push past Sally, Nano and the bouncers would be all over them in the kitchen and they wouldn't get much farther than that. Charlie pressed his back to the alley wall and waited. After about five minutes Nano joined him. "They're gone, Frankie. It's safe."

It wasn't safe, not anymore. He'd never been certain he could trust Delilah; after all, she was Lucius's daughter, and Lucius had become his enemy, and blood ties were always strong, and she'd been working some deal with the Syndonese. "I have to leave here. Tonight. If she just fingered me to the Syndonese I'm a danger to everyone."

Charlie bundled up his few possessions: a change of clothes, his knife, his modest accumulation of dikkas, some ration packs he still had from the lifeboat. He was going to leave by the back alley door, but Momma, Nano, Sally, and Janice cornered him on his way through the kitchen. "You can't leave without saying goodbye," Janice announced and threw her arms around his neck.

Momma gave him a big hug too, and said, "You one of us. We take care of you."

Nano told him, "You go cross town, Frankie, to Delago Street. Find Bennie Freehand's place. Tell him Momma wants him to give you a place to sleep and a job where you ain't too visible. Tell him I'll talk to him personal tomorrow."

It might have been a good plan, but a dozen Syndonese were waiting in the shadows as he emerged from the alley. He gutted one of them with his knife, but the odds were overwhelming, and in short order they had him neatly bundled up in plast manacles. They tossed him into the back of a police van and sped away.

Delilah had betrayed him.

He had a hazy recollection of a beating, not a bad one, because a Syndonese officer intervened and said they were supposed to keep him alive and healthy. Then they drugged him, and kept him drugged, and that made it difficult to keep all the memories straight and in the proper order, and impossible to count the days as they passed. He was almost certain he'd spent some time on a ship, seemed to remember feeling transition a couple of times, maybe more. For a while they kept him in a brightly lit cell, then a dark one, then a bright one again, and finally a dark one. He'd been in a car, in a police van, a shuttle of some kind, and a gunboat, always drugged heavily and just at the edge of consciousness.

There was one strange memory, perhaps just a dream. It had happened recently, maybe, but it kept returning to the forefront of his thoughts. Paul came to mind, and Winston, and Add and Ell, in a dark room, a cell, he was certain of that. A dark cell, possibly even the one he was in now.

"Charles, you have to pay attention." That had been Winston. "We've had to spread around some liberal bribes to get in to see you, and we don't have much time."

"Try to stay alert, little brother." It was the only time in Charlie's memory that he couldn't distinguish Add from Ell.

It was so hard to remember what happened. "Your father . . . certain contingencies . . . event of his death . . . reduce the power of certain . . . enhance that of others . . . protect you . . . dire circumstances arose . . ." Charlie recalled Winston's words over and over again in his mind, hoping to find anything there that meant something to him. Perhaps when the drugs wore off.

"Pay attention, Charlie. Try to stay conscious. Here, sign this. We need your signature. And a retinal scan and a DNA sample for registry."

Charlie couldn't remember if he'd remained conscious, or if he'd paid attention. Paul had said something quite longwinded, and he'd sounded as if he were reading it. Some church mumbo jumbo that involved things like, " . . . by the power vested in me . . ." and " . . . duly consecrated authority . . ." and " . . . in the eyes and heart of the holy authority . . ." Crap like that.

"Pay attention, Charlie. Say, 'I do so swear.' "

"What's going on?" he demanded.

"Damn it, Charlie. Just say, 'I do so swear.' "

Add slapped him hard at that point, or maybe it was Ell. "All right. All right already. I do so swear. I do."

"**W**ake up, asshole."

Something hit Charlie in the ribs hard. He groaned as they lifted him to his feet, cuffed his hands behind his back, and locked manacles on his ankles. The cuffs and the manacles were rusty metal, connected by a rusty chain. That brought back memories, and he realized they'd allowed the drugs to wear off. His guards roughed him up a little, bloodied his nose, split his lip and bruised a few ribs, but nothing serious. Then, surrounding him, they led him out of his cell, and he realized he was back on Turnlee, in the dungeons of the Almsburg Palace.

CHAPTER 14
THE THIRTEENTH MAN

Lucius held court in a grand style. It was little different from the last time Charlie had been dragged before the throne in the great hall. Lucius sat upon his throne, with Goutain at his right hand calling the shots. But now all signs of the fighting were a thing of the past, all nine dukes sat in the ducal gallery, and Delilah, Martino, and Adan sat or stood in their proper places upon the dais.

The guards threw Charlie to his knees at the base of the steps below the throne, and slowly he raised his eyes to meet Delilah's. He silently mouthed the word "bitch," and she cringed.

"So he still has some spirit," Goutain said. He looked around the assembly. "We've done this before, but not everyone was properly present then, so I think it well worth doing again. Adsin, read the charges." Apparently he'd dropped any pretense that Lucius still ruled.

Adsin stepped forward, opened a document, and read from it. It was the same list of charges: high treason, stationing armed troops on the grounds of the Almsburg Palace, violating Turnlee nearspace with armed vessels.

"I object," Duke Rierma cried out, standing. "This proceeding is illegal."

Charlie was as surprised as everyone else. Not surprised that Rierma would want to object, but Rierma was a practical man, and well knew that he could accomplish nothing by doing so. Charlie was a commoner, not granted the same protections as men such as Rierma.

It took several seconds to silence the crowd, then Lucius stood and spoke. "There's nothing illegal about this, old man. Since the crime was committed by the accused on my properties, I have unilateral authority to determine guilt or innocence, as well as the punishment that'll be meted out." Lucius grinned at Rierma smugly and sat down.

Winston stepped out of the shadows behind Rierma, leaned forward, and whispered into the old man's ear. Charlie began to wonder if the wily old man didn't have a trick or two up his sleeve. "First," Rierma said loudly. "You do not have unilateral authority over a duly consecrated Duke of the Realm." That phrase sounded strangely familiar to Charlie. Rierma continued. "Capital guilt can only be decided by unanimous vote of the ducal council. Second, no crime was committed, since, by law, a duly consecrated Duke of the

Realm has the right to bring whatever personal protection he deems necessary, including armed troops."

Lucius rolled his eyes. "Come now, Rierma. I know you're quite old, but I hadn't realized your faculties had begun to diminish so." The crowd responded with a background of suppressed laughter. "This common fool here before us is no Duke of the Realm."

Rierma lifted a document, held it between thumb and forefinger, dangled it before them all, and got their attention. "His Grace, Charles, is a duly consecrated Duke of the Realm, having taken oath before god and the proper witnesses."

Theode cried out, "He hasn't the right to inherit the de Maris ducal seat. He was never legitimized."

Rierma turned slowly toward Theode. "I said nothing of the de Maris ducal seat. Cesare's will legitimized Charles, though without any rights to the de Maris seat or holdings. But he long ago purchased from His Majesty rights to another ducal seat, and the right to determine its inheritance."

"Page," Goutain shouted, pointing at the document dangling from Rierma's fingers. "Bring that here."

A young page scurried across the hall, took the document from Rierma, and scurried back to Goutain, who snatched it angrily from the boy's hands. Goutain read it frantically, and a smile slowly appeared on his face. Then he threw back his head and roared with laughter.

Charlie looked up to Rierma. The old man grinned

and said, "It could be worse, Charlie. You could be de Lunis."

Goutain looked at Lucius. "Your Majesty," he said, and with a grand flourish he bowed to Charlie. "I give you His Grace, Charles, Duke de Lunis." Again he roared with laughter, and when he calmed down he cawed, "The thirteenth Duke de Lunis will fare no better now, for beneath the headsman's ax he'll lie, a frown upon his brow."

Some of the crowd echoed Goutain's laughter, but without enthusiasm, and an uneasy silence descended as Charlie climbed slowly to his feet. Looking at Goutain and Lucius, he could think of only one thing to say. "But should the headsman miss his prey, the thirteenth man will rise. And rule the headsman's ax one day, no limit to his prize."

Goutain frowned at that.

Lucius objected vehemently, maintaining that Charlie wasn't a properly consecrated Duke of the Realm. Gaida protested with such venom that drops of spittle flew from her mouth as she ranted, and Theode threw an absolute tantrum. Charlie simply stood in the middle of the great hall stunned beyond belief. What had Cesare done to him?

Rierma testified that he had reviewed all of the documents several days ago, and had had more than sufficient time to verify their authenticity. Paul testified that Charlie had been duly consecrated. Lucius was forced to admit that, yes, more than four decades ago he had sold to Cesare all rights to the de Lunis ducal seat. Rierma had finally proposed that they remand His Grace, Charles, Duke de Lunis, temporarily into his custody while Lucius and the Nine reviewed the documentation and determined to their own satisfaction if the inheritance of the de Lunis ducal seat was legitimate. For once, the Nine stood as one, and over Lucius's objections, it was done.

They retired to Rierma's suites in the palace—Rierma, Charlie, Winston, Paul, Add, Ell, and Rierma's personal guard. Charlie's first concern was Add and Ell. "You're property of House de Maris. Are you fugitives? Do we need to hide you?"

Winston said, "No, Your Grace. They're no longer property of House de Maris. Your father, in his will, stipulated that upon his death, if Arthur, for any reason, did not inherit the de Maris ducal seat, then Add'mar'die and Ell'mar'kit become the property of House de Lunis."

"We are yours, little brother," Add said.

Charlie asked Winston, "I own them?"

"Yes, Your Grace."

"I don't like owning people," Charlie said. "I don't like slavery. In front of all these witnesses here, I grant them their freedom immediately." For the first time in his life he saw Add's eyes widen with surprise. "Winston, can you draw up the paperwork: unconditionally free, with all the rights of full citizenship."

"As you wish, Your Grace."

"What about Roacka?"

Add said, "He disappeared shortly after Cesare's death and hasn't been seen since."

Rierma issued orders to his guard captain. "Put your people on full alert. Under the circumstances I expect several assassination attempts aimed at both myself and His Grace, Charles." Then Rierma spun and pointed at Charlie's wrists. "And we have a Duke of the Realm manacled in Syndonese irons. Get those vile things off him immediately." Rierma's guard brought in a nuclear torch and started working on Charlie's manacles.

"Why did the Nine stand together on this?" Charlie asked. "Nadama would just as soon have my head."

Rierma poured drinks for them all. "Because, Charles my boy, they didn't stand together. They each voted in their own interest. If all of the documentation is proper and correct, and you are legitimately a Duke of the Realm, then however they allow Lucius and Goutain to treat you, they set a precedent that they themselves can be treated in the same fashion. If Lucius or Goutain take any illegal action against you, it'll unite the Nine as they've never been before. The result would be a bloody war that would cost all sides dearly, including Goutain. This unanimity of self-preservation is the only thing that's holding the Realm together at this moment."

"And is all of the documentation proper and correct?"

"It certainly appears so." Rierma looked to Winston for confirmation.

Ever proper, Winston nodded a bow to Rierma, then turned to Charlie. "Your Grace, your father legitimately purchased the rights to the de Lunis ducal seat before you and Arthur were born. At the time, I don't think he knew exactly what he was going to do with such a valueless property; he was frequently opportunistic that way. Then after Theode was born, he asked me to prepare the proper legal framework for a number of contingencies. One of those was that in the event of his inability to occupy the de Maris ducal seat, and if Arthur, for any reason, could not then immediately occupy the seat himself, I was to initiate a sequence of events that would place you upon the de Lunis ducal seat. I've had most of your life to make sure that this inheritance will be ironclad. And I've made certain that if the Nine don't support it, they'll emasculate themselves. Give them a day or two, and they'll see that."

"Well, now," Rierma said, "they can no longer call us the Nine. I suppose they'll call us the Ten."

Charlie looked at Winston, and for the first time saw an old man without hope. But then something flickered in Winston's eyes. "Your Grace," he said, and dropped to one knee in front of Charlie. "At your father's death I'd have sworn my allegiance to Arthur. But Arthur is not consecrated so I cannot. And I'll not give my allegiance to that snake that now occupies the de Maris ducal seat. Will you accept my oath, Your Grace?"

Winston's question stunned Charlie into silence

and he didn't know what to say. Rierma, standing behind them all, nodded silently to Charlie. Charlie spoke solemnly. "Of course."

Winston bowed his head and placed his hand over his heart. "I, Winston, formerly sworn to His Grace, Cesare, of House de Maris, do solemnly swear before god and man that I give my allegiance to you, Charles, Duke de Lunis. I acknowledge you as lord of House de Lunis, and I swear to defend your rights as holder of all de Lunis properties and as master over its courts, and to abide by your judgments in all disputes."

Charlie had seen the ancient formula spoken many times, had memorized that side of it so he could speak it before Cesare when he'd come of age. But he'd never thought to be on the receiving end, and while he had seen Cesare speak the proper response many times, he was going to have to fake it. He placed a hand on Winston's shoulder. "And I, Charles, the de Lunis, do solemnly swear before god and man to defend your rights and those of your household against all claims and incursions, and to render unto you just and honest decisions in any and all disputes, and to judge fairly as your sworn liege lord." Rierma nodded his silent approval.

Charlie helped Winston to his feet. "Your Grace," Winston protested. "This is not proper."

Charlie laughed. "I doubt there is anyone in Almsburg who thinks there is a proper duke occupying the de Lunis ducal seat."

Paul shook his head vehemently. "You're wrong in that, Your Grace. Besides us in this room, I think there are many here who feel the de Lunis seat is capably occupied. And to that end, I have this . . ." Paul handed Charlie a small package. "It's from your father, though I don't believe it's a gift. He entrusted it to me twenty years ago, with the rather cryptic instructions that I was to give it to 'the de Lunis.' I tried to question him further since the seat was vacant, but he refused to say more than that I should keep it with me always, and wait until there was a de Lunis to accept it. He did say it was extremely valuable."

Everyone looked on expectantly as Charlie opened the package. In it he found a small dagger, more decorative than functional, its handle studded with gems and precious stones. The blade wasn't even plast, merely steel, and its balance was poor. Charlie tossed it to Ell, who caught it deftly and flipped it in the air a few times. "I'd hate to have my life dependent upon this blade," she said, confirming his suspicions. "Even the steel is of poor quality. Perhaps the jewels?" She handed it to Winston.

He looked at it carefully and shrugged. "I'm sorry, Your Grace. I'd guess the jewels are merely colored glass. Worthless."

Paul took the blade from Winston. "If Cesare said it's valuable, then it's priceless in a way we don't understand." He handed the blade to Charlie, then dropped to one knee. "I too would swear, Your Grace."

After Paul, Add stepped forward. "I too would swear, little brother."

Ell gave her a shove. "Now that he's a duke you can't call him 'little brother' anymore."

"Of course I can. He'll always be *little brother*. And I expect we'll continue his training. And I'll expect you not to pull any punches just because he's some duke, little sister."

"Don't call me *little sister*. I'm the older one, by at least a minute."

So the two breeds also swore their allegiance.

"Your Grace," Winston said after they were done. "I personally think it's a rather auspicious beginning. However . . ." Winston paused, looking carefully at Charlie. He had seemed lost until sworn to Charlie. But now that he was a duke's man once more, properly sworn, with his place defined as it should be, he'd returned to being the familiar Winston that Charlie knew. He approached Charlie, reached out, and touched the collar of Charlie's tunic. "However, your attire is not appropriate for your new station." Charlie looked down at his clothing, trampsie through and through: colorful, a bit flamboyant, but filthy, covered in the grime from a half-dozen cells, several days of Charlie's sweat, and some of his blood too. Charlie wasn't sure what about it was more inappropriate, colorful and flamboyant, or torn and bloodstained. Winston looked at Rierma. "Your Grace, would it be possible to call in a tailor, one who could move rather swiftly?"

Over the next two days Rierma's guard thwarted four assassination attempts, all aimed at Charlie. "That's insulting," Rierma shouted. "They don't consider me important enough to assassinate."

Word trickled in from the rest of the Nine that each would support Charlie's inheritance of the de Lunis seat; the legal framework that Winston had structured was indisputable. Add and Ell now shadowed Charlie's every move, as they'd previously shadowed Cesare's. Rierma had put his personal surgeon to work repairing Charlie's injuries. Rierma's surgeon told him the lifeboat's med unit had done a reasonably good job and it would only take a few surgeries to completely restore his face, so Charlie now sported a rather sizable bandage. Since a meeting of the Ten was scheduled for the following day, Winston, Paul, and Rierma took it upon themselves to educate Charlie in all of the legal issues surrounding his new position, plus the customs and rules of the ducal council.

"Your Grace, you have a visitor."

With welcome relief, Charlie looked up. He was seated at a desk absorbed in reviewing the properties of House de Lunis. He owned his ducal estate, which was on an airless moon named Luna orbiting an uninhabited planet in an out-of-the-way system. In fact, he apparently owned the entire system, which included nine named planets or planetoids, a few unnamed planetoids in extreme orbits, various moons and a star named Sol. Archeological evidence indicated that the system had been extensively mined of all valuable elements more than two thousand years ago, and none of the planets or moons was habitable, so the whole thing was worthless. He had a few minor properties on Aagerbanne, Toellan, and Istanna, but according to the records Winston had supplied, none of them brought in any serious revenues, and in fact his holdings on Istanna—a majority interest in a commercial shipping company—were actually losing money. And he didn't have a ship to his name. House de Lunis was the poorest of the Ten, all but destitute.

Charlie looked up from the pile of papers in front of him. "I have a visitor?"

"Yes, Your Grace," the page said. "Her Royal Highness, Princess Delilah, wishes to speak with you."

Charlie bit back the epithet that came to mind as he thought of how she'd turned him in to the Syndonese. He said only, "Tell her I'm unavailable."

"But, Your Grace, it's Her Royal Highness."

"I know that," he said. "Tell her I'm unavailable."

During the next day Delilah tried to see him twice more, and both times he refused her. He didn't see her until he was headed to the meeting of the Ten with his small retinue. He turned into a corridor and there she stood, blocking his path with a retinue of her own that considerably outnumbered his. "Your Grace," she said regally. "I would speak with you."

"Your Highness," he said. "I must apologize that I don't have the time. The ducal council convenes momentarily."

Ell jabbed an elbow into his ribs and hissed in his ear, "Go talk to her, you idiot." She gave him a little shove forward.

Delilah came forward, leaving her retinue behind, and the two of them met halfway, like two generals meeting under a flag of truce with armies at their backs. When she spoke, it was almost a whisper. Clearly she didn't want the armies behind them to hear. "What have I done to anger you so?"

"After betraying me you wonder why I'm angry."

"Betray you? I haven't betrayed you."

"Don't lie to me. On Tachaann you fingered me to the Syndonese."

"No. That's not true. I swear. I mean I know it must have been my fault. I made a scene, and I shouted your name in that bar, and they must have been following me because they picked me up the next morning. But if I'm guilty of anything, Charlie, it's just stupidity."

It was plausible. It could be that simple. But then he recalled her sitting at table five with a Syndonese. "He's the de Maris bastard?" the Syndonese had asked, and Del had replied, "Yes." Charlie put all the ice into his voice he could muster. "No, Your Highness. It is I who am guilty of stupidity, for I trusted you."

He didn't wait for a reply. He stepped around her and started walking. Her retinue parted as he walked through them and he heard his own small entourage rushing to catch up.

"**W**e are assembled here today to vote on several important issues," Nadama said. He had previously been elected as council chair and was running the show. "The first and foremost is to ratify the inheritance of the de Lunis ducal seat. To that end—"

Charlie stood. "I object." He, Winston, and Rierma had considered this carefully. Most of the council would expect Charlie to be completely ignorant of his rights, perhaps an easy mark for some clever maneuvering. "My inheritance needs no ratification, and in fact this council does not have the authority to ratify such an inheritance. Nor is it customary to do so. The only action this council might take in that regard is to consider a dispute concerning said inheritance, and there is no such dispute before this council now." Charlie sat down.

There was a long moment of silence, then Telka said, "He's right."

Nadama took a deep breath and let it out dramatically. "Very well," he said. "Then the next order of business is—"

Charlie stood again. "The next order of business is that I exercise my right to adjourn this council until I've had time to carefully consider all of the matters before it." Now everyone started shouting.

This too they had planned carefully. By law, a newly consecrated duke could table all issues before the council for a period of one hundred days. In an orderly succession the heir, in all likelihood, would've been carefully briefed on the issues and probably would not exercise such a right. But it was still the heir's choice to do so if he felt it necessary, and by law, he need not justify his actions. Also by law, during that period the council could not meet, nor could the king command the heir's presence at court.

Charlie didn't answer any of the shouts, just stood there without expression until the shouting died. In the ensuing silence he sat down without a word. There was some argument, but within a matter of minutes the first council of the Ten in three hundred years ended without ado.

"Your Grace, there's a man here who wishes to speak with you."

At the sound of the page's voice Charlie didn't immediately look up from the accounts of House de Lunis, but held up a hand to forestall him.

Darmczek had shown up a few days ago, sworn himself to Charlie, and told him that all of the Two Thousand—as they were now calling the men he'd shared the chain with—and most of the de Maris servants and much of the guard were prepared to do the same.

Apparently Theode and Gaida had demonstrated their most endearing traits to everyone.

But Charlie couldn't pay any of them. By all rights he should be broke. The holdings on Istanna were losing more money than those on Aagerbanne and Toellan were bringing in. And there were no revenues associated with the Sol system. It was simple mathematics; if you lose more money than you make, you've got a problem. House de Lunis should have been bankrupt long ago, but it wasn't. In fact, the accounts, which were held at a bank on Toellan, always grew—at a modest rate, but they nevertheless grew. Charlie wasn't rich, but he wasn't broke, though he didn't have enough to pay a single servant, let alone vassals, retainers, and an entire house full of servants. Something didn't add up.

Charlie snapped out of his reverie and looked at the page. "I'm sorry. You said there's a man here to see me."

"Yes, Your Grace. But he seems a rather unsavory sort. I've already sent him away five times, but he keeps returning, and he claims to be a friend of yours."

"Did he give a name?"

"Yes, Your Grace. A rather strange name. Nano-who-never-loses, or something like that."

"Nano's here?" Charlie jumped to his feet. "Where is he?"

"He's in the library, Your Grace."

Charlie left the page behind, burst into the library, and found Nano helping himself to a drink and a cigar from Rierma's stash. "Frankie," Nano said, eyeing the cigar carefully. "You now some big-shot duke being, eh?"

"What are you doing here?"

"Momma said you got trouble, and you're family, so we're here to pull your ass out of the fire. But guess you don't need no help." Nano puffed on the cigar and blew a big smoke ring into the air.

Suddenly Charlie felt good. "Tell Momma thanks. But I was in a dungeon in this palace. There's no way you could've gotten to me."

Nano switched to standard. "Frankie, I brought Janice and Sally with me. They can fuck their way into anyplace. And if they need to, they know how to kill good too."

"Momma let Janice and Sally come?"

Nano grimaced. "She don't like the loss of revenue, but the girls begged and pleaded—drove us all nuts—and they were due a vacation." Nano raised a hand, and rubbed his thumb against two fingers in the universal sign of money. "The girls also pointed out there'd be some rich pickings here."

"How'd you get here?"

"In our ship."

"You have a ship?"

"Of course we have a ship. We're smugglers. How do you think we smuggle, up our asses?"

Not only had Momma sent Nano, Janice, and Sally, she'd sent Willie, and Stan Fourhands, pickpocket, lock-pick, computer wizard, a man of many talents. Charlie had Nano retrieve them and bring them up to Rierma's suites. Janice and Sally launched themselves at Charlie and smothered him in kisses. Sally looked at the bandages on his face and her eyes grew big. She turned to Janice. "Hey, they fixed him up. He gonna be pretty on both sides. I got dibs on doin' him first."

Janice shrugged. "I already done him, though I gotta say the way he done me I don't care what his face looks like."

Charlie introduced them to everyone. "A reunion of old friends," Rierma said, "in more ways than one. We'll have a party tonight, and we can all share how we met and became friends."

Sally sidled up to Rierma. "You know," she said. "You pretty good lookin', for a old guy."

CHAPTER 15
INCONSISTENCIES

Charlie needed a ride, literally. It had become a bit of a joke throughout the palace that near-destitute House de Lunis didn't own a ship to transport His Grace to his ducal estates on Luna. Rierma offered him the loan of one of his ships, but Nano volunteered his, saying, "Hey Frankie. We'll take you in our ship. Momma ain't expecting us back for a couple months."

Charlie said, "I don't have any way of paying you back. I'll do what I can, but I have no idea when that'll be."

Nano shrugged and said, "We'll extend credit."

Janice chimed in, "We owe him anyway, 'cause he saved my ass that night."

Sally agreed with her, and the three of them got into a family argument.

Charlie had Add and Ell inspect Nano's ship. Add summed the ship up as, "She's a tramp merchantman, little brother. Looks like a tramp merchantman. Probably runs like a tramp merchantman." So Charlie departed Turnlee in the tramp merchantman *Goldisbest*, a beat-up, decrepit smuggler's scow. On the outbound leg, while trying to clear Turnlee nearspace and set their vector for up-transition, Turnlee customs officials boarded the ship. They were actually Syndonese in Turnlee uniforms, whose only purpose was clearly harassment. They took vids of the interior and exterior of *Goldisbest* and released them to the media, an attempt on Goutain's part to humiliate Charlie. But Goutain had never had to shit in a bucket while chained to two thousand men.

After that, humiliation was a relative thing.

Charlie came to realize that, in an odd sort of way, his near-destitute status provided better protection than a platoon of armed troops. No one considered him a threat, so it wasn't worth the time and effort to do anything about him, though he decided not to depend on that too much. He asked Nano to plot a roundabout course to the Sol system, down-transiting for nav fixes in unpredictable places.

Charlie had nothing to do on the trampsie smuggler. He spent the time reviewing the de Lunis accounts with Winston, and working out with Add and Ell, with an occasional romp in bed with Janice. *Goldisbest* broke down three times, and each time they had to spend a day or two dead in space while Nano and his crew repaired her. Twenty days after departing Turnlee they transited into Sol nearspace.

The Sol system was quite unusual. Eight planets

and one planetoid appeared to have been named after the nine dukes. The de Lunis estate, named Starfall by Cesare, had been carved out of solid rock on Luna, the only moon orbiting the third planet, Terra. There were archeological sites on almost every object in the system, evidence it had been colonized and settled a couple thousand years ago. In fact, there was evidence to indicate that Terra had once held a population of several billion people. But at some point about two thousand years ago it had been the target of a massive bombardment from space. There were large radioactive hot spots all over the planet's surface, its atmosphere was toxic, and its population now limited to a few dozen archeologists willing to live and work in radiation-shielded environments.

There were also a number of prehistory sites on Luna. They'd been similarly bombarded, were now nasty hot spots, but with no atmosphere the contamination hadn't spread to cover Luna's entire surface. The coordinates for Charlie's estates pointed to a location not far from the largest of these in a region known as Mare Crisium, and the gravity on Luna, one-sixth of a standard gravity, was low enough that Nano was comfortable actually bringing *Goldisbest* down to the surface, rather than shuttling them down. Winston provided the keys to the house, security codes that, when broadcast on the correct frequency, activated a number of systems that had shut down while there were no occupants present.

Charlie watched their approach on one of *Goldis-*

best's screens. Starfall nestled high up the side of the rim of a massive, ancient impact crater. The landscape was uniformly gray, with intense shadows, and not until they slowed to a crawl and approached to within a few hundred meters of the estate did Charlie realize what he was looking at. From the outside Starfall was quite grand and big, a palace in every sense of the word, with story after story climbing the side of the crater. But anyone could see that it was old.

Winston told Charlie, "Cesare didn't build it. He got it with the Sol system when he purchased it. He also bought it at fire-sale prices, so don't expect a lot. He did renovate its systems, but I believe a lot of the architecture is outdated."

As they approached, the massive doors of a hangar swung outward. Nano's pilot maneuvered the little ship into a large bay, and set her down gently as the hangar doors closed behind them. Janice's voice blared out of allship. "Frankie, your new place looks pretty cool."

The structure had a sterile, unlived-in quality to it. According to Winston no one had lived within its walls since the demise of the twelfth Duke de Lunis three hundred years earlier. Cesare had expanded it somewhat but never used it, though it had been kept under pressure to preserve the many items that would not survive the vacuum of Luna's surface, and maintenance and cleaning bots kept it clean and dust free.

There were ballrooms, sitting rooms, studies, libraries, enormous suites for guests. Charlie could easily entertain Lucius, the Ten, their retinues, and the entire court from Almsburg, though doing so would bankrupt him before they even arrived. But he was already so close to bankruptcy it didn't matter. It was quite grand, and quite sterile.

What had Cesare been thinking?

They were standing in the middle of one of the ballrooms, all of them, when Sally said, "Whoever made this place musta been thinking a king was gonna live here."

There was a moment of hesitation, then they all turned and looked at Charlie.

Charlie shrugged. "Let's take up residence in one of the suites and leave the rest empty—hopefully that helps keep expenses down. I wish Momma were here. Does anyone know how to cook? I'm hungry."

They found the master suite. It had enough rooms to house ten times their number. Charlie insisted on something smaller, but they argued that he was the *master*. And they argued long enough that he finally gave in.

For the next two days he alternated between pouring over the de Lunis accounts with Winston and Paul, and exploring Starfall's halls with Janice and Sally. The three of them were deep in the bowels of Starfall's cellars on the morning of their third day when Sally called, "Hey Frankie. Look at this."

Sally stood in the intersection of two corridors

holding a computer tablet linked into Starfall's main systems. She turned it to one side, then the other, and her brow wrinkled into a frown. "It ain't on the map," she said.

Janice demanded, "What ain't on the map?"

She and Charlie looked over Sally's shoulder. The tablet's screen showed a three-dimensional map of Starfall, with a small red target pinpointing their present position.

"This hallway here," she said, pointing into an unlit corridor that branched off to her right.

Charlie looked at the map carefully, and she was right. "Probably just an oversight." Nevertheless, he stepped into the dark corridor and the palace's system responded by turning on the lights. They were surprised to find a blind corridor about three meters long that ended in a featureless stone wall. Charlie stopped and stared at it, while Janice stepped up to it and pressed her hand against its surface.

"This is weird," Sally said. "Look at this, Frankie."

Charlie looked over her shoulder again, and now the blind corridor did appear on the map. "As soon as we walked in here it showed up." She turned around, retraced her steps back out of the corridor. "No, it's still there now." Charlie followed her to have a look for himself. "Wow!" she said as he stepped out of the corridor. "It's gone now. Go back, Frankie."

They discovered by simple experimentation that the blind corridor appeared on the system map only when Charlie entered it.

"Frankie," Janice called suddenly. "Come look at this." Janice was at the end of the corridor, running her hand over the featureless wall. "The wall ain't where the wall is."

She was right. It appeared as if Janice's hands had sunk into the stone of the wall up to her wrists. Charlie pressed his hands against the wall, watched his own hands appear to sink into the stone, found that the actual, physical wall was about ten centimeters behind where it appeared to be, and it was as featureless as the apparent wall. "A visual distortion field," he said, looking around for the projector. But whoever had installed it had hidden it well; he found nothing.

"Something funny going on here, Frankie," Janice said.

They showed the blind corridor to Nano, Winston, and Paul, but Charlie swore them all to secrecy, and they agreed not to discuss it or reveal its existence to anyone else. Cesare, even after his death, was up to something.

Late one afternoon Winston showed Charlie some discrepancies he'd discovered in the de Lunis accounts. "You're right," Charlie conceded. "It doesn't add up. And everything points to this shipping company on Istanna: Allston Import/Export. What's interesting is that while they lose money every year, it's always exactly five percent of operations, never more, never less. And you know nothing of this?"

"Your father was quite mysterious about all this. I knew that he'd purchased the rights to the de Lunis ducal seat, and he made some additions to this estate—though I'd never seen it and was not aware of its extent—and I was responsible for the legal framework surrounding your inheritance. But as to the de Lunis properties and accounts, my first glimpse of these records was only after your father's death. Your Grace, in this I'm as ignorant as you."

Charlie thought of the blind corridor in the cellars; the de Lunis accounts were no less mysterious. "I think it's time I paid a visit to Allston Import/Export."

Winston considered that for a moment. "It would be appropriate for a newly installed lord to tour his holdings, to review accounts with key managers. And there's no reason you shouldn't begin with Istanna."

Charlie looked at the paperwork they'd been reviewing. How was he going to tour his holdings when he was broke? Nano would give him a free ride, for a while. But people would expect him to travel in the style befitting a Duke of the Realm. "Oh, what the hell! Let's get Nano and plan a little trip."

They departed the next day and, with the exception of one breakdown that took two days to repair, the transition to Istanna was uneventful. Istanna was a backwater planet, but, like Tachaann, located conveniently between the Realm and Aagerbanne, which was the primary access point for entry into the independent states. Istanna had a reasonably strong economy based on the shipping business, and its merchants were known to be savvy traders. Some said Istannan traders were nothing more than middlemen, adding cost but no value to a transaction. But Cesare had once told Charlie that a good Istannan trader could make deals happen that were otherwise impossible, and that an Istannan considered it a good deal only if all parties were satisfied.

Charlie had decided to travel incognito, using a fake identity to clear customs. They checked into a hotel in the city of Matalan, then sent word ahead that the newly seated duke and owner of Allston Import/Export would be visiting on the following day, and was hoping to meet with Allston's general manager, one Tarak Sague. It was decided that Winston, the two breeds, Darmczek, and Paul would accompany Charlie on this first visit.

Allston's offices were Spartan, at best. A receptionist met them in the lobby and ushered them immediately into Sague's office. The Istannan was a small, neat man, dark hair and complexion, impeccably dressed, though not expensively. He greeted Charlie with a bow and spoke with a clipped and proper Istannan accent. "Your Grace, I've instructed our accountant to have all of our records ready for your review. And I thought you might wish to tour the facility. And if there is anything else that you desire, we are, of course, at your complete disposal. But first, I thought you might wish a cup of tea."

Sague snapped his fingers. The receptionist disappeared and a few minutes later returned with a tray bearing several glasses of hot, black tea, an old Istannan custom. When Add and Ell declined the tea Sague looked at them sharply, perhaps taking insult, so Charlie quickly said, "While on duty they eat and drink nothing that they themselves have not prepared."

"Ah!" Sague said, his manner softening. "The breeds, the bodyguards. I remember them from your father's infrequent visits. So you inherited them from him?"

Charlie sipped at his tea. "Didn't inherit them. They're free citizens now, and sworn to me."

They chatted for a while. Sague expressed his condolences for Cesare's death. They spoke of the news, of the annexation of Aagerbanne and the growing tension between the Realm and the independent states.

"FAR is struggling," Sague said. "Rumor has it they're now limited to what arms and equipment they can steal from the Syndonese occupation forces."

Charlie wondered once more if he might be able to help them somehow, but being destitute he put that thought away.

Sague provided them with copies of Allston's financial reports going back several years. Then, while Winston and Paul closeted themselves with Sague's accountant, the Istannan showed Charlie the facility. At one point, as one of Sague's managers proudly showed them the inventory control system for Allston's warehouses, Sague casually mentioned, "A colleague of mine at Port Istanna Prime told me that you arrived in a rather . . . unusual ship."

Charlie looked at Sague and grinned. "Your colleague told you I arrived in a rather decrepit looking tramp merchantman, captained and crewed by trampsies. Did he not?"

Sague flushed with embarrassment. "I assumed, Your Grace, that the nature of the ship was merely part of the guise of traveling incognito."

"No, Mr. Sague. Since House de Lunis is broke and nearly bankrupt and I don't have a ship of my own, I'm dependent upon the kindness of friends for transportation. And the trampsies are my friends, my dear friends."

Sague's brow wrinkled in a deep frown and his eyes flashed indignantly. "But this is intolerable, Your Grace. Why, you own several ships, or at least your companies do. Mostly freighters, but I'm sure we could refit one of the smaller ones for your personal use. We'll make one available to you immediately. A man in your station must travel appropriately. And where did you get the insane idea that House de Lunis was near bankruptcy?"

Charlie explained their review of the de Lunis books. Sague interrupted him, "No, no, no, no, no, Your Grace. Come with me, please." Sague snapped his fingers, and in moments the little man was marching back to his offices, with Charlie close on his heels having to hurry to keep up with him.

"Your father gave me specific instructions to structure the finances of these holdings this way, though he didn't tell me why, and it was not my place to ask." With Winston and Charlie looking on, Sague paged through screen after screen of account statements. They meant nothing to Charlie.

"Allston itself is moderately profitable, but on your father's instructions, Allston's corporate structure is set up to automatically funnel much of the profits into a numbered investment account on Finalsa. However, in addition to the import and export operations, Allston is a holding company for four other wholly owned subsidiaries, all of which I hold a minority interest in, three of which are profitable, again only moderately so, one of which is not. In fact, before his demise I'd intended to discuss with His Grace liquidation of the assets of that operation. It's a small operation, and by selling it off you'll be able to fund the outfitting of your new ship."

They showed Sague the accounts they'd been reviewing, and the little Istannan responded in a huff. "These too," he said, indicating the de Lunis house accounts, "are per your father's instructions. The expenses of maintaining Starfall were to be properly covered, but no more. The de Lunis accounts were to always appear just barely in the black, though if you wish that changed we could easily divert more into the house accounts."

With Sague's aid they determined that House de Lunis was not penniless. The combined profits from Allston and its holdings didn't make Charlie a wealthy man, especially since he was going to spend a considerable amount outfitting a ship, and the operating costs of a ducal house were considerable, but still it was welcome news. House de Lunis would be the poorest of the Ten, but no longer destitute.

"If Your Grace feels that I've been remiss in any way then I will tender my resignation—"

"No," Charlie interrupted. "You've done an outstanding job, and I hope you'll continue."

Sague's indignation disappeared between one moment and the next. "Well, of course, Your Grace. Your father and I had a working relationship for almost thirty years, and it was always a good one. He recognized that such relationships must be mutually beneficial."

"As do I."

Sague positively beamed with pleasure. "We must get you a ship, Your Grace, one appropriate for a man of your stature. And I certainly can be of assistance there."

"Yes and no," Charlie said. "I do need a ship, but not one that's appropriate for a man of my stature." Charlie had come to understand what Cesare had known all along: for him, there was considerable safety in appearing weak and near destitute.

Sague was scandalized when Charlie asked him for a ship similar to *Goldisbest*. But when Charlie explained the political necessities of his situation, and that he wanted a ship that only appeared decrepit, Sague warmed to the idea. "Sometimes it's necessary to allow the competition to deceive themselves," Sague said. "I can find a vessel with a sound hull, then gut it and refit it in our own shipyards. Trust me, Your Grace. When I'm done it'll have the latest drive and control systems, but still appear to be junk."

"And can you fit it with armaments?"

Sague's eyebrows rose with a question, but he didn't ask it. "All of your holdings that I manage, Your Grace, are commercial in nature, not capable of producing armaments. I'll have to contract with an armaments manufacturer such as Hart & Delorm on Toellan. And that'll be expensive."

"Can they be discreet? Are they willing to install armaments without adding the specifications to the registry documents?"

"I do not know, Your Grace. I have little experience in armaments, but I can make some inquiries."

"No. Don't. Not yet. Let's start with the hull and the refitting. Perhaps my factor on Toellan can help. Let me explore the matter with him first."

Charlie decided to leave Darmczek behind to work with Sague on the specifications for the ship. Darmczek also gave Sague a list of names from the Two Thousand, men he knew could be trusted implicitly, and would jump at the chance to join Charlie's crew. Sague would have his agents contact them and arrange passage for them to Istanna so they could be on hand to crew the new ship when she was ready.

Charlie had Sague transfer some funds to Nano in at least partial payment for *Goldisbest*'s use. Nano said it wasn't necessary, but Charlie ignored him and transferred the money anyway.

However, for all the good news, bad news continued to trickle in. They heard reports that on Aagerbanne, Goutain was trying to brutally suppress FAR by burning slums and executing more civilians, though to everyone's frustration there were no real details available.

They spent four more days reviewing the operations of Allston's subsidiaries and touring each of them. It was on the fifth day, before departing for Toellan, that Sague pulled Charlie aside, saying only, "Before you leave, I must have a private word with you, Your Grace." He pulled Charlie into his office and instructed the house computer to establish a privacy screen, then turned to one corner of the room and approached it carefully. He looked about as if judging his position, then lifted his hand and pressed his palm flat against the wall in an area that was plain and featureless. The room itself seemed to hesitate for a moment, then a small section of wall slid aside revealing a cyberpad. Sague punched some formula into it then stepped back, and suddenly a larger section of another wall slid aside with a loud hiss, revealing a deep recess. Sague approached it, reached within, and lifted out a small package with almost reverent care. He handed it to Charlie. "Your father wanted me to give this to you, or, rather, to the de Lunis."

"When was this?"

"About twenty years ago, Your Grace."

"And did he say anything else?"

"Only that it was quite valuable, Your Grace. Though I did ask him how I was to give it to the de Lunis when there was no de Lunis. But he refused to elaborate, said only that I was to keep it and if there ever was a de Lunis to give it to, then I was to do so at the first opportunity."

Just like with Paul. "One more question. How did you meet my father?"

Sague considered that carefully. "More than thirty years ago, during the Shatee Crisis, when people's lives meant nothing, he gave many of us refuge."

"Thank you," Charlie said.

He didn't open the package until *Goldisbest* had departed and he was alone in his cabin. It contained a cyberkey, a complex electronic and electromagnetic structure about the size of his index finger. It could be activated only by the mating lock to which it was paired, and it in turn would open the lock.

But where's the lock? Charlie wondered.

On Toellan they were met by Aziz Anat Cohannin Meth'kah'hat bin Sabatth duu Donawathat; but, beyond first introductions, no one had time for all that so *Aziz* was good enough for all concerned. Charlie braced himself for the Toellani accent, which included a lisp that hung on certain consonants.

"Your Grathe," he said, rolls of fat bobbing beneath his chin. "It ith tho good to meet your gloriouth prethence." Charlie was pleased how quickly he adapted to Aziz's accent, even as the factotum continued to speak. "You grace my humble presence with your glorious mentality."

Charlie wasn't exactly sure what that meant, though Aziz clearly intended it to be some sort of compliment. The Toellani style could be rather obsequious, though they apparently toned it down when not in their home system.

For a first meeting of such nature it was customary for the Toellani to entertain his guests with a large and extended banquet, with no business discussed the first day. Paul had trouble choking down a few of the Toellani delicacies, some of which were still moving on the plate, but Charlie had eaten worse while starving to death in a prisoner-of-war camp.

The next morning they got down to business, with Winston and Paul reviewing the accounts for the de Lunis Toellan holdings. Aziz escorted Charlie on the customary tour of one of his companies, a manufacturer of ship subsystems: galley, computer, navigation, life support—a rather extensive list. The tour was tedious, but about halfway through it Charlie decided he could now broach the subject that was of most interest to him. "Mr. Aziz."

"Please, Your Grace. I am merely Aziz."

"Well then, Aziz. Have you had any serious dealings with armament manufacturers such as Hart & Delorm?"

Aziz smiled at something. "Well, of course, Your Grace."

Charlie hadn't expected it to be this easy. "Might they be willing to be discreet about certain installations on some hulls I have in mind?"

Aziz laughed almost uncontrollably. "Oh, they might, Your Grace. They might. Your sense of humor is so beguiling."

Obviously, Charlie had tickled Aziz's funny bone in some way. "I am concerned. I need absolute discretion in a certain matter, and if Misters Hart & Delorm cannot provide the discretion I need, then—"

Aziz looked askance at Charlie. "Oh, Your Grace. I do believe you truly do not know. But don't you see, *you* are Misters Hart & Delorm."

It was true. Aziz dragged Charlie back to his own offices. Winston had already started to get some inkling of the truth before they arrived. Then Aziz, with the help of his accountants, guided them carefully through the maze of corporate structure that hid the fact that the de Lunis was the sole owner of the armaments factories of Hart & Delorm. And in fact, there were no Misters Hart & Delorm. All Charlie could think to say was, "Well, I guess Misters Hart & Delorm will be as discreet as I want them to be."

Aziz laughed so hard he had to sit down.

That evening Aziz took them out for dinner, drinks, and a night on the town. It was as they were stepping out of a restaurant that the assassins struck. A man suddenly stepped out of the crowd, wrapped his arms around Charlie, and pulled him to the ground. Charlie lay beneath the man as shots rang out, people screamed, and the vapor trails of powerful energy weapons shattered the night. But the man pinning Charlie to the ground did only that and nothing more. And when calm returned he carefully helped Charlie to his feet. Charlie noticed a couple of men helping Aziz to his feet in the same manner and he turned a questioning look on Add.

She nodded toward Aziz and said, "He has about ten agents constantly surrounding us, little brother. Ell and I have spotted them all, though they think we haven't. Their security is good, so we decided not to interfere unless necessary. And what better place for you when the shooting starts than under a man wearing powered shielding."

One of Aziz's people suddenly appeared before the Toellani and saluted smartly. "We captured one alive, My Lord."

Charlie saw another side of Aziz. "Question him thoroughly. Learn everything he knows. Then kill him."

Charlie looked pointedly at Aziz and said, "I want to know everything you learn."

Aziz insisted on accompanying them to the shuttle port the next morning. On the way Charlie questioned him about the assassin.

"He was a local man, Your Grace, was paid in cash by another local whom we found dead in his home this morning. We can't trace it any further than that."

Charlie and Aziz were sitting in the back of a grav car alone. Aziz handed him a small package, saying, "Your father asked me to keep this for you."

Charlie looked at it. "Did he ask you to keep it for me, or for *the de Lunis*?"

"Ah! You are most correct, Your Grace. It was *the de Lunis* he specified, but twenty years ago there was no de Lunis."

"And did you question him about that?"

"It was not my place to do so. I owed your father far too much to question his motives."

Again Charlie waited until he was alone in his cabin in *Goldisbest* before opening the package. It was another cyberkey, delivered by another loyal business associate of Cesare's. He compared the two keys; each had a different interface, indicating each fit a unique lock. But where were they, these locks? And what lay behind them?

On Toellan, Charlie had learned that while Finalsa and Allison's Cluster had signed a mutual defense alliance with Aagerbanne, they hadn't yet directly intervened in the annexation, and probably wouldn't. However, they'd begun quietly supplying the Aagerbanni resistance, which kept it alive on a day-by-day basis, and the nasty little guerrilla war was proving to be more than Goutain had anticipated. Charlie hoped to learn more from the Aagerbannis themselves.

Because of the turmoil Charlie had Nano down-transit well outside of Aagerbanni nearspace, but close enough to communicate with the de Lunis represen-tative on an encrypted link via transition com. The transition com could communicate over short stellar distances of a few light-years with only a small time delay of seconds, but the absolute limit of its range was about five light-years. Which meant that when they sent a message to Charlie's factor on Aagerbanne, they had to wait an hour for a reply. When it came, a portly little man appeared on one of *Goldisbest*'s screens, introduced himself as Factor Kierson. Next to Kierson stood a beautiful older woman, whom he introduced as Lady Ethallan. Charlie had met her a couple of times, but long ago when he was a child and she a guest of Cesare's.

"Your Grace," she said. "Do not enter our nearspace. It's much too dangerous. This annexation by your king, and occupation by Syndonese troops, has created considerable unrest. I myself am taking advantage of the present chaos to go into exile. However, before I do, you and I must meet, even if only briefly. I have something to give you."

Charlie knew that Ethallan was an old and valued acquaintance of Cesare's, and while she wouldn't elaborate, he suspected that the *something* she had to give him came from his father.

Kierson came back on, gave them a set of coordinates for a rendezvous about two light-years out from Aagerbanne, and a day later they met in deep space. Kierson escorted Charlie aboard Ethallan's yacht, which was, in fact, nothing less than a small destroyer with luxurious quarters for Ethallan and any guests she happened to be entertaining.

Ethallan was as tall as she was beautiful. They

met alone in a sitting room and exchanged pleasantries, but the conversation quickly shifted to the present political situation. "They're raping my world," she said. "They're raping my people, and they're raping our institutions and our customs." She looked into Charlie's eyes with deep sadness, saw something there and flinched. "But then I'm speaking to someone who knows the Syndonese penchant for rape firsthand, aren't I? Five years in that prison camp, wasn't it?"

"I know something of the Syndonese, yes."

She peered into his eyes carefully. "I see you don't need my pity. And I think the Syndonese should fear you."

Charlie grinned. "Should they fear you as well?"

She returned his grin, but hers was hard and angry. "Yes, they should. And perhaps together we can make them fear us even more. They've consolidated their position on Aagerbanne, taken control of all port facilities, utilities, and infrastructure. But I believe they're finding it a bit more difficult than they had anticipated."

Charlie said, "There are rumors you're receiving surreptitious help from certain allies."

"I can't comment on that," she said, "but whatever it might be, it's not enough."

Charlie considered his words carefully, didn't want to offer any false hope. "Maybe I can help. I've recently learned I may have more resources at my disposal than I originally thought."

"Anything you can do will be appreciated."

"I need time," he said. "Buy me time and I may be able to do something."

Her eyes narrowed as she considered his words. "Don't forget that Nadama and Goutain would love to obtain some corroboration that we're receiving assistance from the independent states. If they do they'll use that as an excuse to extend their aggression beyond Aagerbanne. And if you help us and they learn of it . . ." She closed her eyes and shook her head, left it at that.

At her words, Charlie's thoughts raced. "You said *Nadama*, not *Lucius*."

She nodded carefully. "Among the Syndonese we've captured we've noticed a few of them didn't have that atrocious Syndonese accent, though they did try to imitate it a bit. Under neural probe we learned they were really de Satarna regulars. Purportedly, they're here as advisors, but in fact they're playing a much more active role than that. Interestingly enough, we haven't captured anyone sworn directly to Lucius."

"Nadama," Charlie said. He'd suspected that Nadama had been complicit in Lucius and Goutain's scheming; Telka had even implied it when she'd refused to take orders from a de Satarna, pointing out Nadama's lack of surprise when Syndonese troops invaded the palace. But now it occurred to Charlie the Duke de Satarna might be end-running the king. "I wonder if he's working directly with Goutain."

"Probably, and I doubt Lucius is aware of it. Your king has never been terribly astute when it came to these little treacheries. But let's get to the reason I need to meet with you." She turned to a small cabinet, opened it, withdrew a package, and handed it to Charlie, saying only, "From your father."

Charlie questioned her, and like Sague and Aziz, approximately twenty years ago Cesare had asked her to give the package to *the de Lunis*. And like them he had told her it was of considerable value, but would not elaborate on the fact that, back then, there was no de Lunis.

"You're welcome on Luna, Your Ladyship," Charlie offered.

She shook her head. "Trust me, Your Grace. I have my resources, and soon there may be war, and I must be close to my home world when that happens."

Charlie understood that. "Please make sure I know how to reach you. Kierson can arrange the details with my chamberlain, Winston."

She gave him a knowing smile. "I suspect, Your Grace, you and I'll end up on the same side in the coming conflict."

"I think we already have."

Charlie returned to *Goldisbest*, and again waited until he was alone in his cabin before opening the package Ethallan had given him. He was not surprised to find another cyberkey, with a third unique interface: three keys and somewhere three locks. Or perhaps, three keys to one lock, with all three of them required to open it. "Cesare," he said to the empty room. "What are you trying to tell me?"

CHAPTER 16
GENERAL JANICE

It took twelve days to get back to Luna, and when Winston wasn't coaching him on the politics of the upcoming meeting of the Ten, Charlie had spent the time trying to think of some way to aid the Aagerbanni resistance. To do that he needed ships and financing, and while he was no longer destitute, he barely had enough to pay his meager staff, throw a few imperials Nano's way, and employ the spacers he'd need on the ship Sague was refitting for him. Perhaps he could use Hart & Delorm some way.

"Frankie." Nano's voice blared from allship. "We got company. You better come up here."

Only seconds ago they'd down-transited at the edge of Lunan nearspace. Charlie made his way to *Goldisbest*'s bridge without delay.

"They're in close orbit around Luna," Nano said, seated at the captain's console. He waved a hand at an empty couch at the navigation console. Charlie sat down and strapped in. "Two ships, Frankie. They want us to identify ourselves. The smaller looks like a Syndonese, can't be heavily armed. We can take her. Bigger one looks like a tramp freighter."

Charlie scanned the data on the nav console, agreed with Nano's assessment. Neither ship presented any serious danger to *Goldisbest*. "Identify us; tell them you're carrying the de Lunis, the rightful lord of this system, and that he orders them to stand off at a safe distance."

Charlie couldn't hear the conversation between Nano and the unidentified ships, so he waited patiently. Then Nano said, "One of them says he knows you, wants to talk with you. On exterior channel three."

Charlie's implants weren't keyed into the console so he pulled on a headset, switched to channel three, and picked up Roacka's voice in the middle of a sentence. " . . . know the lad well. Taught him everything he knows."

Charlie said, "I think Paul, Add, and Ell would disagree with you on that."

"Charlie, my boy! Damn, you got more lives than anyone I know. When you disappeared we thought you was dead again, then we heard you wasn't."

"And I thought you might be dead. What are you doing with Syndonese?"

"Allies, lad. They hate Goutain even more than you and me."

"And the freighter?"

"Old friends, lad. Old friends."

They truly were old friends: thirty odd members of Cesare's staff, plus more than fifty from the surviving Two Thousand, all of whom had had enough of Twerp and the witch-bitch. Roacka told him there would've been more, but the freighter couldn't carry them all. Roger and Seth were among them, his two closest comrades from the chain and the prison camps, and that was truly a glorious reunion. As for the Syndonese, which included the remnants of more than forty families, Charlie had a difficult time trusting any of them. "Don't worry, lad," Roacka told him. "These people have been treated brutally by Goutain. Every one of them has lost close family to that son-of-a-bitch, and what you see here are the survivors."

After the palace attack, Roacka had gone into hiding. "Laid low, lad, stayed out of sight."

Then he'd heard Charlie was still alive, saw this opportunity, stole the freighter to help transport them all, and they'd transited into Lunan nearspace almost two tendays ago. But with Starfall sealed up tight, and no one there to let them in, they'd been rationing supplies while orbiting Luna and waiting. They'd almost given up hope when *Goldisbest* transited into the system.

Starfall was suddenly alive as it had not been before. Winston took charge of the staff, screening them carefully to ensure there were no spies, assigning them duties similar to those they'd had in Farlight. Charlie found he had servants to help him dress and servants to help him bathe. He dismissed them all, told them to go back to Winston and find other duties. Starfall also had a real cook now; Danya was her name, a plump little woman who was apparently a real tyrant in the kitchen.

Charlie spoke individually with each of them: his new staff, his comrades from the prison camps, even the Syndonese, though he put that off until last. Roacka introduced him to their leader, Drakwin, quite tall, broad shouldered, though otherwise average in appearance. But the man had an intensity to his stare that made him un-average. Later Charlie made some comment to Paul about it, and Paul said, "Yes. It's like the look in your eyes. I see it in the eyes of all of the Two Thousand. I see it in the eyes of men who've been prisoners for a long time."

"Your Grace," Drakwin said when they were introduced, speaking in a thick Syndonese accent. "It is kind of you to give us refuge."

In Charlie's gut he didn't know if he could trust this man. "I haven't said I'll give you refuge yet. Tell me who you are."

One of Drakwin's eyebrows lifted, and he nodded. "In the Republic I was a merchantman."

Roacka said, "In the Republic a merchant ship has to be outfitted much like a light destroyer."

Charlie asked, "Pirates?"

Drakwin grinned as he said, "Na, local customs officials. Goutain gives them a lot of authority, and they'll confiscate just about anything if you're not prepared to stop them."

"Locals are fairly independent, huh?"

"Ya," Drakwin said, and his face hardened. "Goutain leaves it up to them to fund their own government, makes them pay levies and support the local garrison, which are all loyal to him. They steal from us, and he steals from them. They're really just thieves with a badge."

"Got a family?"

Drakwin nodded, and Charlie saw that look in his eyes again. "Wife and two sons. Wife and the youngest are here with me. Don't know where the oldest is, lost him when they confiscated my ship. Don't know if he's alive or not." The look on his face softened for a moment, and there was something familiar about him.

Charlie wondered if it might be possible to sew even more discontent in Goutain's citizens. "Any chance of a popular uprising, a rebellion?"

Drakwin curled his lower lip with distaste and shook his head. "Na, just small groups here and there, mainly the occasional riot when someone's farm or business is confiscated. After they took my ship, and my son, I sounded out some friends about doing something, but we had no weapons beyond a hunting rifle or two."

"How do I know you're not a spy?"

"Put me under probe."

"It's not pleasant. You'd volunteer for that?"

"I been through worse."

Roacka said, "I vouch for him, lad."

Again, Charlie thought he'd met the man somewhere before. "Okay, I'll give you and your people refuge, but I may make you earn it."

"How so, Your Grace?"

"I don't know yet, but it'll hopefully be to Goutain's detriment."

A predatory grin spread across Drakwin's face. "We cannot earn our refuge that way, Your Grace. To earn it we must perform some task or duty."

"But that's what I'm asking of—"

"No," Drakwin said, "it doesn't count. Bringing down the tyrant will be a joy and a pleasure—we'll do that for free."

Charlie suddenly recalled a dim, shadowy booth in the corner of Momma Toofat's trampsie bar on Tachaann: Delilah seated with two men, one a Syndonese with a thick accent. The man had leaned forward into the light and asked, "He's the de Maris bastard?" And while his face had still been obscured in shadows, there was no doubt who that man had been. "It was you—in the bar—on Tachaann—with Delilah—wasn't it?"

"Yes, Your Grace. It was."

"What were you doing with Delilah?"

Drakwin shrugged. "She was hiding with friends, I think on Finalsa. I was hiding in one of the refugee camps on Allison's Cluster."

Roacka said, "That's where we met."

Drakwin continued. "There's a whole underground of information passed around by those who'd like to see Goutain fall. She heard about me, contacted me through friends of friends of friends. We agreed to meet on Tachaann since it's a wide-open port and

Goutain really can't push its government around, neutral territory as it were. She was trying to organize some sort of underground resistance, but she couldn't supply arms and equipment. Goutain's thugs scooped her up the next morning. Why do you ask?"

Charlie tried to recall his last conversation with Delilah, standing in the hallway in Almsburg, the hurt in her eyes as he rejected her. All along she'd been trying to do something big and significant, while all he'd done was try to survive. "I think I've made an ass of myself."

"Probably," Roacka said, smiling.

Drakwin introduced Charlie to the other Syndonese families. Charlie questioned them carefully, delicately, and while none went into detail, each had a story of murdered loved ones. And then he met Madam Carallo, and her two children, both quite young. "My husband's a physician forced to serve that madman. I hope he's well."

She saw the look on Charlie's face, and before he could speak she demanded, "You know something. Don't you?"

"I fear your husband is not well, madam. I owe him a great debt. It was he who helped me escape Goutain's captivity, though I fear he paid for that with his life. But he thought you were dead, all of you. He had heard something of rape and murder."

She closed her eyes as tears trickled down her cheeks. "Oh, he must have heard about Tanya, our oldest daughter. We three escaped—Tanya was not so lucky." Suddenly she straightened her shoulders and the tears stopped. "But I have a daughter and a son left, and I intend that they will avenge their father and their sister."

Charlie put a hand on her shoulder. "Allow your children to grow up happily, not obsessed with vengeance. Leave that to me. I think I might be good at it."

The small freighter that Roacka had stolen was reasonably fit, had a sound hull, a good drive system, and a fairly new power plant—it occurred to Charlie that someday he'd have to reimburse the merchant on Allison's Cluster. Roger felt that with a few modifications she could become a decent light destroyer, so Charlie gave him command of her with instructions to proceed to Istanna then Toellan; Sague could arrange for any infrastructure modifications, and Aziz would handle armaments and shielding through Hart & Delorm. As a skeleton crew, Roger took Seth, the fifty members of the Two Thousand, and all the Syndonese men. Once the two ships were complete—and before returning to Starfall—Roger, Seth, and Darmczek were going to swing by Traxis in a surreptitious attempt to locate any more of the Two Thousand.

With his present resources he couldn't accomplish much, maybe just hinder Nadama and Goutain, slow them down while he looked for more support, more allies. He also needed to keep them from expanding into the independent states where they could confiscate his properties. It wasn't any sort of a real plan, but that was the best he could come up with at the moment. He'd revise it later if he found that support.

Charlie's biggest problem was that he needed a fleet of real warships, not just a few converted freighters. Large warships were a costly matter, though; converting more than two or three freighters would stretch his resources to the limit, and that was nothing compared to the cost of actually laying hulls and building a true warship. He needed something cheaper, and for several tendays now he'd been toying with a new design: a smaller ship with minimal defensive capabilities, its only offensive capability a large store of transition torpedoes. Keep the ship small and maneuverable, give it an overpowered drive, minimal shielding, no defensive batteries, and construct all systems for minimal emissions and maximum stealth capability. Such a ship would depend upon speed and stealth for both offense and defense. "If this Sague fellow can make it," Roger said after reviewing Charlie's specifications, "she'll be a nasty little killer, able to sneak up on her targets and hunt them down." Roger's comments stuck, and when he departed for Istanna he carried the specifications for what they had come to call a *hunter-killer* class warship.

In spare moments Charlie, with Stan Fourhands's help, tried to hack into Starfall's computer system. There were too many things that didn't add up about Starfall, including the blind corridor that didn't appear on the facility map unless Charlie stepped into it. And then there was the computer system itself. Charlie had tried to look into the programming that made the blind corridor appear on the facility map when he stepped into it. He'd been given the codes for ring zero access; there shouldn't be any deeper level of access than ring zero, and yet he'd been blocked from that programming. And as he experimented further he found his access blocked in certain specific ways.

And then there were the cyberkeys. He'd looked for mating interfaces in all the obvious places like the security center, and found nothing that matched. If he had to search every inch of Starfall—floors, ceilings, and walls—he'd be poking around in dark corners for years.

"What is it?" he asked Cesare's ghost. "What are you hiding?"

A few days later a Syndonese heavy cruiser christened *Sachanee* down-transited into Lunan nearspace. At the request of President Goutain, Admiral Santieff had come to pay his respects to the newly seated duke. Speaking to him via transition com Charlie thanked him, told him that he was unable to entertain him at this time, and that he'd let him know when he was able to receive guests.

"No, no, no, Your Grace," Santieff said. He was a smarmy bastard, all smiles and teeth. "We will come now and be entertained. You do not understand. You are not Syndonese."

A warship against Charlie, a handful of servants,

and some Syndonese refugees—no contest. They managed to get the Syndonese refugees disguised as servants before Santieff and his troops landed. Beyond that, Charlie could only grin and bear it.

Santieff landed with about thirty men. They were a rough lot, the kind of spacers that busted up bars and whorehouses. Charlie guessed they'd been carefully selected for such qualities. "Come, come, Your Grace. We must have a banquet. We are your wonderful guests, truly magnanimous guests, and you must entertain us properly. Good food and good drink, and perhaps girls. Do you have girls?"

"None for you."

"Oh, Your Grace. You must adopt the spirit of your guests. His Excellency personally asked me to pay my respects to the new duke. And you must pay your respects to me."

Charlie had few options, so he spoke carefully. "The ducal council will not be pleased that you forced yourself upon me."

Santieff's eyes hardened. "Have we used force, Your Grace?"

Charlie realized the admiral might not be the fool he pretended to be.

Santieff continued. "And is it improper for His Excellency to pay his respects to you through me?"

So far Santieff had not threatened or harmed anyone, and without something overtly inappropriate, the other dukes would shrug it off. Apparently, Santieff understood that. Charlie could only hope the asshole just wanted to harass them for a few days, then leave, just as the supposed customs officials had done when they left Turnlee.

Unable to turn them away, he had no choice but let them into his home. But with Santieff and his thugs wandering about, Charlie went back to carrying a plast knife in one boot and a palm gun hidden beneath his tunic. The twins decided that at least one of them would always shadow him, and as an added precaution, they started sleeping in the anteroom to his bedroom.

The Syndonese wanted food and drink and women. Janice and Sally shrugged, said money was money and they both needed the work, though Nano assured Charlie he'd keep an eye on them. Charlie gave Stan Fourhands permission to pick any Syndonese pockets he could, then he raided the medical stores for sedatives, turned them over to Danya, and told her to be ready to spike the Syndonese drinks if anything happened.

For two days the situation remained reasonably stable, though Santieff kept bringing down more men from his ship each hour until it was obvious nothing remained aboard her but a skeleton crew. At that point they were *entertaining* close to a hundred and fifty Syndonese spacers, who were keeping Starfall's processing stills running at full capacity, and it occurred to Charlie he might be able to turn the situation to his advantage. He called a little council of war with Roacka, the twins, and Winston.

"There's nothing but a skeleton crew up there

now," he said. "And I'd love to take possession of that heavy cruiser."

He turned to Winston. "Tell Danya it's time to spike their drinks. I want Santieff and every crewman he's brought down here unconscious."

He told Roacka, "Start working on a plan to take over that ship. Assume it's badly undermanned."

To Add and Ell he said, "Once Danya's got them knocked out, sweep the place carefully, and if you find any that aren't unconscious, make them that way. I want every one of them bound and gagged before they wake up, and let's pile them all into one room where we can keep an eye on them. And separate Santieff from the rest."

With the help of the servants and the Syndonese refugees it was done quickly. Then Charlie gathered Roacka, Winston, Paul, Add, Ell, and the trampsies for a little tactical conference. "Our problem is that warship in orbit up there. She's probably only got a skeleton crew, but they can still bomb the hell out of us, and we don't have anything to fight back with, though we do have Santieff and most of his crew as hostages. But we'll be better off if we can figure out a way to board her and take control of her."

Roacka hooked a thumb at Add and Ell. "Me and the girls are thinking we can take their boat up, try to bluff our way aboard, then storm the place."

"Frankie," Janice said. "Frankie, Frankie, Frankie, ain't you learned nothing yet? You listen to old General Janice here. Roacka and the girls just need a diversion, and that's where Sally and me come in. Give us about a hour to get those boys in a partying mood, and while we're fucking their brains out, Roacka and the girls here can sneak on board and finish 'em off."

Paul blushed.

"Hey ensign." At the sound of the old NCO's voice, the young Syndonese officer roused from sleep. "The shuttle's approaching, and you gotta see this."

He'd been dozing at the captain's console. He knew he shouldn't do that in front of the men, but then again there were only ten of them left on board, and absolutely nothing happening. "Channel three, ensign."

He put channel three on one of his screens, saw an image of two young women there. Both were quite attractive, and showing a lot of cleavage and leg. One of them asked, "You the man in charge up there?"

Well, at the moment, he was the ranking officer. But as to being in charge, how much was the ship's most junior officer ever in charge? "Yes, I'm the ranking officer."

"Okay, captain. Yer admiral says he's feeling real bad they're having all the fun down there, and you boys ain't getting to share none of it. So he sent me and Sally here, along with a case of some good booze, as a little present for you guys."

"I'm sorry. It's against regulations. I can't allow you on board without a specific order from Admiral Santieff."

"Lighten up, ensign," the old NCO said.

"You too tense," the second girl said, wiggling her breasts at him. "I can make you un-tense, real quick like."

He said to the NCO, "But we should confirm this with the admiral."

One of the girls said, "His admiralship is out cold, nursing one nasty hangover."

The old NCO said, "Listen, ensign. You heard yourself how drunk he was last night, and he ain't gonna appreciate you waking him up to get his permission for this."

"But captain," the first girl said. "It was yer admiral what sent us. I mean, what's a couple of working girls like me and Sally gonna do, take over yer ship from big strong guys like you?"

Charlie looked over Stan Fourhands's shoulder as he stared intently at the readout on the Syndonese screen. "I got access to basic systems, Frankie: life support, medical, drive control, power plant, gravity, navigation. But these military systems are tough. Take me maybe another tenday to hack ring one access to get to weapons, and I don't know about ring zero."

"Don't even try," Charlie told him. "Any mistakes and you could lock the whole system up permanently. The code traps get nastier the deeper you get, and I don't want to take any chances. It's simpler if Sague just flushes the entire operating system and installs a new one."

Charlie leaned back and scanned the bridge of the Syndonese ship. He had a real warship, his first, and acquired rather cheaply.

Charlie didn't dare let any of the Syndonese back on their ship; he had no way of knowing what kind of verbal codes they might be able to activate, or what they might trigger directly through their implants. And in any case, her brig wasn't large enough to hold a hundred and fifty prisoners, and being a warship she didn't really have a hold. But she was stocked with an amazing supply of steel manacles and chain. So in small groups they'd transferred the Syndonese to *Goldisbest*'s hold. Charlie had tried to not feel any satisfaction as they cuffed them in hand and leg irons and locked them to *the chain*. Charlie gave clear orders that the prisoners were to be fed properly and treated in as humane a fashion as possible.

Charlie had agonized over his choices. He didn't have it in him to simply execute one hundred and fifty men, but then if he released them they'd be trained crew that Goutain could eventually use against him. One of the Syndonese refugees pointed out that it didn't matter; Goutain would just have them executed anyway. To get confirmation of that Charlie went to see Santieff in *Goldisbest*'s hold. Santieff was outraged. "You have dishonored yourself with this treatment of your most magnanimous guests. You cannot—"

"Shut up," Charlie said. "I've decided you're right. I'm going to release you."

Santieff smiled his most smarmy smile. "I'm glad

you understand that you must capitulate to Syndonese superiority. And because you have seen your error, I will, perhaps, execute only half of your household. And I'll only have you whipped, not executed."

"Yes," Charlie said. "I'm going to return you to Goutain, all of you . . . cuffed in irons without your ship."

Santieff's smile disappeared, his jaw dropped, and his eyes widened. And in a ship's hold filled with one hundred and fifty prisoners, the sound of a pin drop would have been deafening. During the next two days more than three quarters of them asked to defect and enter Charlie's service. He refused them all. They didn't know it, but Nano was going to drop them in small groups on the nearest Syndonese world, with nothing but the clothes on their backs. They'd have to survive on their own. *Sachanee* and her crew would disappear without a trace, and Charlie and everyone in the de Lunis household would simply deny having ever seen them. It was not unheard of that a ship went out with all hands somewhere in deep space, never to be heard from again.

A few days later, a small liner down-transited at the edge of Lunan nearspace. Seventy of the Two Thousand plus twenty of Cesare's household had chartered it for passage to Luna. So Charlie now had a minimal crew to man *Sachanee*, and he decided to abandon Starfall for the time being. The palace Cesare had given him was grand but indefensible.

CHAPTER 17
THE FOOL RELENTS

Charlie obsessed constantly about the blind corridor. Tomorrow they'd evacuate Starfall, with Nano and his crew and the Syndonese prisoners in *Goldisbest*, Charlie and his household and the members of the Two Thousand in *Sachanee*. Nano would head for the Republic to dump the prisoners, then return to Tachaann with the girls. Charlie would head for Istanna to effect modifications to *Sachanee* and to rendezvous with Roger, Seth, and Darmczek. By rights, Charlie should be getting a good night's sleep before departing, and he had tried, only to toss and turn thinking constantly of Cesare's blind corridor. With the Syndonese spacers trussed up and confined, the twins had stopped shadowing Charlie so closely, though one of them always slept in the anteroom to his bedroom. So it was the middle of the night, and he was down there by himself with a computer tablet for a companion.

He'd already run his hands over every inch of the corridor: walls, floor, ceiling; he'd had to commandeer a small grav lift to get to the ceiling. There were no other visual distortion fields, only the one in the wall at the end of the short corridor, and there were only a few indentations hidden there, and only one of those might be interpreted by touch as a mating interface for a cyberkey, and not one of the three keys he'd been given fit it, no matter how hard he tried. The corridor and the wall had to be related to the cyberkeys in some way. They had to be!

Charlie must have stepped in and out of the corridor a hundred times, watching the screen on the computer tablet, watching the corridor disappear and reappear on the facility map, watching and learning nothing. In another hour everyone would be up and getting ready to depart, and Charlie hadn't slept a wink. He'd be dead on his feet, and he'd have accomplished nothing. On the screen of the computer tablet he expanded the view of the facility map to include all of Starfall, and staring at it he stepped in and out of the blind corridor. The expanded view showed too little detail for him to actually resolve anything of significance, but he could see the little red blotch of the corridor boundaries wink on and off as he stepped in and out of the corridor. It was maddening. What was Cesare trying to tell him?

Finally, out of sheer exasperation he sat down on the floor of the blind corridor with the computer tablet in his lap and stared at the screen. He stared at it for a long time, had actually started to drift off to sleep, had even crossed into that dreamlike state where he wasn't actually asleep, wasn't actually dreaming, but wasn't truly awake either. He could picture the facility map in his mind's eye, the red blotch of the corridor, the blues and greens of the rest of the map, a small amount of red elsewhere here and there. He concentrated on the red, looked at it carefully, realized that there wasn't red *elsewhere here and there*. There was only the corridor in which he sat, and one small red dot; all the rest mapped out in blues and greens.

He snapped awake and looked at the tablet in his lap. He jumped to his feet and jammed his finger onto the other red dot to zoom in on it. At the highest magnification it appeared as a small, cubical recess in the back wall of the security center. He stepped out of the corridor, and the little red cubical recess disappeared along with the corridor. He ran for the security center.

Ordinarily the security center would be under the command of the head of his personal guard, but since he had no personal guard it was under the command of no one, though he had explored it carefully. It was a large control center not unlike the bridge of a warship, though not as cramped and space conscious. From it the entire Sol system could be monitored, not just Starfall itself. If he hadn't been such an impoverished duke, there'd be large defensive batteries on Luna's surface and big weapons platforms in orbit around her. He'd have a couple of warships of his own on hand, and if he ever needed to defend himself and his estate and household from interlopers, it would all be coordinated from the security center. Charlie stood in the middle of it all for a moment, looking down at the tablet in his hands and trying to get oriented. The small cubical recess was no longer visible on the facility map, but he'd memorized its position: in the far wall, behind the security commander's station.

Charlie stepped behind the station and looked at the wall carefully. Waist high, where the cubical recess should be, it was blank and featureless. He pressed his fingertips against it, ran them carefully along the surface: no visual distortion field, but there was a faint pattern embossed there, so faint it wasn't visible to the eye. His fingertips told him it was there, and as he traced it out he realized it was in the shape of a hand, pressed flat against the wall. So he carefully pressed his own hand into the faint indentation.

The security commander's station came to life, and from a speaker the computer said, "Lock sequence initiated." A section of the wall slid aside revealing the small cubical recess. Inside he could see the mating interfaces for three cyberkeys, one of which glowed a faint green. The computer said, "Insert primary key." There really was no choice to make since only one of the three keys would mate with the interface that glowed. Charlie snapped it in place.

The glow there disappeared, and a blue glow appeared around one of the other two interfaces. The computer said, "Insert secondary key."

Again, only one of the two remaining keys mated.

The blue glow disappeared and a red glow appeared around the last interface. "Insert tertiary key."

Charlie did so, the red glow disappeared, the recess closed abruptly, and the computer said, "Insert overlord key."

"What?" Charlie demanded. "There's only three keys, you goddamned pile of circuits. What the hell is an overlord key?"

The computer didn't answer, and try as he might he couldn't reopen the recess.

Overlord key—it had to be the little dagger. *Or maybe not.* He retrieved it from a pocket, removed it from its sheath, and examined it carefully. Ell had declared it useless as a weapon, with a steel blade of poor quality. Winston had said the jewels were just colored glass, pretty, but worthless. Charlie examined each of the stones carefully, and none were loose. He tried to turn or twist each one, in case it was some sort of latch that might reveal a hidden purpose to the blade. He tried to separate the blade from the handle, decided not to pull on it too hard in case he damaged it. Nothing!

He resheathed the dagger, returned it to the pocket, then sat down at the commander's station. He brought up Starfall's operating system, spent the next hour exploring it, and found that nothing had changed. He returned to the blind corridor; nothing had changed there. He stared at the facility map on the tablet; nothing had changed anywhere.

Dejected after coming so close, he went up to his rooms and prepared to leave Starfall.

Charlie chose an indirect route for transition to Istanna. He didn't want to have to identify himself to anyone: the Duke de Lunis commanding a Syndonese warship would raise eyebrows. Sague was enormously helpful, said it would only be a matter of days to make a few key modifications to certain instrumentation, then flush and reinstall Sachanee's operating system, followed by tests to ensure that it was functioning properly. They also scrubbed Sachanee's identity codes and Charlie rechristened her The Headsman. And Sague had been able to round up more than three hundred of the Two Thousand, so they could fully crew all Charlie's ships.

Sague took him on a tour of the orbital shipyard where they were laying the hulls for two of the new hunter-killers. The ships were sleek, but small and cramped, and heavily overpowered so they could move fast when necessary. They stood in the yardmaster's office, looking through a window at the two hulls below them.

"Captain Darmczek expressed some reservations about such ships," Sague said in his precisely worded, clipped manner.

He was hinting at something, and Charlie knew exactly what. Still looking through the window at the hulls he said, "I'll bet he said they're a complete waste of money, and used considerable profanity while saying so." Sague grimaced as Charlie looked his way. "And I'm guessing you share his reservations?"

Sague frowned apologetically. "Not fully, Your Grace."

"I suppose you'd have me build traditional warships."

"There would be less risk in that, Your Grace."

"And how many traditional warships can I afford to build, Mr. Sague?"

"Two, perhaps three, Your Grace."

"And how would I fund such ships?"

Sague spoke hesitantly. "You would have to divest yourself of most of your other holdings."

"Exactly! And the cost of building these?" Charlie waved a hand at the two small hulls.

"A tenth that of one of the larger classes of warship."

"Precisely. And I can crew one with fifty men. And the operating expenses will also be a tenth that of a larger ship. And all one of these ships has to do is put a single transition torpedo in the gut of a larger ship to kill it." Charlie too had his doubts about such small, under-gunned, under-defended warships, but he wasn't going to let Sague know that.

"I'm sure Your Grace knows best. Do you wish me to build more of them?"

"No—I'm not completely crazy," he said with a smile. "These are an experiment, so let's see how they work first. After a little experience with them I wouldn't be surprised if we learned a few things and modified the design."

"Since stealth appears to be a key aspect of the design, Your Grace, I did take the liberty of making some modifications to your initial specification. For instance, we're modifying the control system and drive to allow slow transition velocities. It should be possible to reduce velocity to only a few lights before down-transition, minimizing your transition flare and your visibility to your enemy. Certainly, such a small flare, even if noticed, might not be taken to be a dangerous warship."

"Good thinking. I'm open to pretty much anything that helps us take out the Syndonese."

"Exactly, Your Grace. And speaking of which, the Borreggan situation is proceeding nicely."

Charlie had detailed the next step carefully with Sague. Any serious action he took against Goutain in the coming months would have to be covert, and for that he needed a base of operations unconnected with Starfall, the de Lunis properties, or the independent states. Sague had come up with the idea of Andyne, a large station in solar orbit around the Borreggan primary. It had been a commercial venture based on the assumption that the Realm and the independent states would expand in that direction, and there would then be a need for a station en route that could provide supplies and repairs for commercial shipping. But the expansion hadn't occurred, the commercial venture went bust, and Andyne's owners mothballed her a few decades ago to cut their losses.

Back then Sague had considered purchasing the station so he'd sent one of his agents to review its condition and assets carefully, but had decided against the purchase, seeing no way to recoup his expenses. But when Charlie started talking about a covert base of operations, Sague had recommended Andyne. So two months earlier Charlie had purchased the station for a hundredth of what it had originally cost to build, with the transaction brokered by one of Sague's lieutenants, and Charlie's connection hidden in layer after layer of corporate ownership. Since then Sague had been sending out people and supplies to reactivate the station. Aziz, through Hart & Delorm, had supplied armaments, both for the station's defenses, and for supplies and repairs for warships that couldn't contract for such in normal ports-of-call. In another month it would be fully operational as a station, and in another three as a fully functional shipyard. Though, as both Sague and Aziz were wont to remind Charlie, the cost of such an operation was stretching his financial resources to the limit. To which he replied, "What good is the money if we're not alive or free to spend it?"

Roger, Seth, and Darmczek were already on Toellan getting armaments fitted to Charlie's personal ship and the converted freighter. When Charlie caught up with them he was pleased to learn that, while the freighter would require a couple more months of work, his personal ship was nearing completion. It looked old and outdated, both inside and out, but was, in fact, filled with the most advanced and up-to-date systems, and Aziz had given it some serious teeth, turning it into the equivalent of a midsized destroyer. When she was finished Charlie christened her *The Thirteenth Man*. He ordered Darmczek to command *The Headsman* and take it to Andyne-Borregga, while he took *The Thirteenth Man* to the meeting of the Ten.

Charlie's return to Turnlee wasn't much different from his exit three months earlier. Syndonese disguised as customs officials boarded *The Thirteenth Man* under the pretense of a standard customs inspection. They didn't look closely at anything, merely harassed Charlie and his crew for a few hours before allowing them to proceed. However, in Almsburg he was given a suite of rooms that, while not the grandest, were still acceptable. Someone had helped Lucius understand that none of the Ten would appreciate seeing one of their peers treated inappropriately.

While Charlie's servants were unpacking he sent a page with a note to Delilah requesting an audience. It was time for him to do some serious apologizing. The page returned in short order, the note unopened. "She refused to accept it, Your Grace." He sent the page back, and again the page returned with the note unopened.

He used a different page the third time, and told him to say the note was from Dieter. The page returned with a note from Delilah. It had one word on it, a simple *No*.

Charlie wrote another note, carefully explaining how he'd mistaken her motives on Tachaann and apologizing for the mistake. He got another page and sent him along with instructions to say the note was from Rierma. The page returned in short order with another note from Delilah. It had one sentence on it. He read it and had to rack his brain for a moment to remember that the last sentence on his note had been, *I was a fool*, because it was clearly that which Del's one-sentence reply was in response to:

Yes, you are.

Charlie went to see her. Two pretty young women met him at the entrance to her apartments. He was relieved when they offered him a seat in an elegant sitting room, and told him that the princess would be with him shortly. So he sat there and waited—for two hours he sat there and waited—while a constant parade of pretty, young women came to him at regular intervals to offer him a drink, or a pastry, or *anything Your Grace might desire*, and to tell him that *Her Highness will be with you shortly*. It took him all afternoon to realize she wasn't going to *be with him shortly*, or any time soon, for that matter. He left, calling himself an idiot, realizing he'd gotten what he deserved.

It was a reception for the Ten, all of whom were finally present. There were perhaps two hundred people, sipping at glasses of wine and nibbling on finger food, jockeying for royal position, cutting deals, and cutting political throats. The one-hundred-day waiting period was now over, and the first meeting of the Ten would occur on the following day.

Charlie, Telka, Harrimo, and Rierma were discussing the unrest on Aagerbanne when Chelko joined them. Chelko was Faggan's son and heir, newly occupying the de Jupttar ducal seat. Rierma had warned Charlie that, because of Lucius and Goutain's involvement in the death of his father, Chelko impatiently wanted action now. Chelko was young, and ready to start a war that moment, though being the head of a minor house he didn't have the resources to do so. In a sense he was merely an extreme example of the rest of them. Lucius's stupidity and Goutain's desire to rule the Realm had hurt Telka, Harrimo, and Rierma as much as Charlie, and that gave them common cause.

"What about you, de Lunis?" Chelko asked. "Don't you want to kill that bastard?"

It was plump little Telka who answered for Charlie. "Chelko," the small woman said, "I think there is no doubt what Charlie would *like* to do, but he's not fool enough to speak it aloud. And since he can do nothing at this time, especially since Theode has aligned with Nadama, I'd guess he's smart enough to bite his tongue and bide his time."

Cesare had once warned him that Telka liked to play the plump little scatterbrained woman, twittering and chattering, sometimes aimlessly. Cesare had also pointed out that when Telka had inherited the de Vena ducal seat, it had been a minor house, and through her leadership had grown into one of the three most powerful houses in the Realm.

"You haven't answered my question, de Lunis," Chelko demanded.

"I think Telka answered for me rather nicely," Charlie said. "Combine the de Satarna, the de Maris, and the Syndonese forces, and we don't stand a chance. What I wish to know is why we allowed Theode to usurp the de Maris ducal seat."

Chelko said, "I wasn't even seated."

Tall, thin Harrimo reminded Charlie of Winston when she spoke. "Charlie, you know we cannot intervene in a matter that's internal to House de Maris. It would give Lucius and Goutain the precedent they need to intervene in all our houses."

Telka said, "There's a good cause for you, Chelko. Get Arthur reinstated. We all know who he'd support."

Charlie hadn't realized Theode was behind him until he spoke in that nasally, whining voice of his. "What did you say? What did you say?"

Charlie turned slowly, and Theode stepped into the small circle of people with Gaida on his arm. While Gaida stared daggers at Charlie, Theode said, "You said something about Arthur, and reinstatement."

Charlie looked at Telka, and realized that with her standing there facing him, she had known the two were behind him. He said, "I said nothing of the kind."

"Yes you did. No one else would care about him. He's a murderer."

"Calm down, Theode," Gaida said. She didn't change the expression on her face. "It didn't sound like Charlie's voice." She looked at each of them in turn, but got nothing.

Theode leaned close to Charlie and spit words in his face. "Don't even think about it, because it's never going to happen."

He spun and practically dragged Gaida away.

Adsin took their place. "What was that about, Your Graces?"

Harrimo said, "Theode's just feeling a bit insecure."

Adsin turned to Charlie and looked him up and down. "Your Grace, it's amazing how one's circumstances can change in so short a time."

Harrimo came to Charlie's defense. "Yes, Adsin," she said, snubbing him by not granting him any title, something he dared not do to one of them. "Many of us have had our circumstances change in a short time."

Adsin ignored her and addressed Charlie with a smirk. "Tell me, Your Grace. How is our dear Admiral Santieff?"

Charlie had prepared for that question, though not necessarily from Adsin. Still, the fact that it came from Adsin told him how deeply the little snake was in Goutain's pocket. It also told him that they had yet to realize that Santieff and his ship were missing. "Admiral whom?" Charlie asked.

Adsin frowned. "Santieff. Admiral Santieff, a high-ranking Syndonese officer."

Charlie pretended to think for a moment, then shook his head. "I don't believe I've met him."

"But he was sent to pay you a visit."

"Was he now? Well, I've had no visitors."

Adsin turned and scurried across the room to Goutain.

"What was that about?" Telka demanded.

Charlie grinned at her. "I wouldn't know. But I suspect that our dear Admiral Santieff, and his ship, and his crew, are all going to turn up missing, lost with all hands, as it were."

A little later Charlie and Rierma were alone when an older woman, who happened to be passing by, leaned toward Charlie and whispered, "Don't give up, Your Grace. She is angry with you, but her anger stems purely from her pride, not her heart. And she's being watched closely, which limits what she can say and do." Without another word, she walked on.

"Rierma," Charlie asked, following her with his eyes. "Who's that woman?"

Rierma followed Charlie's gaze. "Ah, that's Lady Carristan, lady-in-waiting to Delilah. It's said she was more of a mother to the princess than Adan."

In the hope of getting Arthur reinstated, Charlie wanted to propose at the meeting of the Ten that they open an inquiry into Cesare's death. Both Rierma and Winston vehemently opposed that on the grounds that Charlie's ducal estates were too weak to force the issue, he'd accomplish nothing, and might open up a precedent that would allow Theode and Gaida to interfere in de Lunis internal affairs. So Charlie swallowed his pride, tried not to think of his brother's predicament, and kept his mouth shut.

The meeting of the Ten went off with only a few minor incidents. Chelko angrily opposed everything that Lucius proposed, and Charlie was pretty sure he'd say black if the king said white. There was nothing of significance on the agenda, though, so on Winston's advice Charlie adopted a low profile and didn't speak out on any issues. He voted his conscience on a few, voted with the majority on the rest, and tried to avoid establishing any visible pattern.

After the meeting, a page delivered a message that Lady Carristan wished to speak with him. Charlie followed the page to a sitting room and found Delilah there alone, though she stood looking the other way and was not immediately aware of his presence. But as the page closed the door she turned toward him, and he watched the look on her face slowly transform from a pleasant smile to a cold, expressionless stare.

"Your Highness," he said.

With only the slightest movement of her lips she said, "Your Grace. I wasn't expecting you."

"I was told to come here. I didn't know you'd be here, and I don't mean to upset you. That said," he went on, moving a bit closer, "I'm not going to waste this opportunity. I've wanted to speak with you, to apologize for our last meeting. I erred badly."

The look she gave him could have cut him in two.

"Yes you did. And my schedule doesn't allow me time to speak with you now."

She walked toward him, toward the door actually, for he stood just within the threshold. She started to step around him, but he back-stepped and put his back to the door, blocking her.

"Do you detain me against my will?" she asked quietly, and he noticed her eyes glance upward right and left, a very cautious, furtive action.

"No," he said, realizing she wouldn't listen to him regardless of what he said or did. He stepped aside. She opened the door and left.

The next morning he departed Almsburg.

CHAPTER 18
SHAKEDOWN

"How's our bogie now?" Charlie asked, seated at *Turmoil*'s command console.

"Coming in hard, sir," Seth answered from the scan console. "Driving at just under two thousand lights, ranging at point-nine light-years. Closest intercept is four AUs, in a little over three hours."

Turmoil was the first of the new hunter-killers. He'd taken her out previously for a shakedown cruise, and to experiment with new tactics: tracking and targeting on warships and merchantmen alike, attempting close approaches without being detected. They were still at the experimental stage, more playing at war games than anything else. They'd been detected once by a de Satarna cruiser and another time by a Syndonese frigate. Both had challenged them and demanded identity codes, then fired on them when they responded with silence and turned to run; *Turmoil* was good at running.

After a month of experimentation he'd returned the hunter-killer to Sague for certain modifications, then another tenday of shakedown, and now it was time to see if they could do anything useful with her, though it still wasn't yet time to start a war.

Charlie could see from her transition wake the incoming ship was big and fast, too fast to be a freighter. "Is she Syndonese, and is she a warship?"

"Too early to tell, sir. Can't really read her signature at this distance."

At least he'd gotten them to drop the *Your Graces* when he was commanding a warship. They were sitting about five light-years off Istanna, in the middle of the shipping lanes to Toellan.

"Can we intercept?"

At the helm, Roger answered, "Yes, sir. Shouldn't be a problem."

Both Roger and Seth had been enthusiastic about the new hunter-killers, seeing all sorts of possibilities, where Darmczek and older COs had seen only weakness.

"Then do so."

Charlie watched his screens as Roger firewalled the sublight drive, accelerating at well over ten thousand gravities. They'd tried this twice now, and both times the incoming ships hadn't been Syndonese. Charlie wanted a Syndonese for a first target—test really.

"Sir, I've got a transition plan for you."

Charlie looked at the summary Roger had sent to one of his screens. They'd up-transit perpendicular to the bogie's vector, hold their velocity at two lights for a little over a quarter of an hour. Two lights should keep their transition wake and flares completely undetectable to a ship in transition, probably even to ships in sublight as long as they weren't close.

"Eighty-one minutes to up-transition, sir."

"It's a good plan, Roger. Do it."

Most of their time would be spent accelerating to, and decelerating from, transition. But Roger's plan would have them directly ahead of the incoming bogie with time to spare.

Waiting, that was always the hard part, watching the minutes tick by. When they finally up-transited Charlie felt that little tickle run down his spine, then again when they down-transited. Then more waiting as they decelerated to kill their perpendicular vector, then more as they accelerated hard to build velocity along the bogie's vector.

"I think I've got a good signature," Seth said. "High probability she's Syndonese, and a warship. A big one, probably battleship class . . . and . . ." A gravity wave rolled through *Turmoil*'s bridge as the bogie's bow wave slammed into her. " . . . here she comes."

"Roger," Charlie said, fighting nausea as his stomach somersaulted. "Remember, let her stern wake pull us into up-transition. Don't force it."

"We've got gravitational instability all over the ship, sir. Some pretty sick people."

Charlie should have thought of that, but too late now. The bogie passed within a million klicks, almost a collision course, then Roger shouted, "Up-transition, sir."

"Go, go, go," Charlie shouted. "We've got to keep up with her. Any reaction from her?"

"No reaction, sir."

More waiting.

"We're stabilizing at two thousand lights, and a little over two AUs behind her."

Turmoil's bridge was silent for several seconds. It took them all that long to realize they'd done it. Then Seth and Roger both let out a whoop, and everyone cheered.

"**H**e's braking strongly, sir, approaching down-transition."

"Helm?" Charlie demanded.

"Three hundred lights, sir, and decelerating."

"Remember, match his deceleration curve down to fifty lights. Then decelerate as hard as you can. I want us down to two lights before we down-transit."

"Two hundred and fifty lights, sir."

It was almost impossible for two ships in transition to detect one another, as long as they both held a straight, steady course and made only small adjustments: long, slow turns, decelerating or accelerating incrementally. But the captain of the bogie had become peacetime careless, had driven straight for Istanna and was now decelerating hard. And with *Turmoil*'s augmented instrumentation, he was handing them an easy targeting signature. She was definitely a big Syndonese warship.

"Two hundred lights, sir."

They'd ridden inside the stern wake of the big ship for a little under a day. That had been hard on the crew, so early on they'd backed off to a distance of five AUs. But now, approaching Istannan nearspace, they needed to correct that.

"One hundred and fifty lights, sir."

Charlie said, "Now hold on to a little extra velocity and start closing the gap. I want to be inside one AU when she down-transits."

"One hundred lights, sir."

"Fire control—status?"

Roacka was at fire control. "As you instructed, lad, a one-megaton transition torpedo armed and targeted for detonation two hundred meters off their bow. Forward and rear transition launchers charged and green-lighted."

Turmoil's hull groaned as a big gravity wave rolled through her, and no one needed to hear Roger say, "We're just under one AU behind her, sir."

"Fifty lights, sir."

Charlie said, "Stay on his tail. Match him exactly."

"Forty lights . . ."

"Hold us at forty, let him decelerate. If he stays in character he'll down-transit at thirty."

With the bogie continuing to decelerate, and *Turmoil* holding steady, they quickly closed with the Syndonese and passed him. This was the critical moment.

To keep their transition flare small enough to remain undetected they had to get *Turmoil* down to four or five lights before down-transiting. But if they started decelerating too soon, the bogie would retake them, and for this maneuver that wouldn't work.

"He's at thirty-five lights . . ."

"Start dumping lights," Charlie said. On his screens he watched the readings for *Turmoil*'s power plant approach redline. Now well out in front of the bogie, they began to decelerate, and with *Turmoil*'s drive-to-weight ratio they decelerated much faster than the bogie, which meant the Syndonese were rapidly overtaking them.

"We're at thirty lights, sir . . . twenty . . . ten. He's just approaching thirty."

"Remember, hold on to as much sublight velocity as you can. And fire control, launch without my command as soon as you have a targeting solution."

"Five lights, sir, and she's getting unstable. And here comes that bogie."

Charlie's stomach churned as a gravity wave washed through *Turmoil*. Then the bogie roared past them, and as her transition wake flooded the ship it slammed them into down-transition.

"All stop," Charlie shouted. "Rig for silent running."

"There she goes, sir."

The bogie down-transited, and almost simultaneously Roacka growled, "Targeted. Torpedo away."

Turmoil's hull thrummed with the characteristic sound of a transition launch. Then only a second later

Charlie's navigational screens went blank as the warhead detonated, the power plant readings dropped off scale, lights dimmed, and shipboard gravity disappeared as all noncritical systems shut down.

"Seth," Charlie said. "What have you got?"

"Detonation was exactly on target, sir, two hundred meters off their bow. They've cut drive and are coasting, don't appear to be taking any action, don't appear to have noticed us. We're coasting at point-nine lights. They're coasting at point-two. I think it worked, sir."

The entire crew breathed a collective sigh of relief. Then someone let out a whoop, and a contagious round of backslapping and cheering followed. It had worked, at least so far. They'd gotten their transition velocity as close to one light as they could before down-transiting, and they'd retained almost one light of sublight velocity, all of which helped minimize their transition flare. They'd also down-transited close to the bogie, and at almost the same moment, so the bogie's much greater flare masked their own. It also masked the launch of the torpedo. Any ships in the vicinity, or any station or planet based monitoring systems, might spot what appeared to be a faint echo of the larger ship's flare. But that wasn't uncommon, and would in all probability raise no concerns. Now, Charlie would have to wait to see if the second part of his plan worked.

Turmoil was coasting at point-nine lights into the gravitational well of the Istannan system, and since *Turmoil* wasn't supposed to exist, they were going to coast right through the system and out the other side before powering back up. During such routine hours Charlie spent a lot of time thinking about Starfall and the *overlord key.* He'd even visited Finalsa recently, to speak to his bankers there, in hopes that they might have a package for him from Cesare. Sague, Aziz, and Ethallan all regularly funneled funds into the same numbered investment account on Finalsa, though none of them had access to those funds or even information on the state of the account. Charlie learned that the money had been carefully invested. There was enough there for him to build a few more hunter-killers, but that was it. Perhaps, now that Andyne-Borregga was coming online, he could expand the shipyard there to something more than repair-and-supply. But that would take months, and in any case, he still had to come up with a way of funding larger hulls if he wanted to oppose Goutain and Lucius with any kind of effectiveness.

The bankers on Finalsa did have a package for him: actually just a sealed envelope, with a chromosome lock keyed to his DNA. And it held the strangest gift of all, a signed document granting Cesare the right to select the husband of Lucius's firstborn daughter, another document willing those rights to the de Lunis, and another certifying registry of both with the church. From the dates on the documents, Cesare had purchased those rights long before Delilah had even been conceived. And with canonical registry, the granting of such rights was a matter of public record. Anyone could dig them up, but only if one knew to look for them buried in the church archives more than thirty years ago. Winston told Charlie it was one of those times, shortly after Martino was born, when Lucius had squandered his personal assets and needed the money. And since he had a male heir, he had little concern for a girl not yet conceived and who might never be born. Charlie would bet that even Lucius, being Lucius, had forgotten this transaction.

To Charlie it was a useless document. He'd never exercise such an option. Nadama and Dieter would probably have him assassinated if he did. And even if that weren't an issue, he would never force Del to be his, and that's what it would amount to.

"Sir, we've just received a coded message from Mr. Sague, for your eyes only."

"Send it down to my cabin."

With no gravity, Charlie unstrapped and pulled his way down to the tiny captain's cabin. Oddly enough, he was more comfortable there than in the big suite of rooms at Starfall. The message was waiting on his personal console. He decoded it, then watched Sague's image report.

Apparently the warship they'd fired on was a Syndonese battleship christened the *Kiralov*. "They believe they triggered a mine, Your Grace. When their captain told me that, I decided to improvise. I told them this system was rather extensively mined during the Kealth incursion about a hundred years ago, and that while we've cleaned out most of the old mines, one does turn up every now and then. He seemed satisfied with that explanation.

"As we hoped, they sustained minor damage and he's demanded immediate service from our shipyard. All is going as planned. Also, we were watching closely and were unable to detect your transition flare. It was wholly masked by that of the larger ship."

Charlie and Sague had hatched their little plot together. Without an atmosphere to carry the shock wave, and with fully operational shielding, a warship should easily survive a small, one-megaton detonation at two hundred meters. But even with only minor damage, the commander of a warship would want to have her systems checked out thoroughly after such a near miss. And with a major shipyard conveniently close at hand, why not have her checked out immediately? As soon as the *Kiralov* docked at Istanna Prime, Sague's people would be all over her, but a special team would be assigned to her core computer system. They'd have to work under the watchful eyes of *Kiralov*'s crew, but Charlie hoped they could learn something useful, though even if they learned nothing, the experiment had been a success.

Once *Turmoil* and her sister ship *Chaos* were completed, Charlie decided to reoccupy Starfall. With his new personal ship *The Thirteenth Man*, the two hunter-killers, the converted Syndonese warship *The Headsman*, and the converted freighter, which he had named *Retribu-*

tion, he could always keep two of the ships in close orbit around Luna, providing the estate with a reasonably effective defense. He'd also decided to maintain the image of being near destitute, and so *The Thirteenth Man*, which appeared on the surface to be little better than a poor man's scow, was the only ship he allowed anyone outside his service to know about. Any of the other ships, when in orbit about Luna, would run silent, maintaining the secret of their existence and ready to deliver a nasty surprise should they receive another visit from a marauding bully like Santieff, or a pirate looking for easy pickings. And as a matter of security, the crews of *Turmoil*, *Chaos*, *Retribution*, and *The Headsman* were aware of only their own ship's existence, and not that of the others. Furthermore, none of the staff of Starfall were privy to the existence of any of Charlie's "shadow fleet," as Roacka had dubbed it.

Every time Charlie returned to Starfall he found more of the Two Thousand waiting for him, and they were often accompanied by a few of Cesare's staff. This time it was Major Pelletier and about a dozen of Cesare's personal guard.

Charlie greeted Pelletier stiffly. "Why now, Major? After all this time why do you suddenly find Theode's service so distasteful?"

A man like Pelletier had resources, and nothing compelled him to remain on Traxis. But after so many months, service to Theode had become implicitly voluntary, and Charlie wondered if he could trust the man.

Charlie had decided to receive Pelletier "under the

eyes of the ducal seat," a saying that meant he'd receive Pelletier seated upon the ducal throne, though no one called it a throne since there was only one throne in the Realm. "Why did you remain?" Charlie asked.

Pelletier lowered his eyes. "I had hoped to do something for Lord Arthur. He was a virtual prisoner in Farlight, constantly under guard by men not under my command. I do believe Duke Theode didn't trust me."

"And what did you hope to do for Arthur?"

"I don't know, Your Grace. I confess I'd never thought through such a situation. One of the men I brought with me wanted to try to kidnap him, steal a ship, and bring him to you. But we wouldn't have gotten far, and in any case I know your resources are limited. Theode would merely have come here in force and taken him back."

"Why did you finally leave?"

"Once they decided to remove Arthur from Traxis, it became clear we could do nothing for him. Though, looking back, it should have been clear from the beginning."

Charlie had allowed only his closest advisors and friends to be present: Winston, Paul, Roacka, Add, Ell, Roger, Seth, and Darmczek. He didn't really know Pelletier, who had joined Cesare's service while Charlie was in the hands of the Syndonese. "You served Theode, who betrayed Cesare and Arthur." Pelletier cringed. "Theode didn't trust you, and clearly he had reason not to. Tell me why *I* should trust you, Major."

Pelletier opened his mouth to speak and hesitated.

The moment drew out, Pelletier standing there with his mouth open, but with no words to say in his own defense. It was Roacka who broke the silence, stepping forward and growling, "I'll speak for the man, lad. He's a good man, loyal. Maybe it was a mistake to stay with Theode so long, maybe not. Who can say? But I have no doubt of his motives."

Add stepped forward. "And I'll speak for him too, little brother."

Ell joined her. "And I." One by one they all stepped forward in a unanimous chorus of support for the major.

Charlie considered Pelletier for a long moment. "Speak for yourself, Major."

Again Pelletier hesitated, then in a rush he said, "I loved your father. I did."

Of all the things Pelletier could have said, Charlie hadn't expected that. "I'll think on the matter," he said, then stood, and without a word marched toward the doors. But in passing he overheard Pelletier whisper to Roacka, "He allows you to call him *lad*?"

"Of course he does," Roacka replied, unable to whisper even when trying to do so. "The day the boy expects me to pull out some *Yer Graces* and *Yer Lordships* is the day I turn him over my knee and spank him like I did twenty years ago."

"Little brother."

Charlie sat on the stone floor facing the featureless

wall at the end of the blind corridor. He'd had another sleepless night, had awakened in the wee hours of the morning and trudged down here to stare at the wall obscured by the visual distortion field. At the sound of Ell's voice he rose to his feet and turned to face her. Add, Roacka, and Pelletier stood behind her. "Major Pelletier may know how to rescue Arthur."

CHAPTER 19
PIRATE'S BOUNTY

Theode was having Arthur removed to the planet Kobiyan, an airless rock in an out-of-the-way system that was a minor de Maris holding, and an ideal place to lock Arthur away forever. With a few modifications and upgrades, Kobiyan could be well-enough defended to make it difficult to crack without a full assault by several warships.

"Why now?" Charlie asked. "Why after all this time?"

Pelletier said, "Apparently, someone made an off-hand remark at a reception in Almsburg about reinstating Arthur, which infuriated him. He kept saying it was you, but Gaida disagreed with him on that. They've both grown quite paranoid about Arthur."

"It was Telka," Charlie said. "And I think she did it on purpose to goad him."

Winston gave Charlie a look as Pelletier continued.

"In any case, the location of Arthur's new prison is to be a closely held secret. Quite simply, he'll never be seen or heard from again."

"How did you learn this *closely held secret*?" Charlie asked.

Pelletier shrugged. "Servants. They hear everything. And a good security chief is wise to cultivate them as sources." Charlie understood that well. His mother had been a servant, and before Cesare had taken an active role in his upbringing he'd been raised by servants, and had been treated as a servant. Servants were ignored until needed, and frequently forgotten even when present.

"There are quite a few in the de Maris household who are loyal to Arthur. And of course Theode and his mother haven't endeared themselves to anyone."

"And Arthur hasn't been moved to Kobiyan yet?"

"No. They've locked him in a hospital room under heavy guard on Traxis Prime to get him out of sight. But that's only temporary while they make modifications to the facilities on Kobiyan to improve security. If we had some firepower we could extract him from there." Pelletier wasn't yet aware of the existence of Charlie's shadow fleet, nor was he aware of the true nature of *The Thirteenth Man*.

It didn't matter, though, and Charlie shook his head adamantly. "If we had the firepower to extract him, as you pointed out earlier, Theode would just come here with more firepower than I can muster and take him back. In any case, it'll be easier to take him from a ship. But how do we do that without them realizing it's me?"

Roacka suddenly threw his head back and laughed, then looked at each of them with an evil grin. Paul demanded angrily, "All right, you old reprobate. You've got some sort of idea, so out with it."

"Well now, churchman," Roacka said, the grin broadening. "I'm reluctant to speak this idea in your hallowed presence because it might offend you."

"Out with it, damn it."

"Ah! A churchman who swears." Roacka looked at Charlie. "I guess that means it won't upset him to conspire with pirates."

The Headsman was an ideal pirate ship. Of obvious Syndonese make, no one would ever associate her with Charlie. Her victims would probably assume that her Syndonese crew had, at some time in the past, mutinied against her officers—Syndonese senior officers were reputed to be brutal disciplinarians—then taken command of the ship and turned pirate. And while piracy was rare in the Realm, it was rumored to be an ever-present problem in the Republic. In fact, Drakwin told Charlie that in the Republic it was also rare, but rumored to be a problem in the Realm. Such rumors would make a real act of piracy all the more believable, and would only work in their favor.

Pelletier still had some sources among Theode's servants. And Theode and Gaida were cut from that caste of arrogance where servants were truly invisible until needed. Apparently, Theode didn't trust many of the crews on his own ships, fearing they still held some loyalty to Cesare's memory, and to his rightful heir. And with only a few captains and crews that he did trust, he couldn't afford to divert one of them for the entire run to Kobiyan. So he'd decided to transport Arthur first to Cathan aboard a de Maris light cruiser, then from there to Dumark by commercial passage aboard the liner *Paradise*, with the last leg to Kobiyan on a chartered merchantman. Arthur would travel drugged and incognito, his itinerary a highly kept secret, and always accompanied by a squad of ten heavily armed mercenaries handpicked by Theode and Gaida.

Charlie scrambled the entire shadow fleet, sent Pelletier, in command of *The Thirteenth Man*, back to the vicinity of Traxis to keep his intelligence sources active, while the rest of them headed for Cathan and Dumark.

Winston didn't want Charlie to join the fake pirate crew on *The Headsman*. He thought Charlie should establish an alibi by making himself publicly visible elsewhere, but Charlie was adamant. "It's Arthur, so I'm going," he said, "and I won't listen to any arguments to the contrary."

Roacka came to his defense. "They'll see *The Headsman* is of Syndonese make, because we'll make sure they do. And they all think Charlie doesn't have access to that kind of firepower. So don't get your panties in a twist."

Charlie carefully hid his smile at Winston's reaction to *that* comment.

Had they been facing a fully crewed man-of-war, there would have been nothing they could do. With Charlie's five ships they might defeat a cruiser, but only after a pitched battle, and then all that would be left of the cruiser would be a cloud of radioactive vapor. But a commercial liner like *Paradise* was a different matter. Furthermore, Charlie had the twin advantages of multiple ships and that no one knew of the existence of hunter-killers and their capabilities.

Using the hunter-killer tactics they'd developed, *Turmoil*, with Roger in command, had picked up *Paradise* as she transited out of Cathan nearspace, and was following close on her stern. *Chaos*, with Seth in command, lay about ten light-years out from Dumark, with *The Headsman* stationary five light-years farther along *Paradise*'s course. Their plan was that *Chaos*, sitting stationary in deep space, could accurately detect the transition wakes of *Paradise* and *Turmoil* as they passed by, then uplink navigational data to *Turmoil* and *The Headsman*. Roger would then correct his course to be right on *Paradise*'s tail, and *The Headsman* would move to intercept *Paradise* as she approached the outer reaches of the Dumark system.

"Got 'em," Darmczek said, breaking the tension on *The Headsman*'s bridge. "*Chaos* reports they've picked up the transition wakes and are in contact with *Turmoil*. And we've got *Paradise*'s vector now."

Charlie felt a general sense of relief wash through everyone on the bridge. His immediate reaction was to start issuing orders, but *The Headsman* was Darmczek's command, so Charlie bit his tongue and sat without comment. Darmczek knew what he had to do, and they had about ten hours in which to do it.

The tension on the bridge declined further as Darmczek barked out orders. They were a quarter of a light-year to one side of *Paradise*'s course. They spent three hours driving hard to build sufficient sublight velocity, then up-transited, pushed their transition drive to the limit for a half hour, down-transited and spent another three hours killing their sublight velocity.

"Two light-years and closing, sir," the navigator barked. "We've got a little over an hour and a half."

Darmczek lined them up on a coarse parallel to *Paradise*'s and they started building up sublight vector. If they succeeded in knocking *Paradise* out of transition, she'd hold on to a lot of sublight velocity, so they needed to build up as much as they could to match her speed when the time came.

"Point-one light-year and closing, sir. We're at a velocity of point-nine lights."

Darmczek pushed *The Headsman*'s sublight drive to the limit. They were a tenth of a light-year in front of *Paradise*, both heading inward toward Dumark, but with the liner in transition she was overtaking them rapidly.

"Com, signal *Turmoil* that we made it on point. They can stand down."

Turmoil's primary purpose had been to help them be sure they were targeting *Paradise*, and not some other wake in the busy Cathan-Dumark shipping lane.

As a secondary purpose, *Turmoil* was there as backup should they be unable to position *The Headsman* properly in front of *Paradise*.

"Fire control," Darmczek ordered. "Arm a ten-kilotonne warhead, target for detonation five kilometers in front of their bow. That should disrupt their transition field nicely. And tell all weapons stations to stand by."

"Sir, she's closing rapidly." Darmczek had positioned them so that *Paradise* would pass about one hundred thousand kilometers to one side of their own line.

"Stand by with that warhead. You've got your targeting solution. Follow it."

The Headsman's hull thrummed with the sound of a transition launch. "Missile away, sir."

The missile only took a fraction of a second to cross the intervening space, and all data from exterior sensors froze momentarily as the incandescent glare of the detonation overloaded them. The tension grew for several seconds as they waited to learn the fate of the liner. "We got her, sir. She's in sublight."

As Charlie's screens came back to life he could see that for himself. The data showed *Paradise* coasting in space, her automated distress systems broadcasting a call for help to Dumark. *Turmoil* had down-transited nearby and was running silent; no sense in letting anyone know of the existence of such ships.

"All forward main batteries," Darmczek barked. "One shot, across her bow, fire." The hull thrummed again to the beat of the transition batteries.

Darmczek continued snapping out orders. "Helm, match their vector. Com, open a channel to *Paradise* and get Drakwin on it."

Roacka had outdone himself, staging the whole pirate thing like a prep-school play. Since they were supposedly Syndonese outlaws, Drakwin, who stood almost two meters tall and spoke with a thick Syndonese accent, would be the infamous pirate Raul the Damned. "Where the hell did you come up with that?" Charlie asked Roacka.

"Just my vivid imagination, lad. I think I should have been a vid writer. Bet I could have made a fortune."

"This is Raul the Damned," Drakwin crowed over the com, sitting at a station near Charlie and hamming it up badly. "Heave to and prepare to be boarded. If you try to run we'll fire on you, and no shot across the bow next time. Lives will be lost, possibly everyone on your ship. Heave to as ordered, and only money will be lost."

They cut the com link and waited for a reply.

"Forward main batteries," Darmczek barked. "Target on their drive and stand by in case they try to run."

Charlie leaned toward Drakwin and said, "Heave to and prepare to be boarded? You've got to be kidding."

Drakwin grinned like a schoolboy. "Saw it in a costume drama once, Your Grace. Always wanted to say it myself."

Paradise had popped out of transition at point-eight lights and one hundred thousand kilometers to one side of their line. *The Headsman* was still decelerating from point-nine lights, which meant they were pulling away from her rapidly, though they were breaking hard to close the distance. They waited several minutes, then Drakwin repeated his message, and this time they got a reply almost immediately.

Someone from *Paradise*, speaking in carefully articulated syllables, said, "Please identify yourself again." They broadcast audio only, no video.

Drakwin snarled, "I am Raul the Damned of the Mexak League. Prepare to be boarded."

The voice that came out of the com said, "A Syndonese pirate! You gotta be kidding."

"I'm not just any Syndonese pirate," Drakwin said. "I'm Raul the Damned. And I answer to no man but the devil and the Mexak League."

Shit, Charlie thought. *We've created a monster.* It had been his idea that Raul should be part of an association of pirates, which they decided to call the Mexak League.

"What do you want?" the fellow demanded, his voice cracking with tension.

The fellow sounded nervous and tense, but not afraid. A crewman on a ship being attacked by bloodthirsty pirates should be just plain scared, and his lack of fear raised Charlie's suspicions.

Drakwin demanded, "I ask the questions here. Identify yourself."

"I'm Captain Chambers, CO, *Paradise*, Dumark registry."

"Well, Captain Chambers, as I said before, heave to and prepare to be boarded."

"You can't do this. We're law-abiding people here."

Charlie switched his com feed to *The Headsman*'s command channel. "Darmczek, he's stalling, probably got his crew rushing to prepare an up-transit. Stand by to put another shot across his bow."

"Aye, Your Grace."

Charlie leaned over to Drakwin and whispered the same message in his ear.

Drakwin spoke over the com link. "Chambers, I'm beginning to think you're not hearing what I say."

Charlie had to crane his neck to see Darmczek amidst the instrument clusters and duty stations in the cramped confines of *The Headsman*'s bridge. Charlie nodded, and a second later heard the thrum of her main transition batteries as they fired another shot across *Paradise*'s bow.

"Okay, okay," Chambers shouted. "Okay. What are you going to do with us?"

"That's better," Drakwin said. "We're going to board you. We're interested in valuables, not people. If there's any resistance, you'll pay a heavy price in lives."

*T*he Headsman had two small gunboats in a hangar bay below decks. Charlie and Drakwin joined Roacka there along with a selected group of spacers who knew how to fight in close quarters. Roacka had chosen to dress Drakwin and a few of his lieutenants in something similar to trampsie attire, loud, flamboyant, and colorful. "Can you swagger?" Roacka asked the Syndonese.

Drakwin rolled his eyes. "I'm Syndonese. What do you think?"

For the rest of them they'd dug up shipboard fatigues in as many different colors as possible, spotted them up with a splash of machine oil here and there, tore a few small holes in them, and sewed patches elsewhere. And for the finishing touch, none of them had shaved for the past three or four days. They made for a rather scruffy looking bunch.

Charlie would play the role of one of Drakwin's lieutenants, and since he might be recognized, he, like most of the boarding party, wore light combat armor, with a helmet and face shield that would hide all but mouth and chin. And as an intimidation tactic, just to ensure that no one on *Paradise* decided to play the hero, Charlie added to the boarding party four marines in heavy, powered combat armor, each carrying large-caliber grav rifles.

It took Darmczek two hours to match *Paradise*'s vector and close the distance between them to a few kilometers. They managed to cram the forty heavily armed members of the boarding party into the two boats without serious crowding.

Once on board *Paradise* they herded all passengers and crew into the main dining salon. Drakwin ordered Chambers to give Charlie a copy of the passenger manifest. He strutted back and forth in front of the crowd while the rest of the boarding party searched them carefully, taking jewelry and any kind of valuables they found; they had to keep up appearances.

The mercenaries guarding Arthur were Charlie's main concern, but as with all mercenaries, their primary loyalty lay with themselves, and when it became clear no one would be harmed as long as no one resisted, they surrendered their weapons peacefully. As they searched each passenger Charlie checked them off the passenger manifest, and, of course, when they were done one name remained.

Charlie and Drakwin played out a little drama they'd rehearsed. Charlie stuck the passenger manifest in front of Drakwin's nose. Charlie spoke Syndonese; Drakwin had carefully tutored him to ensure his accent was accurate.

"Captain," he said, pointing to the one remaining name on the manifest. "This one ain't here."

Drakwin looked at the list, narrowed his eyes dramatically, and turned to Chambers. "Where is this Philip Smithson? He isn't here with the rest of the passengers."

Chambers sputtered. "He's . . . in his cabin."

"And why is he not here? I told you all passengers and crew."

"He's ill, and too weak to stand on his own."

Drakwin pointed at Charlie. "Take my man here to his cabin."

Charlie grabbed two of the armed spacers from *The Headsman* to accompany them, and followed Chambers, who led them to Philip Smithson. Chambers clearly had no idea that Smithson was actually Arthur.

Arthur wasn't ill, just drugged up so heavily he couldn't stand, couldn't even focus on anything, with a stream of drool running down his chin. To complete their little charade, Charlie turned to Chambers and tried to imitate a thick Syndonese accent. "This one, he looks familiar. Did I see him in the vids?"

Charlie keyed his helmet com and spoke for Chambers's benefit. "Captain, we got some sort of celebrity here. Not sure who, but somebody important, maybe worth money."

Drakwin came to Arthur's cabin, took one look at Arthur, and like Charlie, spoke for Chambers's benefit. "I know him, some sort of duke's kid. We're taking him with us."

"No," Chambers said, lunging at Drakwin and grabbing at his arm. "You can't."

One of the spacers put the muzzle of his handgun against the side of Chambers's head. "Yes," Charlie said, "we can. We can do it with you dead, or we can do it with you alive."

Chambers's shoulders slumped; he let go of Drakwin's arm and stepped away. The spacer didn't lower his gun. Drakwin took Chambers back to his crew.

With Arthur supported between the two spacers they got him aboard one of the gunboats. Charlie waited there with Arthur while Drakwin and the rest finished out the pretense of thieving pirates. He hated to do it, but they did need to keep up appearances.

Besides, he could use the money.

CHAPTER 20
COCONSPIRATORS

Charlie didn't have a physician on staff yet, but he did have several experienced medics among his combat troops, a few of which were capable of doing almost as much as any physician, including some delicate surgeries. He asked one of them to give Arthur a thorough exam.

"He's just stoned," the medic said, "though I'll add that he was close to an overdose. A little more and he might have died. He's also suffering from mild malnutrition, though not as bad as what we went through in the prison camps. I'm going to guess the malnutrition is just a side effect of loading him up so heavily on sedatives he doesn't really eat. It'll take a couple days to sweat the tranqs out of his system. Then we make sure he eats well and he'll be back to normal."

Though Arthur was oblivious to any sound, Charlie quietly promised him he'd give Theode some pay-back for this.

As the medic predicted, Arthur wallowed in the drug-induced haze for two more days, and even then it took another two before he had his wits fully about him again. Charlie found him in the officer's mess in *The Headsman* devouring a meal. "Was Theode responsible for Cesare's death?" Charlie asked as he sat down.

Arthur shook his head sadly. "I have my suspicions, but I can't prove anything. Cesare never fully recovered from the injuries he took in the Almsburg Palace, though he should have. But he wasn't dying, just seemed to have aged a lot, became a bit frailer, just slowly withered away. And then one morning he didn't get up."

"Gaida?" Charlie asked.

"Ya, that's what I'm thinking." Arthur stared blankly at the steam rising from a bowl of soup in front of him. "I missed it, Charlie, didn't see it coming. And then the morning father died, Farlight filled with mercenaries taking orders from Gaida, and she accused father's physician, Stallas, of murdering him at my orders. I think Gaida was fucking Stallas."

"Do you remember anything else?"

Again Arthur shook his head. "From then on I was kept in a drugged-out haze."

Charlie felt a knot of cold anger form in his gut. "Let's take this before the rest of the Ten."

Arthur grimaced and pushed the soup away.

"Theode was an acknowledged and proper son of Cesare, legitimately in line to inherit the ducal seat. So the rest of the Ten consider this a squabble internal to House de Maris. By custom, they dared not intervene. That would set a precedent for others to intervene in their own internal issues."

Charlie stood and shouted, "Damn it!" He slammed his fist down on the table. "Then why don't I just go strangle Twerp's scrawny little neck."

"Because you're no longer of House de Maris. You are House de Lunis, and that would be outside intervention, which would force the other ducal houses to support Theode."

"Fuck that bitch," Charlie shouted and stormed across the room. He wanted to hit something, but then he had a sudden thought that helped a little. "But if you had the wherewithal to take the ducal seat back . . ."

Arthur finished the thought for him. "The other houses wouldn't intervene, not openly."

Charlie grinned, and Arthur frowned, clearly not sure what to make of Charlie's attitude.

"Syndonese pirates," Theode screeched. "What do you mean, Syndonese pirates?"

The head of the mercenary team to which he'd entrusted Arthur shrugged. He was a large, ugly man, all hard edges both physically and emotionally. "He called himself Raul the Damned, said he was part of the Mexak League. Definitely Syndonese."

"And you let him take Arthur?"

"We had no choice, ten of us against an entire crew. Some of them wore powered armor and carried assault weapons. And their ship was a Syndonese heavy cruiser."

Theode trembled with rage. With a third of the de Maris old guard leaving his service, and the rest, at best, only reluctantly dutiful, he was becoming more and more dependent on these mercenaries to keep his officers in line. He tried to keep his voice down and failed miserably. "How did a scruffy bunch of pirates get their hands on a functional heavy cruiser?"

The large mercenary shrugged indifferently. "Probably mutinied, killed their senior officers, and took control of the ship."

The man's lack of concern only fueled Theode's rage. "This is a disaster, an absolute disaster."

"My dear," Gaida said calmly, stepping between Theode and the large man. Theode suspected she was fucking him. "Calm down, my dear. I think this might not be as much of a disaster as you fear."

"How do you mean?"

She took him by the arm and led him several paces away from the mercenaries, then spoke softly for his ears only. "I doubt Arthur will be treated terribly well by a bunch of pirates. And of course, any ransom demands they make will be . . . excessive, as far as we're concerned. So we'll have to negotiate, and such negotiations will undoubtedly take years, during which Arthur will probably suffer unthinkable deprivations."

Theode's pulse slowed and his breathing calmed. "Thank you, mother," he said, feeling much better. "Your insights are always so . . . thought provoking." He leaned toward her and kissed her chastely on the cheek. "I do so value your advice."

Shortly after they returned to Luna, Drakwin escorted two other Syndonese into Charlie's office where Charlie and Roacka waited—Charlie seated behind his desk, Roacka seated in a large, comfortable chair to one side. The two Syndonese were vastly different men: one short, balding, slightly overweight; the other medium height, but thin, with a face sculpted of sharply angled features. Drakwin indicated the short, balding one. "This is Sobak. He don't speak standard so good, so I may have to translate."

Charlie stood, stepped around the desk, and extended a hand to Sobak, who eyed him warily. Charlie said in Syndonese, "We can speak in your language then, Mr. Sobak."

"Just Sobak," the man said, extending his hand, though still warily. "You speak Syndonese, eh?"

Charlie said, "I learned a bit before the last war, then had five years of lessons in a POW camp."

Sobak grinned, though it had more the look of a grimace. Drakwin turned to the other Syndonese. "This is Thamaklus."

Charlie extended his hand to Thamaklus, who glowered at him for a moment. The Syndonese reached over with his left hand and gripped his own right wrist, lifted his right arm to about waist high, then let it drop. It flopped down at his side and hung there limply. "It's dead," he said in Syndonese.

Charlie lowered his hand and asked, "How?"

Thamaklus grinned as unpleasantly as Sobak. "Goutain's Security Force interrogated me for a couple of days, though I never did find out why, or what they wanted to know."

"Has it been treated?"

"Who would look at it?"

Charlie turned to Roacka. "Have someone look at that arm. We have advanced medical facilities here; we may be able to do something about nerve damage like that."

He asked Drakwin, "Are there other Syndonese here with untreated injuries?"

Drakwin looked carefully at Sobak and Thamaklus, then back to Charlie. "In Syndon it's not wise to complain."

Every day Charlie learned a little more about life for the ordinary Syndonese. "Please bring them forward. They'll be treated, helped if possible."

The three Syndonese all looked at one another suspiciously. Charlie continued, "Did you tell Sobak and Thamaklus why I wanted to see them?"

Drakwin raised one eyebrow. "Thought it best you tell them."

Charlie turned to the two men. If they were as distrustful as they appeared, then this wouldn't work.

"Drakwin tells me you have no more love for Goutain than I."

The two shared a glance. Thamaklus said, "We try not to get involved. It ain't healthy."

"What if you could make it unhealthy for those who make it unhealthy for you?"

The two men shared another glance, though they still looked at Charlie suspiciously. He continued, "What if I supplied you with arms—explosives and light weaponry—clothing, food, supplies, then dropped you back in Syndon at a place of your choosing? Would you know someone who might make use of such supplies against . . . a mutual enemy?"

A smile appeared slowly on Thamaklus's chiseled features. "We might know someone."

"And could you enlist their aid without telling where you got such equipment, because my name can't come up in this."

"No," Thamaklus said. "We'd have to tell them something, but we'll just lie."

"Good. No civilian targets," Charlie said, "only military and the Security Force."

Thamaklus rubbed his chin with his good hand. "We could work within those constraints."

While reviewing House de Lunis's accounts with Winston, Charlie noticed something odd. "Why am I borrowing from Rierma and Telka?"

Winston opened his hands in a gesture of defeat.

"For one thing, you need the money, especially since you ordered the construction of six more hunter-killers."

"That was a mistake, huh?"

Winston shook his head. "No. If I'd thought it a mistake I'd have spoken up before now."

"Then why not borrow from Sague and Aziz? I'm sure they'd give us a good line of credit."

"That's a resource we may eventually tap, Your Grace. But right now your best defense is that everyone believes you destitute, so no one takes you as a serious threat. And I've been nurturing that impression purposefully. I make sure you're always arrears in payments, but not so much that they call the debt due. And while Rierma and Telka are friendly toward you, you can bet their accountants gossip like market wives, so the word gets around."

"Good thinking . . . I think."

Charlie couldn't sleep that night. His entire staff was working for room and board and minimal pay, as well as the crews on his ships, though that didn't bother him so much concerning the Two Thousand. They'd shared the chain together, and any one of them would give his life for another. But still!

He lay in bed unable to sleep for a while before finally deciding to wander down to the blind corridor once more. He threw on a robe, grabbed a comp tablet, and hit its power switch as he marched out of his room. A groggy-eyed Ell sat up on the couch in the anteroom where she'd been sleeping.

"Go back to sleep," Charlie said as he passed her.

She ignored him, got up, and followed him.

On the face of the tablet he brought up the three-dimensional map of the interior of Starfall, though he knew that the blind corridor wouldn't be visible on it until he stepped into it. But when he did, when he took that step, the corridor didn't appear on the map.

He stopped in his tracks, turned, and stepped out of the corridor, then turned and walked back into it, and where before it would appear on the map whenever he stepped into it, now nothing. He repeated the process a dozen times, stepping into and out of the corridor. And still nothing.

Scratching his head, he wondered for a brief moment if he had imagined the whole thing, but shoved that thought aside. Its appearance on the map had been real, there was no doubt of that, but what had changed? Perplexed and frustrated, he returned to his rooms and dropped the comp tablet onto a dresser next to the ornate dagger Cesare had given him. He tossed the robe over a chair, hoping he'd get some sleep now, but knew he wouldn't.

Charlie had to get Arthur out of Starfall. If Theode and Gaida took a lucky guess, or just decided to drop in to harass Charlie, rescuing Arthur could all be for naught. And thinking about it, he realized he had the perfect place to stash him away. So they departed Luna, and twelve days later—standing on the bridge of *The Headsman*—Charlie pointed to the redundant navigational console where he usually sat, and told Arthur to sit down. As Arthur did so, standing behind him and looking over his shoulder, Charlie asked the young officer seated next to him, "Can you give us an external visual?"

"Certainly, Your Grace. We're only about half a kilometer out so you should get a good view of the whole thing."

On the screen in front of Arthur a massive cylindrical structure appeared, a kilometer in diameter and three hundred meters deep. "Andyne-Borregga," Arthur said, peering intently at the screen. "It's big."

The Headsman was moving cautiously at only a few meters per second toward one of the station's docks. "It has to be big to be self-sufficient," Charlie said.

"And my new home," Arthur added.

Charlie had a busy schedule ahead of him: Andyne-Borregga, Tachaann, Aagerbanne, and then the next meeting of the Ten on Turnlee. And while he'd taken passage from Starfall with Arthur on *The Headsman*, he dared not show a captured Syndonese warship at Turnlee, so *The Thirteenth Man* had accompanied them.

"Has Theode responded to the ransom demand yet?" Arthur asked.

Charlie had let Drakwin play the pirate captain to the hilt. They'd recorded a message from him demanding an outrageous sum for Arthur's ransom, an amount so high that no one would consider paying it. They delivered the message within a tenday of

Arthur's kidnapping, with instructions that Theode could respond by an open broadcast in Cathan nearspace using an encryption key they provided. There followed a flurry of activity by de Maris warships along the Cathan-Dumark run, then absolute silence for a tenday, and finally Theode's reply.

"He wanted to negotiate," Charlie said. "We'll wait a couple of tendays, then Drakwin will respond with dramatic indignation and some threats on your life. He'll even up the ransom demand. We really don't want to negotiate your release, so we're going to draw this out as long as possible."

Still standing behind Arthur, who appeared almost entranced by the image of the space station on the screen, Charlie nodded toward Andyne-Borregga. "No one really knows about this yet, and by the time they do, it had better be able to defend itself."

Charlie had explained to Arthur how he'd acquired the station. "It's isolated, few people have ever heard of it, and those who have don't remember it. The Borreggan system isn't even on most charts. Right now it's defenseless, but we're installing some defensive batteries and active shielding on the outer structure, and when I can dig up the funding I'm going to install a couple of big orbital weapons platforms in defensive positions. And I need someone to run the whole thing. Can you do it? At least until you get the de Maris ducal seat back."

Arthur grinned. "Turn one of your headaches over to me, huh?"

"Yes. Sague needs to get back to his operations on

Istanna, and I need you to take his place, manage the operations here."

The Headsman eased carefully into one of Andyne-Borregga's air docks. Once she cleared the docking bay doors they closed ponderously, the dock crew brought gravity in the dock slowly up to one-tenth standard, and the ship settled onto its landing struts. Large ships like The Headsman couldn't support themselves in full gravity without a constant power feed to her internal gravity generators. One-tenth standard was a nice compromise, permitting the ship to shut down its systems completely, and allowing maintenance personnel to work in the comfort of a gravity well. It was certainly preferable to working in zero-G in vacuum suits in orbit.

Once the bay doors were sealed they brought the dock's internal air pressure up to standard. Darmczek and his crew would spend a good hour securing the ship's systems, though since Darmczek hadn't scheduled maintenance for The Headsman, they'd leave her power plant on a trickle so it could be restarted in short order. Charlie and Arthur were free to go.

A long gantry extended about ten meters above the dock's floor and mated to the ship's main personnel hatch. The twins and Sague waited for Charlie and Arthur there. "Your Grace," Sague said, bowing carefully to Charlie. He turned to Arthur, bowed again, and said, "Your Grace."

Arthur paled. "I'm not the Duke de Maris, Mr. Sague. The honorific isn't appropriate."

Sague winced uncomfortably. "But you're the right-

ful heir to the de Maris ducal seat . . ." He glanced at
Charlie.

Charlie smiled and didn't say anything.

"Come," Sague said abruptly. "Please, I have a tour
prepared for you, as well as a complete briefing."

Only about one percent of Andyne-Borregga's systems were fully operational, which surprised Charlie.
But Sague told him, "However, we've verified and
tested more than half her systems, and they can be
fully operational in a matter of hours. But we're so understaffed at the moment there's no need to bring them
all up. Right now we're focused on testing and verify-
ing status of the rest, and identifying those that need
repair or maintenance. And from what we've seen so
far, there aren't too many systems that require repair,
so if they're not critical, we flag them for later review
and ignore them for the time being. For the rest, we
perform any needed maintenance as part of the testing
and verification, then shut them down until needed."

Charlie didn't want a large staff at Starfall, so with
few exceptions, as refugees of various kinds arrived, he
sent them on to Andyne-Borregga. Sague had a little
over three thousand people working on the station at
the moment—when fully supplied it could easily accommodate a couple million—and he estimated that
with the manpower on hand Arthur could complete
testing of existing systems in under a month. But
equipment for the new defensive batteries and surface
shielding had already begun to arrive from Aziz, and
Arthur pointed out that installation would be a real

construction project, not merely testing and maintenance. He and Sague both agreed that, with the exception of any remaining critical systems, they'd focus
work on the new defensive installations.

Arthur and Sague jumped into the minutiae of the
work, carefully discussing the details of manpower
and resource scheduling. Charlie had no aptitude for
such detail, so he wandered down to check out some of
the work crews. He saw one group using a grav lifter
to muscle a heavy piece of equipment into place. He
moved on and stopped at a window looking out over
one of the station's zero-G vacuum docks. As a group
unloaded equipment from a small merchantman,
someone behind him said, "Commander? That you?"

Charlie turned to find a slightly overweight chief
petty officer facing him, a man with whom he'd shared
the chain. Charlie smiled, and the man frowned as he
suddenly realized what he'd said. "Sorry, Your Grace,"
he said. "I forgot, didn't mean to call you commander,
just—"

"No," Charlie said, sticking out his hand. "For you
and anyone else who shared the chain with me, it'll
always be just *commander*."

The man smiled, began shaking Charlie's hand with
ridiculous vigor, and shouted over his shoulder, "Hey
guys, Commander Cass is here. It's the commander."

In a matter of seconds a dozen men surrounded
him, shaking his hand and slapping him on the back.
He couldn't remember any of their names, but he
knew their faces without any hesitation. "We was just

gonna break for lunch," the chief said. "Wanna join us, Commander?"

They led him to a small cafeteria where they all got trays of simple food. Apparently, word spread quickly and in short order the cafeteria filled with a couple hundred men from the chain. They laughed, joked, ate; Charlie even got into a short dice game with a few of them, lost all the cash he had on hand. It was Sague who interrupted the fun. "My apologies, Your Grace, but it's time to go."

It took Charlie more than an hour to give every single one of them a good handshake and a slap on the back. And when they finally did leave, his hand was a swollen, bruised wreck.

He wouldn't have traded that for anything.

As he and Sague and the twins walked to *The Headsman*'s dock, Sague said, "I believe your next stop is Tachaann, is it not, Your Grace?"

"Yes it is."

"Then Istanna is not far out of your way. It would be advantageous to everyone if you could make a short stop there. There is an important personage there who wishes to meet you."

Sague refused to be more specific than that, and though Charlie trusted the man, it set his curiosity afire.

"May I introduce Mr. Cahntu," Sague said, "chairman of the Istannan Planetary Council?"

Sestimar Cahntu was an ordinary looking man, average height, a little overweight, late middle age, graying hair, simple business suit. He bowed deeply. "Your Grace, it's a pleasure." Like Sague he spoke in the sharp, clipped Istannan accent.

"The pleasure is mine," Charlie said. "You honor me, Chairman Cahntu."

Sague poured them drinks of some fiery Istannan whiskey and directed them to a couple of comfortable chairs in his office. Since the meeting was at Cahntu's request, Charlie let him set the pace, though it was aggravating to have to waste his time discussing local Istannan politics. Eventually, Cahntu said, "I suppose you're wondering why I requested this meeting, Your Grace."

Charlie smiled and said, "Somehow I doubt it was to discuss the controversy surrounding rice subsidies, and the trade imbalance that has produced with Terranzalbo."

Cahntu laughed. "Quite tedious, isn't it? But it plays a role in the coming election. Though I must confess your king's ambitions will play an even greater role."

Charlie didn't want to take that bait. "Which ambitions are you referring to?"

"His annexation of Aagerbanne, of course, and his alliance with Syndon."

Charlie tried to be evasive. "But how does that concern you?"

Cahntu swirled the whiskey in his glass and looked at it for a moment. "The entire Planetary Council, and most of the general populace of Istanna, fears that his annexation of Aagerbanne is merely the first step toward annexation of all of the independent states."

Charlie could see where this was going and wasn't sure he wanted it to go there. "It's no secret that Lucius has ambitions of empire. Why come to me?"

"Because it's well known that you have no love of the Syndonese and that you openly oppose Lucius's warlike inclinations. Because Sague speaks highly of you."

Sague had been mysterious about this meeting, had refused any details in advance, though he had made a point to say beforehand, "During this meeting, should you have any doubts, please be assured that I have divulged none of your activities." The man nodded now, to indicate what he'd said earlier was still true.

Cahntu continued. "And because if Lucius attempts to annex another of the independent states, there'll be war. And perhaps the most important reason: because Ethallan recommended I speak with you."

Charlie couldn't help but show surprise. "Ethallan?"

"Yes. She wouldn't say more than that, but when I expressed our concern to her only a tenday ago, she told me to speak with you."

. . . *only a tenday ago* . . . That was a hint that Cahntu had been in contact with her after she'd gone into exile.

"Tell me, Your Grace. We have a certain need for small arms, light armor, and explosives, things of that nature. And we have the funds to pay for them. Could you recommend a supplier?"

Charlie assumed Cahntu intended to feed such supplies to the Aagerbanni resistance, so he spoke cautiously. "Hart & Delorm on Toellan are certainly capable of supplying the materials you require, and can be quite discreet in such matters. I know them personally, am one of their investors, and I'd be happy to have a word with them."

Cahntu looked Charlie in the eyes, and Charlie felt as if nothing was hidden from the man. Cahntu said, "That would be kind of you, Your Grace."

"And what of you?" Charlie asked. "Should it come to war, is Istanna prepared to fight? Can Istanna field troops and arms?" At that moment Charlie had an idea he'd never considered. "Might Istanna be prepared to enter into a coalition to oppose Lucius and Goutain?"

Cahntu smiled. "Three questions, Your Grace. Three answers. Yes. Yes. And it would depend upon who would be our partners in this coalition."

Charlie shook his head. "Partnerships don't work in war. A coalition would need one leader."

"Of course, Your Grace. And I think we know who that leader should be, though I've only recently met him and don't know him well. But people who do know him speak highly of him, people whom I trust. And I will admit that my first impression of him is good."

Charlie stood politely when Sague ushered Cahntu out of the room. It occurred to him he should find a way to surreptitiously contact the leaders of the other independent states, try the same proposal on them. He decided to broach the subject with Sague on the way to the spaceport. When the Istannan returned he was preparing to leave.

"No, Your Grace. You mustn't leave yet. You have several more meetings."

Clearly Sague had had a similar thought—and the foresight to act on it. So Charlie watched as Sague then ushered in the ambassador from Finalsa, followed by the ambassadors from Toellan, Terranzalbo, Allison's Cluster, and the Scorpo Systems. Charlie met with each of them separately, and with each the conversation was much the same as it had been with Cahntu. Clearly, they'd spoken with one another, if not in a large group then in smaller meetings like these. Charlie made a point of indirectly asking each of them how many capital ships they could supply to a coalition effort, if such a coalition were to be formed, and if war did come. Two ships from one, four or five from another—not a lot, but they could each supply a few. And while he didn't have exact numbers, the total added up to something like twenty or thirty capital ships, plus assorted cruisers, frigates, and destroyers. If he could add a dozen ships of his own, with the element of surprise they could defeat Lucius and Goutain.

He was a soldier, not a politician, but he realized it was time to start thinking like one. Time to be proactive. Time to decide what needed doing, then see that it was done. For the first time he thought he saw a way to win this war that was not really a war. But it would be dangerous, for if any hint or rumor of his complicity were to make it back to the king or any of the Ten, it would be disastrous. Any coalition he formed would fall apart without him, and they'd know that. Goutain or Nadama wouldn't hesitate to pay him a visit at Starfall and drop a few salvos of large warheads on the place, then claim ignorance of the whole incident afterward. He'd be radioactive vapor, and they'd be victorious conquerors.

It occurred to him that there was one piece of the equation missing: the mysterious Kinathin home world, where aging breeds were reputed to retire. For all he knew they didn't have any ships, were just a planet full of peaceful old pensioners. He'd still like to put the question to them, so he tried one last time to broach the subject with Add and Ell. As always, they ignored him and changed the subject.

But with or without the breeds—and even with all of these meetings and plans running through his head—it still wasn't clear to him whether he could actually put such a coalition together. And in the end, he wasn't sure if this had been a wasted trip or not.

CHAPTER 21
COUNTERFEIT LEADER

Soon, a fair number of ships would be docking at Andyne-Borregga to take advantage of its facilities. There would be spacers on shore leave wandering its corridors, and without some form of entertainment, that could become a big problem. As Momma Toofat had said any number of times, "Spacers want girls, booze, gambling, and food, or they get bored. And bored spacers are bad for everyone." So Charlie stopped at Tachaann and cut a deal with Momma to be entertainment coordinator on Andyne-Borregga. She'd open a place or two there herself, and arrange for some of her peers to do the same. She didn't mind the competition because, as entertainment coordinator, she would be allowed to collect franchise fees from the other proprietors. Charlie left Tachaann with one less thing to worry about.

In his small, private cabin on *The Headsman*, Charlie

racked his brains to determine if he'd done anything different the last time he'd gone down to the blind corridor. Darmczek had given him a junior officer's berth, since Charlie refused to displace one of the senior officers. It had a small fold-down desk, and Charlie sat there replaying over and over again the last time he'd gone down to the blind corridor. He hadn't been fully dressed, had just thrown a bathrobe over his underwear, and that was certainly different because previously he'd always been fully clothed. But why would the corridor not respond because of a bathrobe? And it wasn't as if there was something special about the clothing he'd worn; he was certain he'd worn something different almost every time he'd gone down there. So why had the corridor not responded last time?

Darmczek's voice interrupted his thoughts. "Your Grace, we're about ten minutes out from down-transition."

"Thank you, Captain. I'll be right up."

Charlie stood, checked his image in a small mirror, and adjusted his tunic and the wiring for the visual distortion field generator embedded in it. He switched the field on and his image in the mirror changed to that of a middle-aged man, dark hair with gray at the temples, brown eyes, thin tight lips, unsmiling. They'd worked carefully on this image and the persona that would accompany it: Edwin Chevard, a fictitious name, man, and personality.

Charlie switched the distortion field off and his own face reappeared. He left the small cabin, marched down the hall, and climbed the ladder to the cramped confines of *The Headsman*'s bridge. Oddly enough, he was more comfortable in a man-of-war where space was doled out sparingly. Darmczek had reserved one of the redundant navigation consoles for Charlie, and as he sat down and strapped in he felt that odd tingle in the back of his mind that told him they'd just down-transited.

Out of habit, Charlie watched the navigational information build on his screen as shipboard instruments gathered data about nearby space. "Clear to a hundred thousand kilometers, sir," the young navigator seated next to Charlie said.

"Drones out," Darmczek barked, and *The Headsman*'s hull thrummed as she launched her navigational drones. With the drones providing a wider baseline and increased resolution, the navigational data built even more rapidly. No ships in their immediate vicinity, but a couple of transition wakes inbound at three light-years.

"Sir, we've got an incoming signal from a ship at about one light-year," the com tech advised.

"Pass it to me," Darmczek said, and as always his words sounded more like a growl.

Charlie had to lean slightly to one side to see Darmczek through the maze of consoles and instrument clusters. He saw Darmczek's lips move as he spoke through his implants, then he heard Darmczek's voice in his own implants. "Your Grace, the Lady Ethallan."

Ethallan's face appeared on Charlie's screen. Unlike

the last time they'd met, a certain strain had etched crow's feet about the corners of her eyes now. She nodded politely. "Your Grace, I've arranged the meeting as you requested, though my colleagues are distrustful. And, as you requested, I kept your identity to myself."

"Thank you. You know full well that if the king or any of the Ten hear even a rumor of my complicity with FAR, I'm a dead man."

"I fully understand, Your Grace. They're here to meet Edwin Chevard, an old friend and business associate of mine. Though my man Kierson has been with me long enough to know all of my long-term associates, so he's somewhat suspicious of the Chevard identity. But I'm confident he doesn't suspect a disguise, and I've dropped some veiled hints that we were lovers when much younger. In any case, he's loyal and I'm confident he'll be discreet. I do hope you have some good news. The resistance is losing its vigor through attrition and lack of supplies."

"I too hope I bring good news," he said. "We've spotted two transition wakes incoming. Are those your colleagues?"

"I believe so, but we won't know for certain until they down-transit."

Ethallan signed off and the waiting began. Another hour passed before the two ships down-transited, and like Ethallan and *The Headsman*, they chose a position about a half light-year short of the rendezvous coordinates. Caution was the word of the day.

They detected a number of encrypted transmissions between Ethallan and the two new arrivals, then Ethallan contacted *The Headsman* and confirmed that the two ships were her colleagues. All four ships then carefully executed a short transition hop to within a hundred million kilometers of each other. Further maneuvering brought them to within one million kilometers. Again, paranoid caution ruled all.

After tracking the emission signatures on the three ships, Darmczek was satisfied *The Headsman* could outgun them. Of course, that was obvious to them as well, and they'd probably noted that she emitted a characteristic Syndonese emission profile, all of which would make the two newcomers quite nervous. Over Darmczek's objections, Charlie agreed to shuttle over to Ethallan's destroyer-class yacht where they'd all meet.

As Charlie stepped out of *The Headsman*'s gunboat into the small hangar bay of her yacht, she stood nearby to greet him, Kierson standing beside her, two men and a woman standing behind her eyeing him suspiciously. The visual distortion field projected Edwin Chevard's image across Charlie's features, and a programmable vocal implant disguised his voice.

"Edwin," Ethallan said, playing her role beautifully. "My dear Edwin, it's been too long."

Since Edwin Chevard, to all appearances, was of an age with Ethallan, she had come up with the idea that Chevard should flirt lightly with her. So Charlie bowed deeply, kissed her hand as she proffered it, straightened, and said, "All you need do is marry me, dear lady, and I'll cling to your side like your most devoted servant."

She laughed and Charlie found her incredibly attractive in that moment. "You're as shameless as always. Let me introduce you to some friends of mine."

She turned, and with her hand resting lightly on Charlie's arm, escorted him to the woman and two men. Ethallan had provided pictures and briefed him carefully on the three. As she introduced each of them, Charlie reviewed what he'd learned about them.

Colonel Therman Tarlo was tall and handsome and cut quite the dashing figure in his military uniform, complete with gold-braided epaulettes. It was all polish, though, since he was a mediocre military officer at best, put in charge of the resistance's modest combat forces out of necessity when he was much better suited to a peacetime administrative job. But apparently Tarlo was quite aware of his own limitations and let his subordinates, who were better strategists, tell him what to do. Charlie could respect that.

Sandeman Dirkas was a short, fat man, the top of his partially bald head covered in a fine down of hair, his brown business suit rumpled and unkempt. He was the politician, could be quite a firebrand, but more in a calculating way as opposed to a fanatic. His greatest contribution was that he knew how to speak to crowds. Ethallan said he hid behind the image of a rabble-rouser, but was actually more pragmatic when getting the job done, and an expert at cutting back-room deals.

Last was Thea Somal, a frumpy, middle-aged
woman with motherly, grayish-brown hair styled in
an unflattering bob. Like the others, her looks belied
her; she was, in fact, a savvy businesswoman who had
amassed a considerable fortune through her own efforts, and was responsible for much of the resistance's
financing. And while much of her support stemmed
from the fact that Lucius's annexation of Aagerbanne
was seriously hurting her financial interests, it was a
motive Charlie could trust.

They shook hands and exchanged a few pleasantries
before Ethallan led them to her study—a small, private
office that made exorbitant use of space on what was
actually a destroyer disguised as a yacht. While Ethallan served them snifters of brandy, Somal asked Charlie, "So, Mr. Chevard, how long have you known Lady
Ethallan?"

Charlie smiled at her. "We were close friends when
we were much younger, when we were students. Unfortunately, our various responsibilities have meant
that our friendship must endure great distances and
almost continuous separation."

Dirkas asked gruffly, "You're Toellani?"

Charlie sipped his brandy and shook his head. "I
was born in the Realm, but my father had some difficulty with one of Lucius's ambitions, so for many years
now I've called Toellan home."

Tarlo sat down in an expensive looking antique
chair. "I thought I heard the Realm in your voice. And

as to difficulty with Lucius's ambitions, we do seem to share that in common."

Charlie smiled, and purposefully made it an unpleasant smile. "Yes, the enemy-of-mine-enemy thing."

"Is that why we're here?" Dirkas asked. "Because we share a common enemy?"

Charlie shrugged. "In a sense. Let's just say that Lucius's newest ambition is causing considerable difficulty in certain interests of mine."

Ethallan had told Charlie that such a position would resonate nicely with Somal. "So you think we can find common cause?" the businesswoman asked.

Charlie sipped his brandy. "In some areas, yes. I can't provide capital ships or combat troops, not directly. I can't act that openly. On the other hand I've begun a small commercial venture in the Borreggan system that you might find advantageous."

"Borreggan system," Dirkas said. "Never heard of it." He looked to the others one at a time, and each shrugged or shook their head to indicate that they too had never heard of the system.

Charlie continued. "I'm not surprised. Borregga is a gas giant, with no habitable planets, a bit out of the way, but still conveniently accessible."

Somal asked, "And what commercial venture do you have there that'll be of interest to us?"

Charlie smiled at her. "I'm a significant investor in a space station there named Andyne, orbiting the primary. It's a large space station, with a shipyard fully capable of supplying, outfitting, and repairing capital ships. Including armaments."

Tarlo's eyes focused on Charlie as he continued. "Andyne-Borregga is a free port, and its operations staff will not discriminate against any ship because of type or registry . . . although Syndonese ships might find themselves a bit put off by our hospitality," he added with a smile. The others smiled back for a moment, but the mood turned somber again. Charlie continued.

"I've heard that you've been having difficulty of late. That you have ships playing a role in certain disputes, but they can't put into a normal port for supply and repairs. I've heard that your efforts are faltering because of that, and some of you fear you may not be able to continue the struggle. Let me assure you, those ships will be welcome at Andyne-Borregga."

Tarlo looked at Somal and Dirkas and said, "This is exactly what we've needed. This could make the difference."

Charlie spread his hands in a gesture of helpless submission. "Andyne-Borregga is, however, a commercial operation, so nothing is free."

Somal eyed Charlie and spoke cautiously. "Financing of repairs and refitting can be arranged . . . if the prices are reasonable."

Charlie nodded. "It's not in my best interests to gouge you. I need Andyne-Borregga to at least break even, and if you're even partially successful against Lucius and his Syndonese allies—well, we're back to the enemy-of-mine-enemy thing."

Dirkas said, "We also need weapons and armor for our troops." His words mirrored those of Cahntu's on Istanna. "Can you supply that?"

Charlie had anticipated that. "I had heard that your ground forces were faltering as well for lack of equipment, so I've already started some things in motion. I can supply the arms, and introduce you to the ships and smugglers needed to run the Syndonese blockade and deliver them to your people. Again, nothing is free. But since you need a myriad of services we might consider a long-term contract. I should be able to offer you a more attractive pricing structure because of the economies of scale involved."

Somal merely smiled and sipped her brandy.

"One other thing," Tarlo said. "We need experienced spacers, the military kind, not merchantmen. We're undermanned."

That was something Charlie hadn't anticipated, and so he had to think carefully. "I cannot supply such directly, but are you familiar with the men who were in the Syndonese prison camps with the de Maris bastard?"

"The Two Thousand," Somal said.

"Exactly! With the death of Cesare and the disappearance of his first son, Arthur, most refuse to support the new heir to the de Maris ducal seat. There are a few hundred stranded on Andyne-Borregga, working at menial tasks. Given their historical dislike for your enemy, I'd think you'd have no trouble recruiting them. And I have ways of spreading the word to others that if they make their way to Andyne-Borregga, they'll get a chance to fight the Syndonese." Even as he said it, Charlie was thinking that he'd make sure they made their way to the space station.

Somal smiled. "Mr. Chevard, I think we might get along famously."

"That's all I can ask for."

They hammered out the details of an agreement and Charlie returned to *The Headsman* not soon after. With grim determination, they set course for Turnlee and the Almsburg Palace.

CHAPTER 22
NO LOVE LOST

"It's beautiful, isn't it?" Delilah said to Lady Carristan. They were walking in the south rose garden on a lovely spring day, and it felt good just to be out enjoying the flowers and the sun. She plucked a small nasturtium, turned to Carristan, and handed it to her.

Carristan looked pleased at the flower, but, facing Delilah, her eyes suddenly focused over Delilah's shoulder, and she frowned.

"Delilah, my love."

Del turned at the sound of Dieter's voice and found him closing the space between them with long, purposeful strides. "Dieter, how nice to see you," she lied. She couldn't leave her chambers without him shadowing her every move; he insisted on monopolizing her time. She'd even resorted to sneaking out of her chambers upon occasion, like today, but he had an uncanny way of finding her.

Dieter marched up to them, waved a hand at Carristan, and said arrogantly, "Delilah no longer needs you. You may go."

As Carristan curtsied and turned to leave, Delilah wanted to shout, *I'll be the judge of when I no longer need her*, but she bit her tongue, smiled at Dieter, and tried to fake some modicum of warmth. Somehow she had to make this work. Her father and mother had hammered that into her head almost daily. Lucius had squandered his support among the Ten, and now desperately needed Nadama's backing.

For a moment Charlie crossed her mind, and not for the first time she wished she'd been born into a simpler life.

Dieter watched Carristan's back as she walked hurriedly away. "Once we're wed, I think we'll have to replace her."

Delilah had had enough. "I think not," she said, unable to disguise her anger.

"Oh, my darling, I've upset you." He leaned down and gave her a chaste kiss on the cheek. "You're fond of her, I know, but she's not appropriate. You shouldn't worry about such things. I'll handle staffing issues."

Her anger had come to a full boil. "She's not *staff*, and *I'll* choose my own ladies-in-waiting."

He looked at her coldly. "No, you won't." He took her hand, forced her to put it on his arm, and said, "Come. Let's walk. It's such a fine day."

The only way she could resist would be to make a horrible scene, so she held her silence and walked beside him, seething with anger.

I'll make this work, she told herself. *Somehow.*

Charlie struggled to remain awake as the ambassador from god-knew-where droned on about the merits and virtues of Lucius and the royal family. The staff of the Almsburg Palace had remodeled the gallery where the Nine had previously sat in the Great Throne Room, adjusting the seating so it now accommodated the Ten. Unfortunately, that put Charlie clearly on display, whereas previously, with no more status than that of a common soldier, he stood in the throng at the far end of the hall, and could even slip out if he knew they wouldn't call on him.

He turned his head slightly to his right for a glance at the other nine dukes and duchesses. Rierma's head had bowed forward, his chin almost on his chest, his eyes closed; Rierma could get away with that. Theode picked at his fingernails, a smug, bored look on his face. Interestingly enough, there'd been no open talk of Arthur's disappearance, though rumors of every imaginable scenario circulated constantly.

"Little brother," Add whispered in his ear. Charlie cocked his head slightly to indicate he was listening. "If this fool ambassador doesn't finish soon, I'll probably fall asleep on my feet, then tumble forward onto you. Can you catch me?"

Charlie chuckled and whispered, "As you and Ell like to remind me, I'm probably too short."

"That you are, little brother."

Charlie suddenly realized that Lucius was saying something. Apparently, the ambassador from god-knew-where had finally finished and Lucius was thanking him for his gracious speech. The ambassador bowed, backed away, and returned to the diplomatic gallery. As far as Charlie knew, that was the last order of business for the formal court.

Lucius stood and raised his hands for silence. "I have one last item of business not on the agenda," he said. One of the other dukes must have visibly rolled his eyes or something, because Lucius quickly added, "No, I shan't delay you further, just a brief, joyful announcement."

He looked to Adan. She stood and took her place beside him. "It gives Adan and I great pleasure to announce the betrothal of our daughter, Delilah, to Lord Dieter, heir to the de Satarna ducal seat." Delilah, standing behind and to one side of Adan, looked pale and sick, though not surprised. "The marriage contracts have been signed, and properly recorded in the canonical registry."

There were no great cheers or shouts of joy, merely a polite round of applause in which Charlie of course participated. The longer the applause sounded, the paler Delilah's complexion grew.

Charlie had sent a page to Del's chambers with a note asking if she'd receive him, fully expecting to be rejected much as before. But to his surprise, the page returned with a positive response and a specified time later that afternoon when he should come.

He was careful to be prompt, knocking on the door to her chambers at exactly the appointed hour. Lady Carristan answered just as promptly. "Your Grace," she said, curtsying, then backing away carefully. "Her Highness is expecting you."

Carristan led him into a large sitting room. Delilah stood at the far end of the room looking out a window, her back to him. She wore a long spring dress with swirls of lavender colored lace. Carristan backed out of the room, though she left the door open so no one could claim the Duke de Lunis had been in the presence of the princess with no chaperone in attendance. Delilah didn't turn to acknowledge him.

Charlie couldn't think of what else to say, so he tried, "Is it Del or Delilah?"

She turned and gave him an almost shy smile. "You know, Del only exists when you're around."

He crossed the room, but stopped several feet short of her. "I'm so sorry . . . for treating you the way I did. I had the facts all wrong."

She shrugged a little and smiled more openly. "And I took some pleasure in rubbing your nose in it. But I've had time to cool down, and Lady Carristan helped me see . . . how you might have interpreted the circumstances the way you did." Her eyes darted upward right and left, a repeat of the furtive gesture he'd seen before.

He said, "And Carristan told me you're being watched closely."

She shrugged. "It was naughty of me to run away and hide, and to consort with undesirable individuals."

"So you'll forgive me for being an idiot?"

Shaking her head, still smiling, she said, "You men are always such fools. Of course I forgive you."

"I didn't ask your forgiveness for being a fool, rather for being an idiot, which I'll try not to do again. But I fully intend to continue making a fool of myself over a beautiful woman."

The smile disappeared. "Not over me. I'm betrothed."

"So you'll marry Dieter?"

"I must," she said. "Nadama is too powerful, and my father says he needs continuing support from de Satarna." She turned again to look out the window.

Charlie thought of the scenario Arthur had outlined for him some time ago: Dieter marries Delilah, Lucius dies in the not-too-distant future, and heirless Martino has an accident. It was all too plausible, and all too easy.

But Charlie could change that, and he'd thought carefully about his next move. He had the legal authority to determine Delilah's choice of a husband, a right purchased properly long ago. All he need do was bring it to the attention of the rest of the Ten, and the betrothal of Delilah and Dieter would instantly be null and void. There would certainly be some sort of recriminations, for he'd seriously anger Nadama and Goutain, either of which could squash him if it came to that. And his motives would also be questioned, but now—as a member of the Ten—he was less concerned about that. What mattered was what Del wanted.

"What if there was a way," he asked, choosing his words carefully, "a way that you wouldn't have to marry Dieter if you didn't want to? What if there was a proper and legal means to force Nadama and your father, without question, to nullify the betrothal? Do you want to marry Dieter?"

As she stood looking out the window he could see the back of her neck, her shoulders, her face turned ever so slightly so that he had a glancing view of one cheek, and a single tear that rolled down to her chin. She wiped it away with a finger.

"I'm not merely asking an academic question," he persisted. "What would you want done?"

Her shoulders rose as she took a deep breath and let it out slowly. She spoke carefully. "I came to realize long ago that I was nothing more than property of the crown, and that I'd be married off in a way that was good for the crown. Forgive me for being crude, but I'm valued only for my womb and whatever alliance it might attract. And I've come to accept that, though I don't necessarily like it. But there was always the schoolgirl's hope that I might get lucky, find someone who'd satisfy the needs of both love and state. Or failing that, someone who satisfied the needs of state now, and who might grow in time to satisfy the needs of love. Alas, that's not come to pass. But to marry Dieter, that is my fate and I accept it willingly, though not gladly."

She turned back to face him, and he wanted to hold her, somehow make it all better. "If such a way truly existed, I think it best if it never came to light. What I want is of no import here. What I must do is fulfill my duty as a member of the royal family. I've been trained for that all my life."

It was Charlie's turn to hesitate. He could make his own decision, ignore her and try to convince himself that he knew what was best for her. But somehow he knew she would never forgive him for such an act.

He bowed deeply. "As you wish, Your Highness." He straightened, turned, and left the room.

"What was the whoreson doing here?"

Delilah jumped at the sound of Dieter's shout. She'd been staring out at the garden, wondering if she'd made the right decision, changing her mind back and forth, but in the end, she knew she must do her duty.

She turned to face Dieter and said coldly, "He's a friend. And he came to wish me joy of our union."

"Tried to talk you out of it, more likely," Dieter said.

She dared not let Dieter realize how close he was to the truth; he had a nasty streak in him. "Why would he do that?"

"Because he's a mongrel who pretends at nobility, and he wants the crown for himself."

"He's every bit as noble as anyone else in this room, though I'm beginning to think he's more so, and I'll not stand here while you insult him. And what do you mean by *wants the crown for himself*? That sounds as if you believe that by marrying me the crown will be yours, when in fact it'll be Martino's at my father's passing."

Dieter's eyes flashed with guilt, like a child caught in the act of stealing a sweet. He clumsily tried to avoid her question. "You imply that he's nobler than me?"

She saw it now, and she absolutely wouldn't let him evade her. "I asked you a question and you'll answer me. What does my marriage have to do with the crown?"

"Is something wrong, Your Highness?"

Dieter turned at the sound of Carristan's voice. She stood in the doorway behind him, and when he saw her he stormed toward her, clearly in a rage. Her eyes widened fearfully and she backed away. "Out of here, woman," he snarled, his voice sounding like the growl of a predatory animal. "Get out of here." She backed away a step and he slammed the door in her face.

"Don't you speak to her that way!" Now, in private, Del was free to shout at him in turn.

He turned and marched back to her, small bits of spittle flying as he shouted at her. "I'll speak to her any way I want. And you'll start obeying me as you properly should."

"Obey you?" she scoffed. "I don't know what kind of

marriage you think this is going to be, but if you think you're going to get an obedient servant for a wife—"

His face reddened and he lunged toward her, reached out, and grabbed her upper arm in a painful grip. "Don't ever countermand me."

"Let go of me," she said. "You're hurting me."

"This isn't hurting you. When I want to hurt you I'll—"

"Release me, you arrogant pig."

She wouldn't have thought his face could redden further, but it turned absolutely crimson. Then he raised his hand up and back, and she realized he was going to strike her.

"Your Highness!"

Carristan's squeak surprised them both and they froze. With his hand still poised to strike her, Dieter looked over his shoulder. "That woman again."

He released Del, spun, and marched toward Carristan, pointing at the door and shouting, "Get out, get out."

"Don't leave me alone with him," Del pleaded.

Carristan stood her ground, trembling with fear as Dieter towered over her shaking with fury.

"Get out," he snarled.

Carristan's voice wavered as she said, "No."

Dieter spun around, looked at Del with murderous hate, and in that moment she realized if Carristan did leave, she would be in true danger.

"Lady Carristan," Del said, "please don't leave. And Dieter, please *do* leave." It took all her willpower to keep this polite, to not simply yell until the palace guards descended on them. The poor guardsmen would be caught between the heir to one of the most powerful ducal seats and a hysterical royal princess. And all that would come of it would be a nasty scene and embarrassment for them all. Only the mantra *For my father, for my family . . .* kept her in check.

Dieter stood there for a moment, his anger radiating outward like heat from a white-hot cutting torch. Then he spun and marched toward Carristan and the door. If she hadn't skipped aside at the last moment he would have run right into her and knocked her to the floor. She continued to back away as he walked past her, and he slammed the door on his way out.

"**W**hat do you mean by insurgents?" Goutain growled, his voice almost a whisper. "We don't have insurgents in Syndon."

General Tantin knew the symptoms all too well. When Goutain shouted he was to be feared, certainly, but shouting rarely ended with loss of life. However, when the shouting ended, or even worse, when there was no shouting at all, when his voice dropped into that cold, angry growl, someone was going to die. And it was up to Tantin to make certain it was not him. "Yes, Your Excellency. Insurgents indeed! They blew up a local electrical distribution station. And though I confess I've only just been informed of this, last tenday they executed an armed assault on the local security facility, killing half the security forces there. They seem to be organized somewhere in the Rawda Slum."

"Insurgents," Goutain whispered. "Rebels, defying me?"

Goutain had had to return to the Republic for this, and Tantin knew someone would pay a price for that. The president sat behind his desk in the Presidential Residence staring straight ahead, his eyes focused on nothing and his thoughts apparently turned inward. Now was the moment to give him a target for his anger. "Yes, Your Excellency. But most disturbing of all is that it's been going on now for quite some time, and we've not heard about it. I fear that the captain of the local security forces in charge of Rawda has been lenient regarding his charges, and covering up the fact that his indulgence is allowing an escalation of this violence. I'm investigating now and should have a better understanding of the situation before the end of the tenday."

"Don't investigate," Goutain growled. "Execute the fool. Execute him and one tier of officers below him. Then replace them and sweep Rawda clean."

"We haven't yet identified the exact location of the insurgents and their headquarters, Your Excellency."

Goutain shook his head. "I said sweep Rawda clean. Burn it. Kill enough of them and you'll kill the insurgents with them."

He would have struck me," Del said.

Her mother listened calmly, though, seated on one

of the sofas in her private chamber, she was more interested in reviewing arrangements for the betrothal party. Del had quietly dismissed Adan's servants and ladies-in-waiting so they could speak privately. Adan rolled her eyes, looked at Del, and shook her head. "Don't be melodramatic, child. He is your betrothed and you had an argument that got out of hand."

Del was too angry to shout or plead or cry, angry with Dieter and angry with her parents. She'd gotten the same reaction from her father. She spoke barely above a whisper. "Damn it, he would have hit me if Carristan hadn't returned."

Adan stood abruptly, faced Del, and grabbed her by both shoulders. "Keep your voice down," she snarled. "You'll speak of this to no one. This marriage is too important for you to endanger it with wild accusations. I care not if your future husband lacks a gentle hand. You'll marry him, and you'll smile, and if all you can do is pretend at joy when you go to your marriage bed, then you'll do that too. Do you understand me, girl?"

Del hadn't expected anything better from her mother, and she chided herself for even bothering to bring it up. Both Adan and Lucius were desperate to see this marriage happen. "Yes, mother, I understand."

Her mother let go of her, sat down, and returned to her plans for the party. "Next time, don't disagree with him. Let him have his way."

Del thought, but did not say, *There won't be a next time.*

CHAPTER 23
TOO MANY DECEITS

As parties went, Charlie thought the betrothal gala rather dull. Queen Adan had spared no expense and was clearly enjoying herself. The festivities had begun with an elegant banquet. Dieter and Nadama sat with the royal family at the head table, with the remainder of the Ten seated at tables nearby, all on a raised dais. Two hundred guests sat at tables on the main floor, surrounding a large open space where an orchestra provided pleasant background music to accompany the dinner conversation. Dieter sat next to Del, and she seemed distracted. She just toyed with her food, merely shoved it around on her plate, took an occasional bite, and appeared joyless and unhappy.

Goutain was absent this time around, called back to Syndon for some reason, though his Syndonese thugs wandered about everywhere. Rumor had it that a growing insurgency in Syndon itself had created considerable difficulty for Goutain's Security Force, and Goutain had returned to personally clean up the mess. That was the first real justification Charlie had heard for the amount of small arms and other supplies the hunter-killers were delivering to Sobak and Thamaklus.

Displaying a truly sadistic streak, Adan had seated Charlie at a table with Theode and Gaida. Whenever she spoke to him she had to address him as "Your Grace," and each time she looked as if she'd swallowed something unpleasant. Charlie understood fully: her rank within the aristocracy, as the wife of a deceased duke and the mother of a presently seated duke, was still beneath that of Charlie, a seated duke. It had to rankle.

It was one of the few times, in her presence, he had reason to smile. But he kept his expression neutral.

At one of the many lulls in the conversation, Charlie asked Theode, "Any luck yet with the pirates who kidnapped our brother?"

Theode glanced Gaida's way before answering. "We're negotiating with them now. But that scum of a Syndonese pirate is impossible."

Charlie knew the truth of it. It had become clear that Theode was just as happy to have Arthur out of the way. He had no desire to see the negotiations come to fruition. If a bunch of filthy pirates held Arthur indefinitely, or perhaps even murdered him, Theode could wash his hands of the whole matter.

Telka joined them and all the men stood. Not as

traditionally beautiful as Gaida, Charlie still found the plump little woman decidedly attractive, certainly more so than Gaida's sharp-edged beauty. Telka held her hand out to Charlie. He bowed and kissed it properly. "Your Grace," he said. "You grow more beautiful every day."

She chortled and shook her head. "You sound like that old reprobate Rierma."

Theode reached out to take her hand, but she snubbed him by sitting down and ignoring him. Since Theode had sided with Nadama, Lucius, and Goutain, and she'd lost her heir in the matter, her impartiality had shifted decidedly. She did give him a nod, and a cold acknowledgment, "Your Grace."

Protocol did not require her to even recognize Gaida, but she did so without title. "Gaida," she said, almost a slap in the face.

She turned to Charlie and beamed a smile at him. "So, Charlie, you must visit sometime. You'll be most welcome."

"I look forward to it," he said.

"Beware, Your Grace," Theode said. "He's near destitute. He'll probably steal your silverware. If his whore-of-a-mother were still alive—"

Gaida lurched slightly and Theode started. Apparently she'd kicked him under the table.

Telka reached up and ran a finger lightly along Charlie's chin. "Well, his whore-of-a-mother must have been quite beautiful to produce such a handsome young man. Not to mention stealing Cesare's heart. It's said she was the only woman he ever truly loved."

Telka turned a malicious smile on Theode and Gaida. "Tell me, Theode. What of these Syndonese pirates?"

"As you know, they kidnapped my brother," he said, though his indignation didn't ring true. "And I've lost four merchant cargoes in the past month. What of you?"

"I've lost some too," she said, though Charlie knew that was a lie.

Darmczek had had considerable success using the Syndonese warship in league with the new hunter-killers. He continued the tactic of using the hunter-killers to get in close, unseen, then disable a vessel and disappear, while *The Headsman*, a ship of obvious Syndonese make, took visible credit for a lucky or cunning shot. But Charlie's shadow fleet targeted only Nadama, Theode, Karlok, Goutain, and Lucius's shipping. Telka must be trying to avoid suspicion by claiming losses of her own.

Telka said, "I hear Goutain has lost three capital ships to the resistance. One was found hulled and gutted, only a few survivors in lifeboats."

That was news to Charlie. He was only aware of having taken *Sachanee* and converting it to *The Headsman*, and she was a heavy cruiser, not a capital ship.

Theode added, "And only last tenday Nadama lost an entire shipment of military supplies, some heavy weaponry included."

More information Charlie hadn't known. It sounded like Darmczek had been quite busy.

"It's this growing resistance around Aagerbanne," Telka said.

"I don't believe that for a second," Theode said. "I think it's this Mexak League. These Syndonese pirates are much better organized than we thought."

The servants served dessert as a troupe of acrobats joined the orchestra on the floor below them. They all turned to watch and for a time the conversation died. In any case, there wasn't anything of substance they could discuss with Gaida and Theode present. Telka and Charlie spoke of trivialities, and Theode tried to throw out the occasional insult, more to Gaida's embarrassment than Charlie's. He'd learned long ago to simply ignore Twerp, and even though his standing as a duke made it possible to consider responding, he knew that by simply showing restraint, he appeared more noble than Theode.

After the banquet, everyone adjourned to the grand ballroom for polite music, polite dancing, and polite chatter. Charlie thought longingly of his time with the trampsies, who knew how to throw a real party. His mood had also turned melancholy; he really didn't want Del to marry Dieter. He'd thought about it quite a bit and had come up with all sorts of proper political reasons why the union should not take place. But he knew in his heart that such reasoning was actually specious justification for his own feelings. And watching her stand beside Dieter, her back stiff and her face expressionless, he could only think that now he'd probably never have that dance with her.

For the gala she wore a floor length gown of a shimmering pale blue material with embroidered highlights here and there. It was cut to emphasize her figure, cut low enough to expose a bit of cleavage, but not so low as to be provocative. Her hair had been piled elaborately atop her head with the sparkle of small jewels among the curls, but the sparkle had abandoned her eyes. She looked his way, caught him staring at her, and pulled her arm loose from Dieter—actually had to tug a bit forcefully to break loose from his grip. All eyes in the room followed her progress as she marched purposefully, almost angrily, across the floor toward Charlie. She stopped in front of him and faced him squarely. Dieter glared at her but didn't move.

Charlie bowed carefully and she curtsied, saying softly, "No longer the penniless bastard, eh, Your Grace? But I think my father will still disapprove of my dancing with you."

He shrugged and said, "But I'm still penniless. Certainly you must have heard that the de Lunis is near destitute."

She smiled and the sparkle returned to her eyes. "But since Cesare acknowledged you in his will, you're no longer a bastard."

He gave her an evil grin. "I'll always be a bastard, in one way or another."

The sparkle left her eyes and she frowned. "Not nearly as much as others I know."

At that moment the band began a nice, staid waltz. Charlie bowed. "May I have the pleasure?"

She held out her hand and he escorted her onto the dance floor, put his right hand in the small of her back and held her at the appropriate distance. They danced almost woodenly. "You're not having fun," he said.

"I had an argument with my mother, and it soured my evening."

"I was under the impression that mothers and daughters argued frequently."

She breathed an exasperated sigh, and he sensed there was much more to it than a simple argument. Physically holding her like this, it was clear she almost trembled with suppressed anger. She looked at him mischievously and said, "And we'll probably argue again tomorrow about the brazen way I've chosen to dance with you."

"Ah, but I'm one of the Ten, and by custom you must dance at least one dance with each of us. Is that not so?"

She gave him a conspiratorial grin. "But this isn't the kind of dance Del had in mind when she promised one to her spacer."

"What kind of dance did Del have in mind?"

She laughed. "Something lively, not a staid and polite waltz. Maybe even . . . in a crazy place like a trampsie bar."

The music ended and she lingered in his arms for a moment. The smile disappeared from her face, she turned serious, and said, "But we're never going to have that dance, are we?"

Dieter appeared almost magically behind her. Without acknowledging Charlie he said, "My dear, come. You should dance with my father."

She stepped out of his arms. Charlie bowed. She curtsied, turned, and walked away with Dieter.

Charlie spied Rierma across the room with an elegant blonde on his arm. He walked over to them, and said to Rierma, "Your Grace."

"Charles, my boy," he said happily, then leaned forward and whispered, "That robot Nadama is pissing his pants that he didn't get to dance with her first."

"I hope it doesn't come back on her," Charlie said.

The blonde smiled at him. "Your Grace," she said, curtsying deeply. She was a beautiful woman, pale blond hair, blue eyes, expensive floor length gown cut provocatively low in the front, not cheaply done, but still hinting at a graceful seductiveness with which few women in the room could compete.

Since Rierma didn't immediately offer to introduce them, Charlie said, "I'm sorry, My Lady, but you seem to have the advantage of me."

She smiled knowingly. "I think not, Your Grace. Surely you remember me."

Charlie racked his brains, didn't want to insult Rierma by insulting the woman. "Again, I must apologize, but I don't recall having met before."

She smiled and frowned. "I do believe you truly don't recognize me."

She looked at Rierma and he grinned back at her as if they shared some hidden joke. She leaned forward, whispered in Charlie's ear in the street accent of the trampsies, "Frankie, was you asleep the whole time at Momma's?"

Charlie literally took an involuntary step back, looked at her carefully, and it all fell into place: Sally Wantsalot. "Sally!" he said. She smiled at him.

Rierma corrected him. "May I introduce the Lady Sally, Charles, my grandniece? She has come to comfort an old man in his final years."

Charlie looked at the old duke. "Final years, my ass. You're probably going to be around longer than me."

Rierma grinned, looked at Sally, and Charlie could see sincere fondness in his eyes. Rierma said, "But she is a comfort to an old man."

Sally looked back at the old man with the same fondness, and she spoke again without any trace of the street accent. "And he's good to me, Your Grace."

Behind Rierma stood one of his retainers, dressed in de Neptair livery and hovering discreetly in the shadows at the edge of the room. Now that Charlie knew what to look for, he recognized him easily. "Is that Stan Fourhands?"

Rierma grinned. "I believe that's his name."

Charlie said, "Excuse me, Your Grace, Lady Sally."

He walked over to Stan and asked, "How's the pickings?"

Stan shrugged unhappily. "Pretty good." Like the rest of the trampsies he could drop the accent when needed. "It would be better if the old fellow—" he nodded toward Rierma, "—gave me free rein. As it is he'll only let me take from those Nadama and Dieter fellows, and of course from your stepbrother and his mother. And Sally told me if I disobey him she'll cut my balls off."

"Theode and Gaida?"

Stan grinned happily. "Ya, but I do get to rob them blind."

Where Stan went, Nano was usually nearby. "Is Nano here, with *Goldisbest*?"

Stan just smiled. "He's keeping a low profile, doesn't want to be seen."

That meant Nano was setting up some sort of smuggling operation. Charlie turned back to Rierma and Sally, but Lady Carristan intercepted him before he reached them. "Your Grace," she said, curtsying deeply. "May I have a private word with you?"

Charlie asked, "Is there a message from Her Highness?"

Carristan glanced over her shoulder in the direction of Delilah. "No, Your Grace. She doesn't know I'm speaking with you."

Intrigued, Charlie said, "Where can we speak privately, then?"

"Please follow me," she said, then turned and walked away.

He followed at a discreet distance, and outside the ballroom she turned into a servant's entrance, stopped in a dark corridor where they were alone. "Forgive me for such intrigue," she whispered, "but I fear for Her Highness."

"How so?"

"They had an argument, and as I stepped into the room, I'm certain he would have struck her had I not arrived to interrupt him."

"You mean Delilah and Dieter?"

"Yes, Your Grace, he's an animal. And I think she's going to run away, but she has no place to run, except a distant cousin who can only return her to Lucius, or face the king's wrath."

Charlie's thoughts raced furiously. "I don't know what you expect of me, but I can't intervene, Lady Carristan. If I were to aid you, assist you, or advise you in any way that helped Delilah run away, I'd lose the immunity that comes with the ducal seat. And then I too would face the king's wrath."

She lowered her head tiredly and closed her eyes. "I don't know what to do."

"As I said, if I were to advise you inappropriately and you were put to the truth . . ." He was thinking of a deep neural probe, with which they could extract the exact wording of this conversation. " . . . both of us could come to great harm. Out of desperation you may be tempted to seek out certain disreputable characters for assistance, and that would be a terrible mistake. Certainly, you should stay away from the trampsies. You shouldn't seek out a trampsie merchantman named *Goldisbest*, which is, I believe, presently in-system."

Her eyes opened and her head lifted. She looked at him sharply and smiled.

They couldn't put Charlie under deep neural probe, not without clearly damning evidence. On the other hand, Carristan possessed no such immunity. But a neural probe was notoriously explicit, would reveal the exact phrasing of their conversation but not its intent. "And stay away from its captain, a decidedly nefarious character named Nano Neverlose, who can be reached through one of Rierma's retainers, a fellow named Stan Fourhands. He and his crew are disreputable sorts, suspected of smuggling and gunrunning. They'd probably do anything for the right price, so you should definitely not seek passage on *Goldisbest*. And Delilah shouldn't seek refuge with Lady Ethallan of Aagerbanne, who is in hiding as a result of the annexation."

She nodded. "We'll be careful not to do those things, Your Grace. Thank you for your sage advice. Your loyalty to the crown is most admirable."

Charlie returned to Stan Fourhands, pulled him aside, and spoke softly. "I need to speak with Nano right away. And if Her Royal Highness or the Lady Carristan approaches you, be sure to connect her with Nano. But don't tell Sally or Rierma or any of his staff. Rierma mustn't be involved in this, either directly or through Sally."

Stan reverted to his street accent and whispered, "Frankie, what's going on?"

"You'll know soon enough. And afterward you'll have to disappear. If they put you to the truth, they'll hang you. That's why Sally and Rierma can't know anything."

Stan spoke briefly to Rierma, made his excuses and left the ballroom.

"Little brother."

Charlie turned to find Add standing at his elbow. "Ell and I have someone we'd like you to meet."

"Now?" he asked. "I'm kind of busy."

"Now," she said. "It is very important."

The breed wasn't one to exaggerate. "All right, lead on."

He followed her out of the ballroom into a part of the palace reserved for diplomats and other foreign dignitaries. Add stopped at a particular door and knocked on it softly. Ell answered, saw Add and Charlie, nodded, and swung the door wide. Charlie preceded Add into a room filled with Kinathins, all standing and apparently waiting for him. He heard the door shut behind him with a loud clump.

There were Kinathins of every size and age, both male and female, though they were all tall, lean, and muscular, traits engineered into them purposefully. Charlie looked at Add and Ell and raised a questioning eyebrow. They both shrugged.

An older Kinathin woman stepped forward from the group. The Kinathins had been engineered with a high immunity to the effects of aging, at least until the last decade or two of their lives, and at that point they aged rapidly. The fact that Charlie could see crow's feet at the corners of her eyes meant she was quite old. She wore a military uniform with the emblems and livery of Harrimo's personal guard. In fact, the personal guards of several of the Ten were represented, though none from Karlok, Nadama, or Theode (who had replaced Add and Ell with mercenaries).

The older woman's right hand rested casually against her thigh. Her fingers twitched almost imperceptibly, in such a way that one would not notice it if one didn't know what to look for. She signaled to Add and Ell in breed handspeak, *Is he armed?*

Charlie didn't wait for them to answer, and made no effort to conceal his own use of handspeak. He signaled, *Of course I am.* Then he said in breed-tongue, "I'm not stupid, woman. Was I brought here for a purpose?"

The woman's eyes narrowed, which for a Kinathin was an extreme show of emotion. She spoke in standard. "Your Grace, you need not fear any harm."

Charlie smiled and softened his tone. "I know that. I have Add and Ell with me." The twins grinned.

The woman nodded a polite bow to Charlie. "Your Grace, we seem to have gotten off to a bad start. Let me apologize for assuming you were ignorant of our customs. I am Sal'mar'Reyhanna."

As a Kinathin grew and gained recognition for feats of bravery or service or something that Charlie wasn't quite clear on, they added syllables to the last part of their name, which meant the woman before Charlie held some highly elevated rank in the Kinathin class structure. But more importantly, Charlie recognized the middle part of the name. "I'm honored to meet an elder of Add and Ell's family. I value their friendship most highly."

She glanced at the others behind her. "Forgive me, but it would be best if we didn't formalize introductions for all here."

"I'm not sure I understand," Charlie said. "But I take no insult."

"Thank you, Your Grace. May I ask you one question?"

Charlie looked at Add and Ell, both of whom seemed intent on avoiding his eyes. "You may ask. I may not answer."

She smiled at that and nodded toward Add and Ell. "Why did you free them? You owned them. They'd have served you every bit as well without their freedom, and once freed they might have chosen not to serve you at all."

Charlie had to think carefully about that. He'd done it on impulse, and decided to be honest with Sal'mar'Reyhanna. "I didn't think it through at the time, so to be honest I can only guess at my motives. I think I did it because I grew up with them, was almost raised by them. They're my older sisters, you see, and I couldn't stand the thought of owning them. I guess if I truly think about it, I don't really like the thought of anyone owning someone. I've worn chains—real ones—but I can imagine what invisible ones feel like. If they were going to stay with me I wanted it to be because they wanted to."

Add threw in, "We stayed because you still need training, little brother. And I suspect it'll be a lifelong task."

Sal'mar'Reyhanna smiled. "Brother and sisters, eh?" She considered that for a long moment. "And you say you don't like the thought of anyone being owned?"

"Again, to be completely honest, I've had other important things on my mind lately. But if I'm forced to think about it, no, I don't like anyone being owned."

Again, she considered him for a long moment, then seemed to come to some sort of decision. "There is one other here whom you should meet."

She turned, looked behind her and an older Kinathin male stepped forward. "Your Grace," she said formally, "Charles, Duke de Lunis, may I present Sid'nah'sanAfan, ambassador and representative of the free system of Kinatha?"

Charlie was rather proud of the fact that he didn't start or flinch. "I must confess," he said, "that while I'm aware of the rumors—most of which are contradictory—I'm rather ignorant of the free system of Kinatha."

Sid'nah'sanAfan smiled a bit sheepishly. "We do try to keep a low profile, Your Grace. Tell me, are you aware of the custom of Abolition?"

"I am," Charlie said, choosing his words carefully. "After decades of loyal service it is not uncommon for a liege lord to free a Kinathin, give them a pension, and allow them to live out their lives in peace and comfort. I've always found it interesting that we've all heard so little about where they live out their lives."

Sal'mar'Reyhanna said, "Your Grace, perhaps we should confine this conversation to a smaller group."

Charlie shrugged and said, "Certainly."

Sal'mar'Reyhanna ushered the rest of the Kinathins out of the room, though Add and Ell hesitated, looking to Charlie for their cue. He raised an eyebrow in a question, and Add answered, "You're safe with them, little brother. Or rather, if you're not . . ." She looked pointedly at Sal'mar'Reyhanna. " . . . we'll hunt them all down and seek revenge."

Charlie nodded his assent and Add and Ell left, leaving Charlie alone with Sal'mar'Reyhanna and Sid'nah'sanAfan. Sal'mar'Reyhanna beckoned them to comfortable chairs and poured drinks for them. Sipping at his drink, Charlie asked, "Perhaps you could dispel some of my ignorance?"

Sid'nah'sanAfan gave him a diplomat's smile, and said, "A little over two hundred years ago a large group of freed Kinathins pooled their resources and colonized an unclaimed planet on the fringes of explored space. Its first inhabitants were mostly old pensioners, but as the centuries passed the population diversified in age, though it remained exclusively Kinathin and relatively isolated. Kinatha has considerable natural resources, boasts a healthy population, and a strong agricultural and industrial base."

"And why all the rumors?" Charlie asked. "Why have we heard so little of the reality of Kinatha?"

"During our developmental years we thought it wise to distance ourselves from the politics of our far-flung neighbors. But in recent years we've begun establishing diplomatic relations with nearby governments, initially with the independent states since they'd outlawed slavery long ago. Our approach to the Realm was more . . . cautious. At this time the Realm is the only state in which ownership of Kinathins is endemic and systematic. But last year we approached your king in the hope of establishing diplomatic relations. Lucius's initial reaction was to send a flotilla of five warships to impose his will on us breeds."

Charlie grimaced. "Not what you expected, eh?"

"On the contrary, Lucius's reaction was one of many we'd anticipated." He glanced at Sal'mar'Reyhanna. "We've been well advised by our colleagues here, and are aware of his proclivities. It was we who were not what Lucius expected. We are, after all, engineered to be warriors."

Sid'nah'sanAfan grinned. "The entire Kinathin system is heavily defended, and we met his force with more than thirty capital ships. The commander of Lucius's flotilla wisely recognized that force was not an option. Not a shot was fired, and to this day we all pretend that the flotilla was merely a diplomatic escort."

Charlie considered the two Kinathins carefully and asked, "Why are we having this conversation?"

Sid'nah'sanAfan and Sal'mar'Reyhanna exchanged glances, and apparently decided in some unspoken way that Sal'mar'Reyhanna would speak for them. "Your twins thought we should speak with you, and in response to our inquiries, Lady Ethallan said you are a man we can trust."

"Then you're supporting the Free Aagerbanni Resistance?"

Sid'nah'sanAfan did not quickly deny it and considered his words carefully. "We cannot . . . openly . . . support such a struggle."

Charlie didn't miss the careful choice of wording. "Just as I cannot . . . openly . . . support such a struggle."

Sid'nah'sanAfan gave Charlie an appraising look. "Exactly, Your Grace. I'm glad you understand our position."

"But again, I must ask why you've sought me out."

"We seek allies, Your Grace. It's unlikely we'll ever count Lucius as an ally, mostly because of his limitations. But, like us, you are a warrior at heart, and you don't like slavery. And, with the exception of Goutain's interference, it's the Ten who truly rule this Realm. It's simple, Your Grace. We seek allies, and we seek an end to Kinathin slavery everywhere."

"I can support an end to Kinathin slavery," Charlie said. "I can support that quite openly."

Both Kinathins shared another look and smiled.

Charlie left Turnlee aboard *The Thirteenth Man*. Ten light-years out, well outside the range of transition detection, they rendezvoused with *The Headsman*. Charlie transferred over to the warship and *The Thirteenth Man* continued on to Luna, while *The Headsman* proceeded to another destination. One day and ten light-years farther on they down-transited one light-year away from a specific set of coordinates in deep space, far from any solar system. Six large warships awaited them.

Darmczek said, "We're getting a signal and feeding it to your console now."

Charlie, seated at his usual place on *The Headsman*'s bridge, switched on the visual distortion field of the Edwin Chevard persona. The screen in front of him lit up with the image of a naval captain in de Vena livery: dark hair, salt-and-pepper gray on the sides, distinguished appearance—senior navy all the way. Charlie switched on the visual feed from his own console and they both stared at each other for a moment.

"I'm Captain Thessa," the man said, "commanding *Stella's Pride*. And you are?"

"Edwin Chevard," Charlie said. "Pleased to meet you, Captain Thessa. Is Her Grace present?"

"She is, Mr. Chevard. One moment please."

Charlie's screen went blank, then lit up again with Telka's image. "Mr. Chevard, I presume."

"Your Grace, I wasn't sure you'd be here."

"Mr. Chevard, you're an intriguing man with an intriguing message, and so cryptic. And the fact that you could have it delivered to me in the Almsburg Palace piques my curiosity to no end."

On Turnlee, Charlie had had one of Nano's crewmen deliver a simple message to her asking her to meet him at this time and these coordinates, and other than signing it *Edwin Chevard, Free Aagerbanni Resistance*, it gave no other details. "I thought we should talk, Your Grace."

"Don't you fear that I'll take you captive and turn you over to Goutain?"

"A mutual friend told me I could trust you if you gave me the word of House de Vena. The same friend told me you might be interested in . . . comparing notes on the present Aagerbanni situation."

Her eyes narrowed. "And this mutual friend?"

He smiled. "Would prefer to remain anonymous, at least for the time being. But he did tell me that my enemies are also yours."

She stared at him for a long moment, then said, "Yes. Perhaps we should meet in person. May I entertain you on board my ship?" She didn't want to leave the safety of her own ship.

"You would have me subject to your overwhelming force? And what assurance do I have from you regarding my ship, my person, and that of my people?"

"To be clear, you had no such assurances when you came out here, and you're already outgunned by my ships. And yet you came anyway, showing that you have a semblance of trust in my response." She regarded him carefully for several seconds, then said, "But I understand your reticence. So I will say this: Mr. Chevard, as long as you come unarmed, and take no hostile action, you and your retinue will be treated with the utmost respect while you are my guest. You'll be scanned, but only to ensure that you're not armed. You'll not be otherwise interrogated or held against your will. You'll be allowed to depart at any time you so choose, and given a five-light-year head start to prevent pursuit. On this, you have my personal word, and that of House de Vena."

He smiled at the plump little woman. "I look forward to our meeting."

"**S**he's disappeared," Dieter shouted. "Completely disappeared. She and that Carristan woman."

"Calm down," Nadama said tiredly. He was in no mood to deal with his son's hysteria. He poured himself a stiff drink, then poured one for Dieter as well. "Here," he said, handing it to him. "Drink that. It'll calm you."

"I don't want to calm down." He tossed the drink down in a gulp. "How dare she defy me this way?"

"I take it you had an argument?"

"Yes," Dieter said, lowering his eyes like a chastened child.

Dieter had a hot temper combined with a vicious streak that could create problems. "Did you strike her?"

Dieter raised his eyes and looked Nadama in the face. "No."

He was probably telling the truth, but certainly not all of it. "Good, but be very careful. Keep that temper of yours in check until after you're married. Then you can do what you please with her, as long as you don't kill her."

"But she's gone."

"Not for long. Where can she go? Perhaps to some distant relative. We'll just quietly make it known that anyone who harbors her will suffer considerably. And after a few tendays we'll hear from whoever it is. We'll give them a little reward and reel her back in."

At moments like this Dieter took on an almost in-human appearance. "I'm going to kill that Carristan woman, though."

CHAPTER 24
OVERLORD

On his way back to Starfall Charlie stopped briefly at Andyne-Borregga. The transformation that had occurred during his absence was amazing. Roger and Momma Toofat had opened up a large promenade with restaurants, bars, and shops. At present, the shops provided mostly functional supplies and a few luxuries for spacers, the restaurants tended toward simple fare, and the bars provided mostly booze, gambling, and girls. Momma Toofat assured him that, as time progressed and more commerce showed up, all the establishments would attend to more than just the needs of transient spacers. As it was, with warships from the Free Aagerbanni Resistance making extensive use of the new shipyards, and with ships from Istanna, Finalsa, Toellan, Terranzalbo, Allison's Cluster, and the Scorpo Systems all taking advantage of Andyne-Borregga's free port status for gunrunning and other smuggling efforts, Roger told him the station might soon be operating at a profit. Charlie didn't want to damp Roger's enthusiasm so he didn't tell him that wasn't good enough. Even a slight negative operating margin was draining his finances rapidly.

Charlie also learned that ships from the independent states were surreptitiously supporting the Free Aagerbanni Resistance, frequently in direct confrontations. The more they hindered the consolidation of Aagerbanne, the longer it would take Lucius and Goutain to look for their next target. The resistance was slowly heating up into a real shooting war. Certainly more headaches for Lucius and Goutain, but Charlie feared that it was heating up too fast.

He didn't stay on Andyne-Borregga for long—in fact he only had time to sit briefly with Arthur—but left and hurried quickly back to Luna. He needed to be there when Del showed up.

"Where are we?" Charlie heard Carristan say angrily in the reception area outside his office. "This isn't Aagerbanne. Where have you taken us?"

"Just a brief stop," Nano said. "Come. Please."

Carristan had approached Nano under the pretense that Del was nothing more than the noblewoman's servant.

For Edwin Chevard, Charlie had selected a large administrative office in an isolated wing of Starfall on Luna. He had activated it and staffed it with only the most trusted servants and guards. Nano and the guards Charlie had assigned to the two women for their journey had made sure that Carristan and Delilah never got an exterior view, merely the inside of a ship, then the inside of a hangar, then the inside of a maze of corridors. And the rooms Charlie had had prepared for them had no exterior views. Charlie thought he could probably trust Del, but he still didn't know if he could trust Carristan. And Roacka and Winston constantly reminded him that any knowledge of his covert activities should remain on a need-to-know basis, and that even Del did not *need to know.*

The door opened and Nano ushered the two women into the office. Charlie wore the visual distortion field that produced the Edwin Chevard appearance. When Carristan saw him seated behind the desk, she halted abruptly, and swallowed an angry retort. Behind her Delilah stepped into the room, doing a good job of pretending to be the meek servant.

Charlie stood and stepped around the desk. He felt like a schoolboy about to ask a girl on a date for the first time. "Your Ladyship," he said to Carristan, the programmable implant distorting his voice.

"Who are you?" Carristan demanded.

Charlie tried to smile warmly, hoping to alleviate some of her fear. "I'm Edwin Chevard."

"What do you want? Do you intend us harm? My girl here . . ." She waved a hand at Delilah. " . . . is just a servant. Let her go. I'm sure you have no need of kidnapping a mere servant."

Charlie looked at Delilah as he spoke. "Oh no, Lady Carristan, we have no need of a servant. However, we do find it advantageous to kidnap Her Royal Highness." Charlie bowed deeply to Delilah.

Carristan gasped and tried to deny it. To Del's credit, she didn't react in any way, but looked Charlie in the eyes and considered him carefully. She thought the situation over for a few moments, then slowly squared her shoulders. The servant disappeared and the royal princess emerged. "Carristan, my dear, please," she said. "I think there's no use denying it. Mr. Chevard is clearly well-informed."

"We intend you no harm," Charlie said, looking only at Del. "My people will protect you with their lives. You'll be housed, clothed, and fed, and treated as befits your station. Unfortunately, you cannot leave. We support the Free Aagerbanni Resistance here, and the windfall of your captivity is . . . a boon to our efforts, shall we say?"

Del's eyes narrowed, and Charlie wondered if his disguise was as good as he thought. "For the record, Mr. Chevard," she said, "I did not support my father's ambitions. I did not support his alliance with Syndon, nor the annexation of Aagerbanne."

"I'm well aware of that, Your Highness. But you must be aware that your support either way is irrelevant. Your presence here as a hostage, however, is quite relevant to our cause."

Charlie turned to Nano. "Captain Neverlose, please see Her Highness and Lady Carristan to their quarters. And see to it that they're under guard and protected at all times."

"Will do," Nano said. He opened the door and held it for the two women.

Delilah turned, walked to the door, paused on the threshold, and turned back, looked suspiciously from Charlie to Nano. To Nano she said, "I think we've met before."

Nano shook his head. "No, never met."

She smiled, clearly not convinced. She looked again from him to Charlie, then turned and left the room.

Charlie woke in the middle of the night needing to piss badly, staggered tiredly into the fresher, and relieved himself. As he returned to bed he paused at the small dressing table on which lay the computer tablet and the ornate dagger. His last visit to the blind corridor haunted almost every waking moment, and many of his sleeping moments too. He'd racked his brains a hundred times trying to understand why it had failed to respond to his presence.

He threw the switch on the computer tablet, watched the internal map of Starfall appear on its small screen. He stared at the display for several seconds, knew for a fact he'd missed something important, but what? He switched the tablet off, crossed the room to his bed, and sat on its edge staring at the tablet. And the dagger; he stared at that too. He wondered why his eyes kept returning to the dagger, just an ornate piece of junk. He'd suspected it was the overlord key, but that had turned out to be wrong. Cesare had told Paul it was important, so Charlie had never let it out of his sight, stuffing it into a pocket each morning, and putting it on the dresser each night before going to bed. He tried to recall the last time he'd gone down there. He remembered getting up, throwing on the robe, and going down to the blind corridor. He'd done nothing different—except he hadn't taken the dagger. "Shit," he shouted, jumped to his feet, ran across the room, and swept up the dagger and the comp tablet. He ran out of his room in his underwear, swearing, "Shit, shit, shit!"

Ell sat up on the couch where she'd been sleeping and jumped to her feet, a startled look on her face. She followed him out into the corridor where he dodged cleaning bots that only came out at night. Charging down to the lower floors, he took steps three at a time in a headlong dash. He stopped just outside the blind corridor, and Ell stopped beside him.

"What are you doing, little brother?"

"I'm not sure," he said.

He held the dagger in his right hand with the comp tablet in his left displaying the interior map of Starfall. He extended his right arm so the dagger passed into the blind corridor, and the corridor suddenly appeared on the map. He pulled the dagger back out of the corridor, and it disappeared. In, out, in, out, he waved the dagger back and forth, watching the corridor appear and disappear on the map. All along it had been the dagger that triggered the appearance of the corridor on the map, not him. With the exception of that one time he'd always had it stuffed in a pocket.

He sat down on the floor in the corridor with his back to a wall and put the tablet aside, then examined the dagger carefully. The overlord key, it had to be, but again he found nothing to indicate it was anything more than a cheap, decorative blade.

Standing over him, Ell asked, "What is it? What's bothering you?"

He looked up at her and said, "The overlord key, I need—"

He stopped in midsentence as her eyelids fluttered and her mouth opened. In a trancelike state, she stared at nothing for several seconds. When the moment ended, she looked down at him and took a step back. Then she subvocalized into her implants, "Add, get down here right away."

"What's wrong?" he asked.

She ignored him as she told Add their location. In a matter of seconds a breathless and half-dressed Add came running down the corridor and stopped beside Ell. She asked the same question Charlie had. "What's wrong?"

Ell looked at Charlie and said, "Say it to her. She has to hear it in your voice for the implant programming to kick in."

"Say what?"

"What you said to me a moment ago about the key."

"The overlord key?"

Those words had the same effect on Add as they'd had on Ell: the eyelids fluttering, the trancelike state that lasted for only a moment. When Add regained her composure she looked down at Charlie, held out her hand, and said, "May I have the dagger, little brother?"

Charlie extended the hilt up to her. She took it, looked at it for a moment, then pressed the sharp edge of the blade to the back of her hand and made a small cut there. She handed the blade to Ell, who then cut the back of her hand. Both cuts weren't deep, and began healing rapidly due to the genes engineered into the twins' ancestors.

"DNA lock," Ell said as she handed the dagger to Charlie.

He noticed two red smears on the blade's edge. It wasn't a terribly large blade, about the length of his middle finger, hilt the same. As he looked at it, the blade and hilt came apart with a click. There was no hidden compartment, no secret documents that would lead him to concealed wealth and power, but the connection between the two was an odd sort of plug-and-socket type of arrangement.

Charlie rushed up to the security center with the twins on his heels. He sat down at the security commander's station and examined it, looking for an interface that would mate with the dagger. He saw nothing visible, so he put the dagger down and ran his hands over the surface of the station.

"I'm looking for a visual distortion field," he told the twins. "Help me."

He repeated the process at the other stations. Again

nothing. Eventually he and the twins ran their hands over every inch of the security center, every station, console, the floors and walls. They even stood on the consoles and ran their hands over the ceiling. Nothing.

"Computer," he said. "Define the overlord interface."

"This system does not recognize the reference to *overlord interface.*"

He needed to try a different approach. "Computer, define all references to overlord."

"*Overlord* is undefined in this system."

"Damn!"

Dagger in hand, he headed back down to the blind corridor. With the twins standing in the hallway outside it, he stood facing the featureless wall with the visual distortion field. "Cesare," he said, "where is it? What are you hiding? What are you trying to tell me?"

Driven by pure desperation, he laid the dagger on the floor since he had no pockets in his underwear, walked up to the wall, and pressed his hands against it about shoulder high. His hands again appeared to sink into the stone up to the wrists. Something had changed, he realized, something subtle. Perhaps the texture of the wall, perhaps it was ever so slightly different than before, though still featureless and blank.

He started at the top and ran his hands from left to right, dropped his hands down one hand span, dragged them along the wall right to left. Methodically, he repeated the process, slowly working his way down the wall, careful to miss nothing. He was more than halfway down, about waist high, when he found it: two indentations that he could feel, that he was certain hadn't been there when he'd done this once before. That had been before he'd inserted the three cyberkeys into their sockets in the security center.

Two indentations. The visual distortion field hid them from view, and he couldn't really determine any fine detail with his fingers so he had to go on instinct. He picked up the two pieces of the dagger and, going by touch, brought the hilt up to one of the indentations, hoping he could insert it in some way, careful not to force it since he couldn't see what he was doing. Again, nothing.

He moved the hilt to the other indentation, felt a mild pull on it like two magnets attracting one another, carefully let the pull guide his hand. Just before it made contact the pull twisted the dagger slightly, and when it touched the indentation it locked there with a solid click. He tested it, tugged on it, and couldn't remove it.

He lifted the dagger's blade, brought it to the other indentation, felt the same pull, the same guiding twist at the last moment, and it too snapped into place with a click. The visual distortion field disappeared, and the hilt and blade now protruded visibly from the otherwise featureless wall. But nothing else happened. He waited, and still nothing. "Damn it, Cesare. What am I supposed to do?"

He stepped back from the wall, tried to twist or turn or pull the hilt and blade, but met with no success.

He waited for what seemed an eternity and nothing happened.

He turned to the twins. "Do you know anything about the overlord key?"

Both shook their heads as Ell said, "No. There was just some hidden programming in our implants. When you said *overlord key*, I felt a mild compulsion to cut myself with that blade."

"Me too," Add said.

He picked up the tablet, looked at the map of Starfall and nothing had changed. Shaking his head, he turned to leave, and as he stepped across the threshold of the corridor, Cesare said, "Charlie."

He gasped, spun, and there stood Cesare in the middle of the blind corridor, but not really Cesare, just a 3-D projection.

Cesare said, "There were several different scenarios under which Overlord could have been activated. But since this recording is the one that you're seeing, it means I'm dead, someone—probably Gaida and Theode—usurped Arthur's claim to the de Maris ducal seat, and you're now de Lunis."

Cesare grinned. "Sorry about that, Charlie. But it was the only way I could think to save your life under such circumstances. And it was the only way I could think to give you the power necessary to save Arthur's life if he still lives, or to avenge him if he's dead.

"Activate Overlord immediately. With it you can defend Starfall. And remember me to Aziz and Sague and Ethallan. They've been good friends for many years. You can trust them implicitly. And tell them I said, *The thirteenth man will rise.*"

Cesare's image disappeared, and the walls on either side of the blind corridor began to swing shut like two large doors. They didn't grind or creak as they moved, but swung silently with no more noise than the quiet hiss of displaced air. And when they closed there was no longer any indication that the blind corridor had ever existed.

"But how the fuck do I activate Overlord?" he said, though he knew there'd be no answer forthcoming.

"Your father was always quite mysterious," Add said.

Charlie sighed, took a deep breath and let it out slowly, then turned and started back to his rooms. He happened to glance at the face of the tablet as he walked and noticed a small red flashing icon on the map. He stopped, zoomed in on it, and found it located in the security center.

For the second time that night, with the twins on his heels, Charlie rushed up to the security center, dropped down breathlessly into the couch at the commander's console, and said, "Let's try again."

He recalled Cesare's exact words. "Computer, activate Overlord."

Nothing. Just dead silence for several seconds, then the computer said, "Overlord vocal signature confirmed. DNA sequence confirmed. Overlord lock released and initiation sequence activated." There was a pause, then it said, "Diagnostic scans initiated. A full system report will be available in approximately ten minutes."

Ten minutes. Starfall's computational systems were enormously powerful. For it to take ten minutes to run diagnostic scans meant it was scanning one hell of a lot of hardware.

Charlie couldn't sit still. He stood, paced back and forth while he waited for the system to finish its diagnostic run. The twins sat calmly and waited. Goaded by impatience, Charlie stopped and looked at the command console. "Come on, come on, come on," he demanded.

"The system does not recognize the command, *Come on*."

"Oh fuck you!"

"The system does not recognize the command, *Oh fuck you*. However, Your Grace, the diagnostic run is complete. In summary, all elements of the system have been in powered-down and static mode for varying durations ranging from five to twenty-three years, and a considerable amount of maintenance is many years overdue. However, the system is capable of performing at an overall effectiveness of eighty percent, though without further maintenance that will decline rapidly. Do you wish Overlord fully activated at this time?"

While the command console had come to life, Cesare hadn't given him an operator's manual for Overlord, so he'd have to move carefully. He decided best not to activate Overlord until he knew what the hell it was. "Computer, do not activate at this time.

Display an executive schematic of the entire Overlord system, with all Overlord facilities highlighted in red."

Charlie expected to see an enhanced 3-D map of Starfall, with some new pieces of information here and there. But what appeared on the screen in front of him didn't make sense until he realized he was looking at a solar system map. There were eight red blips spaced equally in an orbit around the system's solar primary at an orbital radius twice that of Terra's, another four orbiting Terra along with Luna, though the four blips were at a radius far outside Luna's orbit. The red blips were labeled as platforms one through twelve.

"Amazing," Ell said.

"Overlord," he whispered, almost unable to get the words out. "Give me a detailed specification on platform one."

With the twins looking over his shoulder he spent ten minutes reviewing the flood of data that trailed across the screen. There was so much that he could only scan bits and pieces here and there, and glance briefly at a schematic or two. But it was enough to confirm his suspicions: platform one was an orbital weapons platform, bristling with transition batteries and transition launchers, active shielding, and one hell of a power plant to give it muscle (though no transition drive, and just enough sublight drive to make orbital adjustments over long periods of time). If the other platforms were anything like platform one, Starfall was nicely defended indeed.

"Holy shit!"

"The system does not recognize the command, *Holy shit*."

Ell said, "I thought we taught him better than that."

"Computer," Charlie said. "Download a full Overlord system schematic and specifications to my personal comp. Also download details of the recently run diagnostic scan. Use type-one military encryption so I'm the only one who can access the information."

"It's being downloaded now, Your Grace."

"Computer, lock down all access to Overlord so that only I can view it. And ensure that there are no traces of Overlord within the Starfall system visible to anyone else unless I specifically authorize it."

"As you wish, Your Grace."

CHAPTER 25
SUSPICIONS ABOUND

"Who is this Edwin Chevard?" Goutain shouted. Nadama watched him pace back and forth in front of three of his generals who stood at rigid attention, quaking in their boots. "Only six months ago the Aagerbanni resistance was ready to collapse, and then along comes this Chevard fellow. We should have consolidated Aagerbanne months ago and moved on to the next target by now. Instead, all I hear from you is delays and Edwin Chevard, failures and Edwin Chevard, lost ships and Edwin fucking Chevard!"

Goutain had worked himself into a howling rage. He stopped in front of General Tantin and stood nose-to-nose with him, small bits of spittle splattering Tantin's face as he screamed, "Edwin Chevard, Edwin Chevard, Edwin Chevard! Well, Tantin, what do you have to say for yourself?"

General Tantin's voice trembled as he answered. "We know almost nothing about the man, Your Excellency. It appears he did not exist prior to the advent of these Aagerbanni resistance fighters. That leads me to believe he was not active in politics prior to the annexation."

"You're guessing," Goutain snarled. "I don't let you keep your life so you can give me guesswork."

Nadama sat back, deciding to stay out of it until Goutain finished venting his anger. Nadama had to give Tantin credit; somehow he always managed to survive, while his peers dropped like flies, though this time Goutain's rage did appear uncontrollable. Nadama did hope that Tantin made it through this episode. The man was quite competent, and it was appalling the way Goutain wasted good people.

Speaking of competency. . .

Chevard's name had come up quite frequently of late. He seemed to be involved in almost every facet of the resistance. And yet, Tantin was right: prior to the resistance he had to have maintained an incredibly low profile. "I think it clear," Nadama said, interrupting Goutain's tirade, "that this Edwin Chevard is a false identity."

Goutain turned toward Nadama, struggled visibly to control himself and managed to lower his voice, though only slightly. "How do you mean?"

Nadama tossed the sheaf of reports onto his desk. "These indicate there were absolutely no records of such a man prior to the resistance: no birth certificates, no family records, no tax records, nothing. It's not possible to live and leave so empty a trail."

Goutain frowned and considered Nadama's words for a moment. "I suppose that's true."

To Tantin, Nadama said, "General, I recommend you look to local Aagerbanni civic leaders, politicians, industrial magnates; people of power who cannot easily go into hiding, and who'll suffer in one way or another by the annexation. Don't bother with anyone who's already gone into hiding and is actively supporting the resistance. Such a false identity is only necessary for someone who's attempting to maintain their pre-annexation interests."

Tantin looked to Goutain for approval. Goutain waved a hand at him. "Do it. Just do it, you fool. Can't you think for yourself?"

It had started with her recognition of the trampsie ship's captain, and from that Del had grown quite suspicious of Edwin Chevard. She still wasn't sure where she'd seen Captain Neverlose before, though her life hadn't intersected with trampsies too often. Probably it had been somewhere in Ellitah on Tachaann, which boasted more than its share of trampsies. She just couldn't remember exactly where or when, or under what circumstances.

As promised, Chevard's staff treated both her and Carristan well. Chevard came to see her daily without fail, always asked if there were any problems with her treatment, asked if there was anything else she wanted, and she always told him, "Yes, I want my freedom." And while she was free to live in and roam about a rather large and elegant suite of rooms, there was no question that she was nevertheless imprisoned. She and Carristan had explored the limits of their confinement, found that there were no views of the outside world and only two entrances to her suite from the building proper, both perpetually locked, and with, as she'd seen upon occasion, armed guards stationed beyond. But after the first few days, once she and Carristan realized that Chevard was a man of his word, that they would be treated well, they relaxed. And oddly, even though she was a prisoner, she came to realize that in some ways she was freer now than she had been on Turnlee. Dieter didn't hover relentlessly, oppressively at hand, didn't pop up suddenly when least expected. She had come to fear his temper, and here, that constant, gnawing dread had disappeared. She even felt a bit lighthearted.

Interestingly enough, Chevard was always careful to ask her permission before entering her presence. At first, out of spite, she'd refused and he'd stayed away, and there had been no repercussions. Later she'd agreed to receive him. Occasionally, he'd even joined them for dinner, and it was on the first such occasion that her suspicion of the man had risen to the surface of her thoughts. There was something enticingly familiar about him, though she was absolutely certain she'd never met him before.

"Your Highness, forgive me," Chevard said. "I was boring you."

"No, not at all," she said, bringing her thoughts back to the moment. They were walking through an indoor garden that adjoined several of her rooms. It was styled after outdoor, formal gardens with lovely gravel pathways meandering through flowers and small decorative bushes. Chevard had gotten into the habit of visiting her there and relaying the latest news to her. "I'm sorry. My thoughts drifted for a moment."

There was always a touch of melancholy to the man. "I do apologize that you must be confined so."

She laughed and shrugged. "It's the politics of my life."

"I can't blame you if you resent me for spiriting you away from your betrothed."

She stopped and turned to face him. She had sensed just a hint of jealousy in his tone, as if he needed to gauge her feelings toward Dieter. And there was something very familiar about the way he'd said that, almost as if she knew this man. She stepped in close to him, just a little closer than was appropriate, and took a bit of girlish pleasure in his discomfort. "Dieter and I'll never love one another. Dieter has too much love for himself to spare any for me."

Chevard almost seemed happy at her response. "I'm sorry to hear that," he said, but his words didn't match his tone or expression.

She'd considered this next step carefully. As her

suspicion of Chevard had grown, she'd decided upon a simple test. Before he could react, she closed the distance between them, put her arms around his neck, pressed her body tightly against him, and kissed him. He responded passionately and wrapped his arms around her waist.

By all appearances Chevard was a man in late middle age, but as they held each other, their tongues dancing back and forth almost desperately, she felt him responding like a young man in his prime. The shoulders that she held were the broad, powerful shoulders of a young man, the lips pressed against hers were strong and full, and as she pressed her entire body along the length of him, the unwilling response of his body was not that of an older man.

He suddenly came to his senses, realized what he was doing, and took an alarmed step back from her. "Your Highness, please forgive me. I don't know what came over me."

There'd been something familiar about that kiss, as if she'd kissed him before, and she didn't try to hide her surprise. And then there were his shoulders . . . and Mr. Neverlose . . . who had worked with Charlie in that saloon on Tachaann . . . and Charlie had given Carristan the hint to contact Mr. Neverlose . . .

"Charlie!" she said. She stepped toward him. "It's you, isn't?"

His shoulders slumped, he closed his eyes and lowered his head. She'd heard of visual distortion fields, but never seen one in action until he switched it off.

He opened his eyes and looked at her sheepishly. "I . . . uh . . ."

She wanted to be furious with him, curled her hands into fists and planted them on her hips. "I should be so angry with you."

She knew she didn't sound as angry as she wanted to, and sounded more like she was really happy to see him, which was, in fact, the case. At least Charlie looked like he wanted to crawl under a rock and hide. "Don't you trust me?" she demanded.

He repeated himself. "I . . . uh . . ."

"Wow!" she said. "Mr. Articulate. You should—"

He shut her up by stepping forward, wrapping his arms around her waist, pulling her tightly against him, and kissing her. It was a kiss that made the last one seem rather tame, though now that she knew she was kissing Charlie, she had to admit most of that was her fault.

Charlie, Roacka, Roger, and Seth stood silently in the lift as it plummeted into the depths of the bedrock beneath Starfall. Charlie wanted physical verification of the existence of platforms one through twelve, and of the computer's analysis of their capabilities. It wouldn't do to need such defenses and find that they really only existed in the bits and bytes of the computer. So far they'd boarded five of the platforms, activated them briefly, verified their capabilities, status, maintenance, and repair requirements, then run a quick physical inventory of their systems before shutting them back down. Until they were prepared to properly activate and man the systems, they had to keep them a closely guarded secret.

Manpower turned out to be less and less of a problem. Each platform required a crew of about twenty, since much of it operated under computer control. And every tenday there were more defections from House de Maris and others. There had been something like ten thousand men in various Syndonese POW camps. And while most had not been part of the Two Thousand, they all had suffered similar depravations. Charlie's name had become a symbol for opposition to useless, pointless wars, and the result was a steady stream of highly trained and experienced spacers and their families. And many of the women wanted to serve in the same capacity as their husbands. Charlie's consent to train the women as combatants occasionally raised a few eyebrows, but more often than not was accepted with little more than a shrug.

Cesare had stocked the barracks on the platforms with nonperishable foodstuffs, so that was one issue they didn't have to worry about. But Charlie didn't have enough crewmen to fully operate the platforms' weapons, so he decided to staff them with couples, married or otherwise.

Now that they knew the layout and status of the platforms, each verification team carried a full stock of supplies for the barracks, just in case some of the non-perishables had perished. And Charlie had purchased a number of in-system shuttles to ferry crews back and forth, driving him even further into debt. Winston had warned him that his credit would soon run out.

But what else could he do?

It was Roger who discovered the facilities on Luna in the Overlord schematics. Charlie hadn't noticed them because he'd asked for a schematic of the entire Overlord system, which meant the scale on his screen had been adjusted to view the entire Sol system, and Luna was too small a detail to show up on such a scale except as a single red dot. Roger had been reviewing the locations of Overlord's spare parts inventory with an eye toward repairs on the platforms, and he'd noticed that much of it was located on Luna. So when he'd zoomed in on the Starfall schematics, with the Overlord schematics active, it showed that large defensive batteries pocked the surface of the moon itself, with a number of power plants buried far beneath old, radioactive hot spots, a nice way of keeping them hidden from anything but a detailed examination. But what intrigued them most was a large facility beneath Starfall. To reach it, the schematics directed them to a special lift.

"How deep does this fucking thing go?" Roacka demanded.

Roger answered, "From the schematic, I'd guess about three hundred meters."

They waited several more seconds before the

doors of the lift opened with a whoosh. The lights in the room beyond turned on automatically, revealing what appeared to be a small reception area, with a counter behind which a guard or receptionist might sit. They stood immersed in an eerie silence for several moments, but when the lift doors began to close, Roacka said, "Fuck this," forced the doors to reopen, and marched into the reception area. The only exit visible, other than the lift, was a door to one side and behind the receptionist's desk. Roacka marched up to the door, opened it, and held it for Charlie. "You want to do the honors, lad?"

As Charlie stepped through the door the lights in the room beyond came on, and he found a bullpen of desks, though no indication as to their purpose. There were a number of doors on the periphery of the bullpen, and a quick glance through a few of them merely revealed simple offices. It reminded Charlie of a large operations center of some sort. The far wall appeared to be transparent plast, and as Charlie approached it he called over his shoulder, "Roger, see if you can bring up some of these systems—especially the lights—and find out what we're dealing with here."

Pitch darkness beyond the transparent plast windows hid whatever lay there. Charlie stood there staring into nothing for several moments until Roger called, "Got it." A moment later the room beyond the windows lit up and he tried to make sense of what he saw. The room in which he stood appeared to be a few meters above a warehouse floor, with rows of shelves two or three meters high stretching into the distance. Seth stopped beside him, stood there for a moment with his hands on his hips, then suddenly gasped and pointed to a thin line that crossed the floor below them. "Holy fucking shit. That's a gantry."

The scale of the place suddenly snapped into perspective. "We must be a good ten meters off the floor, and those shelves have to be fifteen meters high." At that scale, that meant some of the hardware racked down there was large, heavy equipment.

"Charlie," Roger said, completely forgetting himself for the moment. The tone of awe in his voice made them all turn his way.

Roger sat at one of the desks, the glare of an active screen reflected in his eyes. "You're looking at just one of four such warehouses, all of the same size. This manifest lists ten completed transition drives in inventory, all of cruiser class or better."

Seth and Roacka both hurried to stand behind Roger and look over his shoulder. Charlie stayed at the plast windows and turned to survey the warehouse while listening. "If I'm reading this correctly there are over fifty large transition batteries, thirty transition launchers, and assorted sublight drives and power plants, all completely assembled, modularized, and ready to be installed in hulls. It looks like there's also enough stocks of smaller spare parts to keep a fleet of thirty or forty warships going for at least a year."

"But no hulls?" Charlie asked.

"No, no hulls."

There wouldn't be. Charlie had asked more as a matter of form. One didn't assemble hulls in a gravity well, not even one as insignificant as Luna's. For just an instant Charlie imagined he could see Cesare's reflection in the plast beside him. "You sneaky bastard, you," he said, and didn't try to hide the smile that formed on his face. "Where are the hulls?"

At the entrance to the apartments Delilah and Carristan shared, Charlie said, "Computer, please inform Her Royal Highness that I wish to see her."

Several seconds passed, then Carristan opened the door and greeted him very formally. "Your Grace," she said, curtsying deeply. When she straightened she gave him a smug look.

Today Del wore a light summer dress that fell to just below her knees, just the tiniest bit transparent, with a few too many buttons undone in the front. *Well, actually,* he thought, stealing another glance at her, *maybe it isn't too many.*

She took his arm as if they were a young couple enjoying a stroll on a clear spring day. "Let's walk in the garden," she said.

She guided him into the indoor garden, with Carristan following several paces behind them. Charlie glanced over his shoulder at the older woman. She returned his look with a knowing smile.

Del said, "You know, she's not going to leave us alone."

"Why?" Charlie asked.

Del shook her head sadly. "After the way you kissed me. Absolutely shameless! My mother would never approve."

Charlie recalled that he hadn't really been the one in control of that kiss. Yes, he'd initiated it, but once begun Del had piloted the ship rather nicely. He considered saying something like, *You seemed to enjoy it,* but decided to keep that thought to himself.

"So," Del said, "you're supporting the resistance?"

"I didn't say that."

"You did when you were pretending to be Edwin Chevard."

Winston, Roacka, and Charlie had discussed how much to tell Del. Charlie wanted to bring her into his inner circle, but Winston was reluctant to do so, while Roacka vehemently opposed the idea. If Del fell into the wrong hands, she or Carristan could be put under deep neural probe, and anything she knew, they would know. "Only need-to-know," Roacka had reminded him.

Charlie didn't like it, but he'd capitulated.

"I do support the resistance," he said, "though, does that really surprise anyone?"

"No," she said, "it doesn't. So what exactly are you doing to support them?"

With more ships each day taking advantage of Andyne-Borregga's facilities, its importance in the opposition to Goutain and Nadama was becoming less of a secret every day. So he figured he could at least share *that* bit of information with her.

Charlie said, "I'm trying to support a free port that FAR can use for supplies and repairs for its ships."

Del stopped in the middle of the garden, forcing him to stop with her. She turned to face him. "That's wonderful. I'm well aware that ships can't operate without some sort of base."

"But it's straining my meager resources to the limit."

"Yes," she said, smiling, "the penniless bastard thing again."

He shrugged. "Still penniless, but no longer officially a bastard."

"So what can I do to help the resistance?"

She caught him off guard with that question. "I'm not sure, but let me think on it."

Long after he left her that day, that question remained at the forefront of his thoughts. He discussed it carefully with Winston and Roacka.

"Let's put her in front of the press," Roacka said, "have her publicly denounce Nadama and Goutain's aggression."

Winston said, "She can't do that because she'd be denouncing her father as well. And it wouldn't be fair to put her in that position."

Charlie decided to get Arthur's advice on the subject, but that would have to wait until his next stop at Andyne-Borregga.

CHAPTER 26
PLATFORM TWELVE

Charlie and Winston met Paul, Roacka, the twins, and Pelletier in Starfall's security center. Charlie had grown to trust Pelletier as Cesare once had, especially since it was because of Pelletier that he'd gotten Arthur back. Like Cesare, he'd made Pelletier his chief of security, and Pelletier had adopted Starfall's security center as his command center, though it was, as yet, badly understaffed. Darmczek and Seth were absent, each captaining one of the hunter-killers and making life miserable for the occupation forces in Aagerbanne. But with the exception of those two, he had his most trusted team together.

Nadama's occupation forces on Aagerbanne had captured a resistance cell, and among the prisoners taken were some Finalsan naval officers there to liaise with the resistance. Interrogation of the Finalsans provided solid proof that Finalsa was actively supporting the resistance. Nadama, Theode, Lucius, and Goutain used that as an excuse to declare war on Finalsa, which did not have the wherewithal to resist the combined forces of the Four Tyrants, a label that had stuck nicely.

Roacka laughed. "Bet old Karlok's pissing his pants that he's been overlooked and it ain't the Five Tyrants."

All knew that the war with Finalsa would be short, resulting in the annexation of all Finalsan territories, unless they could help slow things down. The other independent states continued to support the Aagerbanni resistance behind the scenes, but were now also providing support to Finalsa, and were demanding support from those duchies that did not support the Four Tyrants.

Roacka summed it up nicely. "We're a night-with-a-whore and a hungover afternoon away from open warfare throughout the independent states."

Charlie tried to swallow the uneasy fear that had settled in his stomach. As a naval commander he knew they weren't ready. "We can't risk open war yet. The coalition is only just starting to come together, and we can't fight a war without it. We have tentative agreements, but until we shake the bugs out of working together as a combined naval force, we're just a bunch of independent ships on the same side. They'll eat us alive."

"Maybe we should back the hunter-killers off a bit," Roger said. "Ever since we cut them loose with orders to torpedo as much of the Four Tyrants' shipping as possible, there's been absolute chaos in the shipping lanes through the independent states."

Roacka shook his head. "I say we keep up the pressure. Even Darmczek admits he was wrong about the hunter-killers."

Charlie asked, "They're still a well-kept secret, aren't they?"

Roger grimaced and admitted, "Ya, by and large. They're getting resupplied out of Andyne-Borregga, and spacers get shore leave and head to the bars. And spacers talk, and brag, and other spacers listen and see the hunter-killers in dock."

"Arthur's been monitoring the situation," Winston said. "He and Mrs. Toofat have established a network of agents working the bars on Andyne-Borregga. He says the bragging and general talk from the hunter-killer crews is being met by considerable skepticism, especially since the hunter-killers obviously don't have the firepower of even a small destroyer. And the spacers to whom they're bragging are our allies anyway."

"In any case," Roacka added, "no one has adopted tactics to defend against hunter-killer strategies."

Charlie knew they couldn't keep the secret of the hunter-killers forever. "At some point, someone's going to realize the losses don't add up, and then they're going to start looking for answers, and someone else is going to realize it's the hunter-killers. And that's when we lose our element of surprise."

"But knowing it's the hunter-killers," Roacka argued, "and figuring out their tactics are two different things. Few beyond this room understand their strategy of engagement. But Roger's question still remains, lad: do we back the hunter-killers off? I say no."

"There is another factor, Your Grace," Winston said. Alone in this small, exclusive group, Charlie had gotten everyone but Winston to drop the formal address; Winston would never yield on that point. "Lord Arthur and Mrs. Toofat report that four or five of Duchess Telka's warships are operating out of Andyne-Borregga as privateers. The crews do not wear de Vena livery, nor do these ships fly de Vena colors, but clearly she's entered into the fray, albeit surreptitiously. I think Edwin Chevard's meeting with her yielded excellent results. And I suspect the chaos created by the hunter-killers helps her conceal her own involvement. Should we back off, she may feel less inclined to participate."

Charlie asked, "Is *Chaos* still running arms to Sobak and Thamaklus and their friends in Syndon?"

"Ya," Roacka said, "and she's torpedoing shipping there as well. That, and our Syndonese allies, are making life real unpleasant for Goutain. Those arms are a good investment."

They all looked to Charlie for the decision. He looked at Roger. "We're committed. We can't back off now."

Charlie nodded, then looked to Pelletier. "What about defense here?"

Pelletier touched something on his console and one wall lit up with a large system map. "As you know, with each installation we have to activate it, test it, perform any needed repairs and maintenance, test fire it, calibrate its targeting, restock supplies where needed, then crew it, and in some cases provide training. That said, we now have six of the surface batteries fully active on Luna, those closest to this facility. And since their power plants are hidden beneath large, radioactive hot spots, they're undetectable unless one knows to look for them and so we're keeping them powered and combat ready.

"As to the weapons platforms, we have eight of them fully active, though at your recommendation we've throttled their power plants back to a trickle so they won't be easily visible to any ship entering the system. We can bring them up to full power in about twenty or thirty minutes.

"We've identified three surface batteries and two platforms that require too much repair to bring online quickly, so we've passed them over. We'll go back to them once we've tested all the rest."

Pelletier looked up from his console and met their eyes one by one. "At this point, even though we're only about halfway there, we're ready to defend ourselves against anything but all-out attack by a large force."

"What about spies?" Roacka asked.

"We've identified a few, so we're feeding them misinformation where possible, isolating them where not. But I think it's best to assume we haven't identified them all. Our best strategy at this point is that, outside of this room, no one knows the full extent of our capability. With few exceptions, the hunter-killer crews, shadow fleet crews, surface installations crews, and platform crews are not aware of each other. So any spy that we don't identify may get one or two pieces of the puzzle, but not all."

"It's going to leak out," Charlie said. "We can slow it down, but we can't stop it." And with that thought, the main thing now was speed. At this moment, he had potent military might in the Lunan system, and a narrow window of time during which that fact would remain a secret and he'd have the element of surprise.

"So what's next?" Charlie asked.

"My job's pretty clearly defined here," Pelletier said. "We'll keep going after the platforms and surface batteries one at a time and bring them online as quickly as possible."

Roger added, "By the way, I noticed some discrepancies in platform twelve's schematics, so I'm going to take the team up there next, take it out of sequence. It shouldn't really affect our schedule, but I'm curious to see what's different about it."

As the meeting broke up, Add and Ell pulled Charlie aside. Add said quietly, "We didn't want to speak of it in front of the others, but Sid'nah'sanAfan wishes you to know that Kinatha has quietly sent six warships to support opposition to the Four Tyrants."

Charlie said, "Then we should quietly thank them."

Charlie's implants woke him from a sound sleep. Starfall's computer system said, "Major Pelletier requests your immediate attention, Your Grace. He says it's a matter of some urgency."

"Connect me," Charlie said.

"Your Grace," Pelletier said breathlessly. "I'm in the security center. Come up here, please. Right away."

Pelletier wasn't easily excitable. "I'll be right there."

Charlie threw on a pair of pants, shoes, and a shirt, then sprinted up to the security center, wondering if they were under attack or something. As Charlie rushed into the room, Pelletier, seated at his command console, with Winston standing behind him, pointed at a screen in front of him and said, "Look at that."

Charlie crossed the room, stopped behind Pelletier, and looked over his shoulder; the screen in front of him displayed an image of a large station somewhere in space. "What's that?"

"That, Your Grace, is platform twelve."

"That's no platform."

"No, it's not," Pelletier said, a clear note of wonder in his voice. "It's a prime station, which, I assume, is meant to be Luna Prime."

Charlie snagged a chair and dropped into it as Pelletier continued. "Roger spotted some unusual specifications in twelve's schematics, went up there to investigate. These are vids he took on approach."

Pelletier touched a switch. "Roger, I've got Duke Charles with me. Are you still in the vacuum dock?"

The image shifted to that of four people in vac suits. One of them said in Roger's voice, "You ain't gonna believe this."

The image switched to Roger's helmet cam, and as his head slowly panned the inside of the vacuum dock, Charlie saw two warships docked there. Roger's voice was colored with awe and disbelief as he said, "Looks like a heavy cruiser and a large destroyer. And that's just this dock. There are others that we haven't had a chance to check out yet."

Charlie leaned forward. "What's the condition of the ships? Are they complete? Are they serviceable?"

"Don't know," Roger said. "Don't know. Just got here, so haven't had a chance to do more than gawk and shit my pants."

Charlie and Pelletier looked on as Roger and his team boarded the heavy cruiser. They floated weightless down corridors that were eerily silent and pristine. It took more than an hour, and even then they'd only completed a preliminary examination. It was enough to tell them the ship was complete, with all necessary systems including weapons and drives, though, like the platforms, they'd want to make sure the nonperishable supplies were still viable. That didn't tell them if she was serviceable, and they wouldn't know that until they went through a checkout procedure much like on the platforms.

But if they are. . .

The station itself was about a quarter the size of Andyne-Borregga, its surface pocked with about thirty defensive weapons stations, and clearly meant to be the centerpiece of a system-wide defensive network, as well as the principal transshipment point for all traffic in and out of the Lunan system. Pelletier immediately diverted three more of the platform teams to assist Roger on twelve, and it took them two days to do an inventory of the station. In total, docked on the station were four heavy cruisers, four medium cruisers, eight destroyers, and miscellaneous tenders and other support vessels. All appeared complete, though their serviceability was still unknown. Charlie assumed that, like the platforms and surface batteries, after twenty years of disuse, they would all require some maintenance before they could see active service. Their primary problems were time, manpower, and finances. *Especially* finances.

Cesare couldn't have anticipated the present situation, not twenty years before. Behind Charlie Winston seemed to mirror his thoughts. "As far back as I can remember we bought and sold ships, and commissioned new hulls. There was a constant turnover, but as the years progressed, I began to notice that the number of vessels in the de Maris registry didn't add up to what it should."

Charlie turned away from the screen and looked at Winston. "But how did he get them here without anyone knowing?"

Winston continued to stare at the screen, and he seemed deep in thought. "Back then, Cesare's chief of naval operations was Admiral Tomas Jelliski, who died when you were about ten. They grew up like brothers, were very close. I must assume they worked together to accomplish this."

"But why?" Charlie asked. "How could he have known?"

Winston finally looked away from the screen, and his eyes focused on Charlie. "I don't believe he did. He had me prepare at least a dozen contingencies, some of which included him still alive, most of which involved distribution of the de Lunis properties. As to why, when you and Arthur were quite young your father repeatedly expressed his concern about the future of our civilization. Lucius's instabilities, the growing infighting among the Nine, and the deteriorating balance of power all contributed greatly to his fears. I think he just wanted an ace in the hole."

Charlie turned back to the screen. "Let's focus on the big cruisers, see if we can get a couple of them up and running."

They had enough manpower to fully staff all the weapons platforms and surface installations, but not the ships. Pelletier came up with the idea of cherry-picking experienced spacers from among their crews, and Charlie decided to have Arthur spread the word on Andyne-Borregga that any former experienced de Maris spacer could find work with House de Lunis. In that way, they could crew a couple of cruisers without understaffing the system's defenses.

Sixteen warships! Charlie closed his eyes and thought of Cesare. *Now I have the hulls, you sneaky bastard.*

What other surprises have you got for me?

CHAPTER 27
A MOST LOGICAL PROPOSAL

On *The Headsman*, en route for Andyne-Borregga, the guard outside the cabin that Carristan and Delilah shared stepped out of Charlie's way as he approached. He knocked softly on the door, fearing the coming conversation. Just like Arthur, it was too dangerous to leave Delilah on Luna. He had decided to take her with him to Toellan, then leave her with Roger on Andyne-Borregga. They'd just up-transited out of the Lunan system.

Carristan opened the door. "Your Grace."

"I need to speak with Her Highness."

"Certainly," she said, stepping aside.

Charlie stepped into the small cabin and Carristan closed the door behind him. She had been quite the chaperone, had hovered about Del like a nervous mother whenever Charlie came near. Del sat on the lower of the two bunks dressed in shipboard fatigues.

She stood as Charlie entered, and he noticed she'd cinched the fatigues at the waist, and managed to look gorgeous even in a pair of coveralls.

"Your Grace," she said, smiling at him, but glancing momentarily at Carristan.

"I do apologize for the cramped quarters, Your Highness," he said, "but this is a man-of-war, and space is at a premium."

"Think nothing of it, Your Grace. I fully understand. In fact, I'm happy just to be out and somewhere else for a bit. And I've never been to Toellan before."

He grimaced. "I'm afraid you'll not have much opportunity to see the place."

"But I do so want to."

He really had to stay away from their usual polite banter. He'd come for a purpose, a most unpleasant purpose, and he knew he had to get to the point. "A courier ship arrived at Luna just before we left."

Her face brightened. "You've come to bring me news. But why so solemn?"

As a ship's officer he'd had to deliver bad news before, and he knew the best method was to spit it out. "I'm sorry, but I must tell you that your brother is dead."

She didn't react for a moment, and then the joy and happiness slowly disappeared from her face. Her mouth hung open, and a stream of tears trickled down her cheek. She said only, "How?"

He said, "The death of the heir to the throne was very carefully investigated."

"Yes," she said, dismissing his hedging with her hand. "Tell me *how*."

The courier had brought a detailed report. As unlikely as it seemed, her idiot brother had died by accident. Charlie didn't say this, but he'd learned from the report that Martino and one of his women were experimenting with a stimulant that enhanced sexual pleasure, a powerful drug. The toxicology report showed that he took far too much of it, along with a number of other medications. During their sexual exploits he suffered a massive cerebral hemorrhage and lost consciousness. The woman thought he'd merely passed out—apparently a not uncommon occurrence—so she rolled over and went to sleep. If he hadn't turned off his implants and the physiological monitors in his apartments, the palace's system would have detected the problem immediately and he might have been revived. As it was, no one was aware of the crisis until the woman woke up a few hours later. And by then it was far too late.

Del deserved the truth, though there was no need to dwell on intimate details. "A drug overdose that caused a stroke and a cerebral hemorrhage."

"And there was no foul play?"

Charlie shook his head. "All of the Ten have reviewed the reports in detail, and for once Nadama, Dieter, and Goutain's hands seem clean."

She fell into his arms and began sobbing. "He was a fool, I know. But he was still my brother. And I did so love the poor, misguided idiot."

Charlie just stood there and let her cry for a while,

knowing from personal experience there was nothing he could say to make it easier for her. Eventually, though, he left her with Carristan, the two of them crying together.

Aziz met Charlie as he stepped off *The Headsman*'s gunboat at Toellan's main spaceport. The fat merchant bowed deeply, no small feat considering his girth, and in his strong accent said, "You grace my humble presence with your glorious mentality."

"Aziz," Charlie said. "It's always good to see you."

Delilah and Carristan stepped off the boat behind him, the twins shadowing them both. Delilah had been relentless, pressing him constantly to allow her to see Toellan. He felt somewhat foolish yielding to her wishes, but he liked having her around, and since she and Carristan had agreed to wear visual distortion rigs, they wouldn't be recognized. Charlie introduced them to Aziz. "My niece Anna, and Lady Carristan. May I present Aziz Anat Cohannin Meth'kah'hat bin Sabatth duu Donawathat?"

Aziz simply gushed with joy. "Please. Please. Call me Aziz."

He leaned close to Charlie. "They are both quite beautiful."

Charlie took the opportunity to whisper, "I'd consider it a personal favor if you had your security people keep a close eye on Anna. She's a bit . . . impetuous, and might try to go on an unsupervised lark."

"Of course, Your Grace."

Aziz hustled them into a string of grav limos lined up at the curb, and during the trip across town he made several calls. "My assistant chief of security will take personal charge of the two ladies. He will meet us at your hotel, and take them on a tour of the city while we concern ourselves with our mundane business matters."

At the hotel Aziz introduced his assistant chief of security. The man had a name as long as Aziz's, but insisted Charlie call him Captain Ellas. Charlie explained the agenda to the two ladies, and Delilah said, "That's a wonderful idea." She threw her arms around Charlie's neck and said, "Thank you so much, dear Uncle Charlie."

She took Ellas's arm. "This is going to be so much fun," she said, and marched away with him.

Aziz raised his eyebrows, but had the tact not to say anything.

Charlie and Winston wanted to review Hart & Delorm's books with Aziz and his factor. Since Charlie owned the company, he'd had it outfit the armaments of the eight hunter-killers without billing him, which should have cut heavily into their profit margins for the year. And yet, Hart & Delorm continued operating at its usual five percent profit margin when it should have plummeted into the red.

When they explained the dilemma to Aziz, he frowned and said, "That is most curious, Your Grace."

They sweated over the books for several hours,

broke for lunch, returned, and went back to work. Every time they came close to isolating something unusual, Aziz came up with a logical explanation. About midafternoon they all decided to take a break. Winston and Charlie were alone in Aziz's office, and Winston voiced a concern that had been growing in the back of Charlie's mind. "I fear, Your Grace, that Mr. Aziz is hiding something."

"Yes, that's been bothering me too." Charlie didn't want to believe it of the Toellani. He liked the man, trusted him, and had taken comfort from his long relationship with Cesare.

Charlie tried to recall Cesare's words when he'd activated the Overlord key in the blind corridor. The recorded image of Cesare had said, " . . . . And remember me to Aziz and Sague and Ethallan. They've been good friends for many years. You can trust them implicitly. And tell them I said, *The thirteenth man will rise.*"

You can trust them implicitly. He wanted to, but that didn't seem to be the case with Aziz.

When Aziz returned it was obvious the Toellani businessman felt the strain of their unease.

And remember me to Aziz and Sague and Ethallan.

Charlie stood and approached Aziz, who remained standing. "I want to apologize, Aziz. I've been so caught up in all this paperwork that I forgot, but Cesare left a posthumous message for me." The normally exuberant merchant frowned but said nothing. "He asked me to remember him to you, and wanted me to tell you he said, *The thirteenth man will rise.*"

Aziz reacted instantly. He gasped and shrieked like a woman, "Oh! Oh! Oh!" He paled noticeably and dropped into a chair, desperately fanning himself.

"What's wrong?" Charlie asked.

Aziz could say only that one word in a frightened and trembling voice. "Oh! Oh! Oh!"

"Should we call a doctor?" Charlie turned to Winston. "Winston, call a doctor." Charlie knelt down beside the trembling Toellani.

"No," Aziz said. "No doctor . . . needed." He slowly calmed and his breathing returned to normal. "Cesare . . . long ago . . . asked me to allow a . . . psych block. I owed him so much, I consented."

Slowly, they learned from Aziz that Cesare had had him cook the books for all de Lunis properties under his control. Then the old duke had his physician set a psych block that hid Aziz's own actions from even himself, a block that would only be released when the de Lunis uttered to him the phrase, *The thirteenth man will rise.* And further, should anyone question the accounting, it compelled him to come up with plausible explanations. The result of the accounting manipulations was that profits were continuously funneled out of Charlie's companies into hidden accounts. It made his companies seem less profitable than they were, though Charlie was nothing close to wealthy. But it did support his cover as the poorest of the Ten.

"You are no longer destitute, Your Grace."

From Toellan they transited to Andyne-Borregga, and Charlie immediately sat down with Winston, Roacka, and Arthur in Arthur's office. He'd pulled in the eight hunter-killers, leaving two of them docked at Andyne-Borregga, the other six running silent just outside Borreggan nearspace. Two more were under construction now and would be operational soon. He'd also sent courier ships to Sague and Ethallan, asking them to meet him on Andyne-Borregga. He'd asked Ethallan to arrange for the Free Aagerbanni Resistance leaders to meet Edwin Chevard there, and Sague to arrange for representatives of the independent states to meet the de Lunis there. He'd sent Ell to Kinatha to ask them to send a representative. And Telka had also received an invitation from Edwin Chevard to meet him there, though he wasn't confident that she'd comply. None of them knew that he'd arranged to meet the others. In fact, with few exceptions, none of them knew he was collaborating with the others.

"I tell you, lad," Roacka said. "You got a fucked-up mess on your hands."

"I have to agree with him," Arthur said.

"And I agree with both of you," Charlie said.

Winston said, "But I do have some good news, got it from Pelletier, who got it from one of Theode's servants he's still connected with there. Theode was at Almsburg when Goutain and Nadama had a horrible row. Apparently this war that's not a war is costing both of them dearly, and they're quite upset about it. They can't account for the loss of ships, and since they don't know about the hunter-killers, they've concluded it's sabotage."

Charlie closed his eyes and rubbed his temples.

Arthur asked, "What about the princess?"

"Ya," Roacka grumbled. "She's a complication. What are you going to do with the girl?"

Winston and Charlie had argued about this at some length, and at that moment the older man gave Charlie a pointed look. Winston thought it time for Charlie to openly reveal his right to select Del's husband, while Charlie wanted to forget the documents existed. Charlie sighed, reached into a pocket, and retrieved a copy of the documents. He handed them to Arthur without comment.

Arthur scanned them quickly, started suddenly, frowned and reread them more carefully. When he finished he said, "Holy shit," as he handed them to Roacka. It was one of the few times Charlie had ever heard him swear.

While Roacka read them, Arthur asked Charlie, "These are legitimate?"

Charlie looked at Winston for the answer. The older man said, "I drew those documents up myself. They're properly registered, and ironclad."

When the meaning of the documents finally hit Roacka he roared with laughter. "Your father was a sneaky son-of-a-bitch."

Arthur stood and leaned on his desk. "You told me

earlier Delilah wants to know how she can help the resistance. Well, the answer's rather simple: she can marry you."

"What?" Charlie said. "Me? It says I get to pick her husband, not *be* her husband."

"So pick yourself. You're the best compromise candidate of all the Ten."

"Compromise?" Charlie said, and Arthur laughed. "Besides, she's already betrothed to Dieter. It's not an easy thing to just dismiss that contract."

Winston said, "I didn't write it up, so I'm sure that engagement is not as unbreakable as they think. And more important, with Martino dead, that becomes a dangerous union. It'll divide the Ten almost immediately, could conceivably result in civil war. Whereas you, the de Lunis, with no military resources and near destitute, would be a weak king, which would please the Ten enough to prevent strife. I have no doubt we'd have their support to throw aside her betrothal to Dieter."

"But I do have military resources, and we just learned that, while I'm not wealthy, I'm far from destitute."

Arthur shook his head, shared a look with Winston and Roacka. "Brother, no one but us knows that."

Winston added, "And there's no reason we can't keep up the pretense. At least until after the wedding, and even then we can reveal the extent of your resources over a period of years, allow the Ten to come slowly to an understanding that they have a strong king."

"King." Charlie shook his head, couldn't believe what he was hearing. "I . . . I can't be king."

"Charlie," Arthur said, adopting a calm, almost fatherly, tone of voice. "You're the only man who can thwart Goutain, and the only man who can hold the Realm together without civil war. You've already been running the show all these months.

"You're already our general.

"You *must* be king."

As soon as Sague arrived on Andyne-Borregga, Charlie met him. His reaction to the phrase *The thirteenth man will rise* was far less dramatic than Aziz's. He merely blinked several times, poured a strong drink, tossed it down like a spacer in a bar, then turned to Charlie and calmly said, "You're better off financially than we thought, Your Grace. I do apologize for the deceit, though in my own defense, the deception was your father's."

When Ethallan arrived and he spoke the phrase to her, she fainted, though she recovered quickly. And when Charlie added it all up, his fortune was considerable, though the cost of bringing his military resources fully online would seriously strain that money immediately.

"Your Grace," Delilah said, pulling Charlie away from his thoughts. "You wanted to see me?"

They had space aplenty on Andyne-Borregga, so Arthur had arranged a suite of apartments for Delilah more appropriate to her station. She received Charlie in a large, spacious sitting room.

"Yes," he said. "I wanted to see how you were settling into your new apartments."

She spun around, indicating the room about her. She wore a simple, floor length dress of a light fabric in pale colors, and her skirts flared out with the motion. "They're quite grand, though still a prison, are they not?"

He grimaced. "I would apologize, but it can't be helped. Though, that may soon change."

"Oh, how so?" She stepped in close to him, uncomfortably close, or perhaps too comfortably close. She had to know how she tempted him, how much he was drawn to her.

The way she teased him, he had a feeling she knew *exactly* that.

He stepped back, handed her the same copy of the documents he'd shown Arthur and Roacka. "You should examine these."

Her eyebrows lifted, she took the documents and began reading them as she paced a slow circle around him. He turned to follow her, and as she walked and read, a smile slowly formed on her face. She circled him four times before she finally stopped and faced him. She waved the papers in his face. "Are these legitimate?"

"Very much so," he said. He proceeded to explain how Cesare had acquired them from her father and willed them to the de Lunis, and how Winston had made sure the registry of the documents was indisputable.

"Your father was a brilliant strategist," she said. "I doubt he could have anticipated how this would play out. But still, to have prepared such a contingency." She turned her back to him. "And who'll you choose for my husband?"

"That's your choice," he said. "If you wish, I'll tear those documents up and they'll never see the light of day."

She turned back to him. "How gallant of you, but also foolish. That would leave the choice up to my father, or worse, Nadama. I love my father, but he's merely a tool at this point, and he and Nadama would lead us to disaster."

"Then you make the choice," he said, "and I'll make it official."

"Well, let me see," she said, her voice dripping with sarcasm. "Who are the candidates? There's Dieter . . ." She raised a finger, indicating a count of one. "Besides being a pig, he's wholly inappropriate. With Martino dead, Dieter's too wealthy and powerful to be allowed that close to the throne. The Ten won't allow it." She then proceeded to give a number of additional reasons why Dieter would not satisfy the political needs of the Realm. And as she spoke she took a step toward him, forcing him back a step. "Then there's Telka's heirs," she continued, raising a second finger, taking another step and forcing him to back-step again. The Duchess de Vena was also much too powerful. One by one she eliminated all of the original Nine, raising a finger and taking a step for each until she had him backed against a wall. With nine fingers held up she took a tenth step, and with his back to the wall he could feel her breasts press against his chest as she whispered in his ear. "That seems to leave only one candidate . . . Your Grace." She leaned her head back to look into his eyes, though she didn't step away from him. And standing there pressed against him, she told him why his military weakness and destitute finances made him the only acceptable candidate. "So, you're eligible, your rank is appropriate, and you're weak militarily and financially. In short, you're the only suitable candidate who is no threat to the others."

He marveled at her blue eyes and tried not to stammer as he said, "Winston . . . and Arthur . . . had much the same reasoning."

Her tone turned thoughtful. "But you know, no matter how weak in resources, I don't think you'll ever be a weak king." And with that she kissed him, a long, slow, careful kiss, and whatever parts of her body were not pressed against him at the beginning of the kiss were definitely so by its end.

She suddenly pushed away from him, turned, and walked halfway across the room, then turned back to him. "So, I'll marry you. That's settled. But I have conditions."

She marched back toward him. "One, you'll not

whore around on me. You will not maintain con-
cubines and mistresses. I'm it for you, Charlie Cass.
Agreed?"

He swallowed and said, "Agreed."

"Two, this is the shittiest proposal a girl could imagine. I expect you to go away, think about it, come back,
and properly propose."

She didn't wait for his agreement. "And three, I
expect you to make me fall in love with you. Do that,
and we can be wed."

She turned away from him, marched to the door,
stopped, and turned partially back to him in an all too
familiar pose. She tossed a hip at him, winked, and
said, "We may yet have that dance, spacer."

CHAPTER 28
FEW MASKS REMAIN

"You must tell them, Your Grace," Ethallan said.

Charlie paced across the conference room where he was about to meet with the three leaders of the Free Aagerbanni Resistance: Tarlo, Dirkas, and Somal. Ethallan and Arthur had ganged up on him, arguing for him to drop the fictitious Chevard persona. "I can't declare myself openly. It's too soon."

"She's right, Charlie," Arthur said. "They'll never truly trust an unknown like Edwin Chevard, and will support him only so far as he can provide something they need, like this station and its services. But Charlie Cass, the legendary commander who beat Goutain at Solista, the man who brought two thousand men through the most abominable prison conditions, and brought them home alive. That's different."

"Your Grace, please forgive me for putting it this

way," Ethallan said, "but it'll not be hard to get them to support the de Maris bastard."

"No," Charlie said. "Not yet. Let me try it as Chevard, and if that doesn't work then I'll reconsider."

Since there was too much danger the Aagerbannis might recognize Arthur, shortly before they arrived he left the room. Charlie switched on the distortion field and Tarlo, Dirkas, and Somal entered the room moments later. Since their first meeting, Charlie had met with Tarlo informally a couple of times on Andyne-Borregga, and they shook hands cordially. Dirkas and Somal were somewhat more reserved since this was only the second time Chevard had met them. Ethallan served them tea; they traded bits and pieces of intelligence on the resistance and other activities. It was becoming clear that Goutain's naval forces were stretched to the limit, having suffered a steady stream of losses through attrition.

"But I don't understand," Tarlo said. "We've been comparing notes with the other independent states, and we can't account for the losses he's apparently suffered."

Charlie had thought about this carefully. He needed to show credibility. "It's the hunter-killers."

"I've seen those ships," Tarlo said. "They couldn't engage even a small destroyer."

"The what?" Dirkas asked, looking at Charlie and Tarlo. "What are you talking about?"

Tarlo said impatiently, "They're small warships

called hunter-killers. No more than about a fifty-man crew."

While Tarlo and Dirkas argued, Somal stared at Charlie as if she wanted to see into his soul. He interrupted the two men by tossing a single sheet of paper onto the conference table between them. "That's a list of ships those hunter-killers have destroyed, along with dates, times, and coordinates. They total three battleships, six cruisers, and fourteen destroyers. They don't engage them. They sneak up on them and hull them with a big warhead. Frequently, there are no survivors. And the list doesn't include commercial shipping."

Tarlo picked up the list and looked at it intently. Dirkas turned a silent look on Charlie much like Somal's stare. Still looking at the list Tarlo broke the silence. "This would . . . explain what we haven't been able to account for."

"But it leaves something unexplained," Somal said. "Namely: how do you know this?"

"Because they're my ships."

Somal smiled and nodded. Tarlo looked up from the sheet. "Here on the station, rumor has it that those hunter-killers have something to do with one of the Ten."

Charlie shrugged. "Don't believe everything you hear."

"So why did you call us here?" Somal asked. "This meeting, why?"

"Change of tactics," Charlie said. "It's time for us to

combine our forces, go on the offensive. I think we can put together a coalition. By my estimate, if we all contribute, we can put together an armada of more than a hundred and fifty warships, enough to rout Goutain and end this conflict."

Charlie hadn't expected them to jump and cheer, but they met his statement with silent stares. Dirkas asked, "A coalition. When did this idea come up?"

Charlie shrugged. "Slowly, and only as I began to realize the possibilities."

"And who would provide these ships?"

"You, me, the independent states, Kinatha, some of the ten dukes and duchesses."

"Forgive me, Mr. Chevard," Dirkas said. "But I find it a far stretch of the imagination to believe you could pull together such a coalition."

There it was—exactly what Ethallan and Arthur had told him. Seated at the end of the table, Ethallan met his eyes and lifted an eyebrow.

"You may have guessed," Charlie said, "that I represent certain interests that must remain hidden for the time being." All three of them continued to stare at him. "And I'm guessing that some of you, in fact, have realized Edwin Chevard is a fictitious name and a fictitious person. If I disclose whom I represent, will you give me your words it'll not leave this room?"

Somal and Dirkas nodded, while Tarlo said, "You have mine."

Through his implants, Charlie asked Arthur to join them. The door opened a moment later, then Arthur stepped into the room and remained standing. Charlie switched off the visual distortion field. Dirkas and Somal both started, though it was clear they didn't recognize him. Tarlo didn't react at all.

Ethallan stood. "May I present His Grace, Charles, Duke de Lunis?"

Dirkas grinned. "You're the fucking de Maris bastard."

Charlie stood and turned to Arthur. "And may I present my brother, Arthur, first legitimate son of Cesare de Maris and rightful heir to the de Maris ducal seat?"

Tarlo gave a loud whoop, came around the table, and shook Charlie's hand vigorously, then shook Arthur's. "Now I believe you about the hunter-killers. Can you really put together such a coalition?"

Charlie nodded, but didn't speak the thought that came to mind.

I sure hope so.

Del had to admit to herself that it was pure curiosity. Mr. Neverlose hadn't said anything in plain and simple terms, but from little bits here and there she'd gotten the distinct impression Charlie had had some sort of relationship with one of the trampsie prostitutes. Charlie and Arthur kept Del bottled up rather securely, and didn't allow her out into the station proper. Otherwise she'd go incognito to the trampsie bar where the girls worked. But since that wasn't possible, she'd asked Mr. Neverlose to bring the girls to her.

The two prostitutes were quite exotic and, Del had to admit, quite sexy looking. The one introduced to her as Janice Likesiteasy had dark, curly brown hair that hung to her shoulders, big brown eyes, dark red lips, and a dark complexion. Trina Godowna had a beautifully oval face framed in a wild profusion of frizzy red hair, green eyes, and black lipstick. Both of them wore simple dresses, nothing provocative, and yet they exuded sex appeal from every pore. Their little sister, Becky Neverenough, clearly barely into her teens, was just plain cute in blond pigtails and knee-high stockings.

"Your Worshipfulness," Janice said when they were introduced. Clearly uncomfortable, all three tried awkwardly to curtsy.

"Del," she said. "Please call me Del. And forget the curtsies."

Mr. Neverlose stood uncomfortably at the far end of the room. Del marched toward him and said, "Time to go, Mr. Neverlose. Only we girls allowed here." She ushered him out of the room.

She turned back to the girls. "Can I offer you something to drink? Tea . . . coffee . . ." The three girls frowned so she tried, "Something stronger?"

Becky said, "Ya, I'll take a shot."

"A shot?"

"Ya," Janice and Trina both agreed.

"A shot?"

"Ya," Janice said. "Whiskey, or whatever you got."

Del rang for a servant, ordered a bottle of whiskey and four glasses. It arrived along with a bottle of soda and some ice. The girls each poured themselves a small measure of whiskey and ignored the soda, so Del did the same. They raised their glasses and Janice said, "Here's to ya." They clinked glasses and the girls tossed the whiskey back in a single gulp, even their little sister, so Del followed suit. She wasn't a fan of whiskey, though she'd tasted her share, but not that way. However, she managed to keep it down without spluttering as it burned its way to her stomach.

"Why'd you want to see us?" Janice asked as she poured another round.

"Well . . . you knew Charlie, on Tachaann, and I wanted to meet his friends."

"Charlie?" Trina asked, frowning. "Oh, you mean Frankie. Ya, we know Frankie."

"Ya," Janice agreed. "We call him Frankie. He's a good guy. Nice roll in the sack too."

The girls all got a good laugh out of that, then they tossed back another shot of whiskey. Again, Del followed their lead. "Does he keep you busy that way?"

Janice shrugged. "Not lately. In fact, not for a while. I figured he was getting it somewhere else." She winked at Del.

Del blushed. "We're engaged to be married. Well, as soon as he proposes properly."

"What do you mean, proposes properly?"

Del described the conversation in which she'd agreed to marry Charlie.

"That moron," Janice said. The three girls crowded around her sympathetically. Janice poured more whiskey in her glass. Del tossed it back and was starting to feel the stuff.

"Just like a man," Trina said. "They're all idiots."

The four of them shared thoughts on the idiocy of the opposite sex. The girls asked her for more details on the betrothal, and between shots of whiskey she explained the politics involved.

"Hey," Trina said. "When he's gonna propose right, you make him take you to Momma's place."

Del shook her head sadly. "He and his brother and their advisors won't let me out of these apartments. They say it's too dangerous. And I suppose they're right."

Janice said, "Don't you worry about that. We'll talk to Momma. Nobody says no to Momma. She'll make him come through, and then you gonna get a good proposal."

"But look at you," she said to Janice. "My god you're sexy. How do I compete with you?"

"What?" Janice exclaimed. "Compete with me? Oh honey, you don't gotta compete with me. That man's so in love with you he can't see straight."

"He's in love with me?"

"Course he is. Can't you see it? You must be showing him a thing or two between the sheets, eh?" She and Trina and Becky shared a look and a wink, then threw each other high-fives.

Del blushed, and Janice frowned at her. "You mean you ain't done him yet?"

"Well . . . I . . . um . . . not after the way he proposed."

"Oh sweetheart," Janice said. "That's terrible. I mean, the man's an idiot, we all know that. But that man's gotta go do duke shit. He gotta kill people and fight wars and all that duke stuff. And if he's all tense because he's walking around all day with a hard-on thinking about you all the time, well he's probably gonna kill the wrong people and start the wrong wars. You gotta fuck his brains out."

"Janice!" Becky snapped.

"What?" Janice asked.

"You don't say fuck to a princess. It ain't polite."

"Well then what do I say when I wanna say fuck?"

"You say screw." Becky looked to Del for confirmation. "Ain't that right?"

Janice didn't wait for Del's answer. "Okay then, you gotta screw his brains out, honey. It's your civic duty."

Becky and Trina both agreed with considerable vehemence that it was Del's civic duty to *screw Charlie's brains out*. As they left, Del could tell she wasn't the only one feeling the whiskey.

Out in the hall, just as she was closing the door, she heard Becky say, "You done great, Janice. I think Frankie's finally gonna get laid."

Charlie met with the Kinathins and, one by one, with representatives of all of the independent states. Other than Aagerbanne, the Finalsans were the only ones to enthusiastically endorse such a coalition, obviously because they were the only two states, as yet, under occupation by the Four Tyrants. For the rest, he had to cut deals and make promises. For the Kinathins he agreed to fight tirelessly for the end of slavery in the Realm. For all of them, he had to promise he too would provide warships to the coalition, warships in quantities he didn't yet have.

His one big disappointment was Telka. She alone could provide thirty or forty warships to a coalition armada, and her support would be critical to bring in Rierma, Band, Chelko, Harrimo, and Sig. The five of them, while smaller houses, could together muster another thirty or so warships. But there had been no contact from Telka, no response that she would meet Edwin Chevard here, and her absence—and that of the others—cut the strength of his armada in half.

The night before he was to return to Starfall he had invited Del to dinner at Momma Toofat's, where he'd arranged with Momma for a candlelit dinner in a private room. He hadn't planned on taking her to Momma's, but Del insisted, and when he tried to refuse, Momma came personally and threatened to hit him upside the head with a big rolling pin.

Delilah wore a bright red evening gown cut quite low in the front, even lower in the back, and fashioned from a lacy fabric that was ever so slightly translucent in the most enticing places. Charlie tried not to stare, but couldn't help stealing glances whenever possible.

And of course she caught him at it repeatedly, seemed fully aware of the effect she had on him.

Momma's place on Andyne-Borregga was actually two distinct establishments with separate entrances, a spacer bar on one side and a nice, though certainly not elegant, restaurant on the other. Janice, Trina, and Becky were all giggles and veiled looks as he escorted Del through the main dining room. Del saw them, waved, ran over to them and they all shared hugs. It surprised Charlie to learn that Del knew the girls. The four of them spoke in hushed tones for several seconds, their whispering punctuated by surreptitious glances his way.

Momma broke it up, personally hustled Charlie and Del into a small, private dining room in which a table for two had been meticulously prepared. The table was round with a cushioned bench seat wrapped halfway around it, the two place settings arrayed so that Charlie and Del sat side by side. Charlie thought it best not to tell Del that these were the rooms where the girls took their johns for dinner and drinks. The tables and seating were designed so that if a spacer got amorous in the middle of a meal, the girl was close at hand with no table separating them.

Charlie had no objection to the arrangement.

"You not ordering tonight," Momma said. "Momma Toofat got the dinner all planned out; you just eat."

After Momma left, Del said, "This should be interesting."

"She's a good cook," Charlie said. "I mean, spacers in the bar are happy with slop. But for family, friends, while it's not elegant, it's damn good."

Momma brought in a bottle of wine, accompanied by Trina with the first course. Charlie and Del ate, and they chatted amiably, and he hadn't the faintest idea how to do this marriage proposal thing. Especially since she knew it was coming. Did she expect him to get down on one knee? He'd do that, if that's what she wanted. But that didn't seem like the Del he knew. He wrestled with the idea throughout dinner.

At one point he realized that if he was going to propose to her, he shouldn't be keeping secrets, so he told her about the defenses at Starfall, and the coalition he was trying to put together. Her eyes widened as he spoke, then she leaned back and said, "Aagerbanne, Istanna, Toellan, Kinatha—all of them."

"It's still not enough," he said. "I need Telka and the other duchies. Without them, it's just not enough."

"I might be able to help with Telka," she said. She then got rather excited about the whole mess, and through the rest of the dinner she speculated on how to approach the Duchess. Charlie realized she probably could convince Telka to join them.

They finished the last course, and Momma brought them a couple of snifters with a splash of brandy. He could tell Del really enjoyed the food, and hopefully the company as well.

"My god," she said. "You're terrified."

She'd caught him off guard and all he could say was, "I'm not sure how to do this. I was taught how to be a soldier. No one, especially not me, ever thought I'd be sitting at dinner trying to figure out how to propose marriage to a princess."

She shook her head sadly. "I think your problem is you can't get past the princess thing. Why don't you try thinking of me as just a girl?"

He realized he was never going to get the upper hand in this, decided to just spit it out. "I want you to marry me. Not because of the politics—well there's that too. But I want you to marry me just because I . . . want . . . you . . . to."

She smiled and leaned close to him. As she spoke he could feel her breath against his cheek. "That's a pretty good start, Mr. Cass. Now just ask the big question."

He grimaced. "Will you marry me?"

She frowned and considered the question carefully. "I believe it's traditional to offer me a ring."

"I thought about that," he said. "I could have found someplace here to buy a ring. But it wouldn't have meant anything, and I already have a ring for you. It's back at Starfall, though, so I can't give it to you right at this moment."

She moved even closer so that her lips brushed lightly against his cheek as she spoke. "You bought a ring for me before we came here?"

"No," he said, thinking he'd made a horrible mistake. "It was my mother's. It's the only thing I have of hers. Cesare gave it to her. They say he loved her. And when she . . . died, he made sure I got it to remember her by. I thought . . . you could wear that ring."

She spoke slowly and carefully, her voice a faint whisper in his ear. "Oh Mr. Cass, you just scored big-time points in the romance department."

Charlie couldn't remember how they got there, but he was on his back on the long cushioned seat, she on top of him, kissing him like she'd never kissed him before, softly, tenderly. When they came up for air she said, "Yes, I just may have to do my civic duty."

He wasn't sure what that meant.

But he certainly enjoyed dessert.

Neither of them let it go any further than serious kissing and some heavy breathing, not in Momma Toofat's. Del carefully straightened her somewhat disheveled gown and Charlie his rumpled tunic, and Del used a silk napkin to wipe her lipstick off his lips and cheek. On their way out of the restaurant Charlie saw Becky, Trina, and Janice high-fiving each other. Momma fluttered around Charlie and Del like the mother of the bride. However, they didn't make it out to Andyne-Borregga's commercial concourse because the twins stepped in front of them before they got to the door. Add said, "There's a man here wants to see you. He was smart enough to approach us, smart enough not to attempt to approach you directly. He says you know him, and would want to see him. He says his name is Thessa."

Charlie recalled the name, but couldn't place it. Ell gave him the clue he needed. "He's wearing civilian clothes, little brother, but he's navy all the way."

Telka's distinguished looking senior captain. "Yes," Charlie said. "I do want to see him." He turned to Del. "I'm sorry." To Ell he said, "Please see that Her Highness gets back safely—"

He stopped in midsentence as Ell slowly shook her head. "He wants to see you both. And he mentioned Her Highness by name. He has a private room here, though he wouldn't let us enter it. He said you'll be safe."

Charlie understood. It must be Telka herself in the private room, and she didn't want to be observed by anyone as having personally come to Andyne-Borregga. "We can trust him," Charlie said. Add and Ell both looked uncomfortable with that, but they had no alternative.

The twins led them to another private room, Add knocked on the door politely and Thessa answered it. He bowed to Del and Charlie. "Your Highness. Your Grace."

He stepped aside and Charlie let Del precede him. The room they stepped into was meant for larger private parties, and *both* Rierma and Telka awaited them there. "Charles, my boy," Rierma said. "And Delilah, you look absolutely stunning."

Telka greeted Del. "Your Highness." Del curtsied politely.

The plump little woman turned to Charlie. "Your Grace, or is it . . . Edwin Chevard?"

Telka had also pieced together a fairly good idea of the rest of Charlie's activities, confronted him with them. A frown appeared on Del's face and it deepened as she listened to the older woman. To get Telka's cooperation, Charlie had to tell her about the hunter-killers. To Telka and Thessa's credit, neither of them showed the skepticism that others had.

"You didn't tell me about these new ships," Del demanded angrily. "How dare you, after what we agreed to this evening."

"I told you about the alliance and Starfall's defenses," Charlie said. "It never occurred to me you'd care about ships."

Telka's eyes narrowed; she looked from Charlie to Del and back again. Then she turned to Rierma. "They're lovers, aren't they?"

Del blushed almost scarlet, and Rierma said, "Pretty obvious, isn't it?"

"Absolutely not," Del said. "Not if he's going to keep secrets like that from me."

Telka smiled, took one of Del's hands, and said, "Don't try to fool an old woman, my dear."

Rierma asked, "And what did you two agree to this evening?"

Del's eyes widened and she looked at Charlie. He knew they both looked like a couple of guilty children. She took a deep breath in an obvious effort to calm herself. Then she carefully repeated her reasoning for why Charlie was the only possible choice for a husband. "The perfect compromise candidate, and we're betrothed. But we're not lovers, not yet." She said that almost defiantly.

Telka asked, "But what of your betrothal to Dieter?"

Charlie told them about Cesare's sneaky gift of the right to choose Del's husband. And after a few questions about its authenticity, Rierma slapped Charlie on the back. "Congratulations are in order, my boy. And, I must admit, you *are* the only candidate that none of us will try to have assassinated. At least not right away."

Before they got down to any serious planning, Charlie said, "I should get Arthur in here."

Rierma frowned. "Arthur? I thought he was kidnapped by pirates."

Charlie grimaced and mumbled quietly, "Avast ye maties. Shiver ye timbers, and all that stuff."

Rierma shook his head and his frown deepened. Telka burst into roars of laughter, with tears streaming down her cheeks. "You're also Raul the Damned? Is there even such a thing as the Mexak League?"

Charlie told them about Drakwin. They all got a good laugh out of it, and Telka said, "You're a sneakier son-of-a-bitch than your father." Even Del calmed down, and didn't seem to mind that he'd forgotten to tell her *that* secret as well.

After Arthur joined them, to Charlie's complete surprise, he learned that Telka had already formed an alliance with Rierma, Band, Harrimo, and Sig. "Chelko is too hotheaded," she said. "We can't trust him to be discreet so we'll bring him in at the last minute."

Charlie also learned their alliance had twenty

warships stationed in deep space seven light-years off Andyne-Borregga. "You and this space station are the only things holding this coalition together, so we've decided its defense is paramount."

That was something Charlie had been worrying about for some time now. Thessa and Arthur would review the station's defenses with an eye to coordination with the added warships, and during the next month they'd marshal their forces here in preparation for an assault on the Four Tyrants.

"Please," Del said. "Don't harm my father and mother."

"My dear," Telka said kindly. "Your parents need to be . . . contained . . . not murdered."

They discussed more strategy, and while Charlie was open about pretty much everything, two things he managed to conceal from them were the warships that Roger had found on platform twelve and the improved state of his finances. Telka might object to such a strong king, and Charlie might lose his carefully nurtured status as a compromise candidate. The funny thing was, he really didn't care all that much about being king.

He just didn't want to mess up the chance to marry Del.

Arthur mentioned that they needed to have one of the hunter-killers continue gunrunning for the Syndonese insurgents. Del, Thessa, Rierma, and Telka all started, looking at Charlie with expressions ranging from surprise to calculating assessment. Del asked, "You mean you're behind that, too?"

CHAPTER 29
TRUTH EMERGES

"Your Grace, we've detected several transition wakes incoming at about five light-years. They're at the extreme limit of our detection range, so it's difficult to make out any details yet, but they're driving hard enough to be warships."

Charlie sat up in bed, rubbed at his eyes, and tried to shake the cobwebs out of his head. It took him a moment to remember he was back on Luna, had only returned from Andyne-Borregga two days ago. He looked at his watch; it was the middle of the night.

"I'll be right there," he told Pelletier. Charlie stopped only to splash some water on his face and throw on some clothes.

Pelletier had dramatically transformed the command center. An operator now sat at every console, and a buzz of activity filled the air, while Pelletier occupied an office to one side of the main room. "We've got about a day and a half," Pelletier said as Charlie stepped into his office. Anticipating Charlie's next question, he added, "And no, they're still not close enough for any details."

"What's the status on our defenses?"

"Progress on the Lunan surface batteries has gone better than expected. We've got twenty fully operational, and those are big transition batteries, so they can easily punch through the shielding on a large battleship. And each includes a couple of defensive emplacements.

"The orbital weapons platforms are coming up more slowly because we've focused a lot of attention on Luna Prime, but we've got eight fully operational, and those platforms carry a lot of firepower as well.

"The ships are problematic. Roger's gone through the four heavy cruisers, checked them out fully, and they're all capable of operating at between seventy and ninety percent effectiveness, with no failures in major subsystems."

"Well, that's not too bad," Charlie said. "After six months on deep space patrol, the best of ships is usually down to seventy-five, maybe eighty percent effectiveness."

Pelletier shook his head. "The problem is crews. We've cherry-picked enough experienced spacers from the other defensive stations to make up a crew and a half for the big cruisers, and we're still completely missing some specialists' ratings. Roger's reviewing the qualifications on the spacers you brought back from Andyne-Borregga, but he's only just started."

For several seconds Charlie stared at the data Pelletier showed him, but couldn't escape the painful truth that years of experience told him. "We can't put those ships into combat, if it comes to that—not with new crews that haven't had a chance to shake down yet. That would be disastrous. But maybe there's a way they don't have to fight. Maybe they don't need to be dangerous."

"How's that, Your Grace?"

Charlie grinned. "They just need to *look* dangerous."

"It looks like ten wakes, sir," the technician said, carefully examining the data on his screens. Charlie, Winston, and Pelletier stood behind him looking over his shoulder. "And I'd guess that two of them are large battleships, with some cruisers and destroyers thrown into the mix."

"How far out?" Charlie asked.

"Point-one light-year, Your Grace. Decelerating strongly, I'd say down-transition within the next few minutes, depending upon how they want to play it."

Pelletier's command center reminded Charlie of the bridge of a ship, though this ship commanded far more firepower than any warship. But like on any warship, they spent most of their time waiting.

Charlie asked, "Everything in place?"

Pelletier looked over the technician's shoulder at the screen. Charlie knew Pelletier was nervous about the situation, but professional enough not to show it to his people. "The surface batteries and the shielding for this installation are at full combat status. The platforms, the four cruisers, and *The Headsman* are keeping power drain down, but can come to full combat status in about ten minutes."

"Good."

"Not really, sir. If someone knew to look, they could detect them from the edge of our nearspace, and I don't like that."

"What's done is done. No use worrying over it."

"Yes, Your Grace."

"Sir," the technician said. "They're about two minutes out from our nearspace, sir, and not leapfrogging, so it's not an attack run."

Charlie looked at the data on the screen in front of the technician. He was right. If it had been an attack run, they'd have long ago down-transited a destroyer so it could uplink scan, nav, and targeting data to the other ships still in transition.

"Sir, they're crossing into nearspace now, and . . . ." The technician checked his data. " . . . holding at forty lights, driving into the system in transition."

Charlie could sense relief wash over everyone in the center. No one would make such an approach if they thought any significant defensive capability might oppose them.

"There we go, sir, they just down-transited at twelve AUs. I got ten clear transition flares." The technician worked intently at his console for a few moments. "Looks like two battleships, four heavy cruisers, and four destroyers, and . . . definitely de Maris."

Another ten minutes passed while they confirmed the technician's observations. "They're driving at point-eight lights and decelerating at just under two thousand gravities, sir. That should put them here at Luna with velocity matched in just over four hours."

"I've got an incoming signal, sir," another technician said. "The Duke de Maris wishes to speak with the Duke de Lunis."

"Put it through to my implants, blind copy Winston, and record."

Theode's image appeared in front of him. "Charlie, dear brother," Theode said. "I've come to pay my respects."

Charlie asked, "With a small fleet of warships?"

"Of course, dear brother. How else should one of the most powerful men in the Realm travel, but with a proper retinue? My officers tell me you have Starfall's surface shielding active. Now is that any way to greet your dear brother?"

"It's not a greeting, Theode, merely a precaution. We had no idea who was approaching."

Theode smiled, though it was more a sneer. "Well, it's a precaution that's no longer necessary now that you know it's me, so cut the power feed to Starfall's shielding."

"I won't do that until I know your intentions."

"My intentions are to visit my beloved brother. And active shields are a rather inhospitable way of welcoming me, don't you think? So cut the shields, or I'll cut them with heavy bombardment. We both know that without other defenses, those shields will only hold for so long."

Charlie glanced at Winston, his look a silent question. "It's borderline," Winston said. "It's much cleaner if he makes a hard threat once the shields are down, and especially if he personally threatens you." He and Charlie had discussed this at some length. If it was one of the Ten coming at them, even with a small fleet of warships, there would be unpleasant ramifications if Charlie fired the first shot without provocation. On the other hand, if he could get his guest to make an open threat, Charlie would be free to act. And while the Ten might not support him fully, any repercussions after the fact would be limited.

Charlie turned to Pelletier. "Cut the shields."

Pelletier didn't try to hide his unhappiness as he gave the order. But he was a seasoned officer and knew not to challenge a superior's order. And in any case, they could bring the shields back up in an instant.

"That's much better," Theode said, the sneer unchanged. "My officers tell me we'll arrive in a little less than four hours, and I'm sure it'll be a wonderful reunion. I do hope you show better hospitality than you've shown so far."

They parked the ten warships in high orbits around Terra, Luna's primary. Theode had brought Gaida, and while Theode strutted through the halls of Starfall, Gaida followed him radiating cold disapproval of Charlie and everything associated with him. Theode also brought a bodyguard of twelve armed soldiers, men with a hard look about them. Since Charlie didn't recognize any of them, he concluded they were mercenaries.

Theode insisted on a grand tour of Starfall. At one point, standing on a high balcony overlooking the sterile Lunar landscape, he said, "When you're gone I think I'll use Starfall as a vacation retreat. It boasts wonderful vistas."

Charlie glanced at Winston, who responded with a slight shake of his head—still not enough.

Theode made other veiled references to Charlie's demise, but never came out with an outright threat, and he clearly enjoyed Charlie's helplessness in the matter. After the tour Gaida said, "Well, you've made the place reasonably comfortable. You can show us to our rooms now."

Charlie had thought about this carefully, had structured the tour so they finished in one of the large ballrooms in Starfall, a room with many entrances on all sides. "Rooms? I'm not providing you with rooms. Surely you know you're not invited to stay."

Theode snarled, "It's not up to you to decide if we stay or not. We're staying."

"But it is up to me. I am the consecrated lord of this house, and by law, in this house and on these properties, my word is law."

Theode's temper was actually rather easy to manipulate. He shouted, "Your word is nothing, whoreson. Your word is worth only what I say it is, and my word is backed by these men here." He swept out an arm, indicating the mercenaries. "And the warships I have in orbit."

Charlie smiled, a grin meant to aggravate Theode further. "Are you threatening me, Twerp?"

Theode turned a vivid red, leaned toward Charlie, and shouted in his face, spittle flying from his lips as he spoke. "I told you never to call me that, you son of a poxed whore. I'm not threatening you. I'm telling you the facts. Your days of pretending at nobility are through. I'm here to put an end to you and the games you've been playing with that Chevard fellow."

That was an interesting comment. The Four Tyrants must have assumed Charlie was working with Edwin Chevard. He was glad they hadn't truly put all the pieces together yet.

"Theode," Gaida said, "calm yourself."

Her words might have had some effect, but Charlie widened his grin even further and said, "So, Twerp, you're going to kill me, is that it?"

Theode's voice had grown hoarse from screaming. "I'm going to do worse than kill you. You're going to die slow."

Charlie looked at Winston, who nodded and said, "That should do it nicely."

Charlie stepped back from Theode as if in fear. He subvocalized into his implants, "Pelletier, phase one."

Theode stepped forward, still red-faced with rage and screaming uncontrollably in Charlie's face. For each step he took, Charlie back-stepped, allowing Theode to drive him across the room, slowly putting distance between them and the mercenaries. Winston, to whom no one paid any attention, stepped back against a far wall, leaving Gaida and the mercenaries isolated in the middle of the room. It was then that Charlie's squad of thirty marines, in full combat armor and carrying heavy grav rifles, appeared from several directions at once with their weapons lowered, surrounding the mercenaries. Two marines stepped in front of Winston, shielding him against possible fire from the mercenaries. Two more stepped behind Theode, shielding him and Charlie from the mercenaries, though with his back to the entire tableau Theode was wholly unaware of the situation and continued his tirade.

Charlie thought of Arthur's treatment in Theode's hands. And he thought of Cesare, and knew that Theode and Gaida must have had something to do with his father's death. And finally he thought about all the times Theode had called his mother a whore, and all his restraint fell away.

Almost calmly, he reached out, gripped Theode's throat, and squeezed, cutting the rant off in midsentence. Theode choked. Charlie squeezed harder and Theode thrashed at him, his eyes bulging and face turning purple. Charlie wanted to kill the bastard, knew he had enough strength, backed by enough anger, to crush the little shit's windpipe right then and there. He knew he could do it, but then he saw Winston standing on the far side of the room, quietly shaking his head from side to side. He hesitated, realized that if he didn't do this proper and legal, he'd never be able to reinstate Arthur.

He tossed Theode in a tumble of arms and legs at Add's and Ell's feet, and said, "Keep him quiet."

Faced with overwhelming force, the mercenaries, characteristically inclined to self-preservation as all mercenaries were, raised their hands and did not resist. Charlie's marines quickly disarmed and cuffed them. Add held Theode while Ell held Gaida, so they didn't need cuffs. Theode screamed, "You can't do this. This is illegal."

Winston said calmly, "But it is legal, Your Grace. Since you threatened Duke Charles with murder in his own house, he is at liberty to exercise rather extraordinary powers."

Theode screamed a few epithets at Winston until Charlie said to Add, "Please shut him up."

As Charlie turned to Ell and Gaida, he heard Theode's tirade cut off with a choked gurgle. Gaida gave him an arrogant look and said, "I did not threaten you, whoreson. So detaining me is illegal."

"But you did just slander me, a member of the Ten. I can't stand here in my own house and allow such a thing to go unchallenged." Charlie said to Ell, "Put her under deep neural probe. I want it on record how Cesare really died. We'll worry about the legalities of it later."

"No," Gaida shouted. "You can't do that!" He ignored her screams as Ell dragged her away. Putting her under a probe was a bit of a stretch legally, but if it revealed what Charlie suspected, no one would care.

And then we'll see who was truly the whore, he thought.

In phase one, Pelletier cut all communications in and out of Starfall and started the power-up cycles on the platforms, just as *The Headsman* and the four cruisers from platform twelve began bringing their systems up to full combat status as quickly as possible. They'd split their crew and a half between the four cruisers and were able to man almost all but the weapons stations. As such, the four new cruisers couldn't engage the de Maris warships, but they'd appear on the de Maris screens as fully capable heavy cruisers. If it did turn into a real battle, they had instructions to run. They were also remotely powering up the remaining untested platforms. Like the four cruisers, they were useless in a real fight, but they'd show up on enemy screens as capable weaponry. Their one concern was how long it would take someone on board one of the ten de Maris warships to detect the hot spots appearing in the Lunan system. If it turned into a real battle, they needed ten to fifteen minutes before the shooting started.

Pelletier spoke through Charlie's implants. "Taggart is trying to contact Theode."

"What's our status?"

"Platforms are at seventy percent. Five more minutes."

Charlie started for the command center. "Put Taggart through to me."

Charlie had known Taggart all his life. The man was in his seventies, had probably been born in de Maris livery and was at the height of his capabilities as a senior officer, but he now appeared tense and haggard. "Duke Charles," he said. "I must speak with Duke Theode."

Taggart had earned and deserved respect, so Charlie spoke accordingly. "I'm sorry, Admiral Taggart, but Duke Theode is otherwise engaged."

Charlie could see the strain written in every line of the older man's face. "I'm sorry, Your Grace, but I must insist."

At that moment Charlie reached the command center and dropped into a seat behind a vacant console. To Taggart he said, "First off, I will remind you I'm a member of the Ten, so I'm not inclined to heed your insistence. Still, we are men of honor, and it's not my intention to play at lord of the castle. Instead, I simply ask your indulgence for one moment. I'm going to transmit a recording of my most recent conversation with Duke Theode. Please pay careful attention." He nodded at Pelletier, who responded by throwing a switch.

Taggart watched as the scene in the ballroom played out, including Theode's open and undisguised threat. Charlie spoke before Taggart could say anything. "Because Duke Theode threatened my person with murder in my own house, I am within my rights to hold him until I can deliver him to a tribunal of the Ten. And, as a hostile force, I must insist that you withdraw from the Lunan system immediately." Holding one of the Ten in that way was a stretch legally, but he hoped Taggart didn't know that.

Before Taggart could answer, another man appeared in the transmission with him. He wore a plain tunic without livery, clearly another mercenary. "Listen to me, asshole," the man said. "You give us back Duke Theode right now, or we bomb the fuck out of you."

Taggart grimaced and didn't argue. Charlie now understood. Theode had put mercenaries on the bridge of every ship to ensure the loyalty of his officers, and had placed them over the ranking officers.

Taggart said to Charlie, "We're seeing what appear to be large defensive installations coming online."

Charlie said, "Yes. My house is defended by twelve large orbital weapons platforms, five heavy cruisers, and more than fifty surface batteries." It couldn't hurt to exaggerate a little. "You're englobed, in orbits that make you extremely vulnerable, with subsystems powered down because your threat assessment told you there is no threat. You're badly outgunned." Charlie leaned forward and made it clear he was speaking to the mercenary. "So maybe you should reconsider your decision to 'bomb the fuck' out of us, as you so eloquently put it."

Charlie gave the fellow a nasty grin. "I'm pretty sure you don't want those to be your last words."

The mercenary looked uncertain. Taggart said, "We see no evidence of surface batteries."

Charlie gave Taggart an unfriendly smile. "They wouldn't be all that effective if you could easily identify them, now would they?"

Charlie said to Pelletier, "Phase two."

They'd split the targeting of the operational surface batteries somewhat evenly among the ten hostile warships, with two targeting each of the vessels. Pelletier issued a command and Charlie watched the mercenary's eyes widen as the big transition batteries fired a shot across the bow of each of the de Maris warships.

Charlie asked, "Do you see evidence of surface batteries now?" He let them have a few seconds to think about that, then said, "I must ask you to withdraw immediately. There'll be no more warning shots. The next order I give will be for a continuous barrage by all stations in the system, no quarter given."

The mercenary said, "The fucker's bluffing."

Taggart said to Charlie, "Your Grace, may I have ten minutes to discuss this with my staff?"

Charlie knew the older man had to talk to his other captains, then they had to do something about the mercenaries on their ships. "You have ten minutes, but during that time, if your shields go up, or we detect any increase in power drain on any of your ships, we commence firing."

"Understood," Taggart said. He nodded and cut the connection.

Charlie turned to Pelletier and didn't have to ask. Pelletier said, "The eight platforms we repaired are fully operational."

If Taggart believed that all five heavy cruisers were fully combat capable, and all the platforms were also capable, and there were fifty—not merely twenty—surface batteries, he'd be facing overwhelming odds. On the other hand, if he called Charlie's bluff, some of the active platforms in solar orbit were a couple of AUs distant and could only be marginally effective against ships close in to Luna, and the cruisers were useless. It would be a nasty fight, their principal advantages being the poor deployment of Taggart's ships, and the fact that the platforms and surface installations boasted weaponry heavy enough to punch through even the largest battleship's shielding. Charlie waited in silence, knowing it would be a toss-up if Taggart decided to fight.

Taggart called back in seven minutes. There was no sign of the mercenary. "My adjutant informs me, Duke Charles, that, because of the threats Duke Theode made, you are within your rights to bring the matter before the Ten, but actually holding him is a bit of a stretch."

Charlie shrugged. "Be that as it may, I'm holding him as assurance that you'll leave this system peacefully. And I assure you that he'll be treated well."

Taggart stared at him for a long moment, and it was then that Charlie knew he'd won. Taggart clearly believed that Charlie's overwhelming firepower left him helpless. He simply said, "As you earlier ordered us, we'll withdraw from the system immediately. We haven't begun powering up yet because you might have viewed that as a hostile action. I ask only that you allow my adjutant to remain behind as your guest and Theode's legal advisor."

"Granted," Charlie said, as a sense of relief washed through him. "You may power up your ships one at a time, and one by one withdraw to a rendezvous point of your choosing a minimum of one light-year from heliopause."

Taggart closed his eyes and nodded. "Thank you, Your Grace. And I must apologize for . . . that fellow's rudeness." The mercenary was apparently no longer allowed to roam Taggart's bridge at will.

"Apology accepted," Charlie said. "However, I should mention that because rumors persist regarding Lady Gaida's culpability in Cesare's death, I know she'd want to clear her name, so she's undergoing deep neural probe as we speak. Voluntarily, of course."

A smile formed slowly on Taggart's face. Charlie continued, "I assure you she's not being harmed in any way, but we should shortly have definitive proof of her innocence—or otherwise—and I thought you might wish to personally review the data. If so, you're welcome to remain as my guest."

As Charlie spoke Taggart's smile grew into a broad

grin. "I'd most certainly be interested in reviewing such data, Your Grace."

It took about an hour, but they soon had a clear, irrefutable picture of the cause of Cesare's death, and they transmitted the data up to Taggart and the other de Maris captains. Taggart had his medical staff review the data carefully, then an hour passed with a lot of encrypted communications between the ten warships, though none powered up any major subsystems. When he and Charlie spoke again the man was livid. "That bitch. I suspected, but had no evidence. It shames me."

"Admiral," Charlie said. "I'd say that, since your oath was taken by Theode under false pretenses, your oath is null and void."

"I'm aware of that, Your Grace. I and my captains and my adjutant have discussed it thoroughly. If Arthur were here we'd swear our fealty to him immediately."

"I can take you to Arthur," Charlie said, thinking that if they could get the de Maris forces to join the coalition, they could avoid war altogether.

Taggart started and his eyes narrowed suspiciously. "What do you mean?"

"Arthur has been, and is, my guest at a distant space station I own. And I assure you, he's been treated as the heir to the de Maris ducal seat should be."

Taggart said nothing for several seconds, though his face displayed his changing emotions as he processed that data. To his credit, he asked no questions, but clearly managed to put the pieces together. "This space station, is it Andyne-Borregga?"

"It is."

"Your Grace, Nadama and Goutain are marshaling a fleet as we speak, with the intention of destroying that entire installation. It was their idea that Theode should come here, I think to keep you occupied."

"Oh shit!"

Taggart's voice carried a note of desperation. "We have to go there now. We have to defend him."

Charlie shook his head. "I'll go there, but I'll not take unsworn men with me."

"Then I'll swear to you, on the condition that you release me when I can swear to Arthur. And I'll put these ships at your command."

"Accepted. Let the other captains know." To Pelletier he said, "Let's go save my brother."

CHAPTER 30
MAYBE TOO LATE

With transition coms limited to about five light-years, they immediately dispatched fast courier ships to Andyne-Borregga and to all members of the coalition with news of the impending battle, and the news that Charlie would be bringing a task force of more than ten warships. From what Taggart knew of Nadama and Goutain's plans, they were assuming Theode would completely neutralize Charlie and were in no hurry. So they were taking their time and marshaling their forces carefully. With the distances involved, Charlie was confident that he and most of the independent states could get to the station before the attack force. Telka was bringing in another thirty ships supplied by her alliance of duchies, but that, and the bulk of the Kinathin fleet, wouldn't show up until some time after the action started. That meant that in the initial stages of the battle, based on total number of warships, they'd be evenly matched, but Nadama and Goutain would have a decided advantage in big capital ships and experienced crews. The battle could be lost before coalition reinforcements got there.

They also dispatched one of Taggart's small, fast destroyers back to Traxis. The destroyer's captain would show the rest of the de Maris captains and crews the probe data on Gaida's complicity in Cesare's death, then lead them all to the defense of Andyne-Borregga. They'd probably be too late, but the truth needed to survive whatever happened there.

Taggart was a little pissed when he learned that, of Charlie's five heavy cruisers, only *The Headsman* was in any condition to fight. Though, when he further learned that the problem was really a lack of experienced crews, he offered to thin his own crews a bit, and add them to those already on Charlie's ships. In that way they were able to crew three of the new cruisers, and all three ships would use the time in transit to Andyne-Borregga to run simulations and shake down as much as possible. In any case, they'd hold the new cruisers in reserve until absolutely needed.

One day later they up-transited on a vector to Andyne-Borregga. Charlie's small force consisted of nine de Maris and five de Lunis warships, including *The Thirteenth Man*, all slightly undermanned.

Charlie could only hope it was enough . . .

Thraka had been one of Cesare's retainers for years, but he'd always been a practical man, and long ago had found it quite lucrative to sell information to Nadama. And over the years his clandestine relationship with the de Satarna had grown to include the performance of unpleasant little tasks, which resulted in even higher compensation. When he sent a message to Nadama that Delilah was being held on Andyne-Borregga, Dieter replied with, "Bring the woman to me. Kill whom you must, but bring her to me unharmed." The bonus he promised would be worth almost any risk.

It had taken two months for him to work his way into her immediate service. And though they desperately needed experienced spacers, there was enough confusion on Andyne-Borregga that it was a simple matter for him to hide his own background and avoid shipping out on one of the warships. Interestingly enough, as a former de Maris retainer, he was given a greater degree of trust than many others.

"Your Highness," he said politely as he bowed deeply from the waist. He placed the tray containing a light luncheon for her and her woman on the table in her luxurious little prison.

"Thank you, Thraka," she said. "You may go."

The key to getting her off the space station would be transportation. But there were any number of small tramp vessels making use of Andyne-Borregga's facilities, and he'd had no trouble hiring one with a crew who would ask no questions. The place was, after all, a free port. The ship he'd hired had a smuggling run to complete, but they'd return sometime in the next tenday, and all would be in place then. He'd have to kill a few people, but that was never a problem.

Charlie had one of the new cruisers down-transit three days and fifteen light-years out from Andyne-Borregga. During Charlie's last visit, Arthur had been in the process of setting up relay buoys at five-light-year intervals in a carefully structured globe around the Borreggan system. Each buoy's transition detectors suffered from the same five-light-year limit as everything else, but by properly positioning about thirty of them, each could automatically relay scan data and warn the system of incoming ships out to about fifteen light-years.

The courier ship they'd sent out should have arrived about two days ahead of them. So with the station expecting an assault, fourteen transition wakes driving hard in toward the system, clearly warships all, could easily be mistaken for ships of the Four Tyrants. The cruiser used its transition com to identify them to the station, got a quick briefing on the situation, and uploaded the information to Charlie's small task force. There was a large fleet headed their way from the direction of Turnlee, and the shooting would start in about two days. The cruiser up-transited and rejoined them.

It was frustrating for them all, three days out and

the shooting was going to begin long before they got there. The enemy fleet was too far out for details, so they didn't know if they were coming in with massively overwhelming odds, or something more modest, something Arthur, Darmczek, and Roacka could hold off long enough for Charlie's task force to get there. And once the news spread through the ship, the atmosphere onboard grew subdued and quiet, the pre-battle introspection with which any experienced combat veteran was all too familiar. Two days in transition with no news, but still one day out from Borreggan nearspace, one of their destroyers down-transited and began uplinking information just as the battle began.

Nadama and Goutain came in with a force of almost one hundred warships, along with accompanying tenders, escorts, and scouts. Arrayed against them were the first twenty ships Telka's alliance had supplied, about a dozen ships from the independent states that happened to be in the vicinity, and Charlie's ten hunter-killers, plus the not-inconsiderable defenses of the station itself, including four orbital weapons platforms positioned for close support of the station. It wasn't enough by a long shot, especially considering that Nadama and Goutain's forces had been working closely together for some time now, while Charlie's coalition had never drilled as a combined force. With the strength of numbers and a much better organized command structure, Nadama and Goutain had good reason to be confident. But they hadn't taken into consideration the hunter-killers—still didn't really know of their existence—their capabilities or the tactics they'd use.

They came in using a classic leapfrog attack formation, their ships split up into four waves about five hours apart. One of their scouts down-transited about ten light-years out. With a five-light-year limit on detectable transition phenomena, the scout couldn't detect anything inside the Borreggan system, but it could spot and uplink any activity it observed five light-years out from the system, the traditional point of first engagement. They could only hope that the scout couldn't see, or perhaps just didn't know to look for, the hunter-killers that Darmczek and Roacka had lying in wait there.

The first wave consisted of fifteen Syndonese medium and light destroyers accompanied by ten medium and heavy cruisers. If all followed the traditional strike scenario, two of the destroyers would be well out in front of the first wave, would down-transit just out of range of first engagement and start feeding targeting data to the rest of the ships in the wave. With that information, the first wave would down-transit safely and engage any hostile forces in the vicinity. The destroyers were there for their speed and maneuverability, the cruisers to back them up with heavy firepower if needed. The first wave would clear the vicinity of first engagement and start clearing a swath in toward Borreggan nearspace. With first engagement cleared, and with uplink data from the first wave, the second wave would include heavier ships that should be able to penetrate deeper before down-transiting. They'd finish the job of clearing the way into the system, and the third and fourth waves, consisting of big cruisers and battleships, would down-transit inside Borreggan nearspace and start heavy bombardment of the system's defenses.

The two destroyers leading the first wave down-transited as planned, but to their surprise they detected no activity at the point of first engagement, though they did detect a coalition force of eight cruisers and six destroyers about one light-year farther in. They uplinked the unconventional positions of the coalition warships, and with first engagement apparently already clear, the commodore of the first wave decided to drive right through first engagement and down-transit just short of the waiting coalition forces.

It was just beyond first engagement that the silent and unseen hunter-killers hit them, slamming torpedoes at their transition wakes as fast as they could launch them. In the first seconds of the engagement eight of the attacking ships, including four of the cruisers, took direct hits and blossomed into thermonuclear fireballs. The entire wave down-transited in a confused mess, right in the midst of the nearly invisible, but deadly, hunter-killers, who took advantage of the chaos. They had the advantage that once the shooting started, the incandescent flares of nearby warheads masked their already shielded emission signatures. In the next few minutes they completely destroyed six more enemy warships and heavily damaged seven.

As the mauled remnants of the first wave retreated, desperately trying to signal the following three waves that first engagement had been a rout, the line of coalition cruisers one light-year away up-transited at maximum drive heading straight for the incoming Syndonese. The hunter-killers rigged for silent running and disappeared from everyone's screens.

Roacka and Darmczek's plan had been to completely take out the first wave, then have the line of coalition warships move forward and be waiting at first engagement when the second wave came in, expecting the area to be clear. But the remaining ships of the first wave apparently got their signals through, and five hours later the second wave down-transited early and unscathed, just out of range of first engagement where the coalition warships waited.

To the commodore of the second wave, who was clearly still unaware of the hunter-killers, it must have appeared that he had the advantage of numbers. But after the mauling the first wave had taken he moved cautiously. There then commenced a running battle between the coalition ships and the combined forces of the second wave and the remnants of the first. It turned into an unconventional free-for-all in which most of the lessons of the war colleges were of little use, and each captain had to make up his own tactics on the run. Nadama's and Goutain's ships tried to stall until the third wave could arrive, though the conventional coalition ships found it rather easy to lure them within range of the undetected hunter-killers, all lying in wait as the battle raged about them.

The coalition lost four ships to conventional isolation and englobement tactics, and Nadama lost three. The hunter-killers didn't take just any target, but waited until they could target one of the larger ships. In that way, they managed to torpedo eight big enemy warships before one of Nadama's captains caught on and took out one of the hunter-killers. Then everyone disengaged, and since the hunter-killers were defenseless, and therefore useless without the element of surprise, Roacka withdrew them completely. It was at that point that Charlie and his twelve warships downtransited into Borreggan nearspace.

A *fucking war! What incredible luck,* Thraka thought as he nodded at the guard stationed outside Delilah's apartments. The entire station was in a state of absolute chaos. Anyone with any means of getting outsystem was doing so, and many of those who couldn't, and who didn't have a vested interest in the station's defense, had taken to the public corridors, driven by the classic madness of fear and panic. Thraka could get away with almost anything now.

He'd had to seriously up his bribe to the tramp freighter he'd hired. Her captain wanted to pull out immediately, but Dieter had given him the wherewithal to provide an enticing sum to a greedy man who was used to taking chances. The usual arrangement: half now, half when the fellow delivered Delilah safely to Thraka's employer.

The guard took a casual glance beneath the linen towel on the small tray that Thraka carried. It contained refreshments, exactly the kind of thing the princess would request. And besides, Thraka was trusted. The guard hadn't bothered to search him for some days now, so of course he didn't find the plast knife concealed in his tunic. Thraka had no doubt they'd set up detectors on the threshold, so he dared not attempt to conceal any powered weapons. The guard admitted him to Delilah's sitting room, and he found Delilah pacing nervously back and forth, Carristan sitting in a nearby chair.

"Thraka," Delilah demanded. "What news? Do you know how the battle's going?"

She paid no thought to the fact that he was bringing refreshments she hadn't asked for. He smiled. "They've repelled the first two waves, apparently inflicted serious damage on several enemy warships. And the Duke de Lunis has just down-transited into the system with a sizable force of warships."

She stopped pacing, closed her eyes and took a deep breath. "Oh, thank goodness. But did he bring enough?" She finally noticed the tray he carried and pointed to a small table next to Carristan's seat. "You can put that there."

As he put it down and lifted the linen towel off the tray, Carristan glanced at it carefully, smiled, and said to Delilah, "Thoughtful of you to order lunch, dear."

Delilah frowned. "I didn't order anything. I thought you did."

As Carristan stood to examine the tray's contents, Thraka improvised. "Lord Arthur ordered it for you both, thought that with all the excitement you might be forgotten by the rest of the staff."

Delilah approached them, the hint of a frown forming on her face. She and Carristan looked at the tray carefully and Carristan's frown grew more pronounced. Standing behind them, Thraka casually pulled the palm patch from his pocket. He broke the seal and placed it in his left hand, careful not to expose his skin to the active side. Then, with his right hand, he retrieved the plast knife from another pocket and kept it hidden behind his back.

"I would think," Carristan said with emphasis, "that Arthur would be far too preoccupied to worry about lunch for two rather spoiled women."

Damn these paranoid women, Thraka thought as she turned to face him, one eyebrow lifted in question.

Even to the last, neither of them ever truly understood the danger they faced. Thraka had been careful to stay close to them both, and as Carristan turned he thrust the knife up into her diaphragm just below her ribs. A quick thrust and a twist, paralyzing the diaphragm so she couldn't scream, and slicing through the heart and several major arteries.

With a look of complete surprise she let out a tiny, muffled whimper, looked down at his hand holding the knife in her chest and the blood flowing there. Delilah, slightly behind her, still didn't understand what had happened, the look on her face questioning the strange, agonized look on Carristan's. But before she could react Thraka slapped the side of her neck with the palm patch.

The moment ended. Carristan crumpled to the floor without a sound. Delilah had just an instant before the drug took effect and a look of surprise, fear, and pain washed over her face as she took a breath to scream. But before she could do so her eyes glazed over, she touched her forehead confusedly, and spoke haltingly. "Something's . . . wrong."

"Sit down," he said, "and say nothing, do nothing, make no sound." She staggered back to her seat and did so. The drug thieracin, highly illegal, made her completely obedient to his every command. It occurred to him he could have a little fun, tell her to suck his cock and she'd do so without question. But while she was a pretty little thing, he could buy all the pleasure he wanted after this was over, and Dieter would likely get upset if he found out.

Thraka used the towel from the tray to wipe the blood off his hand and the knife, then turned to the door, beyond which the guard waited. He opened it quickly, spoke in an excited voice. "Come quickly. Something's happened to Lady Carristan. Something terrible."

The guard rushed past him. Thraka quickly closed

the door and followed close behind the man as he dropped to one knee over Carristan's body. He carefully pulled a piece of her garment aside to look at the blood. That was the last move he ever made as Thraka, standing behind him, stabbed the knife down into the man's chest, careful to angle the thin blade so it slipped easily between his ribs. A quick turn of the blade, slicing through aorta and heart, then a heel-palm strike to the back of the head, and the man fell forward on top of Carristan without a sound. Thraka prided himself on being a professional, on knowing how to do these things without creating a fuss.

Again Thraka cleaned off the blood, then grabbed the drugged and obedient Delilah by the wrist and pulled her into her dressing room. He sat her down, carefully scrubbed her face to remove her makeup, pulled her hair back, and tied it in an unattractive ponytail behind her head. From his pockets he produced a small, white lace cap and shawl, common attire for servant women, and adjusted them carefully on her. It wouldn't work if someone looked at her closely, or if she'd been wearing some sort of elaborate gown. But removing the makeup and altering the hairstyle to something unattractive completely changed the woman's appearance. Then add a few visual cues that made everyone immediately think *servant*, and she became virtually invisible, especially accompanied by him, another servant.

Of course, the chaos at every turn helped immeasurably. Thraka pulled the compliant young woman through the public corridors without incident, and met up with two of the men from the tramp freighter. They brought a cloak that covered her even more. And when the docking gantry nudged the freighter away from the station, Thraka breathed a long sigh of relief.

CHAPTER 31
OLD DEBTS

The numbers had improved. Nadama and Goutain had lost twenty-five ships, with an additional ten heavily damaged. The coalition had only lost four, plus two heavily damaged, so first engagement had been an unquestioned victory for the coalition. But that still left Nadama and Goutain with more than sixty undamaged fighting ships, while, excluding the hunter-killers, the coalition had a little over forty, including those with Charlie. And considering the fact that three of Charlie's cruisers weren't ready for battle, and Nadama and Goutain had a preponderance of big battleships and heavy cruisers, the situation was indeed dire. Nadama and Goutain had come prepared to bombard Andyne-Borregga into radioactive vapor.

"Duke Charles," Winston said.

Charlie looked up from his screens. "Yes, Winston, what is it?"

"You need to make a speech, Your Grace. Broadcast it to the entire system . . . and to the enemy."

"I don't make speeches."

Winston smiled like a patient father. "You are the supreme commander of the coalition forces. You need to show yourself to the people fighting for you, you need to tell them what they're fighting for, and you need to tell your enemies why they won't win."

Above all, Charlie understood that he was a soldier, and when Winston put it that way, he could not deny the power of the visible presence of command. They quickly scratched out a few words, though they didn't have time to get elaborate so Charlie would have to fake much of it. And they had to get back into transition so he'd have to keep it short.

They called in a technician, and Winston appeared first on camera to say, "I give you His Grace, Charles, Duke de Lunis, supreme commander of all coalition forces."

Charlie sat down in front of the camera, took a calming breath, and spoke.

"It may surprise you that I, a soldier, do not condone war, but I despise tyranny more, and if need be I will die to eradicate it. I won't claim to be without fault, but my greatest sin is the sin of all commanding officers: I will ask others to die as well. Tyranny is a cancer that will grow if not stopped, and the oppressive annexation of Aagerbanne and Finalsa cannot be allowed to continue."

Charlie and Winston had considered including the

oppression of the Syndonese people in that, but doing so might force them into an offensive war against the republic, and they just didn't have the resources for that. Winston had said, "A good king is always a practical king."

Charlie continued. "We have an alliance that includes all of Aagerbanne, the independent states, and several of the Ten, so today is the day we will stop this tyranny. We are in the right and we will be victorious, but cutting out a cancer can be painful. I long ago learned victory is never grand or sweet. In my experience we will find only relief when the dying has stopped. But fight on, do not waver, and soon we will end this."

After the technician shut off the camera, Winston nodded and gave Charlie an uncharacteristic thumbs-up. The old man's excitement, though, wasn't echoed by Charlie. He felt like a liar, casually promising victory that way.

At the edge of Borreggan nearspace, Charlie sent his small task force to join the coalition forces amassing near first engagement, while he took *The Thirteenth Man*, under the command of a Captain Matula, into Andyne-Borregga. As Arthur and Roacka reviewed the situation in the station's command center, Charlie, still on the destroyer and several AUs out, joined them by way of his implants. Neither Roacka nor Arthur had found time to shave for a couple of days.

As if having a similar thought, Arthur said, "Time. We need time. Your courier ships got the word out, and we've got fifteen warships coming in from the independent states, another five from Aagerbanne, and twenty from Kinatha. But they're all spread out, and will be trickling in one or two at a time for the next four days."

Roacka shook his head and rolled a cigar from one side of his mouth to the other. Arthur wouldn't let him smoke the disgusting thing, so he had to content himself with chewing on the stub that remained. "This'll all be over in four days."

"Maybe we can buy that time," Charlie said. "Nadama and Goutain are regrouping at first engagement. Their obvious solution is to take advantage of their superior numbers, come at us in force, and clear the way into heliopause. Where are the hunter-killers?"

"I pulled them out. They're no good anymore." Roacka still didn't fully understand their capabilities, still hadn't learned to think like a hunter-killer captain. "They're driving in-system now from first engagement, presently about three light-years out."

Charlie asked, "And the nine that remain are relatively undamaged, still stocked with torpedoes?"

Roacka's eyes narrowed suspiciously. "That they are, lad."

Charlie knew they could still play a role, perhaps a significant one. With the numbers against them, they needed every warship at their disposal contributing to the fight. And though some of the enemy captains might understand they were facing something new and unusual, others wouldn't. Even among those who did realize that the rules had changed, Charlie hoped that few could adopt new tactics in so short a time. He could only hope he wasn't condemning the hunter-killer crews to a useless death.

"Have them down-transit where they are, randomly spaced directly in the line of attack from first engagement. Tell them to do everything they can to minimize their transition flares, then run silent and wait for the enemy to come their way. Each hunter-killer captain is to operate independently, wait until he has a solid targeting solution, launch a small salvo of torpedoes, then up-transit, run ahead of the enemy as fast as he can, gain some distance, then down-transit and repeat the whole scenario. Those hunter-killers are fast enough to stay ahead of the advancing enemy, so each ship should be able to get in four or five shots before they reach heliopause. Tell them to make Goutain and Nadama pay dearly for every light-year they gain."

Roacka chewed on the stub of his cigar and carefully rubbed the stubble on his chin. After several silent seconds of consideration he said, "Might work. And let's get some of our conventional warships in there to engage in the traditional fashion. That'll help cover the hunter-killers' tracks."

"Good idea."

Roacka grinned. "I figured I was going to end my days hanging from a gallows, but this just might work."

Arthur suddenly held up his hand, indicating he was listening to something coming in through his implants. He listened for a few seconds, stood suddenly, and said, "Shit." He looked at Charlie and said only, "Delilah," then sprinted out of the room.

Dieter wasn't happy, though in Thraka's experience, Dieter was never happy, not with people like Thraka. Thraka knew he'd always fall short of Dieter's acceptability criteria.

"I told you to bring her to me," Dieter demanded.

"And I would, Your Lordship," Thraka said calmly, "if the men on this ship would let me. But you're on a large warship, in the midst of sixty or seventy other large warships, all of whom'll do your bidding, and that makes these men quite nervous." Thraka didn't add that it made him nervous too. Unlike his father, Dieter was too unpredictable, with a temper that flared too easily, a temper that often led to cruelty.

"You have her, don't you?"

"Oh most certainly, Your Lordship. Once I removed the thieracin patch and the drug wore off, she was quite angry, was . . . quite a handful actually."

"Let me speak with this Captain . . ." Dieter waved a hand impatiently. " . . . what's-his-name."

"Captain Zsutaka, Your Lordship. I'll get him right away."

Zsutaka was no fool. A man in Thraka's profession had to make many choices, and fools were easily led and easily manipulated . . . but could just as easily get you killed. On the other hand, an intelligent man like Zsutaka wouldn't get you killed through simple ineptitude, though he might kill you himself for his own purposes. But Zsutaka was greedy, could be controlled through that greed.

"You were contracted to bring her to me," Dieter demanded.

Zsutaka was the epitome of the tramp freighter captain, slovenly, unshaven, ill mannered, but he knew not to antagonize Dieter. "Your Lordship," he said, his words clipped by an accent Thraka couldn't place. "We were contracted to transport her off the station. We're living up to that contract, and putting ourselves under the guns of sixty warships isn't part of the deal."

Dieter was clearly losing his patience. "Then I'll contract you to do that too."

Zsutaka inclined his head deferentially. "With all due respect, Your Lordship, I'll not accept such a contract."

Dieter snapped his words out. "So you don't trust me?"

Zsutaka lifted both hands palm up and cringed slightly, a gesture of conciliation. "It's not a matter of trust, Your Lordship. We're in the midst of a war, and I'm a cautious man. Caution has kept me and my crew healthy these many years. May I suggest a solution that should work for both of us?"

Dieter did a poor job of hiding his distrust. "Go ahead. I'm listening."

"We'll bring her to a prearranged set of coordinates and deliver her to you there. You may come in a ship no better armed than a destroyer escort or a corvette. That way you can be confident you have us outgunned, and we can be confident that you don't have us so heavily outgunned that you can destroy us before we can make a run for it. And be certain to bring final payment."

Dieter slashed a hand out as if cutting the air with a knife. "Absolutely not."

Zsutaka shrugged uncaringly. "Then we vent her and Thraka to space."

Dieter paced angrily back and forth for several seconds, but finally conceded. "All right. I'll do it."

Charlie saw the scene in Delilah's sitting room through Arthur's implants. Carristan and the guard had both bled out almost instantly. Charlie had seen it before, massive damage to the aorta and heart. Done with a knife that way, it was clearly the work of a professional.

"Where's Delilah?" he demanded.

"We're questioning everyone now," Roacka said. "She seems to have disappeared along with one of the servants, a spacer named Thraka, formerly of de Maris livery, probably someone's agent, though your guess is as good as mine as to whose."

"The shooting's started again," Arthur said breathlessly. "I have to get back to the command center. And you're the admiral of this fleet, Charlie, so you have to focus on the battle."

Charlie's eyes met Roacka's. "Find Del for me," he pleaded. "Find her and get her back."

Roacka nodded carefully. "I'll do my best, lad."

Charlie turned back to the situation summary on one of his screens and tried not to think of Del. Nadama and Goutain had regrouped their forces at first engagement, then started chasing the fleeing coalition forces in toward Borreggan nearspace. The first of the hunter-killer captains got his targeting solution, launched a salvo of two torpedoes, got lucky and took out a frigate, then up-transited well ahead of the incoming forces.

Charlie had to suffer the frustration of every admiral throughout history. Once the battle had begun he could only sit and watch. If he started firing off orders about every little thing to his captains he'd only get in the way, create chaos when they needed the freedom to make their own decisions.

In rapid succession, the incoming invaders encountered five more hunter-killers. The second hunter-killer completely missed his targets, the third caused considerable damage to three cruisers, the forth destroyed a medium cruiser, the fifth two destroyers. The sixth was unlucky, though, taking a large warhead and going out with all hands. And through it all the conventional coalition ships sat back at the extreme limit of their range and took pot shots at the enemy ships with their transition batteries, occasionally scoring a good hit. At that point, the invaders down-transited to regroup again.

"Your Grace," *The Thirteenth Man*'s com officer said through Charlie's implants. "I have an incoming message riding on an old de Maris encryption key from a man who identifies himself as Spacer Turnman. He says it's urgent that he speak with you. He says he can tell you where the girl is, whatever that means."

Turnman? Charlie had to think for some seconds before he recalled the man, one of the snitches from the chain. Charlie said, "Put him through."

Turnman wore de Satarna livery, sat at a console on some ship and had aged considerably in the past year. "Your Grace," he said.

If the man had had anything to do with Delilah's abduction, Charlie swore then and there he'd kill him. His voice came out in a growl. "You know where Delilah is?"

Turnman nodded, though his attitude was not confrontational or adversarial. "I accepted a position on Lord Dieter's staff. I think he was looking to see how he could use me against you, and with no other prospects, I had no choice. The man who kidnapped the princess is one of his agents."

"And you're willing to tell me where she is?"

Again Turnman nodded.

"Why?"

Turnman shrugged. "I'm not proud of what I did, Commander." He used Charlie's old rank, the rank he'd held on the chain. It wasn't uncommon for one of the Two Thousand to do so. "And you could have had us executed, but you didn't, so I figure I owe you this. Maybe it can square things between us . . . a bit."

"Where is she?"

Turnman gave him the coordinates and explained

the conditions of the rendezvous scheduled with the tramp freighter.

"If you're lying," Charlie told him, "I'll find you and kill you myself. If you're telling the truth . . . well, let's wait and see."

Charlie passed the coordinates on to Captain Matula, with orders to, "Get me there, soonest."

Then he contacted Roacka and told him what he'd learned from Turnman. "I'm going after her."

For a moment Roacka looked like he might argue, but before he could say anything, Arthur switched into the circuit and said, "You can't go, Charlie. You're the man running this show. We can't take the risk we might lose you."

Charlie looked at the situation summary on his screens. The recent success of the nine hunter-killers operating independently had improved the numbers nicely, giving him the first real hope they could win this, though it wasn't a foregone conclusion. He said that now, and added, "And Dieter's out there. He's vulnerable. That's a stroke of luck we can't pass up. If I can capture him, we can neutralize Nadama. Even if I kill him, it'll give Nadama pause."

Arthur started to say something, but Charlie cut him off. "This is a battle, brother. I learned long ago that sometimes we have to take risks when an opportunity presents itself."

Roacka grimaced and said, "He's right." It hadn't been an enthusiastic endorsement, but Charlie would take it.

"One more thing," Charlie said. "If Turnman's lying or double-crossing me and I don't get back from this, find him and kill him."

Roacka grinned and nodded.

The invading fleet changed tactics, began sending out small groups of fast ships, leapfrogging one past the other in short micro-transition jumps, attempting to flush out the hunter-killers. It was dangerous since several of the conventional coalition ships could concentrate fire on a single invader, and it also slowed their pace to a crawl.

Five warships from Aagerbanne down-transited on the far side of the system. Charlie ordered them to drive in-system and take up defensive positions near Andyne-Borregga.

Again, all Charlie could do was sit and watch. He had to let his forces fight their battles, and force himself not to call up to the bridge every minute and give Matula orders.

During the next fifteen hours the invaders lost eight more warships, while the coalition lost four conventional warships and two hunter-killers. The invaders inched their way to within one light-year of Borreggan nearspace, and three warships from the independent states down-transited on the far side of the system. Seth Andrews was the captain of one of the hunter-killers that went out with all hands, though he and his crew had been responsible for several successful kills among the enemy's ranks. Charlie said a silent spacer's prayer for him.

It had become a battle of attrition. If they could slowly pick away at the incoming invaders, reinforce their own forces with incoming coalition ships, they might win this thing. But if Charlie couldn't get Del back whole and healthy, it would be a hollow victory.

Charlie waited for a lull in the bridge chatter, then asked Matula, "How far to the rendezvous point?"

"We're about five hours out, Your Grace."

Charlie hadn't eaten anything for hours, and he badly needed a shower and a shave. He decided to take a break. He could monitor the situation through his implants and be back on the bridge in seconds if something developed.

As Charlie headed for his cabin, a little piece of him missed having Add and Ell dogging his heels, and constantly commenting on everything from his stature to his manhood. But in the tight confines of a man-of-war, and with internal security systems monitoring everything, personal bodyguards were considered an inappropriate extravagance, and a sign that the duke lacked confidence in the ship's discipline. Keeping them close at hand would be an open insult to the crew.

He'd gotten his orders—his target—from Goutain several days ago, but he wasn't close enough to the de Lunis to get to him easily, not with those damnable Kinathin twins always hovering close by. But this might be his opportunity. He had no responsibilities that would justify his presence on the destroyer's bridge; after all he was just another Syndonese refugee. But he'd managed to get an assignment in the ship's galley, had been working there when the duke called down and asked them to bring a light meal to his cabin. He'd made sure he was the one delivering the meal.

No power weapons; they'd register too easily on the ship's internal security systems. *A simple plast knife will do the job quite nicely,* he thought as he knocked on the duke's cabin door.

Charlie felt the ship up-transit as he toweled his hair dry; they had a short transition run of a couple of hours to get to the rendezvous point with the tramp freighter. The shower had felt good, even though it was the usual one-minute rush job dictated by shipboard rationing. With his rank he could have ignored rationing, but he'd spent too many years adhering to shipboard regulations to casually violate them now.

At the knock on his cabin door he quickly pulled on a pair of pants, then opened the door. He didn't recognize the man carrying the tray of food—one of the Syndonese refugees—and while he'd seen him about he certainly couldn't recall his name. "Come in. Come in." He waved at the small retractable desk against one bulkhead. "Just put it there, and thanks for bringing it. I'm starved."

"Your Grace," the man said in a thick Syndonese

accent. He crossed the small cabin to the desk, placed the tray on it, and began arranging the meal.

Charlie turned to his grav bunk and the fresh clothing he'd laid out. He could hear the man behind him laying out utensils, removing lids from containers, and arranging the meal. He got a whiff of fresh food . . . and then his implants crashed.

It wasn't a dramatic thing, but when not deactivated or placed in standby during sleep, there was always a constant background of data chatter like someone else carrying on a quiet conversation on the other side of a large room: easy to ignore, to forget it wasn't there, until it suddenly stopped. His implants shouldn't crash like that, cutting him completely out of *shipnet*, isolating him. That just didn't happen, unless someone nearby had intentionally jammed the signal—

He dropped, spun, and lurched to one side, grunted as a knife sliced a searing line of pain across his shoulder. He hit the floor, rolled, and came to his feet just as the man charged into him. Charlie managed to get a grip on the wrist of the man's knife hand. They stood face-to-face, so Charlie head butted him in the nose, sending a spray of blood flying over them both. The man's face screwed up into an ugly grimace as he and Charlie spun across the small cabin like two dancers enjoying a waltz. Charlie's thigh caught on the edge of the small desk and they both went down in a cascade of dishes, food, and utensils. Somewhere in the tumble Charlie felt a sharp, intense pain in his right side. His hand closed on the hilt of a dinner knife and he came to his feet, clutching his side and facing the assassin in a crouch.

The man was a pro, no question about it. He knew how to handle a knife and how to fight. But perhaps he saw the same thing in Charlie and that made him wary. They squared off, stepping carefully in the confines of the small cabin. Time was on Charlie's side; someone would realize he'd dropped out of *shipnet* and they'd come to investigate. Charlie saw it in the man's eyes when he realized the same thing and lunged at him with a thrust.

Charlie deflected the thrust with a palm to the man's wrist, spun, and side-kicked him. Add and Ell would've been proud, except at the moment of the strike an excruciating shock of pain from his side took all the power out of it. It connected weakly. It was something, though—backed the man up a pace—so Charlie charged in and they both went down to the deck again.

It turned into a nasty, brutal struggle on the deck of the cabin, both of them trying to hold the other's knife at bay while using elbows, knees, teeth—anything—to win. To survive. But Charlie was just too weak from the slash wound in his shoulder and stab wound in his side. They rolled over and the man was on top of him . . .

The cabin door burst open. It was the second time in his life when he couldn't tell Add from Ell as one of them lifted the man off him, dislocated his shoulder with a quick twist, broke his arm with a loud snap, then slammed him against a bulkhead. She said to the assassin, "I want you alive so we can talk."

It was Add.

Ell helped Charlie to his feet. "Let's get you to the infirmary, little brother."

CHAPTER 32
CORNERED

Charlie refused to let them heavily sedate him, even though the assassin's knife had punctured a lung. "I'm in the middle of a fucking war," he growled, coughing up blood and trying to ignore the pain.

The ship's surgeon stared at his instruments and said, "Looks like it's a straight puncture. You're lucky he didn't have a chance to twist or turn the knife. We've got to get you into surgery. Now."

"Absolutely not. I told you, I got a war to fight."

Add and Ell looked at each other and rolled their eyes, then looked at Charlie, shaking their heads. Add said to Ell, "I think we're going to have to hold him down, like when he fell out of that tree and broke his arm."

They ganged up on him, and after considerable argument—after Add and Ell threatened to hold him down while the surgeon administered the anesthesia—Charlie agreed to let them give him a local and dope him up briefly, on the condition they brought him out of it as soon as possible. The shooting had started again at the edge of Borreggan nearspace.

He drifted off into a drug-induced haze. A piece of him realized it had been pure fantasy to think he could run a war while under the knife. And when he returned to lucidity an hour had passed.

"I repaired the damage to your lung," the surgeon told him. "It wasn't too bad. But no strenuous activity until we get you into accelerated healing and finish the job."

Charlie ignored the surgeon and immediately keyed his implants back into *shipnet*.

They were blind in transition, but Arthur was providing updates on a continuous feed. The coalition had continued its previous strategy of using the hunter-killers to lie in wait and torpedo unwary invaders. But the invaders had finally realized they were facing something new and different, and were now moving much more cautiously and slowly. The Four Tyrants had lost a large battleship, while the coalition had lost a hunter-killer, a cruiser, and a destroyer. Interestingly, the battleship had been Nadama's flagship, and Nadama was dead. That made it even more imperative that Charlie get to Dieter; capture or kill the heir, and the de Satarna forces would have to withdraw.

In other good news, four more warships from the independent states and three from Kinatha had down-transited into the system and were on their way to join the battle.

"Your Grace," Matula said in his implants. "We're about a half hour out from down-transition."

"Right," he grumbled, trying not to make every word sound like a growl. "I'll be right up."

"Wait a minute," the surgeon said. "You need to spend at least a day in accelerated healing before any exertion."

Charlie didn't try to mask the pain in his voice. "When this is done."

Del had never truly known what it was like to want to kill someone. She'd known rage, fury even, but she was surprised to realize that even then her anger had been nothing compared to this. The man had murdered Carristan right in front of her, and she'd sat there and watched complacently. And Dieter had been behind it. No, nothing compared to this. She embraced the anger and let it fuel her hatred for the man.

They'd kept her locked in a small cabin for several hours. She'd searched it carefully and found nothing she could use as a weapon, though two gravity bunks against the wall and a lot of odds and ends told her it was the cabin of two crewmen. She'd screamed and raged and shouted for the first hour after the drug wore off, to no avail. She'd tried the intercom, but no one answered her. Finally, with her bladder bursting, she begged over the intercom for someone to take her to the toilet. There came no reply over the intercom, but a few minutes later the door of the cabin opened. Any thought she had of resistance evaporated at the hardened look of the two men who waited in the corridor beyond.

They escorted her to what they referred to as the *head* and into one of the stalls there, though one man held the door of the stall open and they both stood there looking at her and waiting.

"Won't you allow me a little privacy?"

The shorter of the two said, "Look, Princess, you can piss with us watching you, or you cannot piss at all, but we ain't letting you out of our sight."

Del lifted her skirts, dropped her panties, sat down and, relieved herself. They escorted her back to the cabin.

She waited for a couple more hours, pacing back and forth in the small cabin. Then, without warning the door to her cabin opened. The same two men stepped into the small space, and before she could react they lifted her off her feet, spun her about, and clamped her wrists behind her back with some sort of manacles. She demanded, "What are—"

The smaller of the two slapped her hard. "You keep your mouth shut, sweetheart. Every little peep out of you gets a slap, and each time it'll be harder."

The big one, standing behind her, reached around her and cupped her breasts in his hands. He massaged them crudely, saying, "She's awful pretty, yuh know. We got a little time. We could have some fun."

Del tried not to let her terror show as the smaller one considered it for a moment, then shook his head. "Nah, Zsutaka'd kill us. We play it straight."

They each lifted her by an armpit and her feet barely touched the floor as they half carried her through the ship. They lifted her through the open hatch of a small shuttle and deposited her in a seat. A few minutes later Zsutaka and Thraka sat down on either side of her. The three of them said nothing, and all Del could do was sit and fume as the shuttle pulled away from the freighter.

"**Y**our Grace," Matula said. "We just got an uplink message that Duchess Telka is within range of the relay buoys and wishes to speak with you. We're in a position to do a quick down-transition."

While in transition Charlie had been monitoring the battle by uplink, a situation in which they could receive, but not transmit. They were prepared to down-transit quickly if they did need to transmit. He knew his greater responsibility lay with the coalition, but he was torn, because to down-transit now might give Dieter the time he needed to escape with Del.

"Do so," he said.

"We're about ten light-years out," Telka told him, once they'd established a conference link with her and Arthur and Roacka. "I have thirty warships, and we'll be there in two days."

Arthur said, "And there are another twenty-five warships coming in from Kinatha and the independent states, ten of which'll be in nearspace within the next ten hours."

Roacka added, "That basically gives us parity now, a decent advantage by the end of the day, and a significant advantage when Her Grace gets here. This thing is over."

"No," Charlie said sharply. "It's not. We're not leaving this to fester and come back and bite us again. It's started, so we finish it here and now."

Telka shook her head. "I won't be part of a bloodbath."

"I'm not planning a bloodbath. But we need to send Goutain back to Syndon with his nose badly bloodied or he'll turn right around and come back."

Telka smiled, clearly liked the idea. "What do you have in mind?"

"Matula, get me a senior de Satarna captain." To Telka and Arthur he said, "Just follow my lead."

Five minutes later an overweight man with gray hair and sweat on his upper lip appeared on one of Charlie's screens. He looked tired as he introduced himself as Commodore Thurston, and while Telka, Arthur, and Matula listened in, Thurston only saw Charlie.

Charlie said, "I'm prepared to offer you terms, Commodore."

"Terms?" Thurston snarled. "You're on the losing side, de Lunis."

"No, Commodore, look again. You're facing a coalition of all the independent states, Aagerbanne, the Kinathin home world, and eight of the ten dukes."

"We have three of the Ten on our side. This is a sham."

"Duchess Telka, care to join the conversation?"

Thurston paled when he saw Telka. She said, "Commodore. I, Rierma, Band, Chelko, Harrimo, Sig, and Charles formed an alliance to oppose your liege lord's designs. And let me inform you that Theode and Gaida are under arrest for complicity in the murder of Cesare. Arthur, who will soon be reinstated as Duke de Maris, is presently in command of the de Maris forces, and has joined our coalition against you."

To Charlie she said—for Thurston's benefit, "Your Grace, my officers tell me we'll be arriving in Borreggan nearspace within the next two days. I have a force of thirty warships which will be at your disposal."

A bead of sweat rolled down Thurston's forehead. Charlie let the man absorb the information for a few moments, then said, "You know the numbers. You can see all the incoming warships and count as well as me. At this moment we have a slight edge in the numbers game. That's going to change dramatically as fifty more warships down-transit in-system, all here to support our coalition."

Thurston stared at him angrily for several seconds and finally said, "Your terms?"

"Withdraw now, leave the rest of this between us and Goutain, and you'll be allowed to retreat unmolested. Return to your bases, stand down, and await a ruling from the Ten on the inheritance of the de Satarna ducal seat. But if you refuse to withdraw, the resulting bloodbath will be on your head, not mine. And it'll be your blood, not ours."

Thurston regarded Charlie carefully for several seconds. "With Duke Nadama dead, I'll have to speak with the other captains, try to get consensus."

Charlie nodded his understanding. "Do so. But don't take too long about it."

"And I'll have to speak to Lord Dieter."

Charlie grinned. "If you can find him, we both know he'll tell you to fight to the death. And if you choose to obey him, we'll happily accommodate you."

They cut the circuit. Charlie said to Arthur and Telka, "You can handle this. I've got to get to Del."

"Go," Arthur said, though Telka, unaware of the situation, frowned.

Dieter had waited a long time for this. Delilah would soon be his, and he'd teach her what it meant to defy him.

By prior agreement, the corvette and the tramp freighter took up positions two million kilometers apart, one-half light-year from the battle at the edge of Borreggan nearspace. Accompanied by a couple of armed spacers, Dieter boarded the corvette's shuttle, which could only do about thirty gravities, then paced impatiently up and down the length of its passenger cabin during the hour it took to get to the point halfway between the two waiting ships. The freighter's shuttle was slower and took even longer to get there. It was a nuisance more than anything, and he'd make that little bitch pay for that too.

His implants informed him he had an urgent message coming in from the corvette's captain. He put it through. "Your Lordship, I received a message from Commodore Thurston. I'm sorry to inform you that your father is dead."

The man waited for some sort of response, as if Dieter would grieve for his father. Dieter simply said, "Is there more?"

"Yes, Your Lordship. Commodore Thurston and the senior officers of your father's fleet are withdrawing from the battle. Apparently, these Andyne-Borreggan pirates have formed some sort of alliance, and their incoming reinforcements have given them an overwhelming advantage."

Dieter didn't care about this battle, and as for his father, he cared only that now he'd inherit the de Satarna ducal seat. "Hold your position. Soon I'll have what I came for and we can leave."

"But Your Lordship—"

"I said hold your position. And don't argue with me." He'd deal with these traitors later.

"Of course, Your Lordship. As you wish."

Dieter had to wait another half hour while the two shuttles mated airlocks. When they finally popped the seals he was fit to be tied. A man he didn't know came through the airlock first; obviously a thug, he wore rather grubby spacer's attire with no insignia. Zsutaka followed him wearing similar attire but with captain's stripes. Behind Zsutaka came Delilah pushed along by Thraka, her hands restrained behind her back. She stopped in front of Dieter, opened her mouth to say something, and he decided to start her instruction then and there. He hit her, not a slap but a solid punch to her face, and she went down like a rag doll. "You fucking cunt," he snarled.

She tried to sit up, but with her hands manacled behind her, she could only thrash around. Thraka looked a question at him and he nodded, so Thraka bent down and helped her to her feet, though she swayed unsteadily and couldn't stand without his support.

"Remove the manacles," Dieter said, and Thraka complied.

"And my payment?" Zsutaka asked.

Dieter nodded to one of the armed spacers, who handed Zsutaka a small case. "All cash," Dieter said. "Aagerbanni currency as you requested."

Zsutaka started to say something but hesitated and suddenly put a finger to his ear, obviously listening to something. At the same moment, the corvette's captain said through Dieter's implants, "Your Lordship, we've just picked up a transition wake, coming in fast from the vicinity of the battle. Its transition signature would indicate a destroyer."

"How far out?" Dieter demanded.

"Less than half an hour, Your Lordship."

Dieter screamed, "What kind of idiot are you, that you can't see a transition wake until it's right on top of us?"

"I'm sorry, Your Lordship, but the nuclear background of the battle has obscured everything. It's only now become obvious—"

Zsutaka was shouting into his own implants. Dieter shouted into his, "Come and get me. Now!"

Everyone pulled out weapons, but Zsutaka shouted, "Hold your fire."

"Yes," Dieter shouted to his men, realizing that in the cramped confines of the shuttle they'd all end up dead. "Hold your fire."

Zsutaka snarled, "Is this a double cross?"

"No," Dieter shouted. "That's one of my enemies coming in."

"Then tell your corvette to hold her position."

Dieter complied, then pleaded, "But we all have to get out of here. That warship has my corvette badly outgunned, and they're not going to be friendly to either of us."

Delilah grinned, though the side of her face had begun to swell and it was a bit lopsided. He wanted to hit her again, but that would have to wait.

"All right," Dieter said, waving a hand at the open airlock. "Get out. Get out. We're both on our own."

Zsutaka and his spacers backed carefully out through the airlock, and they lost more time separating the two shuttles' airlocks without damaging the seals.

As the shuttle pilot firewalled its engines, Dieter ordered the corvette to come in and pick them up, and no doubt Zsutaka was ordering his freighter to do the same. Dieter ordered the corvette to fire upon the freighter and its shuttle; Zsutaka and his crew were scum anyway. The freighter fired back with what little firepower it possessed. The shuttle pilot took evasive action, costing them even more time.

"**D**own-transition."

Charlie closed his eyes and waited, listening to the bridge chatter.

"We're clear, drones out."

There was a delay as the drones gathered and fed them scan data.

"Captain, I've got a small de Satarna corvette off the starboard bow, ranging at one million kilometers, apparently rendezvousing with and picking up a shuttle. There's also an unidentified freighter off the port bow, same range and apparently rendezvousing with and picking up another shuttle. And they're firing on each other."

Matula said, "Targeting solutions on both. I want shots across both bows soonest, and remind those gun batteries the princess is out there somewhere, so we don't start shooting anything until we know where she is."

"Targeting solutions set, sir."

"Fire."

The destroyer's hull thrummed as her main transition batteries slammed shells into transition.

"Com, broadcast a message to both to cease fire, or we get serious. And tell them to stand down and prepare to be boarded. And if they try to run, we shoot to kill."

"Aye, aye, sir."

Things calmed down at that point and the shooting stopped.

The captain of the corvette said he didn't know anything about Delilah. It took some convincing, but the captain of the freighter admitted transporting Delilah, and delivering her to Dieter. "But we didn't know she was being held against her will," Zsutaka said. That was probably a lie, but the main thing was that she wasn't on his ship either.

At that point Charlie personally took over and spoke directly with the corvette's captain. He never got the man's name, but the captain was clearly scared. "You do know that Nadama is dead, the de Satarna forces are withdrawing, and Goutain's remaining forces are heavily outnumbered, correct?"

The man said, "I do. And we'd like to withdraw under the same terms."

Charlie smiled, but it was purposefully an unpleasant one. "I wouldn't have a problem with that, except you're in possession of the person of Her Royal Highness, Delilah, being held against her will, which is a hanging offense."

"Not us," the man said frantically. "Not me and my crew. We're merely transporting Lord Dieter. It's he who kidnapped her."

"And you aided and abetted him."

"No. No. We didn't know what he was coming after."

"Then turn the two of them over to me."

The man thought about it for several seconds, his eyes blinking fearfully. Charlie let him have the time necessary to realize he had no choice. He finally nodded and said, "Okay—" But before he could say more Dieter's image appeared next to his. He stood behind a console in the cramped confines of a shuttle cabin. Del stood in front of him, held there by his left hand gripped in her hair pulling her head back and exposing her throat. His right hand held a knife beneath her chin. Her left eye was badly swollen, a nasty bruise forming around a jagged cut high on her cheek, a trickle of blood inching its way down her face. She looked more angry than scared. "Come and get her yourself, de Lunis," Dieter said, grinning, "or she dies."

CHAPTER 33
MANO-A-MANO, SORT OF

The corvette had a small service bay for its shuttle, but it wouldn't accommodate the destroyer's gunboat, and in any case Dieter was holed up there with Delilah. So they mated the gunboat's airlock to a personnel hatch on the side of the corvette. Matula's executive officer, Lieutenant Commander Jackosa, boarded the corvette first, accompanied by twenty armed marines in light body armor. They insisted that Charlie remain behind in the gunboat with the twins until Jackosa had secured the corvette. No sense giving some fool the chance to become a dead hero by killing the de Lunis.

While Charlie waited he monitored the reports on the battle still raging a half light-year away. The de Satarna forces had withdrawn completely, leaving Goutain and the Syndonese to face overwhelming odds, which had quickly turned into a rout. The Syndonese forces ran, and Charlie gave orders to pursue them until they reached Syndon.

When they got the all-clear from Jackosa, Add and Ell boarded the corvette and led Charlie through the ship past de Satarna crewmen who wouldn't meet his eyes. The last vestiges of the anesthesia had worn off and the pain in Charlie's side had become a nagging reminder that he was only hours out of surgery. They'd pumped him full of accelerated healing drugs, which meant that in another day or so he'd be as good as new, but not today. Add and Ell led him directly to a hatch leading to the shuttle service bay, where the corvette's captain waited flanked by two of Charlie's marines.

"Your Grace," the man said, bowing his head and averting his eyes. "As the heir to the de Satarna ducal seat, Lord Dieter has access codes on this ship that not even I can override. He's locked himself alone with Princess Delilah in the service bay. He says he'll open this one hatch briefly, but if anyone but you comes through it, or if we don't allow it to shut behind you, she dies."

There was some heated discussion between Add, Ell, and the marines about how they might storm the service bay, since of course it was unthinkable that Charlie would go in there alone, even for the princess. As they argued, Charlie thought about the POW camps and the chain. He knew it was an irrational thought, but he'd always felt that he'd let three thousand men die on that chain, that somehow he'd let them down.

And while Add and Ell and the marines were confident that Dieter was bluffing, they didn't know Dieter like Charlie knew Dieter. No, he wasn't going to let Del down too.

"Enough," Charlie said. "I'm going in. That's the end of it."

Ell spoke in an icy tone, "Absolutely not. You can't—"

Charlie cut her off. "The decision's made. It's done."

"I won't let you." She stepped in front of the hatch and stood there facing him, fists on her hips. "You'll have to go through me."

Add calmly approached her, put a hand on Ell's shoulder, and said, "It's time we trust that little brother has learned his lessons well."

Ell looked dumbfounded; Add, always the critical one, and never satisfied with either of them. Add continued, "Sister, I always knew that one day he'd have to kill this Dieter, and that day has come. But he doesn't have to go in there unprepared or unarmed." Her lips curled upward in a very menacing grin.

Add and Ell both retrieved knives from various places on their own bodies, planted one in each of Charlie's boots, one up his left sleeve. Ell then rifled through a medic's kit, retrieved an injector and several vials. "I can see in your face the pain is back. This'll fix that."

She pressed the injector against the side of his throat and pulled the trigger. Mercifully, the pain disappeared. "But any new wounds will hurt, and any exertion will tear open your old wounds, which'll hurt like hell, and you'll start bleeding out. So if you do tear them open, you have to finish it soon after that."

Add just stood by, nodding her approval. When Ell was finished, she stepped back and looked Charlie up and down. Charlie had a thought and said, "One more thing. Give me a kikker."

Everyone there looked at him skeptically, but Ell didn't question him, again searched through the medic's kit and found another vial. She loaded it into the injector and shot it into his neck.

As the flood of combat drugs washed through his system, he took a deep breath and let it out slowly, had to force his own control over the aggression hypes that made him feel like some sort of super human. To the two of them he said, "As soon as that hatch closes with me on the other side, get a plast torch and start cutting your way in. Either I and Del will be dead and you'll need to cut your way in to kill Dieter, or Dieter'll be dead and you'll need to cut your way in to let us out."

He turned to the corvette's captain. "I'm ready."

The man spoke to Dieter through his own implants, and moments later the hatch cycled open with a soft hiss. Charlie pushed it open and peered carefully into the cramped confines of the service bay. The shuttle filled most of the bay, a squat, ugly shape with only a few meters of space around it, the walls lined with tool cabinets. The large access hatch through which the shuttle had passed was at the far end of the bay. Once Charlie was in the service bay, Dieter could end it quickly by opening that hatch, venting Charlie to space with he and Delilah protected inside the shuttle. But Charlie wasn't worried about that. Dieter wanted to do this personally. That was Dieter.

Charlie looked right and left, leery of a possible ambush just inside the hatch, stepped through it and allowed it to cycle shut. The bay was silent, the shuttle's airlock wide-open.

The situation was all wrong. If Dieter just dropped the whole matter, released Del, claimed he was only obeying the orders of his now dead father, the Ten would have no alternative but to let him inherit the de Satarna ducal seat. But provoking this situation, there was only one way this could end: with Dieter dead. The only thing he could hope to gain was to take Charlie with him. Was giving up his own life actually worth that? Charlie feared the de Satarna heir was willing to do exactly that.

I'm dealing with an unstable personality, he realized, *the most dangerous kind.*

He glanced briefly into the shuttle's open airlock, keeping an eye over his shoulder at all times. Dieter and Del weren't there, and as he glanced around the shuttle bay again he heard a feminine grunt and footsteps on the other side of the shuttle, so he started edging his way around it, moving slowly and carefully, alert for an attack. He'd just passed behind the tail section when he heard a rustle of fabric up ahead, another muted grunt and what sounded like a brief struggle. He moved toward the commotion, edging along the curved side of the shuttle. Again the sounds of a struggle, then Del shouted, "He's not alone, Charlie."

Charlie ducked and dove to one side just as something hit him between the shoulder blades with an excruciating thud, knocking him to the deck. A heavy wrench clattered to the deck beside him, would have killed him if it had hit him in the back of the head. He tried to ignore the throbbing pain high on his back and struggled to climb to his feet, but a hand gripped his hair, lifted him, and slammed him face-on against the side of the shuttle, his chest and face pressed heavily against it. He heard the sharp, characteristic hum of a power knife, then his attacker yanked his hair and jerked his head back. The fellow placed the paper-thin blade a hair's breadth from his throat. "You know what this is," the man said.

Charlie froze. With the cutting edge of the blade enhanced by power, the knife could cut through steel or plast effortlessly. Even a child could cut Charlie in two with no more than the flick of a wrist.

Dieter called, "Don't hurt him too much, Thraka."

Del growled, "You bastard."

He heard them struggling, then Dieter and Del stepped into view, Del held in front of him, a knife at her throat.

Holding the power knife at Charlie's throat Thraka searched him thoroughly, found every weapon the twins had given him, and in short order disarmed him completely. Then, holding his left arm in a lock behind his back, Thraka pulled him away from the side of the shuttle and stood him in front of Dieter.

"Well, well," Dieter said happily. "I always knew I'd have to kill you, de Lunis."

Del struggled against him. He said, "Don't struggle, my dear betrothed, or I'll have Thraka cut him up slowly, piece by piece."

Del stopped moving, though there was no fear on her face, just anger and fury.

Dieter's left hand reached in front of her, gripped the neckline of her dress and ripped it downward, tearing it and exposing one of her breasts. She stood rigidly in his embrace as he massaged it clumsily, like an untalented sculptor crudely trying to shape clay. Dieter smiled at Charlie triumphantly, and there was clearly a bit of madness and hysteria in his eyes. "She's mine, you son of a whore, always will be. You'll never touch her. She's all mine, and I'll use her as I see fit."

Still clutching at her breast with one hand, with the other he lifted the knife high and clubbed her in the side of the head with the hilt. She crumpled to the deck unconscious. He stepped over her and walked toward Charlie saying, "There. We can get to her later."

As long as Thraka held the power knife at his throat he could do nothing. Behind Dieter, the first hint of a cherry-red glow formed near the bottom of the hatch he'd come through. He had to stall, give them time to cut their way through. "Give it up, Dieter," he said. "You haven't done anything yet that can't be undone.

Give it up now and you can still inherit the de Satarna ducal seat."

Dieter looked him up and down scornfully. "You're a sorry excuse for nobility."

That was ironic, Charlie thought, for he'd have said the same thing about Dieter, but for completely different reasons.

"You're favoring your left side, de Lunis," Dieter said. He reached out, pulled at Charlie's tunic, and sliced it with a quick slash of his knife, exposing some of the bandage beneath it. "Aha! It appears you've been injured. Now where exactly is it under all these bandages?"

Dieter wanted Charlie to see the blow coming so he took his time curling his fingers into a fist and drawing his arm back. Then he slammed his fist into Charlie's gut. Charlie grunted and doubled over, but Thraka kept him from falling. "Be careful, Thraka," Dieter said. "Get rid of that power knife. I'd hate to end this too soon by accident."

The hum of the power knife disappeared. Thraka straightened Charlie up and held both his arms behind his back in a painful lock.

Dieter grinned happily. "Now, I don't think I hit your wound with that one. How about this one?" Again he broadcast the punch as he hit Charlie in the ribs, and again Charlie grunted with pain.

"No, I think I still missed. Maybe this one."

He drew his fist back slowly, and this time the blow

landed right on the newly repaired wound in Charlie's chest, and he screamed in agony, nearly blacked out. "Yes," Dieter said. "I think I've found it."

Dieter hit Charlie again in the same spot, and again. At some point he blacked out momentarily, awoke lying on his side on the deck curled into a fetal position, his bandages now soaked with blood. Dieter stood over him, Thraka standing behind him, and behind both Charlie thought he caught a glimpse of movement where Del lay in a heap on the deck.

"Come on, de Lunis," Dieter said, waving a hand at Charlie impatiently. "Get to your feet. I always knew it would come down to you and me, one-on-one, and I expected more of a fight." He grinned maniacally, his eyes practically devoid of sanity.

Charlie realized that getting to his feet might be more than he could handle. Blood seeped through his bandages, puddling on the deck. He coughed and spit more blood. Slowly he rolled off his side onto his stomach, and caught another glimpse of movement where Del lay on the deck. He had to keep Dieter and Thraka's attention away from her and the airlock.

He took his time, knowing that just before he made it fully upright, Dieter would attack. He lifted himself onto his elbows, then pulled his knees up and struggled to his elbows and knees. He paused there for a moment, buying time, then pushed off his elbows to his hands and knees, and glanced behind them at Del. Her eyes were open, calculating.

He moved slowly and got one foot on the deck,

paused there for a moment, his left foot, right hand, and right knee on the deck, his left hand clutching at his side, sticky with blood. He took several shallow breaths, readying himself for the attack, knowing he could probably ignore the pain for one strike, but that would be it. Then, slowly, he began to rise, and out of the corner of his eye he saw Del climbing quietly to her feet.

Dieter came in intending to kick him, but Charlie dropped back to the deck in a spin, struck out with a sweeping kick, and caught Dieter in the side of the knee. Dieter went down howling with pain. Charlie crawled over to him as Thraka stepped in to intervene. But behind Thraka, Del rose up holding the wrench Thraka had thrown at Charlie. It was the length of her arm and she could barely lift it, but she swung it high over her head in a long, arcing blow, and with a grunt slammed it into the top of Thraka's head. The wrench impacted with a sickening, meaty thud. Brains and blood spattered all over Del, Charlie, and Dieter, and Thraka dropped to the deck.

Dieter scrambled to his feet, favoring his left knee, circling Del carefully. Charlie tried to rise, fell back to his hands and knees as the deck swayed dizzily beneath him, and he coughed up more blood. Del tried to defend herself with the wrench, but it was much too heavy for her to wield easily. She swung it once, but Dieter stepped inside her guard and punched her in the face, knocking her to the deck. She landed in a heap on top of Thraka's body. Dieter kicked her viciously and she cried out.

Dieter marched over to Charlie, retrieved his knife from the deck, and hauled Charlie to his feet. "You fucking son of a whore," he shouted, holding the knife to Charlie's throat, spittle flying into Charlie's face. Charlie was helpless as his head spun crazily and pain hammered at the wound in his chest. He coughed up more blood.

"Wait," Del shouted. "Wait."

Dieter spun to face her, holding the knife at Charlie's throat.

She pulled herself slowly to her feet, a plast knife held in her left hand. Her right arm had clearly been injured, because she clutched her right hand painfully to her side in a fold of her dress. Standing there with her dress torn, one breast exposed, the side of her face swollen, covered in bits of Thraka's brains and blood and bone, she was the oddest, most beautiful creature Charlie had ever seen. "Don't kill him," she said to Dieter. She said it in a seductive, almost alluring way. "Don't hurt him and I'll come with you willingly."

Dieter hooted and laughed. "Why do I care if you come with me willingly, since you're going to come with me no matter what?"

She smiled, cocked her head coquettishly and limped toward them. "Because if I'm not willing, then the only way you'll ever have me is rape. Over and over again, just rape, just the same old thing day after day, and don't you think that'll get a little boring?"

She stopped two paces away. With the knife in her left hand, she reached up and cut her own breast, not a deep cut but enough to draw a little blood. She tossed the knife aside, reached up again and smeared her own blood on the tips of her fingers. Then, oh so seductively, she rubbed the blood on the tip of her tongue, traced it across her lips. "But with my . . . cooperation," she said in a low and sultry voice, "I could get very inventive, and you might find pleasures you've never imagined."

Still clutching her right hand in the fold of her dress, she smeared more of her blood on the fingers of her left hand, held it out to Dieter and walked slowly toward him. Dieter dropped Charlie to the deck, completely entranced as she touched the blood delicately to his lips. His tongue darted out, tasted the blood, and he almost swooned.

Charlie lay on the deck, unable to believe his eyes. But he saw it a second before he heard it, the hilt of Thraka's power knife in her right hand hidden in the folds of her dress. They all heard the hum as she threw the switch. Dieter's eyes widened for just an instant, and Del's face turned into a mask of fury and hatred. She grunted angrily as she jammed the blade up into his chest. She punched it up directly into his spine, then stepped back and slashed upward and out to the side. The blade half severed Dieter's torso and exited just under his left armpit. The momentum of Del's slice carried her hand and the blade right through his arm just below the shoulder, severing it completely.

Dieter's severed arm thudded to the deck. He stood there for a moment, staring at it stupidly, blood flowing in a massive cascade down his torso. And then he crumpled down into a pathetic heap on the deck. He groaned, gurgled, blood forming a giant pool on the deck around him. He tried to say something, only managed to produce a choking, wet murmur and a froth of blood on his lips. Del ignored him, kicked his knife away, touched the switch on the power knife and it went silent. She tossed it aside.

She stepped over to Charlie, knelt down beside him. "How bad are you hurt?" she asked, as Dieter continued to gurgle and drown in his own blood.

"Not good," he said.

"Can you wait a minute or two before we get help?"

"Why?"

She nodded toward Dieter, who still struggled and gurgled. "If he gets help immediately, they're good enough, they just might revive him, and I'm not going to let that happen. Let's give him a few minutes to bleed out, make sure he's really dead."

Charlie looked in her eyes. "Remind me . . . never to . . . piss you off."

She grinned, and her eyebrows lifted excitedly. "We could spend the time making out, necking and petting like school kids." She suddenly remembered her exposed breast, blushed, and lifted the torn fabric of her dress to cover it. She leaned down farther and kissed him, a gentle kiss that promised more.

When their lips parted she said, "You came and got me. That was stupid. I'm glad you did, but the Realm doesn't need me. Not as much as it needs you."

"But I need you."

She smiled. "I know. I like it that you need me. And I need you."

She kissed him again. Dieter had been silent for some time. She glanced his way and said, "That should do it."

Charlie couldn't get to his feet on his own. She helped him up and he had to lean heavily on her. "Come on, spacer," she said. "Let's go have that dance."

EPILOGUE
THE SPACER GETS HIS DANCE

Enrik Adsin was never heard from again. It was believed that President Goutain had him done away with, though nothing could ever be proven.

Goutain's military forces were badly mauled at the battle of Andyne-Borregga. Of the fifty odd warships he brought to the battle, only eight made it back to the Republic of Syndon, and those all had heavy damage. He made a number of speeches about the injustice of the Realm's unprovoked attack on the Republic. But he'd lost considerable support among his Syndonese sycophants for his failed attempt to turn the Realm into a puppet kingdom. The Syndonese insurrection gained further momentum, and one year after the battle the military overthrew him in a bloody coup and he was never seen again. His successor, President Tantin—formerly General Tantin—gave a number of long-winded speeches touting peaceful cooperation with Syndon's neighboring states, though since it was Tantin, his words were viewed with considerable skepticism.

Gaida and Theode were confined to a small de Maris estate and lived out their days in comfortable, though isolated, imprisonment. But with all her dreams dashed, Gaida finally went mad, murdered Theode, then took her own life.

The nine dukes reinstated Lord Arthur as His Grace, Duke de Maris, and for centuries the de Maris ducal seat remained one of the strongest in the Realm.

With the demise of both Nadama and Dieter, the nine dukes found a distant cousin to inherit the de Satarna ducal seat, though he was far from strong. And after the disastrous battle of Andyne-Borregga, which severely weakened House de Satarna, it never regained its status as the preeminent duchy in the Realm.

Old Rierma married Lady Sally, made an honest woman out of her—or perhaps she made a dishonest man out of him, though he'd openly admit he had always been quite dishonest. It "turned out" she wasn't his niece after all, but a highborn and elegant noblewoman of unquestionable repute, concerning which he was able to produce considerable documentation. In any case, he married her and made her the Duchess de Neptair. Rumors surfaced that he and she frequented a rather disreputable trampsie saloon, and had been seen dancing an undignified, and quite lively, jig. Interestingly enough, she seemed quite happy, and in his later years he always had a smile on his face. After his death at a ripe old age, Duchess Sally proved to be one of the most formidable women in the empire.

To Janice's surprise, Charlie never did "do duke shit": start wars and kill people, though she wouldn't have held it against him if he had, because that's what dukes did. She and Becky and Trina eventually found husbands and got out of the business, though they took great pride that their daughters were chosen to follow in their footsteps, and the young girls benefitted considerably from their mothers' years of experience.

Because of Charlie's near-destitute status, the other nine dukes were quite comfortable with his betrothal to Delilah, and they were married in a magnificent ceremony to much celebration throughout the Realm. When the Ten forced Lucius, because of his follies, to abdicate, Charlie and Delilah were crowned king and queen. It surprised no one that Charlie turned out to be a strong king, though it did surprise some that Delilah was an equally strong queen.

Within a few years, because of the instabilities in Syndon, and as it leaked out that Charlie was a far stronger and more powerful king than anticipated, several of the independent states petitioned King Charles for protectorate status. And from that day the Lunan Empire was born, with Charlie and Delilah the first emperor and empress.

Delilah, mercifully, did not have the willpower to wait for the nuptials before fulfilling her civic duty, much to Charlie's delight—and hers too, for that matter. In fact, performing her civic duty was a responsibility she and Charlie took quite seriously throughout their lives.

Del and her spacer finally did have that dance, at Momma Toofat's, and it was no sedate waltz.

ACKNOWLEDGMENTS

I'd like to thank Betsy Mitchell for whipping both me and my book into shape; Karen for both supporting my dream and being my most valuable critic; and David Pomerico, and the whole team at HarperCollins, for believing in an indie, and turning the book into something to be proud of.

ABOUT THE AUTHOR

Trained as a scientist with a PhD in Electrical Engineering (specializing in laser physics), **J.L. DOTY** has been writing science fiction and fantasy for over thirty years. He has nine published novels, including the three series: *The Treasons Cycle*, *The Gods Within*, and *The Dead Among Us*. Born in Seattle, he now lives in Arizona with his wife and three cats. He writes full-time now and continues to focus on speculative fiction, but never with lasers as a weapon, since most writers invariably get that wrong.

Discover great authors, exclusive offers, and more at hc.com.